PRAISE FOR
AMANDA SCOTT'S
SCOTTISH ADVENTURES

BORDER LASS

"4½ Stars! TOP PICK! Readers will be thrilled . . . a tautly written, deeply emotional love story steeped in the rich history of the Borders. Scott's use of real events and people enables her to subtly move readers into the characters' mindsets, which greatly enriches the story."
—*Romantic Times BOOKreviews Magazine*

"5 Stars! A thrilling tale, rife with villains and notorious plots . . . Scott demonstrates again her expertise in the realm of medieval Scotland. She combines a passionate love story with a detailed understanding of those dangerous times . . . a fascinating story. I highly recommend *Border Lass*."
—FallenAngelReviews.com

"Scott excels at creating memorable characters . . . A good read."
—FreshFiction.com

BORDER WEDDING

"4½ Stars! TO............................ters leap off the pages, ...is more than entertain........................rical romance as it was................................
—*Roman........BOOKreviews Magazine*

more . . .

"A fun, light read . . . Scott's vivid attention to details makes you feel as if you are indeed visiting Scotland each and every time you pick up her delightful book."
—ArmchairInterviews.com

"A winner . . . Few authors do medieval romances as consistently excellent as Amanda Scott's . . . brings to life the late fourteenth century."
—HarrietKlausner.wwwi.com

"Well-written narrative and dialogue . . . exciting plot . . . *Border Wedding* proves great stories of Scotland don't only arise out of the Highlands."
—RomRevToday.com

KING OF STORMS

"4 Stars! An exhilarating novel . . . with a lively love story . . . Scott brings the memorable characters from her previous novels together in an exciting adventure romance."
—*Romantic Times BOOKreviews Magazine*

"Passionate and breathtaking . . . Amanda Scott's *King of Storms* keeps the tension moving as she continues her powerful saga of the Macleod sisters."
—NovelTalk.com

more . . .

"A terrific tale starring two interesting lead characters who fight, fuss, and fall in love . . . Rich in history and romance, fans will enjoy the search for the Templar treasure and the Stone of Scone."

—**Midwest Book Review**

"An engaging tale with well-written characters, and a wonderful plot that will keep readers turning pages . . . Fans of historical romances will be delighted with *King of Storms*."

—**TheRomanceReadersConnection.com**

"Enjoyable . . . moves at a fast pace . . . It was difficult to put the book down."

—**BookLoons.com**

"Intrigue and danger . . . Readers will enjoy the adventures and sweet romance."

—**RomRevToday.com**

"Enchanting . . . a thrilling adventure . . . a *must* read . . . *King of Storms* is a page-turner. A sensual, action-packed romance sure to satisfy every heart. Combine this with a battle of wits, a test of strength, faith, and honor, and you have one great read."

—**FreshFiction.com**

KNIGHT'S TREASURE

"An enjoyable book for a quiet evening at home. If you are a fan of historical romance with a touch of suspense, you don't want to miss this book."

—LoveRomanceAndMore.com

"Filled with tension, deceptions, and newly awakened passions. Scott gets better and better."

—NovelTalk.com

LADY'S CHOICE

"Terrific . . . with an exhilarating climax. Scott is at the top of her game with this deep historical tale."

—Midwest Book Review

"Enjoyable . . . The premise of Scott's adventure romance is strong."

—Romantic Times BOOKreviews Magazine

"A page-turner . . . her characters are a joy to read. *Lady's Choice* is sure to delight medieval historical fans."

—Romance Reviews Today

"Plenty of suspense and action and a delightful developing love story . . . Another excellent story from Scott."

—RomanceReviewsMag.com

more . . .

PRINCE OF DANGER

"Phenomenal."
—*Romantic Times BOOKreviews Magazine*

"RITA Award–winning Scott has a flair for colorful, convincing characterization."
—*Publishers Weekly*

"Exhilarating . . . fabulous . . . action-packed . . . Fans of fast-paced historical tales . . . will want to read Amanda Scott's latest."
—*Midwest Book Review*

"Amanda Scott is a phenomenal writer . . . I am not sure if perfection can be improved upon, but that is exactly what she has done in her latest offering."
—*RomanceReaderAtHeart.com*

LORD OF THE ISLES

"Ms. Scott's diverse, marvelous, unforgettable characters in this intricate plot provide hours of pure pleasure."
—*Rendezvous*

"Scott pits her strong characters against one another and fate. She delves into their motivations, bringing insight into them and the thrilling era in which they live."
—*Romantic Times BOOKreviews Magazine*

A HIGHLAND PRINCESS

AMANDA SCOTT

Border Moonlight

FOREVER

NEW YORK   BOSTON

Copyright © 2009 by Lynne Scott-Drennan
Excerpt from *Tamed by a Laird* copyright © 2009 by Lynne Scott-Drennan.
All rights reserved. Except as permitted under the U.S. Copyright Act of 1976, no part of this publication may be reproduced, distributed, or transmitted in any form or by any means, or stored in a database or retrieval system, without the prior written permission of the publisher.

Cover design by Claire Brown

Forever
Hachette Book Group
237 Park Avenue
New York, NY 10017
Visit our Web site at www. HachetteBookGroup.com

Forever is an imprint of Grand Central Publishing.
The Forever name and logo is a trademark of Hachette Book Group, Inc.

Printed in the United States of America

First Printing: January 2009

10 9 8 7 6 5 4 3 2 1

ATTENTION CORPORATIONS AND ORGANIZATIONS:
Most HACHETTE BOOK GROUP books are available at quantity discounts with bulk purchase for educational, business, or sales promotional use. For information, please call or write:

Special Markets Department, Hachette Book Group
237 Park Avenue, New York, NY 10017
Telephone: 1-800-222-6747 Fax: 1-800-477-5925

To the real ladies Nancy and Averil,
wonderful friends and boon companions

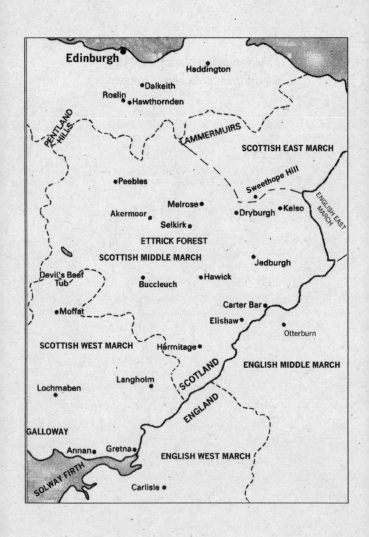

We'll have moonlight again!

—Scotts of Harden, motto and reivers' cry

Author's Note ————

For readers who appreciate assistance with meaning and pronunciation:

Buccleuch = Buh-CLOO

East, West, or Middle March = Border jurisdictions on each side

Hawick = HOYK

Of that Ilk = of the same. Sir John Edmonstone of that Ilk = Sir John Edmonstone of Edmonstone

The Douglas = the (Scottish) Earl of Douglas

The Percy = the (English) Earl of Northumberland

Prologue

St. Giles Kirk, Edinburgh, 1386

"No."

The young bride's single decisive word silenced the rustling of the noble wedding guests' movements and whispers.

The priest, having just asked the stout, elegantly dressed groom if he would take fourteen-year-old Lady Sibylla Cavers as his wife, now shifted his gaze to her.

"My daughter," he said sternly, "I was asking his lordship if he would take you as his wife. Prithee, keep silent until I address you."

The wedding guests saw only her slender back and thus could not read her expression. But her very posture expressed her indignation.

Her hip-long, wavy auburn hair glinted golden in the glow of the cressets on the arcade separating the new south aisle from the nave. That aisle, as most of Edinburgh knew, owed its existence to the generosity of the bride's father, Sir Malcolm Cavers, Lord of Akermoor.

The groom—nearer Sir Malcolm's age than Sibylla's—

turned to gape at her. His jowls were aquiver. His thick lower lip protruded.

Ignoring him, she faced the priest. "It cannot matter how Lord Galston answers you, Father," she said as firmly and clearly as before. "I do have the right to refuse him, do I not? My godfather said I do."

"A good daughter obeys the commands of her *father*," the priest declared.

"I *am* a good daughter, but I *don't* want Lord Galston for my husband. The Douglas, my godfather, said I need not have him. Was he wrong?"

The priest stared at her, his heavy frown making most of the spectators glad he had not directed it at them.

They held their communal breath, fearful of missing a word.

Heads turned toward Sir Malcolm. He stood at the foot of the chancel steps, his grim profile visible to nearly everyone save the bridal couple.

His face flamed red and his jaw jutted forward.

The priest looked at him. The bride did not.

"My lord," the priest said. "You know the answer to her ladyship's question. What would you have me do?"

Grimacing, Sir Malcolm shook his head. "*Ye* can do nowt," he muttered.

The lady Sibylla turned, gathered her skirts in a graceful, swooping gesture, and descended the chancel steps. Head high, acknowledging no one, she turned toward the south aisle.

As the congregation watched in stunned silence, she walked with dignity far beyond her tender years outside into Edinburgh's High Street.

Selkirk, Allhallows' Day, 1387

As fifteen-year-old Sibylla Cavers walked beside her father toward the altar of the wee kirk, she saw that he had invited few guests. But she could scarcely blame him after what had happened the first time he'd arranged for her to marry.

With the banns mysteriously omitted this time, just two lay brothers and a few curious citizens were in the kirk that drizzly November day to view the sacred rite and help alleviate the damp chill. Shivering, Sibylla studied the handsome young man who awaited her with the priest at the altar.

She had never met the bridegroom before. But, as her father had promised, this one did seem a better choice for her than the aged Lord Galston. For one thing, this man was only six years older than she was, surely a better match for her than any rotund graybeard.

The dark-tawny hair beneath his plumed blue velvet cap was neatly trimmed. His expensively clad figure boasted broad shoulders, slim hips, and legs both powerful-looking and shapely in their dark hose. His eyes seemed a bit fierce under jutting eyebrows darker than his hair, but fierce eyes did not scare Sibylla. At first glance, she thought him intriguing.

She had enjoyed a few mild flirtations, and was growing used to men of every age—including her brother Hugh's friends—making clear their approval of her beauty. So she waited for that familiar look to appear on the face of her intended.

He continued to regard her without any change of expression other than what seemed to be a touch of chilly impatience.

Aware that she had inherited her mother's generous wedding portion on that lady's unfortunate demise ten years before, Sibylla eyed the young man more intently as she offered him a warm smile.

He remained coldly somber.

At the chancel steps, her father moved away after declaring himself willing to give her in marriage. With easy grace, she went up the steps, stopped nearer her bridegroom than the priest had indicated, and said confidingly, "You might at least smile, sir. You look as if you are attending a funeral."

Instead, he glanced irritably at the priest. That worthy said, "My lady, you should look at me and not speak except to repeat your vows."

Ignoring him, Sibylla smiled again at her intended. "My father told me you were all eagerness, sir," she said. "But you never came to visit me, and now you do not return my smile. In troth, I begin to doubt his word."

"This discourse is unseemly, Father," the groom said. "Pray, proceed."

"Nay, then, do not, Father," Sibylla said. "I will have none of him."

As she turned away, her erstwhile bridegroom said testily, "Where do you think you're going?"

"Home," she said. "You do not want me, and I do *not* want you."

"By heaven, no one humiliates me like this!" he exclaimed.

Without word or pause, Sibylla picked up her skirts and left the kirk.

The words he shouted at her then rang in her ears for days afterward:

"I'll *never* forgive you, you impudent snip! You will rue this day!"

Akermoor Castle, Lothian, April 1388

After each of her two aborted weddings, Sibylla had faced her furious father and endured his rebukes. She knew she deserved them, if only for disappointing him, and had felt profound relief that his reaction had not been more violent.

On both occasions, after he had roared at her, she had tried to explain her reasons. But Lord Galston's having been too old for her and his successor too coldly arrogant had not impressed Sir Malcolm.

The third time, she recognized her error sooner. The ceremony was to take place at Akermoor, so she simply sent a message downstairs to the priest and did not show herself. Accordingly, she expected Sir Malcolm's wrath to engulf her.

"What manner of complaint can ye have this time?" he demanded. "In sooth, ye said Thomas Colville suited ye fine."

"I had seen him only at court with companies of people," Sibylla replied. "Thomas seemed charming then and kind. But since he has been here at Akermoor, I have found not one thing about which we can talk."

"Ye'll talk enough *after* ye're married!"

"He leers at the maidservants, sir, and cares only for his own wishes," she said. Fearing that Sir Malcolm would see nothing amiss in that either, she added, "He also complained unceasingly that Hugh was not here to bear him company."

"Any man prefers the company of other men," her father retorted. "His wife is meant to look after his home and his bairns, no to demand his constant attention. Moreover, if ye meant to refuse him, ye should have said as much before now."

"I did, sir. You did not listen. Apparently, that, too, is the nature of men."

"I'll stand nae more of your sauce!" he roared. "Your sister Alice will soon need a husband, and although I'd a mind to see ye wedded afore her, ye've had your chance, Sibylla—three of them! I'll do nae more for ye. Ye'll always have your home here, but ye'll look after Alice till she weds and then ye'll look after yourself and me. So look now at your future, ye foolish lass, and weep for it!"

But Sibylla did not weep.

Instead, as usual, she took matters into her own capable hands.

Chapter 1 ———————————

The child's scream shattered the morning stillness.

Whipping her head toward the sound, which had come from a short distance away near the river Tweed, nineteen-year-old Lady Sibylla Cavers reined in the dapple-gray gelding she rode. Pushing back the sable-lined hood of her long, dark-green wool cloak, she listened, frowning, her eyes narrowed. For the first time since leaving Sweethope Hill House that morning, she wished she had brought her groom, but as the land from Sweethope Hill to the river belonged to the estate, she had not.

She often rode alone, and having but recently recovered from an illness that had kept her in bed for a fortnight, she had wanted to savor her freedom.

The scream came again and seemed closer.

Spurring the gray, Sibylla rode toward the river until she saw through a break in the trees lining its bank a tiny, splashing figure a quarter mile to the west. Caught in the river's powerful, sweeping spring flow, it moved steadily toward her.

Without hesitation, Sibylla wheeled her mount eastward and urged it to a gallop, hoping it could outrun the
river to the next ford. With hood bobbing and long, thick,
red-gold plaits flying, she listened for more screams to tell
her the child was still alive and help her estimate how fast
the river was carrying it along.

Her sense of urgency increasing with every hoofbeat,
she leaned low along the gelding's neck and urged it to
go faster.

The ford was not far, if it still was a ford. She knew only
what she had gleaned about the Tweed during the princess Isabel Stewart's eight-month residence at Sweethope.
But her experience with other rivers warned her that even
trustworthy fords that had remained so for years could
vanish in a heavy spate, and tended to do so just when one
most urgently needed to cross to the other side.

At present, the Tweed was a thick, muddy brown color
and moved swiftly, carrying branches, twigs, and larger
items in its grip. Some distance to the east, she saw a
long, half-submerged log that had snagged near the opposite shore just short of where the river bent southward.
Branches with enough clinging dry leaves to look like
spiky plumes shot off the log in all directions, making
it easy to see. Other objects swept past it though, as the
child would if she could not intercept it.

The ford lay just ahead now with sunlight gleaming
on water-filled ruts of the worn track approaching it. Although the river was higher than usual, hoofprints in the
mud indicated that, not long before, horses had crossed
there.

Reining the gray to a trot and turning in fear that she
would see nothing but churning water, she observed with

profound relief that the child still splashed, albeit with less energy than before. Its strength was rapidly waning.

At best, she would have only one chance to save it.

Reaching the ford, she urged the gray into the water. The horse was reluctant, but she was an experienced horsewoman.

She knew it was strong and reliable. Forcing it into the swift flow, wishing again that she had brought her groom, she discovered only when the gray was in nearly to its withers that the water was deeper than she had expected.

Nevertheless, the horse obeyed, leaning into the river's flow to steady itself.

Keeping firm control of it, she fixed her eyes on the child, urging the gelding forward until the child was splashing directly toward them.

When the little one was near enough, Sibylla resisted trying to grab one of the thin, flailing arms with her gloved hand. She grabbed clothing instead, praying the cloth would not tear as the water fought to rip the terrified child from her grip. The river thrust hard against the horse, eddying angrily around the already skittish beast.

The child proved shockingly heavy and awkward to hold. Just as she thought she had a firm grip, the gelding shifted a foreleg eastward.

The combination of the child's waterlogged weight and the river's mighty flow pulled the little one under the horse's neck and forced Sibylla to lean sharply to retain her grip. Before she knew what was happening, she was in the icy water.

Long practice compelled her to hold on to the reins.

The startled horse, already struggling to return to firm ground, jerked its head up, nearly yanking the reins free. Sibylla's skirts and heavy cloak threatened to sink her, and the combined forces of the river and the child's weight dragged her eastward with a strength impossible to resist. Worse, the child had caught hold of her arm and, shrieking in its terror, tried to climb right up her.

Sibylla let go of the reins and, submerging, used her left hand to release the clasp at the neck of her cloak as she tried desperately to keep the child's head above her, out of the water, and find footing beneath her. The water filled her boots and thrust one off. She kicked the other one away.

Although her feet had briefly touched bottom as she kicked toward the surface and the cloak's weight vanished as the river swept it away, she could find only water under her now. Whatever had remained of the ford was behind them.

Pulse pounding, trying not to swallow the cold, muddy water churning around them, Sibylla fought to breathe and to keep them both afloat. But the river, determined to keep them, swept them inexorably toward the sea.

Simon Murray, Laird of Elishaw, returning from Kelso with his usual, modest tail of six armed men, had forded the Tweed sometime earlier on his way south to Elishaw. Having also heard the screaming child, he had turned back at once.

By the time he and his men reached the riverbank, the screams were well east of them, but Simon easily spotted the frantically splashing child. Beyond, in the distance, he discerned through the shrubbery a lone rider in a dark-green cloak racing along the opposite bank. Whoever it was, with the river as high as it was, and the current as strong, that rider would need help.

As Simon turned east, one of his men shouted, "M'lord, look yonder! There be another lad in the water!"

Glancing back to see more splashes, Simon shouted, "You men do what you must to rescue him. I'm going after the other one. Hodge Law, you're with me!" he added, singling out the largest and strongest of his men.

Giving spur to his mount with mental thanks to God that he was riding a sure-footed horse of good speed, Simon followed the narrow, rutted track along the river-bank. Watching through trees and shrubbery as well as he could in passing, he tried to keep one eye on the child and the other on the green-cloaked rider.

As he rode, he wondered how two bairns had ended up in the river. If they'd been playing on its banks, they wanted skelping—if they lived long enough. If not . . .

Half of his mind continued to toy with possibilities as it was wont to do when faced with any problem. But as he drew nearer, he saw that the other rider was female and realized that, before, the shrubbery had hidden her flying plaits.

Forgetting all else, he focused his mind on how he could aid her.

When she forced her mount into the river at the ford where he and his men had crossed, he noted how nervous the beast was and how deftly she controlled it.

As that thought crossed his mind, she leaned to grab the child racing toward her, and although he saw with approval that she grabbed the front of its garments rather than trying to catch a madly waving arm, he doubted that any female would be strong enough to hold on to it in such a current. She would have to let go.

He spurred his horse again, his vivid imagination warning him what would happen split seconds before she fell in.

She bobbed up straightaway, still gripping the child. But the current had both of them and was flowing fast enough to make him fear he could not catch up in time, let alone get ahead of them as he must if he were to help them.

The woods lining the river were thicker where its course bent southward, but he knew it would bend east again half a mile later. He could shorten the distance by cutting across the field. Then, *if* the two could avoid drowning before he got to them, and *if* his horse could avoid putting a foot in a rabbit hole or worse . . .

Sibylla held on to the child by sheer willpower. She resisted fighting the current, tried to relax, and put her energy into kicking and keeping her head and the child's above water as she let the river carry them.

She hoped she could keep her wits together long enough to think what to do, but the icy water made it hard to breathe, let alone to think. Although the child seemed lighter with the water bearing them both, she knew they did not have long to survive unless they could reach one of the river's banks.

Adventurous by nature, Sibylla had grown up at Akermoor Castle, which boasted its own loch a short way to the west and the Ale Water to the east. Having likewise enjoyed the blessing of an older brother determined to teach her how to survive the commonest perils of Border life, and to look after herself, she was an excellent swimmer and had acquired the ability to remain calm in a crisis.

She knew she could not successfully fight the child and the strong current, so to divert the child she commanded it to help them stay afloat.

"Kick hard!" she shouted, managing to shift her grip to the back of its clothing near its neck. By floating the child on its back, keeping her right arm straight, and bending her wrist sharply, she could keep its head up while she paddled with her left hand. Her body shifted almost onto its side, but she found it easier to kick hard in that position with the child kicking its legs above hers.

Desperation kept her going, and for a wonder, the water had pushed her skirts nearly to her hips, enough for the fabric to resist wrapping itself around her legs.

Sibylla was tiring fast though, and knew she could not go on indefinitely. They had to find something that would float and to which they could cling.

She could barely see where she was going, but she knew they were rapidly approaching the river bend. Without intent but because of the way she held the child and because she faced the south bank of the river, she had drawn close enough to it to be wary of nearby boulders poking their heads out of the water.

Much as she wanted to feel firm ground beneath her again, it occurred to her that letting the river smash them into a boulder might kill them both.

Telling herself sternly that such a collision was more likely to injure them than kill them, and that injury would be better than drowning, she tried to judge how safely she could ease them closer. Only then did she remember the half-submerged log.

Debris in the water consisted mostly of branches,

twigs, and other useless stuff, none of it large enough to provide support for them both.

If she could grab the log, they could at least gain a respite. They might even manage to drag themselves out of the water if the log lay near enough to the shore.

She had no doubt she could manage that feat for herself. But her grip on the child made everything else gruelingly awkward. Other than reminding the little one to kick, and muttering occasional brief encouragement as she fought to swim and to breathe, Sibylla had barely spoken.

The child, too, was exhausting what energy it had left in kicking, and she knew she dared not waste her own lest she need it later.

As a result, she did not even know yet which sex the child was.

It was wearing thin breeks rather than a skirt, but its fragile bone structure seemed feminine, as did its willingness to obey her. Despite the attempt to climb up her when she fell in, a single stern command to kick hard and look for something they could grab to keep them afloat had been enough.

Such simple trust in her made Sibylla determined not to give up. She had no illusions though. She had to get closer to shore for them to have any chance at all.

~

When a break in the trees showed Simon he was a little ahead of the victims, he shouted at Hodge Law to stay near the river, to be at hand if they managed to make it to shore before the current swept them around the bend. Then he turned his horse to cross the open field, hoping to get farther ahead of them beyond the bend.

He had ridden just a short way, however, when a shrill whistle made him look back to see Hodge waving frantically. As Simon wheeled his horse, he saw the big man thrust himself off his own mount and vanish into the shrubbery.

Simon put his horse to its fastest pace, wrenched it to a halt near Hodge's beast, and flung himself from the saddle. Following Hodge's huge footprints through the shrubbery to the riverbank, he saw the big shaggy-haired Borderer trying to step onto a half-submerged log with a multitude of dead branches thrusting from it.

Seeing the sodden, bedraggled woman clinging to a branch and the child clinging to the woman, Simon said, "Take care or you'll end in the river with them!"

"I'll no be going aboard it, m'lord," Hodge said. "The blessed log be so unstable I'm afeard me weight will dislodge it from what's keeping it here."

"Will it take my weight?" Simon asked as he drew near enough to see for himself that the log rocked like a ship at sea.

"I'm thinking I could hold it steady enough for ye," Hodge said. "Like as not, though, ye'll get a dousing."

"I won't fall in," Simon said, noting that the woman had not spoken or even tried to push away the heavy strands of muddy hair that obscured most of her face.

She was shivering, clearly exhausted and using the last dregs of her energy to hang on. The child, too, looked spent. But although its arms were around the woman's neck, it seemed to have sense enough left not to choke her.

He moved up by Hodge, who held on to a stout branch. The log looked like part of a good-sized tree, but it lay too far from shore for him to step onto it. He'd have to leap, and the damnable thing was bound to be slippery.

But if anyone could hold it steady, Hodge could.

"Mistress, heed me," Simon said as he shrugged off his cloak and tossed it over a nearby shrub. "I am going to jump on that log whilst my man holds it steady. When I do, I'll take the lad from you first. Can you hang on a while longer?"

"I shall have to, shall I not?" she murmured, still barely moving.

"Have faith," he said more gently. "I won't let the river have you. Hold fast now, Hodge. Don't let the damnable thing get away when I jump."

"I've got it, sir."

The woman looked up as Simon set himself to leap, her eyes widening.

They were an odd grayish brown, matching the muddy water. Her plaits and the loose strands that concealed so much of her face—soaked through as they were and doubtless painted with mud—were a similar color. Her lips were blue.

Despite her bedraggled appearance, she seemed familiar. He wondered if she resided on one of the estates near Elishaw.

Shifting his mind to getting safely on the log, he put one hand on a sturdy branch, picked a flattish spot as the best place to land, and leapt.

The log was indeed slippery, but he kept his balance by grabbing a strong-looking upright branch. Holding it with his left hand, he bent toward the child, saying, "Reach a hand up to me, lad. I'll pull you out."

The child shook its head fervently, clinging tighter to the woman.

"Come now, don't be foolish!" Simon said curtly. "Give me your hand."

"Obey him," the woman said quietly. "He will not harm you or let you fall."

"Them others t-tried to hurt us," the child said, teeth chattering. "S-sithee, they said they was j-just drowning puppies. But them puppies was us!"

"His lordship only wants to help us get out," the woman said as calmly as before. "I'm gey cold, and I know you are, too. We must get warm."

"Come, lad," Simon said, forcing the same calm firmness into his own voice.

"Me name's Kit," the little one said. "And I'm no a lad."

Stifling his shock that anyone would throw such a wee lassock into a river to drown, Simon said in a gentler tone, "Come now, reach up to me, lassie. I want to have you out of there so I can help the kind woman who rescued you. You do not want her to freeze hard like a block of ice, do you?"

Biting a colorless lower lip, Kit obeyed him, and as he grasped her little arm, he warned himself to be careful. As stick-thin as she was, he feared her arm might snap in a too-tight grip.

Balancing himself and trusting Hodge to keep the log as still as possible, he braced a knee against the upright branch and squatted. Then he used both hands to lift the child. Despite her sodden state, she seemed feather light.

"There now," he said as he held her close. "Not so bad to be out, is it?"

She was silent, staring over his shoulder at the large, shaggy man behind him.

"That's Hodge Law," he said. "He only looks like a

bear, lassie. He'll be gey gentle with you. I'm going to turn now and hand you across to him."

"I've me cloak ready for her, m'lord," Hodge said, reaching to take the child as Simon leaned out as far as he could and handed her across to him.

Turning back to the woman, Simon saw that she had begun to ease her way to the end of the log. "Be careful, mistress," he warned. "That current is deadly."

"You need not tell me that, sir," she said in a harsh, croaking voice. "I've been its captive now for what seems like hours."

"Not as long as that," he replied. "I saw you fall, and I'd wager you were in no more than five minutes, mayhap ten by now."

She gave him a sour look, and the sense of familiarity increased. He had been wrong about her being from a tenant family, though. Her manner of speech revealed considerably higher birth. In any event, he wanted her out of the water.

Hodge was trying to shift wee Kit under his cloak without letting go of the log, and Simon realized with growing concern that they had no idea how long the child had been in the water before they had heard her scream.

The log tipped precariously, making the woman gasp.

Simon said, "I'm getting off, Hodge. I'll hold the log whilst you wrap that bairn up. As thin as she is, it will amaze me if she does not sicken from this ordeal."

"Aye, sir," Hodge said, firming his grip on the branch he held until Simon was ashore and then relinquishing it to give his full attention to warming the child.

That they had not seen the second child go by gave Simon hope that his lads had plucked it from the water, too. It occurred to him that although Kit had said "us," revealing knowledge that the villains had thrown someone in besides herself, she seemed unconcerned about the fate of her companion.

As these thoughts teased him, he watched the woman, who was managing deftly now that she no longer had to worry about Kit. When she had made her way around the end of the log, he extended a hand to help her from the water.

Her exit was not graceful. She had lost her shoes, the bank was nearly vertical, and she kept tripping on her soaked skirts. How she had swum, let alone held on to the child, he could not imagine.

By the time he got her out, Hodge had wee Kit swaddled tight in his voluminous cloak and was holding Simon's out in his free hand.

Taking it from him, Simon wrapped it around the woman and pulled the fur-lined hood up to cover her head. As he did, he saw that her eyes were not muddy brown but a clear, reflective gray. He said, "The sooner we get you to a fire and see you both well warmed, mistress, the less likely you are to—"

He broke off in consternation as she gave him a bewildered look, lost what remained of her color, and fainted. Had he not been tying the strings of the cloak, she'd have fallen flat. As it was, he barely caught her before she hit the ground.

"Sakes, m'lord," Hodge said. "What do we do now?"

Simon did not reply. He was staring at the woman in his arms.

As he'd caught her, he had scooped her up into his arms so abruptly that the hood had fallen off and the strands of loose hair that had hidden her face had fallen back, too, giving him a clear view of her features.

He had met her only two or three times before, but he recognized her easily.

"Ye look as if ye'd seen a boggart, m'lord. D'ye ken the lass then?"

"Aye," Simon said curtly.

Although he saw Hodge raise an eyebrow, clearly expecting explanation, Simon said no more but strode off with her toward the horses instead.

He was hardly going to tell Hodge Law what even his own family did not know, that just three years before, he had nearly married the woman.

⁓

Slowly becoming aware of hoofbeats and motion, Sibylla realized she was on horseback and that someone was holding her in front of him on his saddle. His hardened, muscular body supported her securely and moved easily with the animal.

She had no doubt who he was.

Perhaps this will teach you, the next time you try to drown yourself, to do a proper job of it, she told herself with a touch of amusement, doubtless born of exhaustion or incipient hysteria.

Of all the people who might have rescued her, the one who had was the would-be bridegroom she had humiliated in Selkirk three years before, the man who had fiercely warned her afterward that he would someday see that she got her just desserts.

To be sure, due to her service with the princess Isabel and his with Isabel's brother the Earl of Fife, now Governor of the Realm, they had met a few times since then but always in company, where he had behaved with chilly civility.

He had spoken to her only once, and she had never been alone with him.

Forcing herself to stay relaxed so he would not know she had regained consciousness, she peeked through her lashes, hoping to see where they were and judge how far she was from the safety of Sweethope Hill House.

Since the hood of the thick woolen cloak that enwrapped her covered most of her face, she could not see enough of the passing landscape to do any good. She gave silent thanks that the princess and her other ladies were away from home, thus sparing her any awkward explanations. She also prayed that her chilly dousing would not make her sick again.

She was warm at least, warmer than by rights she should be after such an experience. The cloak was not her own though, because the river had swept hers away forever. And her other garments—warm or not—must still be wet, because had anyone tried to strip her, surely she would have wakened.

Worry for her horse stirred until her usual good sense assured her that the beast had likely run back to its stable.

The hood's fur lining felt soft against her cheek and smelled comfortingly of cinnamon, cloves, and something else she lacked the energy to identify. The smooth, loping gait of the horse soothed her, and whatever Simon Murray had threatened years ago, she knew he would keep her safe . . . until he could safely murder her.

Simon stared straight ahead, his face carefully devoid of expression but his thoughts whirling like water spouts as memories formed, renewing emotions they had stirred in the past, some as strong in the minute as they had been at the time.

He remembered the damp, gloomy day in Selkirk as if it had been yesterday. Looking back, he recalled the sense of pride he'd had that he was doing his duty. He had believed in his liege lord, the Earl of Fife, and Fife's wanting him to marry the elder daughter of the Laird of Akermoor had been sufficient cause to do so.

A man obeyed his lord, and that was that. He had been proud, too, though, that Fife had singled him out from all the other men who served him.

As for his bride-to-be, what more had she been than the chosen vessel, singled out from all the families with which Fife might have wished to ally himself?

But not only had she disdained the honor, she had done so in a way surely calculated to make a fool of Simon. How disappointed she must have been to have had such a small audience! But Fife and Sir Malcolm had each had reason for that.

Despite the small number of witnesses, her rejection had dealt Simon's self-esteem a massive blow. Just two days past his twenty-first birthday, he had been thinking himself a man at last, as well as one of value to his family and to his lord.

The lady Sibylla had shattered that image in less than half a minute.

In days following, he had imagined hundreds of things he might have said or done at the time, or afterward, to punish her. None had seemed sufficient.

His only consolation, although he had not learned of

it until months later, was that the impertinent snip had spurned another before him. Lord Galston had died soon afterward, leaving his vast wealth and estates to the distant cousin who was his heir. Simon had hoped that the lass recognized her loss and mourned it, for Galston had agreed to settle the bulk of that wealth on his wife. It had not taken much thought, though, to realize that most likely the lass had not known about that.

Men did not discuss marriage settlements with their daughters. Moreover, he had also learned over the years that such arrangements usually benefited the Earl of Fife, and now the Crown, more than they benefited those more nearly concerned.

The fickle lass had then spurned another of Fife's men, but Simon knew naught of the settlements for that one. Fife did not encourage his men to confide in each other.

His warm burden shifted slightly and moaned, so he tightened his grip. It would not do to let her fall. She had already injured herself, for he had seen a reddened lump forming on her forehead and knew she must have struck it on something. At present she was sound asleep with her head against his shoulder, and although he remembered her eyes widening at first sight of him, and knew she had recognized him, she was relaxed, apparently trusting him.

An image rose then of her racing to beat the child to the ford. He'd say one thing for her: She had an even better seat on a horse than his sister Amalie did.

He also had to admire her courage, but he was not ready to forgive her. Nor, now that he had his hands on her, was he ready to let her go. He was older, his emotions more carefully guarded, but he still had a score to settle with her.

Over the past few years, from one cause or another, Fife's crest had lowered in his estimation, but he had only to think of that day in Selkirk to feel the humiliation of Sibylla Cavers's insolent rejection burning through him again.

Chapter 2

"You, there! What are you doing in here?"

The woman's imperious tones seemed to come from far away, but Sibylla felt an immediate quickening of guilt. Was she not at Sweethope Hill House, where she ought to be? To be sure, she had no memory of arriving, but—

"You have no business in this chamber, girl," the authoritative voice went on. "Begone, and do not let me catch you here again, or"—Sibylla struggled to collect her wits—"it will be the worse for you."

"I told her she could stay."

That deep, masculine voice was not distant but very clear, very firm. Nevertheless, it certainly ought not to be in Sibylla's bedchamber.

Her eyes flew open.

She was lying on her side in a cupboard bed, and the first thing she saw was the waiflike child standing beside it, her thin hands clutching each other at her narrow waist. Now that she was dry, one could see that her hair was short, softly curly, and very fair. Her face was pinched and drawn, her pale blue eyes wide.

Following the child's gaze to an unfamiliar doorway,

Sibylla saw Simon Murray of Elishaw, watching her. A fashionably attired woman with a long, horsey face bridled like an irritated mare beside him.

Sibylla thought vaguely that she ought to recognize that face and the English lilt in the woman's voice. Where had she—?

Abruptly, she realized the woman was Simon's mother, Lady Murray.

The villain had not taken her to Sweethope Hill House. Instead, he had ridden a greater distance with her, to Elishaw Castle, his home.

Her ladyship stood stiffly, cheeks afire, but controlled herself enough to say, "You do not know this child, sir. It could be diseased."

A movement from the child drew Sibylla's gaze. Indignation had turned the wraithlike little figure almost as stiff as her reluctant hostess.

"Shhh," Sibylla murmured.

"Ye're awake!" the child exclaimed. "Praise be, for I feared ye were—"

"I told you she was just sleeping, Kit," Simon said, snapping Sibylla's gaze back to him. He had spoken so gently that she would not have believed it was his voice had she not looked in time to see his lips still moving.

"I am at Elishaw, am I not?" she asked him, astonished to hear the feeble croak of her voice and feel its roughness. Her throat was sore.

"I thought it best," he answered coolly, as if that were that.

"Oh, but I must—" As she started to sit up, pain sliced through her head, inside and out, making her shut her eyes.

She reached to find a lump on her forehead as she continued trying to sit. But in the brief time she'd had her eyes shut he had closed the distance from doorway to bed. Putting a firm hand on her shoulder, he pressed her back to the pillows.

"Lie still," he commanded. "I have sent for our local herb woman to provide something to ease your pain. You've taken a hard knock to your head."

"That log . . . no, a branch clouted me as I was trying to keep the river from impaling us on another. Faith, I scarcely remember! How long was I unconscious?"

"Just a short time," he said in that maddeningly cool tone, as if what had happened had been quite ordinary. "You stirred shortly after you fainted, and—"

"I never faint," she replied, firmly suppressing the discomfiting memory of coming to in his arms. "Doubtless, I suffered a delayed reaction from the blow."

She was thinking with gratitude that her voice sounded stronger, more like her own, when his sharp gaze locked with hers. As she gazed back, her confidence faltered. His hand still touched her shoulder, and she was vaguely aware of its warmth there, but she seemed to lack strength enough to speak or look away.

She had known his eyes were dark and had thought them merely dark brown. They were not. They were a deep, almost fathomless green and strangely hypnotic.

She often felt as if she could look into a person's eyes and know his mind, but one would never see deeply enough into Simon Murray to see anything but green.

As faintly as when she was first awakening, as if the sound came from a great distance, she heard Lady Murray say, "Simon."

He glanced at his mother, straightening as he did, and

broke the spell. For spell it must certainly have been, Sibylla thought, to have rendered her speechless.

Speechlessness was *not* one of her normal characteristics.

Though he had taken his hand away, her bare shoulder still felt warm where he had touched it. *Bare!* She tugged the coverlet higher.

That brief glance was the only response he made to his mother before he looked back to say, "It may be rare for you to faint, but you did. You stirred shortly thereafter, murmured something unintelligible, and then you slept."

"The blow must have rendered me unconscious," she repeated firmly.

"It did no such thing. You will shortly recall that we had a brief conversation before you fainted. I do not doubt that the blow made you dizzy or that you fainted from sheer exhaustion, which accounts for your sleeping so deeply and so long. The difference was notable, so I did not try to wake you. I knew sleep would do you good and that you'd travel more comfortably so."

She frowned, only to wince again as she said, "I've no memory of that ride."

"You stirred when I dismounted here at Elishaw but went back to sleep before I carried you upstairs," he said. "You are in my sister Amalie's chamber."

"But who are you?" Lady Murray said, moving to stand beside Simon and making Sibylla feel more vulnerable than ever and a little uneasy. "You look familiar," her ladyship added. "I am sure we have met somewhere."

"At Sweethope Hill, my lady, when you visited Amalie last summer before she married," Sibylla said, avoiding Simon's gaze. "She and I are friends, although I've seen little of her since she married Westruther. I am Sibylla Cavers of Akermoor."

"I do remember you," Lady Murray said. "But 'tis no mystery that I did not know you, as bedraggled as you were when my son carried you in. He said you'd fallen into the river. We could learn no more, because you slept even whilst Tetsy and another maidservant undressed you and put you to bed."

"It was kind of you to look after me," Sibylla said.

"I doubt that anyone at Sweethope Hill told me your name. In troth, I am quite sure that I never heard your surname. Did you say Cavers?"

"Not now, madam," Simon said. "We ought not to have wakened her. She should rest until the herb woman comes."

"But I don't need her," Sibylla protested. "I am rarely sick, sir. If you will just send someone to gather a handful or two of willow bark and boil some water to steep it, I shall be my old self in no time. And, pray, ask someone to find something dry for me to wear so I can get up. I detest lying abed."

"Nonetheless you will stay where you are until you have recovered from your adventure," he said.

Her lips tightened. She was grateful for his hospitality but annoyed with herself for having shown weakness before him—or, indeed, before anyone.

Softly, he said, "You would do well to think carefully before you defy me."

She glowered, looking him in the eyes again, only to wish she had not.

This time, his mother broke the spell, saying, "Do not waste your breath arguing with him, my dear. He rarely alters his decisions."

"Then he should learn to be more considerate of other people's wishes," Sibylla said, still watching Simon. More tartly, she added, "Why did you not take me home to Sweethope Hill, sir, instead of bringing me all the way here?"

"Would you have subjected this child or her brother to crossing that river after their ordeal?" he asked, laying a hand lightly on the little girl's head.

"Her brother! Do you mean to say there were two of them in the river?"

"Aye, and thankfully, my men were able to save the lad," he said. "Due to the rains we've had, the river is still rising, so I decided that Elishaw was the most suitable place to look after you. You and the children will be safe here."

He turned away and, with a touch to his mother's arm, urged her back to the doorway. As he did, Sibylla noted a tightening at one corner of his mouth, but whether it was from vexation or triumph she did not know.

He shut the door without looking back, and a nearby sigh of relief reminded Sibylla of the child's presence.

"I was sure the lady would send me away," Kit muttered.

"I warrant she would if she could. But if his lordship said you could stay—"

"He did, aye," the child said, nodding. "He brought me up here himself."

"Then you may stay," Sibylla said. "Have you any other name but Kit?"

The child shrugged. "That be all they call me."

"Where is your brother, Kit?"

A cloud passed over the thin little face. "Dand do still

be asleep, mistress. I thought he were drowned. He's not, but the laird would no let me stay with him."

Wondering if the boy was in dire straits, Sibylla said bracingly, "Recall how deeply I slept, Kit, and I am fully grown. If they think he needs a good sleep to make him well, they may fear that with you in the room, he might waken."

"He might, aye," Kit said thoughtfully. "Mayhap ye should sleep more, too, mistress. The laird said ye need your rest."

"I'm wide awake," Sibylla said. "And I do not like lying abed if I need not."

"They took your clothes, though," the child pointed out.

"They did." Recalling then that Simon had said she was in Amalie's bedchamber, Sibylla began to sit up, only to feel her head pound and lie back again. She said, "That kist near the door . . . Do you see others like it in here?"

"Aye, two more," Kit said with a gesture.

"Prithee, open them and tell me what they contain."

"Should we do that, though? Them kists dinna belong to us."

"We should," Sibylla assured her. "The lady whose room this was is a friend of mine. If she left clothing here, she would want me to make use of it."

As she spoke, she wondered if Amalie's clothing would fit her.

Amalie—now Lady Westruther and happily expecting her first child—was several inches shorter, plumper, and more buxom. Her skirts would be too large around the waist and would hang shorter than fashion decreed. But Sibylla thought they would fit well enough to sustain her modesty.

She wanted to get up, but she was not wearing a stitch of clothing.

~

"I do not know what you can be thinking to have brought that young woman to Elishaw," Lady Murray said to her eldest and sole remaining son as she followed him down the winding stone stairs to the great hall. "She is a Cavers of Akermoor! Doubtless, she is that dreadful man's daughter."

"She does have a father," Simon said, weighing how much he ought to say.

"I do not admire flippancy," Lady Murray said with her customary, majestic air. "You know that she must be the daughter of Sir Malcolm Cavers of Akermoor. Moreover, you have been very glib, sir, about why you brought her here."

"As I explained, the river was too high to make a crossing safely with an unconscious woman and two bairns to protect," Simon said. "Also, I'd heard that Isabel departed a fortnight ago for Galloway to visit his grace and the Queen."

"More likely to create trouble for your liege lord," Lady Murray observed. "That surely was her purpose the last time she traveled to Galloway."

"That was nearly three years ago, after James Douglas's death," Simon said, suppressing familiar irritation. "She was seeking then to protect her widow's rights."

He was aware that he was unlikely to sway his mother from a position based on her strong belief that his destiny, and therefore Elishaw's, lay in his long service to Robert

Stewart, Earl of Fife and now Governor of the Realm in place of their crippled, disinterested King.

Because Sibylla Cavers served Fife's sister, who was often at odds with him, Lady Murray surely believed Fife would disapprove of Sibylla's presence at Elishaw.

As the widow of James, second Earl of Douglas, Princess Isabel had been entitled to lands deeded her in their marriage settlements and to a third of the income from other Douglas lands that James had owned or controlled as earl.

Fife had hoped to acquire Isabel's Douglas lands for the Crown, but Archie the Grim, now third Earl of Douglas and more powerful than any Stewart, had acted swiftly and honorably to protect those rights for her. Archie continued to provide her with knights and men-at-arms to protect her, too, just as James Douglas had.

Fife had hoped to arrange a second marriage for Isabel to one of his loyal adherents and thereby control both her and her property, but the Douglases had outmaneuvered him by hastily marrying Isabel to Sir John Edmonstone of that Ilk, a loyal if somewhat muttonheaded follower of Archie's.

Despite Isabel's inconsolable grief over James's untimely death, she had agreed to the hasty marriage to avoid battle with Fife. But she had married Edmonstone only with an understanding that she need not live with him.

According to Simon's sister Amalie, Isabel thought Edmonstone uncouth, too fond of his whisky, and worst of all, a paralyzing bore. So she had taken up semipermanent residence with her ladies at Sweethope Hill House in Lothian.

Entering Elishaw's empty great hall, Lady Murray

moved to one of the two tall, narrow windows that over-looked the bailey and gazed silently out on the yard.

Simon waited, knowing she had more to say. She had a magisterial temperament, and he had often observed how patiently she let his late father bluster on about what he would do or not do. When the flow had run its course, she would exert her influence to persuade him that he meant to do something else altogether.

Since Sir Iagan's death eight months before, Border-ers who knew them had made clear their expectation that she would continue to rule at Elishaw, that Simon, having lived under her thumb or Fife's all his life, would be no match for her.

But Simon's experience with her had taught him to keep his thoughts to himself until he could decide if any-one else wanted to hear them. The result was that he had weathered service with the Earl of Fife more successfully than most.

Subsequently, his experience with Fife had curbed his hitherto volatile temper and taught him to bide his time until he knew what the opposition's most potent argu-ments were and how fierce a verbal battle might become before joining a discussion. Therefore, he believed he was well equipped to deal with his mother.

His respect for her judgment was great. After his fa-ther's death, he had accepted her advice on many issues. But he was master of Elishaw now.

Realizing she was determined to outwait him, and not wanting to stir coals with her yet, he said, "You would fight to retain your rights here just as Isabel fought for hers, would you not, madam—if that were necessary?"

She turned then and met his gaze, her expression soft-ening. "I'd have no need to fight you, my dear, whilst you remain Lord of Elishaw." Thoughtfully, she added, "Such knowledge was comforting eight months ago, but I own, it does now afford me concern. We have seen, have we not, how quickly lives may end—first James Douglas, then your father and our poor Tom."

When she paused, he looked away, unwilling to let her see the pain he felt at the still-strong memory of his younger brother's death.

Recollection of their father's demise just days before Tom's was likewise strong, but Sir Iagan had lived a good life, and a longer one than most men enjoyed in such dangerous times. And Sir Iagan had most likely died in a fall from his horse.

Tom had barely reached his majority before meeting his death in a violent, villainous attack while on a journey to their sister Meg's home in Rankilburn Glen.

If, as his sister Amalie believed, Sir Iagan's death had been violent, too, no evidence of that had come to light. Nor did Simon expect to find any. He suspected that the violence of Tom's death had influenced Amalie's thinking, and he could not blame her. He felt considerable responsibility himself for Tom's death.

"I have distressed you, Simon," his mother said.

"'Tis nowt, madam," he assured her.

"It was not my intention, but you must know that 'tis time you were wed. Recall that James Douglas left Isabel with no child to comfort her, and himself with no suitable heir. You now find yourself in danger of leaving Elishaw similarly unprotected. I do not fear for myself. I think of your sister Rosalie, and so must you."

"I do not suppose you bring up this subject because you think I ought to wed the lady Sibylla," he said, trying to sound thoughtful rather than provocative.

She stiffened. "Certainly not. You know that your father and Sir Malcolm Cavers never got on. I mention the need for you to marry only because, despite being master here for eight months, you have not yet begun to seek a wife. Yet you could find yourself beset by raiders or thieves and foully murdered tomorrow, just as Tom was. However, we do need to discuss the lady Sibylla," she added. "What do you mean to do about her? It is most unsuitable to keep her here."

"I disagree," he said coolly. Keeping the lass where she was, was slight punishment for what she had done to him but too tempting an opportunity to abandon yet. "Whilst you are at Elishaw, madam, none will condemn her presence here."

"If you do not mean to return her to Sweethope Hill, one must suppose that you will inform Sir Malcolm that she is here. I warn you, sir, I will not allow that man to set foot inside this castle. Your father would writhe in his grave."

Simon met her gaze but remained silent until color tinged her cheeks. Then he said quietly, "If I send for Sir Malcolm, madam, he will come here as our guest."

Recovering swiftly, she said, "I do not set myself against you, my dearest. You command all here, as you should. But you have heeded my advice now and again, so I thought you understood that certain things just *are* as they are."

"I understand that you and my father took a dislike to Sir Malcolm long ago, but I never sought to know the reason. Perhaps now you might tell me."

"There is no need for that," she said, her color deepening. "You need not invite him here, after all. Akermoor lies nearer to Sweethope Hill than to Elishaw, so if you want him to fetch her, doubtless you will prefer the convenience of his collecting her there. Recall, too, that you extended an invitation to my cousin Cecil Percy to visit us with his family. So you will not want to be traveling any far—"

"Sakes, madam, you usually conceal your intent better," Simon said. "Cecil Percy's man did not say when Cousin Cecil means to visit or that he will bring his family. He said only that he sought to learn if we would receive him."

"That is true, and again you are right to rebuke me," she admitted without rancor. "I should not have spoken so plainly. But I have never made a secret of the pleasure it would give me if you were to marry an English girl. And Maria Percy . . ."

When she fell silent, Simon knew she had noted his increasing irritation. It was a measure of her displeasure at finding Cavers's daughter in her house that she had spoken openly of her hope that he'd marry an Englishwoman as his father had.

To add another Percy wife to the Murray kindred would, she believed, allow them to strengthen the neutrality that Elishaw under his father and his grandfather had maintained through years of Border strife. Lady Murray held that neutrality dear even now, with a truce in effect that allowed nearly free access across the line.

"I do still wonder, sir," she added, "at your decision to bring the girl here."

In truth, Simon wondered, too. His explanation *had* been glib, because he had not thought about his reasons before bringing Sibylla to Elishaw. In truth, he had been more than glib. His explanation had bordered on prevarication.

The Tweed *was* running dangerously high. But had Sibylla or either child been in danger of dying, he knew he would have risked the crossing to get them indoors where a fire and attentive servants could aid them as quickly as possible.

The truth was that he had succumbed to his long-held desire to teach her that humiliating people could be dangerous. And his mother had unwittingly given him an idea of how he might provide her with yet another little lesson.

Chapter 3 _____

Sibylla watched as Kit moved methodically from kist to kist. Someone had rinsed the mud from the child's hair, she noted enviously, leaving a halo of soft flaxen curls. The little blue tunic and skirt she now wore were clean, too.

Although the outfit was clearly a castoff and lacked decoration, its fabric was fine enough to have clothed one of Simon's sisters. Sibylla thought it must be a splendid dress by the child's standards, yet Kit seemed oblivious of it.

"Have you found nothing suitable yet?" Sibylla asked her.

"Nobbut stuff ye couldna wear out o' this room," Kit muttered without looking up from the large basket through which she was searching. Moments later though, she looked up, smiling. "Here's summat that might do, me lady."

Rising with swift grace, she dragged out a heap of scarlet fabric that proved to be a kirtle of figured silk with a dagged neckline and hem, and front bodice lacing of bright yellow silk.

Although the rich scarlet was doubtless a wonderful color for Amalie, with her raven tresses and hazel-green eyes, Sibylla generally preferred shades of green, gray, yellow, or russet. However, if it fit her she would not care what color it was.

No one had done much if anything about her hair, and the bed clothing revealed as much, for it smelled of river mud and bore streaks of the stuff. Whoever had undressed her had taken her clothing but had not tried to wash her. Her skin felt stiff and rough, as if caked in dried mud.

What she wanted was a hot bath and a chance to wash her hair thoroughly with fragrant soap. But she knew enough about Simon Murray to be sure he would not allow such a luxury until the herb woman had pronounced her fit enough.

"Hoots, then, are ye getting up?" Kit demanded when Sibylla began gingerly to sit up. Moving nearer, red kirtle in hand, the child said sternly, "Ye ken fine that the laird did say ye should stay in bed."

"The laird did say that," Sibylla said, clutching the covers to her breast and keeping an eye on the closed door. "But I'll feel better on my own two feet. Mercy," she exclaimed as she put them to the cold floor. "I've no shoes!"

"Nay, ye lost them in the river. Ye've nae shift or hose neither. But I did see summat like a shift in one o' them kists. If ye want—"

"I don't care about a shift," Sibylla said. "Just hand me that kirtle and go stand by the door. If anyone tries to enter whilst I'm putting it on, keep them out."

Kit's light-blue eyes widened at the command, as if she knew it would be hopeless to try to keep the laird out. But she went obediently to the door. "Shall I peek out, then?" she asked. "Might be, I'd hear them on the stairs."

"Nay, but if you do hear voices, warn me."

A mental picture of Simon throwing open the door and striding in urged her to don the kirtle swiftly, although she hoped that even he would not barge into a female guest's bedchamber. Her lack of footwear was more disconcerting.

They had stripped off her wet stockings, the floor was cold, and she could not go downstairs without something to cover her feet. On a warmer day she might not care, but she felt sure that her formidable hostess would condemn such unmannerly behavior and knew it would be wise to consider her ladyship's feelings.

Tying the yellow laces, she said, "Did you see no shoes or slippers, Kit?"

The child shook her head. "Nae netherstocks neither."

"Mayhap a hairbrush or a comb?"

"Aye!" Kit darted back to one of the other kists, plunged her hands in, and pulled out two silver combs.

"Those will do," Sibylla said. Turning to pour water from the ewer into the washstand basin, she tried not to think what it would feel like to drag a comb through her stiff, filthy tresses.

"Them combs will pull like Auld Clootie," Kit said as Sibylla dampened a towel and gingerly dabbed dirt from her face with it. "I could help ye, though."

"Aye, so you could," Sibylla agreed. "If we each take one strand at a time and begin at the end, working our way upward, we can comb out a little at a time. That way, we may not pull out all my hair."

Kit giggled, but when Sibylla had washed her face and hands, they both climbed back up on the cupboardlike bed with their combs. Sitting close together, propped up with pillows, they went to work on her hair.

They were going to make a mess, she knew. But a maid would have to strip off the bedding anyway to wash it and would shake everything out when she did.

"Whilst we do this, would you like to tell me how you came to be in the river?" she asked Kit a few minutes later.

"I did tell ye," Kit said. "Them men said they was a-drowning puppies."

"Dreadful, but why would they want to drown you and your brother?"

Kit concentrated closely on a stubborn snarl in the strand of hair she was combing. Then she said grimly, "They were the deevil's men, that's why. I hope they burn for their wickedness and dinna *ever* find us again."

"But how did they find you at all? Do you know who they were?"

Kit shook her head, her gaze fixed again on the stubborn hank of hair.

"Kit, you must know why they behaved so badly. Were you doing aught to attract their attention, or anger them?"

Kit shrugged. "Just walking by the river and . . . and talking a bit is all."

Watching her, wondering if she knew more and just did not want to tell, Sibylla tried another approach, saying gently, "What is your brother's name?"

Kit had worked her way halfway up the strand she held and got onto her knees as she murmured, "Dand . . . They do call him Dand."

"I warrant his Sunday name must be Andrew then."

Kit shrugged again. "I call him Dand. D'ye think he'll die?"

As Sibylla started to assure her that God would not be so cruel, she hesitated, knowing it would be crueler to raise her hopes with what might prove a lie.

Instead she said, "Whilst his lordship . . . the laird . . . was here, we should have thought to ask him how Dand is faring." Wondering then if Kit had intended to divert her with the question, she said, "Have you a Sunday name, Kit—Cristina perhaps?"

Shaking her head, she said, "Just Kit is all."

The door opened abruptly, and Simon appeared at the threshold, looking first concerned and then annoyed.

"What are you doing out of bed?" he demanded of Sibylla.

"Mercy, sir, I am still on it," she said calmly. But she set aside the comb and stood to face him, feeling infinitely less vulnerable on her feet, bare or not. "I am a woman grown, sir," she added then. "I'm fully capable of knowing my own mind."

"Nonsense," he said. "No female ever knows her own mind."

She might have retorted, but his gaze had shifted. He was staring at the scarlet kirtle she wore, and she realized that without a shift beneath it, its fabric was too thin to conceal details of her body. The lack had not concerned her before, but with Simon staring so, she felt naked again. Heat flooded her cheeks.

"Be this the young lady wha's sick then, me laird?" a high-pitched, quavering voice inquired from behind him.

His body had been blocking the entrance, but an old woman peeked around him. She wore a long black wool scarf draped over her unkempt, grizzled curls, and had tossed the long end across her meager chest and over the other shoulder of her faded gray tunic. In her visible hand, she carried a small black sack.

Her voice had startled Simon, and Sibylla hid a smile as he stepped hastily aside to make way for her.

"This is the lady Sibylla, Mistress Beaton," he said. "She

knocked her head hard against a tree branch. I want you to do what you can to ease her pain."

"Aye, sure, and so your lad said, me laird. I've brung a potion to give her."

"What manner of potion?" Sibylla asked. "'Tis naught but a headache, so a distillation of willow bark should suffice, or mayhap a mug of steeped yarrow."

The woman cocked her head. "D'ye ken summat o' herbs, me lady?"

"Some," Sibylla said. "Willow and yarrow are both good for pain."

"Aye, sure, if such pain be from fever. But willow stays *all* fever, including the heat o' lust in a man *or* woman. So, as ye're young and bonny, ye'll no want willow. Yarrow be good for most ailments, but me own potion o' rectified wine wi' camphor and spirit o' sal ammoniac be gey better. I'll give it a good shake and—"

"Mercy, you do not expect me to drink such stuff, do you?"

"Nay, me lady. I'll just rub some on me hand and hold it hard on the injury till the potion dries."

"I can do that for myself," Sibylla said, trying not to recoil at the thought of the old woman pressing hard on the knot the branch had left on her forehead.

Looking at Simon, she said, "Prithee, sir . . ." Recalling that he believed he owed her punishment and was unlikely to be sympathetic, she paused there.

To her surprise, he said, "Thank you, Mistress Beaton. You may leave that bottle with us. How often should her ladyship apply this treatment?"

"Until the pain be gone, o' course." She seemed about to protest her dismissal, but after a second look at his stern face, she patted her sack and said, "I've other things, too, me laird. A good eyewash, and dried betony leaves from the monks at Dryburgh Abbey for a tisane, aye, oils o' rosemary and marjoram, and clover for—"

"Thank you, mistress, but the headache potion will be enough," Simon said.

"Wait, sir," Sibylla said, smiling now at the herb woman. "We'll take the clover, the rosemary, and the marjoram, if you please." She looked at Simon, who shrugged and nodded, surprising her.

Gratefully the herb woman accepted the coins he gave her and handed him the potion bottle and the other requested items from her bag.

When he had summoned a servant to show her out, he shut the door and turned back to Sibylla. Then, with a glance at Kit, he said, "I want to speak to the lady Sibylla privately, lassie. Go downstairs to the first door you will come to and open it. I believe Dand is awake now, so you may visit him until I finish here."

Soberly, Kit nodded. Then she looked at Sibylla.

"Go along, Kit," Sibylla said. "The laird cannot eat me."

"Aye, but he may try," the little one said fearlessly. Then, with a quick, wary look at Simon, she hurried past him and out the door, leaving it open behind her.

Simon shut it and turned back to face Sibylla.

A tremor shot up her spine. So much, she thought, for her foolish assumption that he would observe the proprieties.

Cocking her head, she said, "Surely you know you ought not to be alone with me in here, my lord. Think what people would say."

"I don't care what they say."

"I do."

"Do you?" He regarded her thoughtfully before he said, "I should think a lass with such concerns would not have marched out of that wee kirk as you did."

"I was not then a member of Isabel's household," she reminded him. "I could lose my place with her if she should learn I'd been alone with you in a bedchamber."

"Doubtless, my mother's presence here at Elishaw will protect you."

She dared to shrug much as Kit had and saw with unexpected satisfaction that his eyes opened wide. Their fathomless green color fascinated her anew. How unfair, she thought, that a man should have such beautiful eyes. And, too, his lashes were dark, absurdly long, and lushly thick. Most unfair, indeed!

Giving herself a mental shake, and realizing she had instinctively braced herself to step back, she said, "Surely, you've outgrown your fury with me by now."

"I warned you I would not."

"An overproud, angry lad's warning," she countered, undaunted. "That wee kirk was well nigh empty. They read no banns, the priest had not yet said your name, and none who saw us that day will have spoken of it except perhaps my father. And I am very nearly certain that he did not."

"I believe you. But I also know that was not the only time you did such a thing. You did it the year before in front of a crowd at St. Giles in Edinburgh."

"So I did," she agreed. "I also did it the following year just before Otterburn when I refused to marry Thomas Colville of Cocklaw. It pains me to admit that I did not even present myself at the altar to face him," she added with a sigh.

"I knew about Colville but not that particular detail,"

he said with a disapproving grimace. "You prove my case for me."

"I must agree that I do not care much for *some* proprieties," she admitted. "In troth, I am burning now to ask why no one in your family seems to know that you and I nearly married each other. However, inasmuch as I may owe my life to you today, I expect that *would* be unmannerly."

"It would, aye," he said. "But what makes you think no one knows?"

Dryly, she said, "Your mother is not one to keep such knowledge to herself. Nor, if she did know, would she have greeted my arrival as she did. The most telling evidence, though, is that Amalie has never spoken of it or shown any indication that she knows about it. Do you mean to say someone in your family *does* know?"

"Nay, I've told no one."

"But your father must have known. Did you not have to discuss marriage settlements? Mine never shared such information with me, but I believe such a discussion is commonplace before any marriage."

"It is, but I was fully of age and capable of managing my own settlements."

"How could you? You had not yet inherited Elishaw. Surely Sir Iagan would have had to agree to any decision about the land."

"Aye, sure, but I made no agreements about Elishaw, and your father was content with the things to which we did agree."

"Which were?"

He raised his eyebrows. "I don't see how that can be any affair of yours now. By marching away as you did, you effectively rendered those agreements moot."

"Call it unmannerly curiosity then," she said. "Or is

there aught about those agreements that you do not want to reveal?"

She saw that she had angered him again, and the knowledge made her head throb. It had been aching all along, but she had ignored it, well aware that she had exacerbated the pain herself by standing as long as she had.

"I should not have said that," she admitted ruefully.

He was watching her closely again, and he said with an indecipherable but decidedly different note in his voice, "The settlements contained nowt that was out of the ordinary. Sir Malcolm agreed to settle a generous dowry on you and to arrange that you would inherit something more than half of the Akermoor estates if—"

"Faith, sir, I had no right then to *any* Akermoor estate. You forget that until Otterburn my brother, Hugh, was still alive!"

"Aye, sure, but just consider the nature of Sir Hugh's duties as a knight," Simon said matter-of-factly. "With extreme hostilities then between Scotland and England, the likelihood was high that he might die young—as of course he did."

She gasped at the rush of anguish produced by so cruel a reminder of Hugh's heroic death during Scotland's victory over the English. The image her imagination produced of the unseen event was nonetheless stark in its clarity, as always, stirring both outrage and resentment.

Ruthlessly suppressing both, she abruptly shifted the focus of her questions, saying, "Tell me this, my lord. How much had the Governor of the Realm to do with those marriage settlements of ours? You and Thomas both serve him, after all, and I believe that Lord Galston was likewise an ally of his."

His silence answered her question. "I see," she said, putting a hand to her pounding head as a new wave of dizziness struck her.

Simon shook the bottle he held. "Get back on that bed before you fall down."

Stiffening, ignoring her pain, she said, "I dislike being ordered about, my lord. You would do better to make polite requests."

"Would I? Then, pray, my lady, get back on that bed *if you please*, or I will pick you up and put you there." His expression had not changed. "Is that better?"

Knowing he meant every word and was capable of doing as he threatened, she abandoned the remaining shreds of her dignity and got back on the bed.

"Lie back," he said.

"But I—"

He loomed over her and, without setting the bottle aside, pressed her to the pillows, holding her down as he put his face close to hers and said, "I will *not* let you do harm to yourself through nowt but more of your damned stubbornness."

"Let go of me."

"Not until you understand that you will stay in this bed because I command it. If you refuse, I'll take every stitch of clothing from this room to see that you do. Do you understand me?"

"I do," Sibylla said angrily, glad she had had the good sense *not* to say those two words when she had stood at the altar with him three years before.

"Do you promise?"

"Aye, my lord," she replied meekly.

He eyed her shrewdly. "If you hope this sudden docility will persuade me that I need not take the clothing, you are going to be disappointed."

As that was exactly what she had hoped, she wanted to smack him.

~

Her expression provided a mirror to her thoughts, but Simon wished he had not touched her. He'd wanted to shake her the minute she had defied him but restrained himself, not just because of her injury but also because the thought of putting his hands on her had stirred feelings that had nothing to do with vengeance.

When he got close to her, though, and she had made it plain that she would argue with him for the pure sake of argument, he had been unable to stop himself.

To have escorted the herb woman upstairs, expecting to have to waken the lass, only to find her standing before him in the too-revealing red dress, had been a shock to his sensitivities. He had recognized the kirtle as Amalie's but only because, when Amalie had first worn it, the dagged neckline had been a new and daring fashion, and Amalie was particularly buxom.

Fashion had decreed then, however, that the lace edging of the wearer's shift should peek out between the jagged bits, and thus it had covered more of her.

Sibylla was taller and slimmer than Amalie, and clearly had not realized how much of her soft, mud-dusted but nonetheless tantalizing breasts the dagging revealed. In the chilly bedchamber, her nipples had stood out as if eagerly inviting his touch.

Sakes, but they still stood out, lying back as she was, and he could see that she wore nothing beneath the enticing red silk. Collecting his wits, he reminded himself sternly that she deserved whatever he might do to her but said only,

"If you will stay as you are, I'll take the stopper out of this bottle."

She grimaced, then said bitterly, "'Tis hard to retain one's dignity when every facial movement brings pain. But pray, sir, do not remove that stopper."

"The stuff is useless with the stopper in."

"I do not want that potion. I cannot bear the smell of camphor or sal ammoniac separately, let alone together. If you want to help me ease this pain, hand me the vials of oil she gave you. I want to smell them to be sure they are pure, but either marjoram oil or rosemary will do me more good than that horrid potion."

He obeyed, watching her pull out the stoppers and sniff each vial's contents suspiciously. She chose the second over the first.

"Which is that?" he asked.

"The marjoram. One rubs it on the wound, but I suspect the scent does more than the oil itself to ease what ails one. Rosemary oil is similar, but I find marjoram more soothing. If you are willing to aid me more, pray ask your cook or someone else you can trust to steep the clover Mistress Beaton gave you gently in hot but not boiling water and make a cloth poultice from it, wringing the poultice out well. You can then send it back up with the child. It will give her something to do."

"Will it?" he said, making his tone stern again. The lady Sibylla was mistaken if she thought she could command at Elishaw. "I'll have Tetsy bring up the poultice," he added. "She is one of the maidservants who put you to bed. Kit needs rest as much as you do. My cook's wife will look after her. She can keep warm by the kitchen fire and nap in the chimney corner if she likes."

"How is her brother?" Sibylla asked. "I've not clapped

eyes on him yet, you know. Is he older than she is or younger?"

"He must be eleven or twelve, but he's a thin lad and worn to the bone. Unless Kit is gey small and fragile for her age, I suspect she is only six or seven."

"I doubt she can be as fragile as she looks," Sibylla said. "She is very self-possessed for one so young, and she is *not* the one in bed."

"She lied to us, though, by omission if not by design."

"About what?" She had put several drops of oil from the vial on two fingers and began now to rub it on her forehead, flinching when she touched the knot.

He felt an impulse to offer to do it for her but suppressed it, saying, "The lad told me those men pitched him into the river first."

"But how can that be? Kit came downriver well ahead of him."

"Aye, but he said they flung him well upriver. He was trying to swim across to the other side when Kit leapt in, doubtless with some crazy notion of saving him. But the river swept her away. The men had thrown rocks at him, Dand said, so he'd pulled hard for the opposite bank, seeking shelter. When he heard them shouting and saw what Kit had done, he hurled himself after her."

"No wonder the poor laddie is spent," Sibylla said. "But what did the men do then? If they did not throw Kit in, did they try to save her?"

"Dand said they rode after her but when they met another horseman, they all turned back and rode away at speed. I'm thinking they must have been a band of the English raiders who have been plaguing this area and lands to the west of us. I'd like nowt better than to catch and hang them all."

"I saw no other rider," she said. "But I had come from

Sweethope Hill and was approaching the river when I heard Kit scream. Do you suppose the other rider Dand saw had seen you and your men crossing the river?"

"If he was acting as a lookout for them, he must have seen us approaching the ford," Simon said. "Growth is thick on that bank between the river and the track. For him to see us would have been gey easier than for us to see him or his horse."

She nodded, winced, and he shook his head at her. "Go to sleep," he said. "'Tis plain you are not yourself yet, so for once, do as I bid you."

"I don't like doing as I'm bid," she said grumpily. "Moreover, I'm filthy, uncomfortable, and my head itches from mud as much as it aches with pain. And this bed is now as dirty as my body is."

He could see that her hair was tangled and dull looking, but he could not think of her body, still mud spattered or not, without stirring thoughts he dared not think.

Believing she would not stay awake long if left to herself, he said brusquely, "Just lie back and rest as well as you can. I'll send Tetsy up when your poultice is ready, and I'll have someone bring up hot water and clean bedding then, too."

"A bath, too," she pled.

"We'll see," he said. "The herb woman said you'd likely be dizzy from that knock you took, and I saw you sway just before you returned to the bed. It would not do for you to fall and hurt yourself again."

"Sakes, I'm not a bairn," she protested.

"You're beginning to sound like one," he retorted. "You may as well accustom yourself to resting, because I mean to see that you do. I promise you, you won't leave Elishaw until I am persuaded that you are fit."

With a sigh, she said, "Very well, sir, but I do not take well to confinement. So if you expect gratitude—"

"I don't," he said curtly. "I expect obedience. Bearing that in mind, give that kirtle to Tetsy when she comes in to make the bed, and tell her to bring it to me."

On those words, he turned and left the room, taking care to shut the door without banging it. He did not want her to guess how much it disturbed him to see such visible expressions of pain on a woman he was sure usually hid such feelings.

Sibylla watched Simon go with mixed emotions. She was glad to be alone and to rest against the pillows without feeling at a disadvantage. But she was *not* happy about her confinement to the bedchamber and did not mean to give up the only clothing she had. She had to think how she could avoid his taking it from her.

Uncomfortably aware that he meant well and she was probably just suffering from her usual fierce resentment of pain or illness, she shut her eyes and inhaled the mintlike scent of the marjoram oil. It was one of her favorite fragrances. She used it in scent bags in her clothes kists and frequently used the oil in making her perfumes.

Sweet marjoram grew wild in the tall grass of the hills near Akermoor Loch, where one rarely had to search for it. Its strong scent announced the presence of its small, clustering purple flowers well before one trod on them.

Relaxing, she let her thoughts drift back to Simon and how much more human he seemed than the day he had stood in the wee kirk, looking as cold as winter and as if he were about to bestow a grand privilege on her by marrying her.

She clung to that thought, breathing in sweet marjoram. The fragrance reminded her of her pillows at Sweethope Hill. She would remember to drip some of the oil on the clover poultice when the maidservant brought it up, and on the fresh pillow slip, too, when she changed the bedding.

～

Simon walked into the small chamber that opened off the landing below Amalie's room and found the two children murmuring to each other.

He was tempted to question them further about the men who had thrown at least one of them into the Tweed. But he knew he would learn more by talking to them separately. The lass, when she turned to him, looked less confident than when she was with Sibylla, and much wearier.

Her eyes widened as he stepped nearer.

"What will ye be doing with us, laird?" she asked bluntly.

"I don't know yet," he replied. "For the present, I mean to let you both rest and eat. Art hungry yet, Dand?"

"Aye, sir, I'm peckish," the lad said.

But for their thin faces and a certain wiry fragility they shared, the two did not look alike. The boy's hair was almost as dark as Amalie's, and Kit's was flaxen light. The two provided a stark contrast, but so did he and his dark-haired sisters.

Dand's look of wary curiosity was a dead match for Kit's.

"And you, Kit?" Simon said to her. "Are you peckish, too?"

"I am, aye," she admitted.

"When did you eat last?"

She kept silent, but Dand said, "We had a bit o' bread afore them villains came on us, sir, and our barley porridge this morning. But I dinna think Kit ate any o' that. Ye must be starving, lassie."

"I said I was hungry."

"Well, you may come with me," Simon said. "I'm going down to the kitchen to ask them to make a poultice up for the lady Sibylla, and you may watch how they do it so you will know how to make one yourself one day." Noting that she looked cold, he added, "The kitchen will be warm, too."

She followed him silently but was clearly glad to warm herself by the kitchen fire. However, she showed no interest in his discussion of food, hot water, and clover poultices with the cook and Tetsy. Still, she did seem content to stay with them, and Simon was hungry. After giving his orders to the cook and Tetsy, he went upstairs to take supper with his mother.

Chapter 4 _____

Sibylla awoke to the click of the door latch, startled to note that the light in her room had diminished considerably. Seeing a slender, uncertain young maidservant at the threshold in a white cap and a plain blue kirtle, she said, "Are you Tetsy?"

"Aye, m'lady."

"Come in, then. How long have I slept?"

"No so long, but Cook said he'll send up your supper if ye want it, and I've brung your poultice." She stepped to the bed with the small cloth packet, saying as she handed it to Sibylla, "It smells good, that."

Sibylla was starving, but she wanted a bath more than she wanted food.

As she placed the poultice gently on her forehead, she said, "It does smell wonderful, aye, and 'tis still wonderfully hot. Thank you, Tetsy. Did the laird tell you to order hot water for me as well?"

"Aye, m'lady, but he said no to disturb ye if ye were

sleeping. I'll tell them to bring that water straightaway, though." She hesitated. "Um . . . I'm to tell ye ye're no to wash your hair, m'lady. The laird did say it wouldna dry and 'twould be better to wait another day, anyhow—till ye're feeling better, he said."

"Did he?" Sibylla said. "I'll warrant you dislike men who decide what is good for you and what is not as much as I do, Tetsy. Do you not?"

The girl's mouth twitched, and when Sibylla smiled, Tetsy grinned back. "Me brother Jed's gey like the laird in that, m'lady."

"Is he?"

"Aye, and now that he's captain o' the guard he always kens best, does Jed, though I shouldna say such. And, certes, but I'd no defy him," she added.

"Well, I have slept much today," Sibylla said. "Doubtless I shall have trouble sleeping tonight unless I get up and move about. Have them bring up lots of that hot water now so I can wash off the worst of this dirt before I eat my supper. Then mayhap you can come back afterward to tell me when everyone else has left the kitchen. They do leave the kitchen empty at a good hour, do they not?"

"Aye, m'lady, as soon as they tidy it after supper and get the bakehouse fire going. The baker's lad tends to that, and he sleeps by that fire to be sure o' having good coals for the baker's morning breads."

"What about the kitchen fire?"

"They bank it down afore the scullery maids finish tidying the kitchen."

"Mayhap we'll stir that fire up again then," Sibylla said.

"M'lady, we daren't!"

"Don't worry, I know what I'm about in a kitchen,

Tetsy, and barring this sore and unsightly lump on my head, I am perfectly fit. I want you to come and fetch me when the kitchen is clear, because whether the laird wills it or no, I mean to wash my hair and have a bath tonight. I expect there must be a screen to set before the kitchen fire if the baker's lad sleeps round the corner."

"Och, there is, aye," Tetsy said, wide-eyed. "But ye mustna do it. The laird be a proper devil when—" She clapped a hand over her mouth.

Sibylla chuckled. "I served in Princess Isabel's household with Lady Amalie for nearly three years, Tetsy, so I have heard much about your laird. He *is* a proper devil, but he does not scare me."

"Mayhap he should, m'lady," Tetsy said. "I tell ye, it doesna do to vex him. What's more, he bade me fetch the kists from here and said I'm to take that kirtle to him, too, so ye'll ha' nae clothes to wear. Did I no obey him, he'd make a great rant o'er me. Then he'd tell Jed I'd been ill-doin', and Jed would do worse to me!"

Realizing she had frightened her, Sibylla said, "I vow that you will not suffer for my ill-doings, Tetsy. Leave me with this poultice now, and see to that hot water. I want fresh bedding, too. I will *not* sleep in this filthy bed."

"Nay, m'lady. The mistress did give orders for that after she saw the state ye were in. The laird did, too, so I'll see to the bed whilst ye sup."

"That will do then," Sibylla said with a smile. "Oh, but if you must take this kirtle, prithee find me a robe I can wear if I must get up to use the night jar. The laird cannot want me to freeze."

Looking relieved, Tetsy nodded, picked up one of the kists, and hurried away.

In the great hall, servants had set up privy screens on the dais at the north end of the chamber, separating the family table from the constant murmur of conversation in the lower hall, where servants and men-at-arms supped at two long trestle tables.

Simon sat in the two-elbow chair that had been his father's. A gillie had moved it from its normal position at the center of the high table to the end nearest the big hooded fireplace in the center of the long east wall.

Lady Murray and Simon's youngest sister, Rosalie, sat one on each side of him, his mother facing the lower hall and Rosalie with her back to it.

Nearly fourteen, Rosalie had lost her little-girl plumpness and the freckles she had hated as a child and was bidding fair to become a beauty. Roses bloomed on her soft, smooth cheeks, and her dark plaits gleamed in the candlelight. They were not as dark as Amalie's but were nearly as glossy.

Looking up to meet Simon's fond gaze, she smiled and said, "Why did you not invite the lady you brought here today to sup with us? I want to meet her."

"You did meet her, last fall at Sweethope," he said. "She is the lady Sibylla Cavers. She must rest now, though, and her clothes are a mess," he said, recalling that he had tossed her riding clothes in the scullery sink. "You will see her soon."

"I do remember her, and I'm sure I can find her something to wear," Rosalie said eagerly. "I know Meg left some things, and so did Amalie."

With an image of Amalie's red kirtle on Sibylla, Simon said, "Lady Sibylla is taller than Amalie—taller than

Meg, too, I think. But see what you can find, lass." He turned to his mother, who was looking thoughtful and had paid little heed to them. "Mayhap you can suggest something Sibylla might wear, madam."

"I shall see what we have," Lady Murray said. "You may come up with me after supper, Rosalie, and we will look. Then I mean to prepare a message for my cousin Cecil Percy. You were right, Simon, when you pointed out earlier how remiss I was in not requesting more details about his visit."

"It cannot matter," Simon said. "He is welcome whenever he comes."

"He will *feel* welcome only if we are prepared for him, and to be prepared we must know the number in his party," she said. "Had his messenger not left as soon as he'd got permission for Cecil to visit, I'd have sent my query with him."

"Do not all of our kinsmen know they are welcome here?" Rosalie asked. "Why did our cousin have to apply for permission to come?"

Simon kept silent as Lady Murray explained in more detail than she evidently had before that although the present truce was to last ten years, even truces often failed to keep the peace. Therefore, when Scots traveled to England or the English to Scotland, courtesy or wisdom generally prompted them to seek safe conduct in the form of an invitation from someone, preferably a nobleman, in the host country.

"But one need not give a safe conduct whilst English reivers are stealing one's cattle, as they have been, need one?" Rosalie asked, looking at Simon.

"One must first prove that the reivers *are* English," he told her. "Fresh beef tempts men on both sides of the line when their families are hungry, and although I've looked for the men responsible for the raids in this area, so far I've found no evidence to prove they are English. In any event, we don't suspect Cousin Cecil."

"But if they are not English, who could they be?"

"They could be men from either side of the line," he said. "Our own father once stole Scottish beasts when an English army was marching on Scotland."

"*Father* did that?" This time Rosalie looked at Lady Murray.

Austerely, her ladyship said, "Your father thought— quite justly, in my opinion—that if the English came through Elishaw, rather than see them seize all of our beasts to feed their army, other Scots should share the loss."

"The problem now," Simon explained, "is that these raids threaten the truce. Scots nearly always assume the reivers are English and the English that they are Scots. The victims then launch a raid on the other side of the line and hostilities can quickly escalate. Even small raids may eventually lead to all-out war."

"But if someone steals a man's kine, should he not try to get them back?"

"Aye, sure, but the more proper way to do so is to report the theft to one's laird, who then reports it to the march warden. But without proof or admission, an injured party can do nothing to redress his grievance against Scottish reivers before Scottish wardens, let alone across the line."

In the pause that fell, Lady Murray said thoughtfully, "I believe I shall recommend to Cecil Percy that he come one month from now. And," she added with a near challenging look at Simon, "I shall insist that he bring his family, particularly his daughters, and spend a fortnight or longer with us."

"Ask him to bring his sons, too, madam," Rosalie said with a merry twinkle. "If Simon decides not to marry an Englishwoman, mayhap one of my Percy cousins will form a desire to marry me. I am old enough and fast growing older. Moreover, I think it would be most interesting to live in England."

Lady Murray patted Rosalie's arm as she said, "You are indeed old enough to marry, dearling, but I should dreadfully miss your companionship. And your poor father, as you well know, thought you still a trifle young for marriage."

"I am nearly two years past the age of consent!"

Simon said, "Enough, lassie. We'll decide when it is right for you to wed."

She pouted, but then her gaze met his, twinkling again. "I expect you'll want to be rid of me soon enough once you marry, sir. In any event, I have not met many gentlemen yet. You must tell me how I shall contrive to do so."

"We will discuss that another time, but not tonight," he said. "I have duties I must see to before I sleep, and the day has already been long."

His mother announced that she had eaten all she wanted and told Rosalie that they could look for clothes that she could take to the lady Sibylla on the morrow.

Simon was tempted to suggest that they wait another day to provide Sibylla with clothing, but he knew he could not keep her in bed much longer.

He stood politely as his mother and sister left the dais. Then he went down the nearby service stairway to the kitchen to confer with his cook about poultices—and to direct a scullery maid to see that someone attended to

Sibylla's riding dress and the red kirtle—before going out to see Jed Hay and discuss the puzzling increase of raids in the area. The two men talked long, sharing a jug of ale.

Thanks to Tetsy's efforts, Sibylla's bed was clean and she had washed her face and body as well as she could with damp cloths. She donned a clean robe, and had eaten her supper when the maid returned, lugging a fresh pail of hot water.

Sibylla eyed it askance. "What is that for?"

"Ye said ye're loath to get into a clean bed wi' your hair such a mess, m'lady. I would, too, so I thought mayhap we could wash it up here in yon basin."

"I've much too much hair for that wee washstand basin," Sibylla said, vexed that the girl had not realized how badly she wanted to feel clean again. "In troth, Tetsy, I want a bath. Is the kitchen empty yet?"

"It is, aye, m'lady, but 'tis no use. I did ask Cook about fetching a tub up here, but the laird did tell him nae one is to bathe tonight. He said it were too cold."

Sibylla raised her eyebrows. "It will not be too cold in the kitchen."

Tetsy shrugged. "Mayhap it will not, but we canna go down there."

"You need not go with me," Sibylla said. "But although I did the best I could earlier with a cloth and the warm water you brought me, my skin still feels as if it may crack, and my hair . . . Where do they keep the tub?"

Tetsy's eyebrows shot upward. "Sakes, m'lady, it takes two men to carry it!"

Sibylla sighed, eyeing the pail of water with irritation. "Thank you for bringing that water, Tetsy. I know it was heavy, but I cannot bathe or rinse out my hair in that wee basin. There must be a scullery sink and hot water still on the hob."

"In the kitchen? Aye, mistress, o' course there be a sink, and a big kettle of water always sits on the hob. Even a banked fire does keep it warm all night. But did anyone find us a-stirring up that fire, they'd be telling half the castle about it."

"Then here's what I mean to do," Sibylla said. She paused before adding, "I forgot you dare not go with me. I should say no more, so you can say honestly—"

"Nay, m'lady, I'd best go with ye. Ye canna do it alone."

"Bless you!" Sibylla said, feeling guilty for relying on Tetsy's kindness but nonetheless determined. "I swear I'll not let you suffer for helping me," she added.

Whether Tetsy believed her or not, she led the way down the service stairs with her pail. Sibylla followed, her robe tied tight, her bare feet protesting the cold stairs. She carried her poultice so they could claim to be refreshing it if necessary.

At the hall landing, Tetsy peeked in, nodded, and motioned her on.

"Is the kitchen the lowest level of the castle?" Sibylla whispered.

"Aye, save for the dungeons."

Sibylla experienced a mental image of Simon casting her into a dungeon and leaving her there. *Let him try,* she thought, grinning.

The kitchen was as warm as she had expected and the bakehouse behind its fireplace wall even warmer. The bakehouse proved to be a small room with a big fireplace boasting cavelike openings in the rock wall at each end of the fire bed.

Taking swift inventory of the empty chamber, the kitchen, and the scullery at its far end, she said, "If you can find a large basin, Tetsy, we'll start rinsing my hair in the bakehouse. I doubt the laird will visit the kitchen at such an hour, but someone may, so we dare not use that sink for long. Where is the baker's boy?"

"I saw Jack in the hall, m'lady. If he comes down, I'll tell 'im we dinna want folks talking about us being in here. He'll say nowt."

"Good, then set your pail on the baker's table, and find that basin." A thought occurred to her. "There *is* a drain in the scullery sink, is there not, so we can use it to empty the basin when we're ready to sluice the last of the dirt from my hair?"

"There is a drain, aye," Tetsy said. "But ye'll want yon sink clean when ye use it later, so I'll empty our basin outside. Yon scullery door opens to a path betwixt the walls with a drain that carries water straight to the cesspits."

"Go then and take this poultice with you," Sibylla directed. "Set it in a bowl of water from the hob. It can steep there whilst we work in here."

Tetsy hurried to obey, clearly nervous, and Sibylla fidgeted, too, listening for any approaching footsteps. The maid soon returned with a large basin.

"Set it on the table," Sibylla said. "We'll use the water from the pail first, so I can begin working the dirt out whilst you refill the pail. Find towels to wrap my hair in afterward, too. I've brought combs, so we can dry it by this fire."

After Tetsy had poured water over Sibylla's head and

gone to get more, Sibylla worked with the mass of loose hair in water that half filled the basin. That water was soon filthy, and she could do little with the back of her head.

Hearing Tetsy's returning footsteps at last, she said, "Pour more water over the back of my head, will you? Then you can empty this basin."

"Sakes, mistress, we'll be sloshing water all over the baker's table!"

"We'll scrub the dirt off, and the table will dry by morning," Sibylla said, squeezing her eyes shut as water ran into them. "He'll never know."

Tetsy said no more but continued pouring slowly while Sibylla worked the hair at the back. When the pail was empty, Sibylla gathered the wet mass of hair into her hands, squeezing as much of the dirty water out as she could.

"Now, take the basin and empty it," she directed. "Then bring it back and fetch clean water from the hob to rinse me again." She wished she could help but was well aware that while Tetsy could plausibly explain being in the kitchen, *she* could not. And if Simon caught them both, Tetsy might suffer for helping her.

Their process was not ideal, she thought, holding the mass of dripping hair as Tetsy hurried off with the basinful of dirty water and the empty pail. It was the best they could manage, though, and it gave her great satisfaction to be doing something for herself in defiance of her stern rescuer's obstructive nature.

Tetsy had been right about the sloshing. Water streamed off the table to the flagstone floor and into a shallow, curved alcove at the near end of the table. Dubiously eyeing the water's depth, she hoped the floor could also dry by morning.

A large flour bin and a wooden tub that doubtless held lard or goose grease were all that stood on the alcove floor, but smaller supplies occupied two shallow shelves. Baker's utensils hung from iron wall hooks, as did baskets of fruit and nuts.

Most of the spilled water had pooled at the innermost part of the alcove curve, where the flagstone floor met the wall. Water there was nearly an inch deep, so they would have to sop it up with a towel.

As the thought crossed her mind, she saw in the dim glow cast there by the fire that the water was rapidly disappearing. With relief, she decided that a crack between the flagstones was eliminating that problem for them.

Tetsy returned with more water and a second basin, saying, "Two will serve us better than one. If ye'll hold your hair over one, I'll pour this water for ye."

She did so, and had paused to let Sibylla work her hair so the clean water would remove the remaining dirt, when a voice in the kitchen startled them both.

Straightening to grab the pail from Tetsy, Sibylla whispered, "See who that is. Say you were steeping my poultice and stepped in here to warm yourself."

Tetsy nodded, but as she went into the kitchen, Sibylla heard the voice again clearly—Simon's voice. Backing against the wall, dripping and feeling just as a child in mischief might, she wondered what she could say to him if he caught her and how on earth she could protect Tetsy from the consequences.

Simon touched Kit's shoulder and pointed to the pallet in the chimney corner. "See, lassie," he said. "Cook fixed you a good place to sleep till we can return you to your family. He's left you a quilt, too, so you'll be comfortable."

"Aye, laird, but I'd rather stay with Dand. He seems none so well yet."

"Then we must let him rest as much as he can," Simon said. He had not liked the look of the lad, who had swallowed more of the filthy river water than was good for anyone. Hodge said the boy had thrown up most of what he'd taken in, but he had exhausted himself swimming after Kit.

After a long but unproductive discussion of raiders with Jed, Simon had gone to check on the lad and found Kit curled up beside him in the bed. He'd have left her there had Dand not looked up at him with pleading eyes.

"I need t' piss, laird," he muttered hoarsely when Simon raised his eyebrows. "But I'm afeard I'll wake her if I move."

Setting down his candlestick, Simon scooped Kit up. "She ought not to sleep here with you in any event," he said. "I think you've caught cold, and she may catch it from you. Can you get up by yourself? The night jar's in yon corner."

Dand hastily assured him that he could manage, but his progress to the jar was unsteady. Simon said nothing, waiting patiently until the boy was back in bed.

Kit wakened as he carried her down to the kitchen, but he thought she would fall asleep again quickly in the chimney corner.

She eyed the shadowy space dourly, muttering, "It be dark there."

"Not as dark as Dand's room," he said. "The glow from

those coals and from yon bakehouse archway will let you see well enough." As he spoke, he noted a change in the glow and saw Tetsy appear in the archway.

She bobbed a jerky curtsy. "I'll look after her, laird," she said. "I-I came down to fix another poultice for her ladyship."

"In the bakehouse?"

"Nay, sir." She gestured to the kitchen fire. "'Tis on the hob by yon kettle. I'd stepped into the bakehouse, looking for Jack, when I heard your voice."

"Is her ladyship not settling in comfortably for the night?"

"Her head be troubling her," she said. "But yon poultice will set her right."

He nodded. "Then, whilst you wait for it, you may bear Kit company. I warrant she'll fall asleep before that poultice finishes steeping, won't you, lassie?"

"Aye, sir," Kit said with a mournful sigh.

"Get you into the chimney corner now. I'll straighten the quilt for you."

He did so, bade them both goodnight, and adjourned upstairs to the room where he customarily dealt with the castle accounts as his father had before him.

He sat for a time staring at the accounts by the light of several candles, and wondered if the lady Sibylla had found an effective way yet to tidy herself.

Although Tetsy would do all she could to help, he knew he had doubtless annoyed his guest considerably by not allowing her to do as she pleased. The thought drew a rare smile from him.

Sibylla heard Tetsy tell Kit firmly that she had things to see to in the bakehouse. "So you shut your eyes like a good bairn, and go to sleep."

Rejoining Sibylla, Tetsy clutched a hand to her throat as she muttered close to Sibylla's ear, "I tell ye, me heart won't bang right again till morning, m'lady. I doubt the lassie will hear us pouring water, but we'd best not talk."

"What lies the other side of that alcove?" Sibylla asked her just as quietly, pointing to where the water had disappeared.

Tetsy stiffened and seemed to lose color.

Putting a hand on her shoulder, Sibylla whispered, "I thought there might be a door in there, but I cannot find any latch."

"A door?"

Tetsy whispered so quietly that Sibylla could barely hear her, but she did not need to. She could see that Tetsy was prevaricating.

"Do you know of such a door?" she asked.

Tetsy shook her head hard and pressed her lips together.

"I expect I was a fool then to think there might be one there," Sibylla said with a smile. "Help me finish this now."

Looking relieved, Tetsy obeyed. They were silent then until she had piled Sibylla's hair atop her head, wrapped a towel round it, and Sibylla straightened.

"Prithee, move that stool to the—" Breaking off, she stared in dismay at a lad of about ten summers, who had appeared silently in the archway.

Following her gaze, Tetsy murmured, "That be our Jack, m'lady. This be the laird's guest, Jack. She got mud in her hair, and we've been getting it out, but ye're to say nowt. Ye've been watching the men dicing in the hall again, have ye no?"

The boy nodded and moved to the wood basket. Glancing at Sibylla, who smiled at him, he put more fuel on the fire, pulled a narrow pallet to the floor from where it leaned against the wall, and lay down upon it, shutting his eyes.

Tetsy and Sibylla exchanged looks of amusement, but Tetsy said, "I dinna think we should use the scullery wi' these bairns here, so shall I fetch more water?"

Sibylla wanted to rinse every grain of dirt away, but she realized that Tetsy was more nervous than ever about her part in the business and felt increasingly guilty at having put her at risk.

"Do you worry that he will come back?" she asked, knowing Tetsy would understand that she meant Simon and that they would be giving nothing away to Jack or to Kit if the latter were still wakeful in the other chamber.

Tetsy nodded fervently.

"Then you tidy up whilst I rub the dirt off this table and do what I can to dry my hair. We'll go up as soon as you've put everything away," Sibylla said.

The fire was hot, but her hair was by no means dry when Tetsy returned.

"Ye'll catch your death," she said.

"I can plait it and sleep perfectly safely with it still damp," Sibylla assured her as they passed through the kitchen toward the service stairs. "I have often done it, although I know some people do think—"

"Be ye going to leave me here, then?" a small, quavering voice inquired from the chimney corner.

Turning to find Kit sitting with her knees tucked up to

her chin and her quilt clutched around her, Sibylla said, "*You* are supposed to be asleep."

"Nay, I dinna like all them shadows in here. Nor I dinna ken the lad yonder. I'm no afeard," she added firmly. "I just dinna like it here."

Tetsy said, "I can take her up with me, m'lady."

Sibylla began to nod, but Kit scrambled upright and said eagerly, "Or I could sleep on the floor in *your* chamber, mistress."

Looking into the pinched little face, Sibylla could not refuse. So although Tetsy moved to protest, she forestalled her, saying cheerfully, "Then that's what we'll do, Kit. But we must be gey quiet going upstairs."

Chapter 5 _____

Saturday morning arrived with gloomy, overcast skies. Simon arose early, broke his fast, and plunged into his duties. First, he sent messengers to Sweethope Hill and to Sir Malcolm Cavers with the news that Sibylla was safe at Elishaw. He also sent one to Dour Hill, England, with Lady Murray's message to Cecil Percy.

As he crossed the pebbled bailey, he felt the sense of pride that usually struck him, after he had been away, when familiar Elishaw landmarks came into sight through the forest surrounding the castle. Concern for his rescued charges the day before had delayed the reaction.

Beyond Elishaw's southeast wall, two peaks known as Hartshorn Pike and Carlin Tooth rose as tall, silent sentinels. They were landmarks Simon had trusted since childhood to lead him home if he ever lost his way in the forest.

He had climbed them and explored them, learning the value of knowing his environs as he gazed on the vast panorama of Border landscape. From the Pike and the Tooth, one could see into England and know how near the enemy lay. Now, living again at Elishaw, truce or no truce, he kept watchmen posted on both peaks.

While he had served the Earl of Fife, England's nearness to Elishaw had meant little to him. He had spent most of his time then in Stirling or Edinburgh. Moreover, Sir Iagan had remained strictly neutral in Border affairs, aided by Lady Murray's resolve that he follow the same course his father had.

Her ladyship was English and kin to the great Northumberland Percys. So the Murrays possessed strong connections on both sides of the line. Despite such allies, though, Elishaw had suffered occupation more than once.

Simon did not mean to let that happen while he was master. But he was beginning to learn how difficult it was to remain neutral.

The Governor of the Realm had little patience with neutrality and had had his eye on the castle for some time. He had made it plain even before Sir Iagan's death that he expected Elishaw to declare for Scotland.

The Earl of Douglas, more powerful than the Governor but thought by many to be his ally, agreed with him.

Simon had been Fife's man absolutely until Fife had tried to seize Hermitage Castle, a Douglas stronghold. Acting on the Governor's behalf, Simon had found his sisters Meg and Amalie at Hermitage, guests of the princess Isabel Stewart, then married to the second earl.

That discovery had shaken Simon but not as much as the later discovery that Fife expected him to force his sister Amalie to marry a man she detested, and to dower her with a sizable piece of Elishaw land.

Simon's belief in honor and loyalty had kept him faithful even then. But Fife, failing to force Amalie to marry his henchman, then set his sights on Rosalie as the wife his man should have. Simon had flatly refused to permit the marriage.

He had scarcely seen Fife since then, or the Douglas. Either one of them—or both, if they chanced to be of one mind—would make a formidable enemy. And now, with one of the mighty English Percys soon to visit, he suspected that their leader, the Earl of Northumberland, would likewise want to know where he stood.

Therefore, he had little time left to decide what Elishaw's future position would be. The cold, miserable winter had given him a respite. But it had been warming for weeks.

Abruptly pushing these thoughts aside, he wondered how his reluctant guest was enjoying her confinement.

As he thought about her, it occurred to him that at her first near-wedding, to the aged Lord Galston, Sibylla had not been much older than his little sister was now. She had been barely a year older than that when he had expected her to marry him.

"My dearest, whatever are you doing, staring at the wall like that?"

Startled, Simon turned to find his mother with her thinly plucked eyebrows arched even higher than usual. "Forgive me, madam," he said. "I was woolgathering. But I have sent your messenger on his way to Dour Hill."

"I have something to say to you."

Stifling a sigh, he set himself to listen patiently to whatever it might be.

Sibylla had broken her fast in her bedchamber, sharing with Kit the fresh-baked rolls and beef that Tetsy brought them. Noting how carefully the child tried to imitate the way she broke her bread, Sibylla hid a smile.

Tetsy, straightening the bed, looked over her shoulder to say, "I'll take the lassie to the kitchen with me when I go, m'lady. And I'll keep her with me tonight. Will ye be wanting to get back into bed after I've made it?"

"Nay, I will not," Sibylla said. "And I want more suitable garments to wear than this robe."

"Och, aye, and I'm a fool for no telling ye afore now! Her ladyship did say she'll be sending some things along as soon as she attends to some other matters."

"I'll be very grateful to her," Sibylla said, wondering how far down Lady Murray's list the clothing would be.

She did not wonder long, because shortly after Tetsy had taken the protesting Kit to the kitchens, the door opened with no more ceremony than a rap to reveal a grinning, dark-haired girl. She looked so much like Amalie that even had Sibylla not met the lady Rosalie before, she'd have known her at once.

As they exchanged greetings, Rosalie said, "I've brought you some clothes."

"Bless you, shut that door then and help me dress," Sibylla said eagerly. "If I have to wait until Tetsy finishes her other chores, I'll go mad."

"Will you, in troth?" Rosalie said, her dark hazel eyes sparkling.

"I am sometimes prone to exaggerate," Sibylla admitted. "But your odious brother has kept me shut up here with naught to wear since I arrived. I yearn for fresh air and a brisk walk."

"Simon said you had hurt yourself, and you have a dreadful lump on your head. Does it not still ache?"

"Aye, if I heed it. But I am stout enough to get up, and although he insists I should stay in bed, I have also been aching for sensible conversation. So tell me about yourself and about Elishaw. Sithee, I came here once before, but it was whilst you were at Scott's Hall awaiting the birth of Meg's wee daughter."

"I remember, aye," Rosalie said as she laid a gray silk kirtle and another the blue-green color of a forest pond on the bed.

"I like those colors," Sibylla said.

"My lady mother said they would suit you."

"Do you mind helping me dress?"

"Not if you want to talk," Rosalie said. "I almost never have anyone but my lady mother to talk to. Oh, servants, of course. But she does not approve of my talking much with them."

"Does she not? Faith, I learn more from servants than from anyone else," Sibylla said. "They always know what is going on."

Rosalie giggled. "'Tis true, and I own, I do converse often with many of them. We ought not to gossip, of course."

"Pish tush," Sibylla said, doffing the borrowed robe and reaching for the lacy shift Rosalie held out. "Without gossip, Rosalie, the world would be a tedious place, especially for women. So, tell me about Elishaw and its people. Tetsy has told me a little, and your mother, too. But I think she does not like my being here."

"I doubt she dislikes you," Rosalie said, handing her the blue-green kirtle. "She is just determined that Simon shall marry an Englishwoman."

"Mercy, does she fear that I want him?"

"She does not like surprises, and you are beautiful. You've a lovely figure!"

"Well, I've no intention of marrying your brother," Sibylla said. "I'd not have him if he wanted me, which I promise you, he does not."

"I doubt he's given it a thought," Rosalie said. "But your being here is a distraction, especially now. Sithee, Mother is hoping that when her English cousin comes to visit soon, he will bring his daughters. For my part," she added with a mischievous smile, "I hope he brings his sons."

After that, conversation marched as informatively as Sibylla had hoped. She encouraged Rosalie to bear her company for the rest of the morning. And when Rosalie went downstairs for the midday meal, Sibylla went with her.

Having listened to his mother's comments on his management of everything from his guest to matters he had learned to leave to his steward, Simon entered the hall, hoping she would not begin again. Much as he respected her years of experience in seeing to things his father had overlooked, his patience was wearing thin.

Thus, when he saw Sibylla standing beside Rosalie at the dais table, her blatant defiance of his orders stirred no more than well-concealed amusement.

The blue-green gown she wore suited her coloring. Her hair was simply plaited and looked more natural than it had the last time he'd seen it, albeit not as shiny as he knew it could be.

As he was wondering how it had been possible to make it look so much better with only a pair of combs and some water, his mother's entrance diverted him. Had he been fool enough to think Sibylla was there at her invitation, Lady Murray's expression would have banished the thought. Since he had thought no such thing, it merely increased his amusement.

⁓

Sibylla made her curtsy to Lady Murray as Rosalie, likewise curtsying, said cheerfully, "As you see, madam, I have invited Sibylla to dine with us. I knew you would be pleased to see that she has nearly recovered from her swim in the Tweed."

Lady Murray said coolly, "You must not make light of such an act, my dearling. Lady Sibylla risked her life, flinging herself in after that child as she did."

Sibylla had been eyeing Simon, trying to judge if her presence displeased him. When she could not tell, she felt a twinge of disappointment. But Lady Murray's comment drew her attention. Hostess or not . . .

As the correction leapt to her tongue, Rosalie laughed again and said, "My lady mother jests with us, Sibylla. Faith, madam, I know you too well not to be sure you applaud Sibylla's courage as much as you would that of any lady so quick to act in such a case. Rescuing that child was exactly what you'd have done yourself had you been there. Come now, own that I am right."

To Sibylla's amazement, Lady Murray's cheeks turned pink as she murmured, "You are kind to say so, my dearling."

Sibylla glanced at Simon.

His gaze collided with hers as he said, "I would not call that a kindness, madam. You are too wise to cast yourself into a rain-swollen river. Nor should *you* attempt such a foolish thing, Rosalie. Certainly not until you learn to swim. I trust, Lady Sibylla," he added, "that you will not encourage her to emulate your actions."

"I have no concern that she might, my lord," Sibylla said. "Rosalie seems as sensible as her mother and is surely able enough to learn to swim if someone would exert himself to teach her . . . as my dear late brother, Hugh, taught me."

Still watching her as he moved to sit in the two-elbow chair at the end of the table, Simon said dryly, "I see that you are more your usual self today."

She smiled and took the stool Rosalie patted, so they faced Lady Murray with the lower hall behind them and Simon at the end on Rosalie's right. Sibylla was glad they did not sit with the women all at Simon's left, facing the hall. But she thought he might have preferred more formality just then.

Conversation was desultory, with Simon polite but distant, as if his thoughts were elsewhere. His attitude gave Sibylla the urge to prick him with a pin to see how he would react. She had begun to realize that however angrily he had shouted at her in the kirk that drizzly long-ago day, he was no longer a man who so readily revealed his emotions.

Lady Murray, too, remained distant and rather stately, but at least she took part civilly in the conversation. Simon spoke only when someone addressed him.

Rosalie provided a stark contrast throughout with her cheerful, even merry attitude. When she demanded in an abrupt but teasing way to know if Simon had removed himself from them in spirit if not in body, his expression softened.

"I'm still here, lassie."

"Aye, well, if I were to behave so, I warrant you'd have something to say."

"Rosalie, that will do," Lady Murray said. "It is not your place to take your brother to task. Nor should you show him such disrespect."

"I noted no disrespect, madam," Simon said gently. "She is right to remind me that I would reproach her for such behavior. Moreover, she will heed my rebukes more readily if I do not set her such a poor example."

Silence greeting these words, he added, "Do you want to swim, lassie?"

She grinned. "I expect I could learn if *you* were to teach me—"

"Mercy, dearling, do not suggest such a thing," Lady Murray said. "Had one of your brothers or your father taught you when you were a bairn, such a skill might have benefited you. But now that you are turning into a young lady, Simon's teaching you to swim might stir unpleasant talk."

Sibylla glanced at Simon and raised an eyebrow.

"No," he said firmly. "You are not to teach her, either. My mother is right. That, too, would stir talk, and once begun, who can say where it might lead?"

"What you mean is that anyone teaching me would cause gossip," Rosalie said. "But Sibylla says that without gossip, this world would be—"

With a speaking look, Sibylla had silenced her.

"Do finish telling us what she said," Simon prompted gently.

With an apologetic look at Sibylla, Rosalie said, "Just

that without gossip, the world would be a tedious place, sir."

"Especially for women," Sibylla murmured provocatively.

"I will thank you *not* to put such notions in her head," he retorted.

"Will you?"

His lips tightened again, and conscious of Lady Murray's similar expression, Sibylla decided she had better exert herself to soothe her hostess.

Accordingly, she smiled at her and said, "The sauce for this beef is excellent, madam. I have learned many things about herbs and spices at home and with Isabel, but I cannot tell what your people add to this to make it so delicious."

If Lady Murray did not melt at such praise, she did condescend to discuss several recipes with Sibylla. As their conversation progressed, she put Sibylla in mind of Lady Averil Anderson, the princess Isabel's chief companion. Both were sensible, competent women who refused to suffer foolishness or flattery. But neither did they dismiss compliments sincerely offered.

As they were all about to leave the table, Lady Murray said to Simon, "How does the lad fare, sir? Need I concern myself with his mending?"

"He has caught a cold," Simon said. "He told me he felt sick before he went into the river, but he's worse now and still very weak. The lassie is well, though. I've put her in the kitchen to aid the cook."

He excused himself then, and the ladies adjourned to Lady Murray's solar.

At a loss for what to talk about that would not renew her ladyship's hostility, Sibylla recalled Amalie's saying that her mother admired Isabel. Seizing the first chance to mention Sweethope, she described some of her service there.

Rosalie aided her efforts, asking impertinently at one point if Sibylla would not rather find a husband. That gave Sibylla the opportunity to say truthfully that she believed she was unsuited to marry.

"Surely, that is for your father to decide," Lady Murray said.

"I'm sorry to admit, madam, that he has thrice tried to provide me with a husband. He is persuaded now, as I am, that I must remain unwed. He says I am not sufficiently biddable. In troth, though, none of them pleased me."

"Faith," Rosalie exclaimed. "You sent away three suitors! I wish I might have just one! Who were they?"

"Hush, my love," Lady Murray said, relieving Sibylla of the need either to prevaricate or to admit that Simon had been one. "A polite person does not inquire into the intimate details of another person's life."

"Well, *I* shan't do anything so bird-witted. I *want* to marry!"

"In time, you shall," Lady Murray said.

Later, after stopping to look in on the sleeping Dand and put a few drops of marjoram oil on his pillow, Sibylla explored the castle. She talked to the people she met and visited the kitchen, where she asked the cook if he had some dried catmint to steep as a drink for Dand to ease his breathing.

Assured that he would see to the lad, she looked for Kit and found the little girl content—by daylight—to aid the cook and the cook's helpers. The kitchen area was busy though, as was the bakehouse, providing no hope of ex-

ploring the alcove. Sibylla decided she would have to find
another way to learn what lay beyond it.

Tetsy's reaction to her comment about a door had persuaded her that something of that sort existed, but Tetsy
had said no more. Sibylla chatted with others but took
pains to avoid stirring annoyance or curiosity. As a result,
although she learned a few interesting things, not one had
to do with the alcove.

Reminded as she dressed for supper that Tetsy would
keep Kit that night, leaving Sibylla alone after everyone
else retired, Sibylla considered the alcove with fresh enthusiasm. Except for the taciturn Jack—who might well
watch the dicing again—no one would be in the kitchen
after the servants had finished cleaning it.

The day had been warm for the latter part of April, and
the lump on her forehead, although more colorful, had diminished in size. As she tidied her hair, she wondered if it
was worth asking Simon again if he would let her bathe.

Deciding she would do better to ignore him, she considered how she might satisfy her curiosity instead.

~

As Sibylla joined Lady Murray and Rosalie in the hall a
short time later, her ladyship surprised her, saying, "I've
arranged for us to take supper in my solar."

Aware that she was disappointed not to sup with Simon,
Sibylla decided she was taking too much pleasure in their
verbal jousting. To continue might irritate his mother and
lead others to wonder if a match were in the offing.

Neither she nor Simon wanted to initiate such rumors.

Supper might have taxed her ingenuity for conversation had she not learned of Lady Murray's pride in her

kinsmen. That subject served well until Rosalie asked her ladyship to tell them more about Cecil Percy's sons.

It would have been obvious then to a lesser intelligence than Sibylla's that Lady Murray did not want Rosalie to marry anyone yet. She changed the subject and soon announced that it was time to retire.

On the way to her bedchamber, Sibylla met Kit coming downstairs.

"Where have you been, lassie?"

"Talking wi' Dand, but he fell asleep. So I went to see were ye back yet."

"Where is Tetsy?"

"In the kitchen. She said I could visit Dand."

"You should go back to her and see if you can help," Sibylla said.

"She'll be coming to ye anon. I'll just wait wi' ye."

Sibylla agreed but bade goodnight to both assistants an hour later, assuring them that she would sleep well. As soon as they had gone, she got up, lit a fresh candle to replace the stub Tetsy had left burning in the dish, and put her clothes back on.

Carrying her useful clover poultice lest anyone ask why she was up, she went quietly down the service stairs to the kitchen.

Through her conversations that day she had learned that maidservants who lived in the castle slept in tiny chambers under the ramparts. Most of the men slept in the great hall or on pallets outside in the bailey.

As she passed the hall landing, she heard voices and a bark of laughter that told her the men were playing some game or other. Sending up a prayer that the baker's lad was with them or otherwise engaged, she hurried on her way and soon saw that she had judged her timing well. The kitchen and bakehouse were empty.

The baker's fire burned almost as fiercely as it had after Jack had fueled it the night before, assuring her that wherever he had gone, he would not return for a while. Accordingly, she dipped a pewter mug into the kettle on the hob and took it into the smaller chamber. In the storage alcove, she hiked up her skirts, turned so she would not block the firelight, and squatted. Spilling water from the mug to the floor, she watched it flow under the wall.

Her earlier explorations had revealed that the alcove wall was part of an eight-foot-thick exterior wall. Years before she had learned that some Border castles had siege tunnels and had even seen two of them. Holding her candle to the stones, she soon found the straight lines that might indicate the entrance to a passageway.

Turning next to the hooks set into the wall with an apparently random hand—holding towels, oven rakes, utensils, rags for removing hot pans from the oven, and other baker's paraphernalia—she tested each one to see if it would move.

One did seem loose, but try as she might, she could not make it serve her purpose. Shifting her candle, she noticed an odd, shadowy crack in the masonry beside the hook just below it. Pushing it hard to that side, she felt a click. With slight pressure, the rock wall opened away from her into pitch-black space.

Having seen a basket of tallow candles in the kitchen, she hurried to get some, hoping that four would be enough.

Fearing she might lock herself out if she shut the door all the way from the other side, she took a sack of walnuts from its hook, stepped through the opening, and edged the door shut as far as it would go without latching. Then she wedged the sack against its base so it could not swing open of its own weight.

Hoping Jack would not notice the wider crack and that she could come back the same way without disturbing him, she turned and followed the narrow tunnel.

The floor was uneven and the silken shoes Rosalie had given her with the kirtle were thin. Also, the ceiling was low, stirring her dislike of confinement. But if she was right about the tunnel's purpose, she had found an exit from the castle that would take her outside its walls with no one else the wiser.

A short time later, she sensed a change in the atmosphere and the air smelled fresher. Soon afterward, she emerged into thick shrubbery.

She was in the forest, well outside the castle clearing.

The night air was still, and she heard water flowing nearby. Peering through leaves and past branches, she saw moonlight glinting on calm water. With more moonbeams piercing the dense canopy of trees overhead, she blew out her candle and decided to leave her extra ones at the opening.

Easing her way to avoid scratches, she emerged from the worst of the thicket and turned to see torches burning on the distant ramparts behind her. Judging that she had come a quarter mile from the wall, she took care to leave no path through grass or shrubbery as she moved farther away from the opening.

She knew enough to take note of a pair of boulders in direct line with the narrow body of water. Beyond it, a single tall tree completed the line.

Certain she could find the opening again, she continued into the clearing.

Minutes later, she stood by a long, oval pond doubtless fed by the burn she heard chuckling nearby. The pond was mirror still, reflecting the bright full moon in silvery patches wherever its beams touched the surface.

Trees and shrubbery remained dense around the clearing. Despite the flickers of distant torchlight, she was sure no one at the castle could see her. Likewise, no one would look for her at that hour or in such a place.

Smiling mischievously, she pulled off her shoes and dipped a bare toe into the water. It felt warm, but she knew that was because the air was colder.

Nevertheless, grinning in anticipation of ridding herself of the last vestiges of the muddy Tweed, she stripped off her clothes.

Chapter 6 _____

Simon, riding back to Elishaw after taking supper with a man near Hobkirk, was enjoying the stillness of the spring night and the glory of the full moon. Seeing torches ahead on the castle ramparts, he realized he was eager to get home.

His horse was eager, too, and would have broken into a lope had he let it. Both he and the animal knew the way, but bright moonbeams piercing the forest canopy interfered with a man's night vision and could make shadows ahead look like gaping holes in the track. So he curbed the animal's impatience and his own.

Drinking in the night air, he listened for night birds and other common sounds of the forest, as any wary lone rider should.

The night was unnaturally silent.

Feeling safe in his own territory, he had ridden to Hobkirk without his usual tail of men. Continuing silence suggested that he might have made a mistake. Then moonlight through shrubbery ahead on his left revealed unusual movement.

A narrow track just yards away, little more than a deer

trail, led to a clearing that had been one of his favorite childhood haunts. However, poachers also favored the rill-fed pond there as an excellent source of trout and an inviting place for deer to drink, keeping them still long enough for a steady bowshot.

Reining in his horse, Simon quietly dismounted and led it on to the narrower track. Looping its reins over a shrub, knowing the well-trained animal would stand patiently until he returned for it, he moved silently but swiftly along the narrow path until he saw that the intruder was no poacher.

Seeing Sibylla stirred anger even sharper than poachers would have stirred.

As he strode nearer, he was stunned to see that she stood barefoot on a granite slab at the edge of the pond, dipping one foot into the water.

Wondering why she had not simply put in a hand to learn how cold it was, he watched in amazement approaching alarm as she straightened and untied the front lacing of the blue-green kirtle that hugged her shapely body so well.

Numerous thoughts sped through his mind as he stood fascinated, watching her. How had she got past his guards? What had possessed her to leave the castle?

Had the clout to her head affected her senses? Certainly she must be mad to strip off her kirtle as she was doing and endure the cold night air in only her shift?

She caught hold of the shift and pulled it off over her head, dropping it atop the discarded kirtle at her feet.

He could hardly breathe. The moon overhead painted her slender, curvaceous body alabaster white. The smooth surface of the pond reflected her figure as if it were a moving statue. Doubtless, she would catch her death from such insanity.

He ought to order her to put her clothes back on, scold her, and take her back to the castle. But he could not move. Nor, in truth, did he want to break the silence.

He had seen when she was just fourteen that she was a beautiful woman. But he had never guessed how beautiful. Her profile was magnificent, her breasts high and perfectly sized to fit a man's hands. Her waist looked small enough for his hands to encircle. But her hips swelled wide below it, womanly and enticing. His hands flexed, yearning to test the softness of her breasts and bottom cheeks.

With his blood racing, his cock stirred, teasing him with the knowledge that she might have been his for three years and more by now to use as he pleased.

His memory promptly presented him with the image from the altar in Selkirk and his determination never to forgive her. A voice in his head murmured that he could punish her as severely as he liked for the wantonness her actions displayed now, and no one would blame him. As his guest, she was his responsibility.

Sakes, it was practically his duty to teach her the error of her ways!

He took a step forward and saw that she was doing the same. To his shock, she waded into the water up to her hips before she stopped. He had expected a shriek or some other sign that the water was as icy cold as he knew it must be.

Other than the water's whispering as she moved, she had not made a sound.

Recalling that the granite slab dropped off just ahead

of her and that the water was much deeper there, he moved more quickly to the clearing.

At its edge, he stopped with a gasp when she drew a deep breath, put her hands up, and plunged headfirst into the pond.

In his experience, women did not put their heads under water by choice, even women who could swim. He half expected to have to rescue her again, but knowing that she could swim gave him pause.

Although her defiance of his orders had stirred the impulse to punish her, he realized that the ideas racing through his head, of shaking her or worse, were images of childish retribution. They were precisely the "angry lad's" reaction she had once deemed his original threats to be.

As if that were not enough to stop him, his body's immediate, sensual reaction to those images reminded him sharply that just touching her was dangerous for him.

She had attracted him from the moment he'd seen her at the altar. To be sure, half of that attraction had been his belief that Fife wanted him to marry her so Fife could draw Sir Malcolm Cavers into his growing circle of allies.

Fife had offered Simon her generous marriage portion and possibly larger inheritance as a reward for his cooperation. Simon had thought it a sign of favor, an excellent way to increase his holdings, and a way to please his liege lord.

Her beauty had struck him so hard that he realized now, with glaring hindsight, it was one reason he had reacted so furiously to her rejection.

But that was in the past. Her foolhardiness now had gone beyond what any man responsible for any female should tolerate. She deserved censure not only for defying him but also for risking her safety at night in surroundings that must be wholly unknown to her. Moreover, if she *was* trying to drown herself—

Her head broke the surface, stirring sharp relief in place of what had been dawning fear. She seemed oblivious to her vulnerability as she sat with her back to him on what he knew was a flat boulder near the center of the pond. Her upper half was out of the water, doubtless freezing as she tried to wring out her long hair.

Although she must have combed or brushed the bits of dried mud from her hair and scrubbed the worst of it from her body, she had clearly not been satisfied.

Doubtless, too, she had wanted to defy him again as she had by leaving her bedchamber before he had given her leave. He could understand her dislike of confinement, but to have left the safety of the castle alone was folly.

It would serve her right if she caught her death of cold.

If nothing else, she deserved a good fright.

⁓

Sibylla knew she could not stay long where she was. The chilly air was raising goose bumps on her flesh, and experience told her that by the time she got her kirtle back on, she would feel chilled to the bone. She would be cold then until she could get back through the tunnel and warm herself by the bakehouse fire.

She had been gone too long already. Unless Jack was still in the hall or had fallen deeply asleep, he'd surely see her. The thought stirred a resigned smile.

A lad who doubtless faced sound whipping if he shirked his duty would not sleep heavily enough to let the baker find his fire out in the morning. Moreover, although she had brought four candles, she had put out the lighted one on seeing the moon and had brought no tinder box. The tunnel was nearly straight, and she did not fear its darkness, but it would take her longer to return than it had to come out.

Still, the night wooed her with its magical, peaceful beauty. The moon's reflection on water still gently rippling from her swim fascinated her.

"What the *devil* do you think you're doing out there?"

The voice thundering out of the silence startled her so that she plunged back into the water without turning to be sure it was Simon. She hoped she was wrong but knew it was he the minute she surfaced, because she heard him scolding.

He stood at the edge of the pond, arms akimbo, so even before the water had drained from her eyes she knew he was furious and heard as much in his voice.

It was not as loud as when he had startled her. But the spate of his words resembled the sort of muttering thunder that warned of a storm to come.

She had looked forward with interest to their next confrontation, but she had not expected to endure a second one without clothing. Nevertheless, as she collected her wits, she noted again that he was a particularly fine figure of a man.

His hair was tousled, and he had shoved his dark cloak back off his broad, powerful-looking shoulders and chest. He had his hands on his hips, and his snug-fitting trunk hose displayed his muscular legs well. His eyes flashed, his jaw looked rock hard, and his deep voice remained thunderous as he continued to scold.

She paid no heed to what he said. But his fierce expression warned her he might be capable of more than hurling words at her, reminding her of what Hugh had done when he'd caught her swimming alone. Sitting had been painful for days.

Simon had that same look on his face. Belatedly, it occurred to her that she ought to have suspected he might treat defiance of his orders as Hugh had.

"Come out of there at once," he commanded.

Tempted to suggest that he come and get her, Sibylla bit back the words. She was certain he would do it.

Instead, she said with amiable calm, "You are right in all that you have said to me, sir, but I am chilly now and need to put my clothes back on. If you will turn your back, I will get out. However, I will not display myself for your—"

"Don't try me too far," he warned. "It astonishes me to learn that you possess even a modicum of modesty. Just moments ago, you showed no concern about displaying yourself to anyone who might have been looking."

Knowing it would be a waste of words to tell him she had not expected anyone to come upon her there, she kept silent. She also took care not to look into his eyes, lest he capture and hold her gaze as he had before.

As it was, he took a precious long time to turn his back but did so at last.

Scrambling out of the water, she snatched up the shift to dry as much of herself as she could and hoped that if he grew impatient enough to turn around, she could cover the important bits of herself with it.

Even with his back to her, she could feel the effects of knowing he had watched her. Despite the chill, her skin burned with awareness that he had seen her naked. How long, she wondered, had he watched before he had spoken to her?

"What brought you here?" she asked as she stepped into the ring of discarded kirtle and quickly yanked the garment up.

When he began to turn, she whirled to give him her back view as she laced it, blessing Lady Murray for choosing dresses she could do up herself.

She would *not* have wanted to ask Simon for help. Just the thought of him touching her made· her skin flame hotter.

He said, "I was riding back from Hobkirk, and I know this pond. When I saw movement here through the shrubbery, I thought someone might be poaching."

"I did not realize the pond was visible from the road," she said.

"It is not, most of the time," he said. "The woods are dense here. But a trick of light, or mayhap the night's stillness, revealed your movement. It does not matter how *I* came here, though," he added. "*You* should not be here."

"I could not resist the chance to enjoy a half hour's freedom," she said.

"To have come by yourself was unwise. The reason I was away tonight is that reivers—mayhap the same men who tried to drown the children—lifted one of my men's beasts. He sent to inform me of his loss and, I believe, to learn what I mean to do about it."

Glancing over her shoulder at him, she said, "You believe?"

"Aye, well, he did not have the temerity to make the demand, but I'd wager he'd have liked to. It is as well he did not, for I knew not what to say to him," he added. "Until recently, we've had few such problems hereabouts."

She turned, tying off her laces as she said, "Because of your neutrality?"

He looked surprised but said, "I expect you heard that from Amalie."

"One hears much from numerous sources, sir. Surely, you know that in times of strife many complain of Elishaw's neutral position."

"I do know that, aye," he said. "But I do not mean to talk of Elishaw, my lady. I mean to talk about a young woman who defies her host in matters relating to her safety, and does so when she knows that raiders infest the area."

"You have already made yourself plain on that subject, sir." She shivered as she slipped on her thin shoes and bent to retie their ribbons.

Discerning nearby movement, she looked up to see that he had doffed his cloak and was striding toward her. As she straightened, he glanced at her shoes.

"Those shoes are hardly suitable for walking in these woods," he said as he draped his cloak over her shoulders.

She did not reply other than to thank him for the cloak, still cinnamon-scented and warm from his body. She could hardly say the tunnel floor had not hurt her feet. Nor could she say she had noted no discomfort in walking the twenty or so yards from its entrance. At the time, she had thought only of concealing any sign of her passage.

Meeting his piercing gaze, she told him the truth. "I was just seeking brief freedom, my lord. I did not consider the danger or the distance."

"My horse stands a quarter of a mile that way," he said as if he had never lost his temper. "We'll have to fetch him, but I'll put you up to ride the rest of the way."

She did not think he was being kind. One did not think of Simon Murray as a kind man. She was not certain now that he really *had* lost his temper.

He had spoken that first sentence loudly, doubtless to frighten her. But what had followed had been frosty displeasure quite unlike her father's fiery rants.

However, Simon did not care about her as Sir Malcolm did. Simon was just angry that she had defied him.

They walked for a time before he said in the even tone he had used since she had begun dressing, "How did you get out of the castle?"

She knew it had been foolish to hope he would not ask. But she had hoped anyway, because she had no sensible reply and dared not tell him the truth.

Were the truth to expose only herself, she would tell him. But she could not tell him how she'd found the tunnel without revealing her visit to the bakehouse with Tetsy, or that a look on Tetsy's face had told her that a secret existed.

"Well?" he said.

"I walked, of course."

"How did you get past the guards at the gate?"

Not above a white lie or even a gray one in a good cause, she said glibly, "The gate stood open and I walked out, of course. No one saw me."

"I see. That is too bad."

Recognizing bait when she heard it, she grimaced as she asked him why.

"Because I must now hang the men responsible for such neglect."

Sibylla's temper ignited. "You can't do that!"

"Of course I can. I have the power of the pit and the gallows, just as your father has at Akermoor. In times like these, when even a truce cannot protect us from raiders, I *must* hang careless guards."

"If you do such a thing, you will be guilty of a great wrong, because those men were not at fault. No one is but me. I promise you that, on my word of honor."

"Women have small understanding of honor," he said.

"I understand it," she said. "I got out by myself, sir. I shan't tell you how, but I will swear on anything you like that your men had no part in it."

"Is that supposed to impress me?" His tone was icy enough now to stir more goose bumps on her skin. "You lied to me at least once in claiming that the gate was open. You cannot expect me to believe you now."

"I don't suppose I can," she admitted. "What I say is nonetheless true."

He did not speak again, and they reached his horse a short time later.

"I can walk," she said. "The ground is soft, and the exercise warms me."

"We'll go faster if you ride," he said. Allowing no further discussion, he put his hands at her waist and lifted her to his saddle.

It was as well, she thought, that he had done it quickly and without comment, because she could still feel the pressure of his hands on her waist and ribs. She was able to think about little else until the gate came into view.

As she had expected, a chill had enveloped her body soon after she stopped walking. But as they approached the gate and saw it swing open to receive them, one look at Simon's grim expression set her heart pounding. She kept silent.

He made no comment either, merely nodding when the two guards gaped in surprise at her as they greeted him.

She stared straight ahead, but her sense of humor stirred when she recalled that it was the second time the guards at Elishaw had seen her arrive on Simon's horse, wrapped in his cloak, with wet, tangled hair.

Whether he liked it or not, if they had recognized her, word would spread.

In the bailey, a lad ran to take the horse, and Simon lifted her down as effortlessly as he had put her up. Then, with a hand at the small of her back, he guided her past the main entrance and around the stable to a narrow walkway that opened between the outer wall and the rear of the keep.

She murmured, "I trust you won't cast me into your dungeon."

"Don't tempt me," he said. "The entrance to the dungeons is from the bailey, however. We are going to the kitchen, where one of the fires will still be going, so you can dry your hair. You should not go to bed with it wet."

Sibylla's breath stopped in her throat. Having small reason to trust such thoughtfulness, she felt sure he must have realized how she had slipped outside.

Even so, she did not tell him that she often went to bed with damp hair.

⟋⟋

Simon's thoughts had returned to the men at the gate. Their expressions had told him more plainly than Sibylla's promise had that they had not known she was outside the wall. Had they let her out, they'd have looked to him when they saw her, to judge how angry he was at having found her outside the gate.

Instead, they had gaped at her as if they could not

imagine how she came to be with him—or as if they did not even know who she was.

He recalled then that although guards the previous day had seen him carry her in, the hood of the cloak in which he and Hodge had wrapped her might well have prevented a clear view of her face.

In any event, the guards tonight had not looked at him with the fearful expressions he'd expect to see had they had any responsibility for her escape.

His sister Amalie had said Sibylla often seemed to know things that others did not. Indeed, she had assured him that Sibylla was *not* a witch, although admitting that some had called her so. Sibylla simply gathered information where she found it, Amalie had explained, and put it to good use.

He wondered with a touch of dry amusement if Amalie might have underestimated Sibylla's powers.

As he descended with her to the kitchen, his mind continued to seek an answer that fit with what he knew of her and of Elishaw. He found it impossible to believe that she had donned a disguise clever enough to slip past his guards without their having questioned her. Moreover, the blue-green kirtle was the same one she had worn earlier. If she had donned a disguise, where was it?

She had not even worn a cloak. He'd had to provide one again. Gratitude for that act alone ought to have loosened her tongue, but she had barely said thank you.

Having given her the cloak out of courtesy and *not* because her shivering had disturbed him, he assured himself that letting her dry her hair was more of the same.

She clearly spared no thought for such practicalities, but he did hope she might note his civility and decide she owed him an explanation.

Sibylla's apprehension grew with each step they took toward the kitchen. As Simon guided her through it to the bakehouse chamber, she felt as if it were harder to breathe. Jack was asleep on his pallet but woke when Simon prodded him gently with the toe of his boot.

Dismayed, the boy darted a glance at the fire, then looked at his master.

"Go up to the hall, Jack," Simon said. "I'll fetch you when we've finished here. Meantime, I'll take good care not to let your fire go out."

Jack looked relieved, but Sibylla's tension increased tenfold.

Deciding not to allow Simon to continue whatever game he was playing, she said as the boy's footsteps faded in the distance, "Why did you send him so far? He could easily have dragged his pallet into the kitchen."

"I wanted him beyond earshot whilst we talk," he said.

She swallowed. The chamber seemed smaller than it had the previous night.

It dawned on her with horror that the door to the tunnel was still ajar.

She dared not look, but she recalled that the alcove was shadowy. The flour bin and lard barrel surely blocked any view the ambient, flickering firelight might throw on so narrow an opening. But he'd have only to put a hand to the door to discover she had left it off the latch.

"Have you a comb?" he asked.

"Nay," she admitted. Then, forcing a smile, she added, "It won't be the first time I've used my fingers."

"Wait here," he said, striding back into the kitchen.

Crossing quickly to the alcove, she pulled the tunnel door to, taking care to hold the latch open, lest it make a noise loud enough for him to hear as it tripped over its catch and fell into place. Then, instead of moving from the alcove to the fire, she stepped toward the archway and met him as he returned.

"I should have known you wouldn't wait as I told you to," he said.

"Curiosity is my besetting sin, sir. But you've found a comb!"

"And a brush," he said, showing her. "My sisters keep them down here for drying their hair. I was not certain I'd find them, but I did."

"Thank you," she said, accepting the implements. "You may leave me to dry my hair if you like. I can easily find my way back to my bedchamber."

"It does not suit my notion of courtesy to leave a female guest to wander the halls of this castle alone any more than to let her traipse about the forest at night. And I still have more to say to you."

Words flowed from him as she pulled a stool to the fire and began to brush her hair. She listened as politely as she could, given the irritation she felt at his continued attempt to command her and a waning hope that he would not mention the tunnel.

Yearning to have the matter over and done, she nearly spoke of it herself at one point. But she held her tongue, and when he pressed her harder to tell him how she had got out, she let her temper show.

"I have said I will not tell you, sir. I meant that."

"I mean what I say, too," he retorted. "However, if you will not tell me, I warrant you will tell your father."

"My father!"

"Aye, I sent for him this morning to come and fetch you."

"But I'm going back to Sweethope Hill as soon as I can persuade you to lend me a horse! Isabel's people must be frantic by now."

"I sent a messenger to Sweethope as well."

"Thank you," she said, feeling both relieved and exceedingly guilty that she had not thought earlier to ask him to do so. "Even so, sir—"

"Mayhap your father will take you there," he said. "I took the liberty of informing him that Isabel had left you there by yourself. I also suggested that that decision might not have been the wisest one she has made."

"Did you?" she said grimly, wishing she could snatch him baldheaded. "How very thoughtful."

"It was, aye," he said. "Is your hair dry yet?"

"Yes," she said tartly, although it was still very damp.

When he reached to test the truth of her words, she gave him a look that ought to have incinerated him on the spot. It did not, nor did it stay his hand.

He gripped a handful of hair, gave her a look, and said, "We'll let it dry a little longer, I think."

He leaned against the nearby wall, silently, his arms folded across his chest. She still felt lingering heat all through her from his just having touched her hair. He was gazing around the chamber as if he had not seen it before. When he peered into the storage alcove, she shifted her own gaze back to the fire.

Setting down the brush a few minutes later, she deftly plaited her hair and said, "It is dry enough now, sir. We can go."

He made no objection, nor did he feel her hair again.

Halfway up the stairs, she realized he could not be certain that she knew of the tunnel. Therefore he could not test the door or ask her about it without revealing its existence to her if she did not know. Now that she had shut it, even if he found the wee sack of walnuts she had put against it, he could not be sure how it got there.

He saw her to her door. Only as she was politely bidding him goodnight did the unlikely chance that he might know nothing about the tunnel occur to her.

She was pondering that thought as she opened the door to the bedchamber and stepped inside. By the light of the guttering candle she had left burning in its dish, she saw Kit asleep on the rag rug in front of the washstand.

Quietly stripping and donning the robe to keep warm, she thought about the evening behind her as she draped the blue-green kirtle over a pair of kists to air.

In sending for Sir Malcolm, Simon had doubtless meant to punish her more. It was annoying, but she could do nothing about it.

What was less understandable was her strong mental and physical reaction to Simon himself, in the woods and afterward. She had enjoyed their verbal sparring from the outset, and she had definitely reacted to his pushing her back on the bed the day before. But she'd felt unusually vulnerable then and had believed her reaction nothing more than that.

More puzzling was the knowledge that she'd have found it hard to reject his touch had he tried to do more that night than feel her hair to see if it was dry.

Deciding she was indulging in foolishness to think such things about a man who didn't like her, Sibylla gazed affectionately at the sleeping child for a long moment and then returned her attention to preparing for bed.

Chapter 7 ─────────────

After a quiet Sunday, due to Lady Murray's English insistence on observing the Sabbath, Sir Malcolm Cavers arrived Monday afternoon with a tail of a half dozen men. The Murrays and Sibylla were just finishing their midday meal.

Having given his men orders to inform him if anyone approached, Simon excused himself from the table after a gillie murmured the news in his ear.

Informing the others that guests had arrived, he said, "You will want to linger at the table, madam. Anyone arriving at this hour cannot yet have dined."

"To be sure, we will stay to welcome them," Lady Murray said. "But I cannot imagine who has come. It cannot be Cecil Percy, for I told him most particularly that he should come in four weeks' time."

"How many have come, Simon?" Rosalie asked when he did not reply to Lady Murray's less direct approach.

"The lad said seven, mostly men-at-arms," he said. Catching Sibylla's eye, he held her gaze briefly but looked away when she wrinkled her nose at him.

Satisfied that she had guessed her father was his chief

visitor, he strode from the hall to greet Sir Malcolm. As he crossed the threshold to the stairs, he heard his mother repeat her declaration that she could not imagine who had come.

~

Sibylla turned to Lady Murray and said, "I believe your son sent for my father, madam, a rather highhanded act as I'm sure you will agree. Apparently, he thinks I am not safe at Sweethope and require more protection."

"Sir Malcolm Cavers? Coming here?"

Detecting a note of strain in place of her hostess's usual stately aplomb, Sibylla said, "I believe so, aye. Does that displease you?"

"Nay, nay," her ladyship said with an airiness belying her words. As if she realized it, she added brusquely, "Certes, my dear, you are too young to be all alone as you have been since Isabel left Sweethope. She ought never to have left you so."

"I was sick, my lady, but hardly alone. As you must know, the Douglas provides Isabel with two knights and fifty men-at-arms to serve her, and more when she travels. She left twenty trustworthy men to guard Sweethope in her absence."

"Bless me," Rosalie said, awestruck. "Twenty men to look after you!"

Lady Murray looked disapproving, but Sibylla said with a grin, "They do provide protection for us, Rosalie. But their chief duty is guarding Sweethope Hill House. We also have a number of maidservants. I'd like to pretend that I manage the entire household in Isabel's absence, but of course I do naught of the sort."

"Do you not?" Lady Murray said absently, her gaze drifting to the archway.

"No, madam," Sibylla replied. "Her steward and housekeeper look after all of us, along with her stablemaster and other servants. I was relieved to learn that Simon had sent to tell them I was safe here."

"I am sure you were, but mayhap you should refer to him as Lord Murray in front of our guests and . . . and our servants, my dear. One does not want to give the wrong impression of your presence, as you might by referring to him so familiarly."

She did not look at Sibylla as she spoke, and although Sibylla's back was to the lower hall, she knew her ladyship was watching for Simon to return with Sir Malcolm. The privacy screen shielded that end of the table from the hall, but Lady Murray's position afforded her a view of the entrance archway at the far corner.

It puzzled Sibylla, though, that her ladyship stared with such intensity.

Demurely, she said, "I pray you will forgive me for the lapse, madam. I am so accustomed to Amalie's calling him Simon that I've often done so myself. Also, I was not sure he referred to himself as Lord Murray, as Sir Iagan did not."

"My husband was justly prouder of his knightly title," Lady Murray said, her gaze still fixed beyond Sibylla's shoulder. "Your father is, too, is he not?"

"He is, aye."

"Both of them inherited baronies but won knighthoods at great risk. Simon has served the Earl of Fife in many ways but has not yet won his spurs. So he takes his title rightly as a baron, and you will call him so if you would please me."

Sibylla murmured her willingness to do so but was not sure Lady Murray heard her. The woman's ears were as attuned as her eyes were to the archway.

Moments later, Simon returned with Sir Malcolm. As was the latter's custom, he was talking heartily as they entered.

". . . so I was astonished to get your invitation, Murray! But I took your news most gratefully. I'd no notion my lass was alone at Sweethope. Never thought it! But ye were gey long-headed to think I'd not like it. I do not, not one whit!"

With a slight grimace, Sibylla arose and turned to watch the two men make their way between the trestle tables where the castle servants ate.

"Good afternoon, my lord," she said to her father as he mounted the dais and bestowed a kiss on her cheek. "I trust you had a pleasant journey."

"Aye, lass, aye, and ye're looking fine but for yon bruise," he replied bluffly.

He was not as tall as Simon and was bulkier through chest and stomach. But he'd been a handsome man in his prime and remained so despite a fondness for food and drink that had taken a toll on his figure. His once dark auburn hair had grayed at the temples, and his fashionably pointed beard bore gray streaks. But it was trim and tidy, and the silvery eyes his daughter had inherited were still wont to twinkle.

The current craze for tight, varicolored nether hose did not flatter him, but his clothing was expensive and well cut. He was a proud man but carried his pride and his impressive lineage lightly, and with an endearing touch of humility.

Despite his flaws and his tendency to make hasty decisions with which Sibylla could not agree, she had great affection for him. Now, however, he eyed her with stern disapproval as if trying to decide how to begin expressing his feelings.

A sound from behind her diverted him and drew a smile of pure delight.

"Annabel, by my faith, is it yourself?" He swept Lady Murray a deep bow. "Had I not been so grateful to see my lassie safe and sound, I'd have seen ye at once! That I failed is nobbut the measure of my concern for the naughty puss."

"I believe my son sent for you to fetch your daughter, sir," Lady Murray said, a touch of strain still evident in her voice.

"He did, aye, and I am glad of it and sorry she has been a trial to ye," Sir Malcolm replied, clearly oblivious of her tension. "I've nae doubt ye still mourn your husband and younger son, madam. Such a tragedy to lose them both as ye did!"

"It was, indeed," she said. "But my son has taken command here and does very well. Do you stay with us long, Sir Malcolm?"

Her manner, Sibylla thought, suggested that a short stay would be wiser.

Sir Malcolm said as cheerfully as before, "I dare not, lest your husband's ghost haunt me. He and I did not get on, as ye ken fine, m'lady. Ye may not have been aware of that, lad," he added in an aside to Simon. "Your father did not welcome me here, so I mark well your kindness to my lass. Still, I thought it best to leave her younger sister at home, rather than tax your hospitality."

"You are welcome at Elishaw, Sir Malcolm," Simon

said. "I do not fight my father's battles, especially when I do not know their cause."

"Trifles, I promise ye, lad. Nobbut foolishness we need not discuss here."

"Do take this seat, sir," Simon said, indicating a back-stool near the center of the table and signing to a gillie to move his two-arm chair from the end to the place between Lady Murray and Sir Malcolm.

As the two men sat, and servants hurried to provide Sir Malcolm with food, Simon added, "My lads will bring in your men when they are ready to eat."

Sir Malcolm nodded, but his attention had drifted back to Sibylla. "I ken fine that ye must be disappointed I did not bring Alice," he said. "Ye've not clapped eyes on the lass for nearly a year, but I warrant she were glad to bide at home."

"She is not sick, I hope," Sibylla said.

"Nay, just put about by the grand marriage I've arranged for her. As she is nearly fifteen, most would say she should have married long ago."

Aware of Rosalie beside her, Sibylla chose her words with care. "If she is put out over your choice for her husband, sir, mayhap you should heed what she says."

His brow furrowed and his bushy eyebrows knitted as he fixed a stern look on her and said, "Ye'll be keeping such opinions to yourself, my lass. Unlike *you*, Alice will do as I bid her."

Sibylla felt Rosalie stir and said hastily, "I am sure she will, sir."

"Faith, Sibylla, do you *frequently* disobey your father?" Rosalie asked.

Sibylla turned to her with a quick smile, but before she could speak, Lady Murray said, "Such a question of our guest is most improper, dearling. Prithee, wait until someone addresses you before you insert yourself into a conversation."

"Yes, madam, I beg your pardon," Rosalie said. "And yours, my lady."

"Aye, sure," Sibylla said. She sensed that Lady Murray's curiosity was as strong as Rosalie's and knew that both had recalled her three suitors. She could only pray that her ladyship's strong sense of propriety would keep her from asking Sir Malcolm about them.

Simon drew Sibylla's gratitude then by inviting Sir Malcolm to share any news he had from the capital. As Sir Malcolm continued to eat while they talked, the men effectively shut the women out of their discussion.

Enduring only a short time of this two-way conversation, Lady Murray said into a brief silence, "I hope you will forgive me, Sir Malcolm. I have much to do to see that all is in readiness for your stay. My daughter has duties to see to as well."

"To be sure, my lady," he said genially. "I've no doubt my lass will aid ye both. She'll not want to listen to us discuss men's affairs."

"But heed me, Sibylla," he added as Lady Murray arose and everyone else, perforce, did likewise. "Murray has explained how ye came to be here, and I'll have much to say about that anon. Ye'll return with me to Akermoor tomorrow."

"It is good to see you, sir," Sibylla said with a smile. "I look forward to talking more with you."

He gave her a speculative look but did not question her meaning.

Noting a shrewder look on Simon's face, she avoided

his eye as she and Rosalie followed Lady Murray from the hall.

"Is there some way I can aid you in your duties, madam?" Sibylla asked as they reached the stairway.

"Quite unnecessary," Lady Murray said. "I shall alert our housekeeper, although I expect Simon has already done so. Unlike most men, he is efficient about such things after years of anticipating Fife's wishes. We will adjourn to my solar."

Rosalie said, "I *am* sorry for speaking out of turn, Sibylla. But you did tell us about your suitors, and I just wondered if you often dare to disobey your father."

Sibylla hesitated, waiting for Lady Murray to quell her daughter again. When she did not, and did not forbid Rosalie to join them in the solar, Sibylla said, "We can discuss that more if you like, lassie. But not, I think, here in the stairwell."

In the solar, she waited until Lady Murray had sent a gillie with her message to the housekeeper. Then, with the door shut behind him, she said, "Do you object if I answer the lady Rosalie's question, madam?"

"Not at all," her hostess said, arranging herself on a cushioned back-stool and drawing her tambour frame close. "I own, bad manners or none, I am curious, too."

"Well, I don't often disobey, but I've told you how unsuited I should be to the wedded state," Sibylla said. "That, of course, was why my lord father said what he did. After his third attempt to arrange a marriage for me failed, he told me I would end my days at Akermoor in the manner of most unmarried maidens."

"Which is to say, as a servant in your own home," Lady Murray said.

"Horrid!" exclaimed Rosalie. "But you live with Princess Isabel."

"Thanks to my brother and my very kind godfather."

Lady Murray frowned. "Who is your godfather, Lady Sibylla?"

"Archibald Douglas," Sibylla said.

Rosalie squeaked, "The Earl of Douglas?"

"He was not yet the earl," Sibylla said. "But he was cousin to James, the second earl, and James was Isabel's husband. Also, as Lord of Galloway, Archie was gey powerful in his own right."

"That explains your acquiring a place with Isabel," Lady Murray said. "The Douglas has afforded her particular attention since her husband's death. Indeed, he pays more heed to her than members of her own royal family do."

"I need not tell you, madam, that the princess is well beloved by most of her family. It is only one or two of her royal brothers who would cause her grief."

"One in particular, I believe," Lady Murray said with a sigh.

"Aye, madam," Sibylla agreed. "I know you think highly of the Earl of Fife and that your son has long and most loyally served him, but . . ." Recalling Rosalie, she said, "But I should say no more about that."

"Do you not like the Earl of Fife?" Rosalie asked.

Lady Murray said, "Such things are complicated, dearling. But in plainest terms, we here at Elishaw strive to get on with everyone. The more allies a family has, especially powerful ones, the less likely it is to suffer in times of strife."

Rosalie thought for a moment. Then she said, "Will

you have to give up your position with the princess now, Sibylla, and become your family's servant?"

"Oh, no," Sibylla said. "My place with Isabel is secure, and I must soon rejoin her. She was to stay at Turnberry only until the royal court moved from Stirling to Edinburgh. And according to what the men were saying earlier, the court *is* in Edinburgh, so I expect the most convenient course is for me to join her there."

"But how will you do that?" Lady Murray asked, frowning. "Surely, Sir Malcolm will have something to say about it."

"I don't doubt he will have much to say, madam, but I must fulfill my duty to Isabel. Once his temper calms, he will soon come to understand that, I think."

"I believe he will," Lady Murray said, her frown turning thoughtful.

⁓

After the women left the hall, Simon maintained a desultory conversation with Sir Malcolm until the latter had eaten his fill. Then, signing to gillies to clear the table, he suggested that his guest might like to see more of Elishaw.

"I'd like to, but I'd prefer to hear more about how ye found my daughter."

"Then we'll walk outside, where we can talk privately," Simon said.

"I've a notion ye want to quiz me as well," Sir Malcolm said as they went downstairs. "Seems providential, this. Have ye taken an eye to my lass again?"

"No, sir, nor would it do any good if I had," Simon said. "She made her position clear years ago, and I see no indication that she has altered it. Nor," he added firmly, "have I changed my views. You may recall what I said to her then."

"Roared at her, more like. But she's a stubborn one. Defiant, too. Whilst our Hugh were alive, she'd go to him first and have him plead her case with me. He indulged her too much, did Hugh. In troth, though, I was as wax in the lassie's hands, too. Bless me, but I ought to have taught her obedience."

"There are tried and proven ways, sir," Simon suggested.

Sir Malcolm grimaced. "I'm not a man of violence with my lasses, sir. 'Tis no use expecting that from me. I roar, though, and Alice—bless her—submits to roaring. But Sibylla just stands and looks at ye, waiting for the storm of 'ye won't' to pass before she says, 'I *will*.'"

"I warrant you are not the first man ruled by a stubborn daughter, sir," Simon said, vowing again that no woman would ever rule him.

"Sithee, lad, she's the spit of my dear wife, rest her soul. Not in temperament, mind ye! My Mary were as gentle as a woman could be, but our Sibylla looks so much like her that . . . Well, I'm a weak man, is all. That'd be what ye're thinking."

"Nay, sir," Simon said, although he was. "I should tell you, however, that my mother does not know I once nearly married Sibylla."

"I suspected ye'd said nowt to them at the time, so it does not surprise me that ye've told them nowt since."

"Doubtless you've guessed that I feared if I did tell them, they would forbid the match. I had good reasons of my own, too, to agree to it."

"Fife, of course. I cannot blame ye for that when gain-ing an ally in the man was my reason for accepting the suit. I knew ye'd not be doing the thing without him guiding your steps, and your close access to him was desirable to me. As to not wanting to tell your mother . . . Sakes, me own sweet Mary could be a terror if she learned of such things after the doing, so I'll not tell Annabel on ye. When she was young, she was the soul of competence and good sense, but folks tell me now that she's known better for her managing disposition."

"She is still a competent woman, sir, and gey shrewd," Simon said mildly. He wished he could in good conscience quiz the man about Lady Murray's younger days and learn how well he had known her. Instead he said, "I value her opinions, but I own, I'd liefer she not hear about that arrangement from anyone but me."

Sir Malcolm smiled wryly and said, "Take my advice, lad, and tell her at the first opportunity. I'd not put it past that contrary puss of mine to let summat slip."

"She has not done so yet," Simon said. "Nor did she tell my sister Amalie, although Amalie served with her in Princess Isabel's household."

"Even so . . ." Sir Malcolm paused.

"Sakes, sir, you're taking her home tomorrow. With the river Tweed between us again, I doubt we'll see much of either of you after that."

Two hours later, a rider from Edinburgh arrived with a message for Simon from the Governor of the Realm. He was to join the royal court as soon as possible.

～

When Sibylla left Lady Murray's solar later that afternoon, she saw no sign of Sir Malcolm or Simon. Returning to the solitude of her bedchamber, she pondered how she might gain her father's permission to rejoin Isabel in Edinburgh.

As fond as she was of Sir Malcolm and of Alice, and as pleased as she would be to see the latter, she could not let the two of them immure her at Akermoor.

One way or another, she would rejoin Isabel, and quickly, before Sir Malcolm should take it into his head to order her to stay home. Even Archie the Grim was unlikely to support her in defiance of such a command.

"Mistress?"

Startled, Sibylla turned to find Kit behind her on the stairway.

"Faith, lassie, how do you tread so lightly?"

"If nae one hears ye, nae one tells ye to do summat ye dinna want to do."

"Is that why you disappeared again this morning before I awoke?"

Kit looked around as if she feared someone were listening, then whispered, "Tetsy's no happy an she finds me in your room. She shoos me away."

"I expect she thinks you ought not to creep into my chamber at night, as you have, without an invitation," Sibylla said gently.

"Aye, sure," Kit replied. "She said I must no . . . must *not* do it again, but I dinna . . . do not like sleeping wi' Tetsy. She snores louder than Dand does."

"I am sorry to hear that," Sibylla said. "I shan't be here much longer though, Kit. My father has come today, and he means to take me home with him."

Kit's face fell. "Where do ye live then?"

"A place called Akermoor, on the other side of the river Tweed—where you and I met." The child's silence and solemn face made Sibylla want to reassure her. "You and Dand will be safe here," she added. "The laird will look after you."

"Aye, but I like to sleep with ye in here," Kit said. "D'ye think my hair will one day grow to be as long as what yours is?"

"If you do not let anyone cut it, it will," Sibylla said, opening the door to her chamber. "You may come in if you like. Is your hair always kept short?"

Kit shook her head. "I cut it m'self t'other day."

"Why?"

Kit shrugged. "I just did. Ye dinna have anything to pack up, do ye?"

"Not much," Sibylla agreed, hoping her hostess would not object if she took the two kirtles with her to wear on the way. "Now that I think of it, do you happen to know what became of the riding dress I was wearing when I fell into the river?"

"It got ruined," Kit said. "The laird took it away and put it in the scullery sink, and then a scullery maid rinsed it out and hung it by the fire to dry. It shrunk to bairn's size, Tetsy said. She said it be fine wool, too, and they ought to ha' asked her ladyship's woman how to dry it. Tetsy were fearful ye'd ask after it afore now."

Sibylla would miss the riding dress, which had been a favorite. But she could order another made in Edinburgh. Boots were a more pressing matter. A day's ride in a pair of silken slippers was unthinkable.

It occurred to her that she would need more than boots and a riding dress in Edinburgh, because her father was unlikely to agree to return to Akermoor by way of Sweethope Hill. Sweethope lay miles northeast of Elishaw, while Akermoor lay nearly as far to the northwest.

Her father would say, and rightly, that she had garments aplenty at Akermoor. That they were all years out of date would not matter to him. And, since he assumed she would stay at Akermoor, he would say that it should not matter to her either.

Her sister would have fashionable clothing, to be sure, but unless Alice had grown since the last time they'd seen each other, she was smaller in every way.

When the princess arrived in Edinburgh, the matter would resolve itself. Isabel was of a similar size and generous with her cast-off clothing, and the lady Susan Lennox was also much the same size as Sibylla.

Lady Susan was not as generous as Isabel. But Sibylla had no doubt that she would be pleased to lend her clothing if only to feel superior in doing so. Such things mattered much to Lady Susan and not at all to Sibylla.

The best course, she decided, would be to send a messenger to Sweethope from Akermoor to request that they send a selection of her clothing to Edinburgh.

The trick, of course, would be to get to Edinburgh in the first place.

Kit had wandered to the washstand and was refolding the towel there. When she turned and scanned the room, Sibylla felt a touch of amusement at the child's determination to serve her.

"I wish I could take you with me, Kit," she said impulsively. "I think you will make a fine attire woman for a lady one day, especially if you continue to improve your manners and speech as I have noticed you doing here."

Flushing, Kit nibbled her lower lip, but Sibylla thought she was pleased.

When Tetsy entered a short time later, she threw up her hands at seeing Kit. "I vow, m'lady, that bairn be like smoke," she said. "One minute ye see her; the next she's vanished. I've told her she's no to follow ye about, but nae one misses her in the kitchen. She's no been trained for scullery work, and she's too small to reach the sink anyhow without she has a box to stand on."

"Never mind, Tetsy. You may let her sleep here again tonight. I must go home tomorrow, and I warrant Kit will behave just as you like then."

"Och, aye, I ken fine that ye're going, and I must tell ye that yon dress—"

"Kit already told me that my riding dress shrank. I hope you did not throw it away, though. Someone smaller can still make use of it."

"They will, aye, for the laird did say to give it to Cook's wee daughter."

"An excellent notion."

"Aye, but he be leaving, too. The Governor did summon him to Edinburgh."

"Did he?" Sibylla said, her thoughts racing. "How providential!"

⁓

When Simon entered the hall for supper that evening, his family and one of his guests stood at their places by the dais table, awaiting his arrival. Sibylla, however, came to meet him as he stepped onto the dais.

She wore a gray kirtle with a pink sideless surcoat over it, and he noted that tonight her eyes were silvery. The dark rims of her irises emphasized the effect.

"May I have a word with you, sir?" she said so quietly that she doubted anyone else could hear her.

"Certainly," he said in much the same tone. "How may I serve you?"

Keeping her back to the others, she said, "You mean to depart soon for Edinburgh and, I suspect, will take the Selkirk road, which passes near Akermoor. I had hoped I might persuade you to escort me there to rejoin Isabel."

"You know I cannot do that without your father's permission," he said. "But how is it that you are so well informed? I have told no one of my plans."

Eyes twinkling, she said, "The wind whispered the news to me."

Recalling that Amalie had said some folks thought Sibylla might be a witch, he nearly believed it just then.

Then, as he took his seat, Lady Murray said in her customary stately tones, "I have decided that Rosalie and I shall accompany you to Edinburgh, sir. She is old enough now, I believe, to attend the royal court."

Chapter 8 _____

Sir Malcolm said to Simon in surprise, "Bless me, Murray, d'ye go to Edinburgh, then? If so, ye're bound to go by way of Selkirk."

"That is my usual route, aye," Simon said.

"Then ye'll stay the first night at Akermoor. We lie but two miles off yon Selkirk road. After your kindness and hospitality to my lass, I'll hear of nowt else."

"Looking after the lady Sibylla was no trouble, sir," Simon said, sensing his mother's immediate tension. "In troth, you need not—"

"Simon, you know our lady mother dislikes traveling more than fifteen miles in a day," Rosalie said. "It is kind of Sir Malcolm to invite us, is it not?"

"It is, aye," Simon said, glancing at her and wondering at his mother's unusual silence. The pause, however, was all Rosalie needed to continue.

"I should like to see Lady Sibylla's home," she said eagerly. "I want to meet her sister, too. If she has not yet turned fifteen, she is just a year older than I am and I know few girls so near me in age."

Simon turned to Lady Murray. "What think you, madam?"

"Two miles off the main road is four miles out of our way," she said. "Doubtless, you will prefer to ride on to Selkirk."

Sir Malcolm said, "Whilst one always respects your judgment, my lady, that would mean riding twenty-two miles the first day. I'm thinking ye'll be content to stop a few miles sooner, especially if ye've packing yet to do before we depart."

"We are not so fragile, sir, nor so lacking in forethought," she replied. "We have prepared for Rosalie's court appearance this year, and I set my women to packing as soon as I learned of Murray's intent. We will be ready when you are."

"Aye, then I'll tell ye this, lad," Sir Malcolm said. "A good hill track leads north from Akermoor past an ancient Roman camp. It fords Ettrick Water west of Selkirk and the Tweed not far beyond. 'Tis shorter and will take less time than if ye have to ride all the way to the Abbot's Ford at Melrose to cross them both."

"That route is unknown to me," Simon said.

"Aye, well, I'll see ye safely on your way," Sir Malcolm said with a chuckle. "Once ye clap eyes on Ettrick Water, ye'll ken fine how to go."

Sibylla remained quiet, but Simon's memory of their earlier conversation diverted his attention to her. Her gaze met his with a twinkle. Then she smiled.

That smile sent a jolt of heat through him. As he collected his wits, Sir Malcolm said, "Yon Roman road affords some grand views of the Vale of Tweed."

Rosalie's gaze, Simon noted, had fixed itself on their mother.

Tempted to look at Sibylla again, he resisted the urge and said to his mother, "If you have no objection, madam, I would like to try that route."

"My dear sir, you are master here. We will naturally submit to your will."

He wished he could believe her, but she sounded too submissive, so he suspected she would make her true wishes known before the night was done.

She was not normally an early riser, but he hoped she would not expect him to delay his departure, because he wanted to deal quickly with Fife's wishes. He hoped to distance himself more from the Governor, but also, with raiders growing more daring, he did not want to be long away from home.

~

Agreeing to Lady Murray's suggestion that they meet in her solar in half an hour's time, Sibylla returned to her bedchamber to wash her hands and face.

To her surprise, Tetsy and Kit were in the room when she entered.

Tetsy greeted her with a smile. "Her ladyship did say ye'd need a proper riding dress, boots, and a warm cloak against the chill," she said, gesturing to a light brown, hooded cloak on a wall hook, leather boots on the floor beneath it, and a tunic and skirt of russet-colored Say cloth that lay draped across the bed. "I've put out a fresh shift for ye, too," she added.

"Thank you," Sibylla said, watching as Kit busily tidied the washstand. "I see you have your helper with you again."

"Aye, m'lady, she's willing enough, I'll say that for her.

Come along now, lassie, if ye're done there," Tetsy added, turning toward the door.

"I'd like to keep her a moment longer, Tetsy," Sibylla said. "Prithee, do not forget that I have given her leave to sleep in here again tonight if she likes."

Assuring them both that she remembered, Tetsy nodded and was gone.

"Kit, I have good news," Sibylla said, measuring a boot against one silk-shod foot for size. "His lordship and Lady Murray are going to Edinburgh when I leave here, and my father and I will ride with them. I thought you might like to go, too."

"Och, nay," Kit said, her eyes widening. "I'd liefer stay here—wi' Dand."

"Sithee, I thought that, as we traveled, you might see familiar country. You might even see your home if we pass by it. Or someone we see may know you."

Kit shook her head fiercely. "The bad men may see me and take me away. That be what they said they'd do, so I'd liefer stay here. Tetsy says I've gey much to learn afore I'll be much good to anyone. I want to learn, m'lady."

"But his lordship . . . all of us— We'll see that no harm comes to you."

Kit shook her head again, clearly frightened, so Sibylla did not press her. She sensed that more was amiss than fear of the raiders. But as tight-lipped as the child was, she doubted she would get anywhere by demanding an explanation.

It occurred to her that she ought to have consulted Simon before inviting Kit to go with them. And, as she hoped to go on to Edinburgh with the Murrays, she ought also to have consulted her hostess about Kit.

With time to spare before meeting Lady Murray in the

solar, she went in search of Simon and found him still on the dais in the great hall, talking to his steward. A number of his men were already laying out pallets in the lower hall.

"Your father decided to retire early, Lady Sibylla," Simon said, flicking a frowning glance at his men. "His chamber is on the floor above yours. 'Tis the room you slept in last fall when you stayed here with Amalie."

"I was looking for you, sir, not my father," she said.

He looked mildly displeased but dismissed the steward, saying to him, "I'll rely on you again to see to everything whilst I'm away. You know my ways now."

The man bowed and left. Before Sibylla could speak, Simon said, "I've told you I cannot take you to Edinburgh unless your father agrees. You should speak to him."

"I want to discuss another matter with you," she said.

"Art ready, then, to tell me how you slipped out of this castle?"

She was finding it easier to meet that penetrating look of his. "I suspect you know how," she replied, her own direct gaze challenging him to deny it.

"I would hear the words from you."

Satisfied that he dared not mention the tunnel without first being sure of her knowledge, she said, "I won't invite more reproaches from you, sir, so if you have a new charge, make it. I believe you dare not, lest you find yourself in error and provide me with information you'd liefer I not have."

His look of puzzlement came so swiftly and sincerely that, although it vanished as swiftly, she wondered if it was possible after all that he did *not* know of the tunnel.

He said, "I do not like this game, lass. I would have the truth from you."

"You threatened to make my father ask me," she reminded him.

To her astonishment, a rueful smile appeared, the first smile she had seen from him. It was small, but it powerfully altered his features, adding light to the fascinating green eyes and revealing just how fine-looking a man he was.

He said, "I apologize for that, Sibylla. I fight my own battles. If you did not come to tell me how you got out of the castle, what did you want to say to me?"

"I'm concerned for Kit," she said.

"She seems content enough here," he said.

"Aye, but she should not be, sir. She's but a bairn away from her family for four days now. Yet she does not even talk of them. After you agreed to stop overnight at Akermoor, I invited her to go with us. I know I should have asked you first, but I thought she might see familiar countryside or kinsmen along the way. It seems odd, does it not, that no one has come looking for her or Dand?"

"It does," he agreed. "I've had men out since we arrived. They have found no one missing a child, but I did warn them all to be cautious. I feared they might otherwise reveal to the men responsible for their near-drowning that both she and Dand survived. I want those villains for hanging," he added grimly.

"Kit refused my invitation, though. She insists she wants to stay here."

"Doubtless she is still afraid of the raiders."

"So she says, but why should she be? She must know that you and your men—and I—will do all in our power to protect her and find her family."

"Mayhap she does not want us to find them."

"Don't be daft," Sibylla said sharply.

When he stiffened, she grimaced and said, "I am sorry to speak so rudely. But I dislike leaving her here without knowing what frightens her so."

He shook his head. "You have let your imagination run amok. I gave orders to my steward, the housekeeper, the cook—aye, and Tetsy—to keep a close watch over Kit and Dand, too. You can trust my people, even if you don't trust me."

"It isn't that—"

"Whatever it is must keep," he said curtly. "We should not stand talking like this with only my lads in here, so unless you mean to tell me how you got out of the castle, I'll bid you goodnight. Speak to your father if you want to go to Edinburgh. I'll take you if he approves. Rosalie will be delighted, and I'm sure my mother will be pleased to take you under her protection."

She was not so sure of the last bit but nodded and thanked him. Although she was glad to have accomplished part of her plan to rejoin the princess, she was frustrated about Kit. She also felt oddly uneasy about her discovery of the tunnel.

What if he did not know it existed?

Such ignorance seemed unlikely for the master of El-ishaw. So perhaps he just wanted her to confess what she had done so he could tell her again in that maddeningly righteous way he had—that *all* men had—how much at fault she had been.

In her experience, whatever a woman did or wanted to do, a man would nearly always say, "Don't." So far, though, she had held her own against him.

In fact, and despite her better judgment, she was beginning to find him intriguing. His confidence and the loyalty his people showed him made him more so, as did her increasing sense that he was physically as attracted to her as she was to him.

Nevertheless, his flaws were many. He consistently dismissed her thoughts and opinions, while certain other qualities—particularly his assumption that he was always right—annoyed her to exasperation.

Congratulating herself again on her good sense in refusing to marry him, she went to the solar where she found Lady Murray occupied with her needle, silks, and tambour frame. Rosalie, her ladyship said, had retired for the night.

Sibylla soon wished she had work of her own to occupy her hands. When she offered assistance, Lady Murray denied having anything "suitable" for her to do, so she exerted herself to be tactful and soon drew her hostess into deeper discussion.

Being truly interested in her comments about household management, Sibylla began to note an occasional smile as her ladyship became more informative.

They had chatted for nearly an hour when Simon entered and said with a chill in his voice, "Pray forgive us, Lady Sibylla. I want a private word with my mother."

She could see that he had himself under rigid control. Even so, he looked more dangerous than usual. "I hope nothing awful has occurred," she said.

"Nowt," he replied. "I mean to leave tomorrow soon after we break our fast, though. I want to reach the Teviot by midday and Akermoor by midafternoon."

"I can be ready whenever you like," Sibylla said. "Your lady mother has kindly provided me with boots and a riding dress, for which I am most grateful."

"I'd wager you are. They baked your dress overlong by the fire, I'm told."

"They did, aye," she agreed, turning to make her curtsy to his mother.

Simon opened the door for her, and as she passed him, her body seemed to tingle. She feared she was blushing. Trying to read his expression, she decided he was definitely angry. But she did not think his anger was with her.

"Goodnight, my lord," she said. He nodded, his thoughts as he shut the door visibly shifting back to the issue that had brought him to the solar.

Curiosity surged, making her wish with all her heart that she could put her ear to the door. But it was stout and heavy, and it opened off a passageway that servants used continually. She dared not linger near it.

Simon faced his mother, feet spread and hands behind him, as he strove to curb his impatient temper. Long experience warned him that losing it with her would gain him nothing. Moreover, he doubted that she bore the responsibility for his outrage if, indeed, she even knew about any tunnel.

"Madam, I've come to ask how it is that a fact regarding Elishaw, of which I had hitherto heard not one word, has come to my attention only this past hour."

"Indeed, my dear?" She set her needlework aside and folded her hands.

"I had occasion this evening to ask Jed Hay if he knew a way by which someone other than a supernatural being might enter or leave this castle without passing through the gate, and—"

"Whatever can have prompted such a question?"

"You would doubtless call it masculine foolishness," he replied glibly. "But imagine my surprise when Jed said he thought such a way might exist."

"My dear Simon, do take a seat," she begged. "I cannot continue to look up at you this way without crippling myself. As to Jed Hay, one can only infer that he spoke of the tunnel. One does understand your displeasure at his alluding to it in so offhand a way, though," she added as he drew up a stool.

He sat without breaking his silence, knowing she would fill it.

Frowning, she said, "Although Jed is captain of our guard, he should *not* know about that tunnel. Your father and men he trusted dug it in utmost secrecy. Everyone else involved had died by the time he did, so one wonders how Jed learned of it."

"He'd heard a rumor about it years ago from an uncle of his who worked here," Simon said grimly. "What I want to know is why no one told me about it."

"I thought your father did tell you."

"If he had, madam, I would not be so angry now."

She frowned. "I do remember we had an invigorating discussion about it just before you came of age. I said he should tell you, because it was your right to know. But he did not like doing so whilst you were so thick with the Earl of Fife."

"Sakes, he wanted me to serve Fife."

"Yes, and he hoped Fife would continue to respect Elishaw's neutrality, but he never trusted him. And, although he respected your loyalty to the man, he did fear that if you knew about the tunnel and Fife decided to seize Elishaw for the Crown . . ." She spread her hands as if the rest went without saying.

"Did he also fear that you might tell the Percys?" he asked curtly.

She bristled. "Your father had no cause to distrust me, sir. I may have been born a Percy, but when I married him, I became a Murray. My children's needs and those of this castle will always come first with me. Your father understood that."

"But he did not trust me," Simon said, trying to ignore the stab of pain and bitter regret he felt. "Did he honestly think I might betray my own family, my own heritage? And if he did, madam, how did you come to forget that I knew nowt of it? I should think you'd remember *any* time he'd failed to follow your guidance."

"Do not take that tone with me when you speak of your father, Simon," she said severely. "I *would* have recalled such a time, but that was not one. He agreed to tell you, deciding as I had that it was your right to know and believing as I did that you would honor his trust. If he failed to confide in you, you must blame yourself."

"Why should I?"

"I'd remind you that he saw little of you after you came of age until the affair at Hermitage Castle three years ago, after the Scottish victory at Otterburn. When he *did* see you at Hermitage, the circumstances were not such as to persuade him to trust you. I shall not recount for you what you and your brother did there—"

"You need not," Simon replied, tightening the rein on his temper. "And I need not defend obeying my liege lord. Fife had reason to take Hermitage. It is Scotland's greatest Border stronghold, and he believed James Douglas had grown too powerful. His rivalry with the Percys—our cousins, madam—was creating chaos in the Borders. Fife said James and Hotspur both needed taming."

"James Douglas troubled no one after his death," she said. "However, your father helped foil Fife's attempt to seize Hermitage and opposed his notion last year of dowering Amalie with Elishaw land. Has it occurred to you, my dearling," she added, "that of the three Murray men at Hermitage that day, two are dead?"

"Five Murrays were at Hermitage that day," he said. "You cannot have forgotten that Meg and Amalie were there with Isabel."

"I remember," she said. "I would submit, though, that Meg's marriage to Buccleuch protects her, thanks to his influence and powerful connections. Amalie, too, is safe now that she has married Westruther. However, when I think that Fife did try to force her marriage to that dreadful creature of his . . ." She shook her head.

Simon forbore to remind her that she and Sir Iagan had also tried to make Amalie marry Harald Boyd, or that Simon himself had played a role.

Meeting her gaze, he found it surprisingly sympathetic.

"I know your feelings have altered since then, dearling, as mine have," she said. "So you must take especial care in Edinburgh. Men who arouse the Governor's anger rarely live long afterward, and you must have vexed him sorely."

"I can look after myself," Simon said, ignoring a tingling along his spine as he said it. "At present, madam, I want only to know where that tunnel lies."

"Why, it leads from the bakehouse storage alcove into the woods southeast of the castle," she said. "One shifts one of the alcove wall hooks to unlatch the door."

"Why from the bakehouse?" he asked. "I should have

thought a tunnel from the dungeons would have been more sensible and easier to keep secret."

"Also, more logical to find from inside," she said. "Part of the kitchen is also underground and lies close to the curtain wall. Digging the tunnel there was easier."

"Do my sisters know of it?"

"Mercy, no. We never had need to tell them. Indeed, I've not spared a thought for it myself in years. No one has, I expect."

Simon did not tell her how mistaken she was. But he did wonder how—if Amalie could not have revealed it to her—the lady Sibylla had discovered such a close-kept secret within twenty-four hours of her arrival.

Perhaps Sibylla *was* a witch, he told himself as he bade his mother goodnight.

That thought amused him, but his amusement faded when he realized that with servants and men still up and about preparing for the next day's journey, he could not go to the bakehouse chamber and search for the tunnel entrance at once. Nor, with Jack sleeping there, could he go down later in the night.

Such exploration would require forethought and so must await his return.

⁓

The next day's journey to Akermoor proved pleasanter than Sibylla had anticipated. Having traveled with Lady Murray once before at a plodding pace made necessary by her ladyship's apparently customary insistence on a horse litter, she had expected to endure the same slow pace to Akermoor.

However, her ladyship astonished everyone by electing to ride.

Sibylla had also expected Sir Malcolm to seize his first opportunity to speak his mind to her. But he, too, surprised her. The only pertinent comment he made was to say, as they rode side by side for a time, that he hoped she had fully recovered from the illness that had kept her at Sweethope Hill.

"Aye, sir, I'm rarely sick, as you know," she replied. "In troth, I was the last to succumb to the illness that struck us, which is how Isabel came to leave me."

"I feared your swim in the Tweed might have made you sick again," he said. "But, barring that bruise on your head, ye're looking gey hardy."

"I am, sir," she said. "Tell me more about Alice and this man she is to marry."

He shot her a look from under his eyebrows that told her he was pleased with himself. "I warrant ye'll recall young Colville of Cocklaw."

"Aye, sure, I do," she said, her heart sinking at the memory of her third rejected suitor. "But Thomas Colville is too old for Alice."

"So I thought, although a man's age has less to do with his fitness for marriage than his fortune does. However, Colville has a younger brother."

"But Thomas is heir to Cocklaw."

"Aye, sure, he is, and 'twas foolish of ye to reject your chance to be mistress there, just as ye were foolish to spurn Galston and his wealth. Thomas is to marry a great heiress now and will control her vast estates, but his brother inherits their mother's property. 'Tis a tidy place, albeit not as large as what Thomas will have."

"I hope the younger Colville is a better man than his brother, sir."

"He's a God-fearing man and has gelt, so he'll do for Alice. In troth, 'tis more than I'd expected for her, with her share of what I'll leave being gey smaller than yours if ye marry. And now that I'm seeing ye with young Murray again—"

"Do *not* let your thoughts turn in that direction, sir," Sibylla begged. "He has not forgiven me for rejecting him. Nor is he likely to," she added a little dismally. "Also, his lady mother knows naught of that day, so prithee . . ." She looked at him.

"I've told the lad I'll say nowt, but I wish I'd made sure of *that* match," Sir Malcolm said. "I'll not be making such a mistake again. Nobbut what Alice will do as she's bid. She's agreed and the date for the wedding is set, so I'll hear no sighs and such over yon plaguey lackwit that was cheeking up to her last year."

When Sibylla inquired further about the lackwit, Sir Malcolm's temper flared. "Ye'll not be stirring talk of rebellion in your sister's head, Sibylla, or by the Rood, I'll lock ye in your bedchamber till after her wedding. D'ye hear me?"

"Aye, sir," Sibylla said and tactfully changed the subject.

⌒

Simon glanced back several times at Sibylla and her father, riding just ahead of the servants and men-at-arms. He was curious about their conversation. Overall, he was bored, but his mother and Rosalie rode behind him, and he could not think of a tactful way to drop back to ride with Sibylla and Sir Malcolm.

Knowing he did not care a whit what Sir Malcolm might be saying, he saw it as an ironic turn of fate, shortly after they entered Teviotdale, when the older man urged his mount past Lady Murray and drew in beside him.

"I could see ye were aching for conversation, lad, and I'm not one for spending whole days with the ladies. If ye'll permit me, I'll ride with ye for a time."

"You are welcome, sir," Simon said. "I must thank you again for offering us your hospitality at Akermoor."

"Faugh, I'm glad to have ye. In troth, I miss my son Hugh most when the emptiness of the place gets over me. Servants, even a daughter as loving and obedient as our Alice, cannot compensate a man for the loss of his only son."

"Hugh died a hero," Simon reminded him, trying to keep his own sense of loss at bay. "You must be proud of him."

"Aye, sure, but I'd be that proud if he were still here," Sir Malcolm said. "I did not ride with ye to talk of myself. I heard ye've fallen out with the Governor."

"Our relationship remains cordial, sir. He recognizes my duty to my family, and to Elishaw, and knows I remain as loyal to the Crown as I've ever been."

"Ye don't want him as an enemy, lad."

"I know that. But I am no danger to him."

"D'ye mean to say then that the Murrays will nae longer maintain their so-determined neutrality, but will now favor only the Scots?"

Recalling that Sir Malcolm had accepted his offer for Sibylla because of the ready access he had to Fife, Simon said warily, "I foresee no trouble any time soon to test our neutrality. The truce with England has lasted more than two years now."

"Such as it is," Sir Malcolm said. "I ken fine that ye're plagued with raiders in your part of the Borders, just as folks to the west have been. And whilst English raiders are crossing the line, we Scots will ever retaliate."

"As will the English whenever our lads cross the line," Simon said.

"Aye, but 'tis English reivers doing the crossing now."

"Have you proof of that, sir? I'd remind you, it would not be the first time minor incidents of reiving had been made to look more threatening than they are."

"D'ye mean to suggest someone may be stirring trouble on purpose?"

"I don't know," Simon admitted. "I'd suggest only that the truce is as likely to succeed as to fail. Should it fail, I will decide my course."

Sir Malcolm nodded, and they talked of other things until they reached the river Teviot north of Hawick and stopped for their midday meal.

Sibylla had been listening with amusement to Rosalie's stream of questions about the royal court and her mother's surprisingly patient answers.

At one point, Rosalie said, "You did not tell me where we will stay, madam."

"Simon has chambers in the castle," Lady Murray said. "I suppose we will stay there as your father and I often did."

Knowing that Fife's gentlemen had cramped quarters, Sibylla said, "Isabel also keeps rooms there, madam. As she has not yet replaced Amalie, she'll have an extra one. So if his lordship's chambers are not adequate, let me see what I can do."

"That would be very kind, my dear," Lady Murray said with a gracious nod.

The afternoon was pleasant and the distance from the Teviot to Akermoor just five miles through low hills. Two hours after they had eaten, the castle came into view, giving Sibylla an unexpected surge of pleasure.

Akermoor Castle sat high above Wolf Burn on a rocky knoll that protected all but the west front of the castle and provided a solid foundation for its square, four-story keep and the two round, five-story towers flanking it. Watchtowers on corbels made the two towers look as if they wore peaked hats.

On the west front, a walled forecourt protected the entrance. Gates opened for them into the court, where a raised portcullis guarded the archway to the door.

As Sibylla watched, the door opened and Alice Cavers stepped out, waving excitedly. Waving back, Sibylla realized she was glad to have come home.

Chapter 9 ————————————

The forest surrounding Akermoor reminded Simon of Elishaw. The primary difference was the way Akermoor perched above the trees on its granite knoll. The track up to it was a good one but dropped off precipitously to the burn below, so anyone trying to attack the castle would be at a distinct disadvantage.

The distance to the water was about three hundred feet at the track's highest point. A siege might be possible, he thought, but if the tower were well stocked . . .

"Have you a source of water inside?" he asked Sir Malcolm.

"We've a spring in the cliff just above us, aye," that gentleman replied.

"How far are we from the loch?"

"A mile, no more, by yon track," Sir Malcolm said, pointing to a narrow dirt path into the woods. "But come in, lad. I'll show ye the whole place."

Dismounting in the forecourt, Sibylla hurried to embrace her sister, who met her laughing. Alice also had their father's light gray eyes but was half a head shorter than Sibylla, very fair, and of a willowy shape and build.

"I am so glad you're home," she said to Sibylla. "I've missed you."

Introducing her to Lady Murray and Rosalie, Sibylla said, "The Murrays were very kind to me, and they stay only one night before riding on to Edinburgh to join the royal court. We must show them our finest hospitality."

"Oh, how I wish I could go to court," Alice said, looking at Rosalie, her envy plain to see. "It has been so dull here, and everyone else is going somewhere!"

"Your turn will come," Sibylla said, her attention drifting to Simon and her father, who had dismounted and were heading toward the stables together.

"I know I shall go one day, Sibylla," Alice said. "But our lord father says I must marry first, and I—" Breaking off, she glanced at Lady Murray. "Forgive me, madam— and Lady Rosalie, too," she said ruefully. "I should not be talking about myself. Do come inside and I will show you where you may refresh yourselves."

"Thank you, Lady Alice," Lady Murray said. "I am sorry you will not be going to court. I had hoped that you and our Rosalie might become friends."

"I'd like that, aye," Alice said, smiling at Rosalie. "I have two cousins my age, but I rarely see them. 'Tis a pity I am not to go to Edinburgh."

Sibylla said, "Someday, dearling, but let us go in now." She accompanied them to the chamber Lady Murray and Rosalie would occupy that night. Waiting until her ladyship's woman joined them, and assured that their baggage was on its way up, Sibylla said, "Now you may take me to your room, Alice love, and tell me all the news." With their ladyships' door shut behind them, she added quietly, "I want to hear all about this young Colville our father tells me you are to marry."

Alice's face fell but she silently led the way to her bedchamber and shut that door. Then she said, "Sibylla, Edward Colville is horrid!"

"I own, although Father wanted me to marry his brother, I have never met Edward. Sakes, I scarcely knew Thomas Colville."

"I'm sure Thomas was just as bad, but you were so brave, Sibylla, refusing him as you did. I just wish I could refuse Edward."

Recalling her father's threat to lock her up if she encouraged rebellion, Sibylla said cautiously, "But why do you want to refuse him? Father says he has property, and if he *is* like Thomas, he is handsome. What makes him so horrid?"

Alice shuddered dramatically. "He is the sort of man who says what he thinks people want him to say and then behaves as he wants to behave."

"How do you mean?"

"At Yuletide, when we were all at Ferniehurst together in a large company, he heard our father express admiration for the Bishop of St. Andrews," Alice said. "Straightaway Edward began to act holier than I expect it has ever occurred to the bishop to act. One might have thought he aspired to take holy orders himself."

"Perhaps he does. Many younger sons go into the Kirk."

"Edward has no such intention," Alice said, grimacing. "One has only to see the way he leers at anyone in a skirt to know that."

"He is exactly like Thomas then. So why did you agree to marry him?"

Alice rolled her eyes. "I'll tell you how it happened. Father came to me and asked if I was a good, obedient daughter. I thought I must have displeased him, so I assured him that I am as obedient and dutiful as I know how to be, which is *true*."

"I know it is, dearling," Sibylla said.

"Aye, well, then Father asked what I thought of Edward Colville."

"And you said . . ."

"I told him I scarcely knew him but he had done naught to attract my liking. Father frowned heavily, the way he does, making my knees quake. So I said, 'Faith, sir, what would you *have* me say of him?' "

"And he said . . . ?"

"That he expected me to agree that Edward was a worthy young man that any marriageable maiden would rejoice to have as a husband."

"Mercy, Alice, did you agree?"

"I did not! I told him I could not say such a thing without lying. Faith, but I had no reason to *like* Edward Colville, let alone to call him worthy."

"What did our father say to that?"

"That he is sure I will be very happy with him as my husband. So you see—"

"I do *not* see," Sibylla said. "Surely, you disagreed with that, too."

"I did, aye, and he began bellowing at me. You know his way."

"I do. But the law will side with you."

Alice shook her head. "Nay, then, it won't, because I've

told him every way I know. But he went ahead as if I had agreed to everything. We marry in August."

"But—"

"I saw how *your* behavior infuriated him each time *you* refused a husband. He regarded it as a personal affront that you sought the Douglas's aid to defy him."

"Mayhap he did," Sibylla agreed, ignoring a twinge of guilt. "I did what I believed I had to do, Alice. I did not think of it as defiance but as taking my own path rather than fading to dust here at home."

"But to do such a thing *was* defiance, and I have no one to aid me. I wish you had come home when Hugh died," she added wistfully.

"I suppose you do, but I did not learn of his death for weeks. Do not forget that Isabel had just lost her husband, too. By the time the news of Hugh's death caught up with me, we were in Galloway," Sibylla said. "But I have visited twice since then. And Father seemed gey pleased to see me at Elishaw. He did not even scold me much for falling into the river Tweed."

"Sakes, neither of us could imagine how you came to do such a thing!"

Sibylla described her adventure, and the two spent a cozy time talking of Kit and Dand and the household at Elishaw. If Sibylla passed over the master of Elishaw, noting only her gratitude that he had appeared in time to help her get Kit out of the river, she doubted that Alice noticed any lack.

Alice made no further reference to her own situation as they chatted, and Sibylla did not press her. She knew that her sister lacked the fiercely independent spirit that had inspired Sibylla to reject each of their father's plans for her future.

Alice would not defy him, but she had given her sister food for thought.

Sibylla hoped she was not emulating Isabel's tendency to see Fife's hand in any ill. But, since Fife *had* tried to marry her into the Colville family, she believed he might also have had a hand in Alice's betrothal. Had he not tried to marry young Rosalie to his man Harald Boyd after failing to force Amalie to marry him?

With these thoughts in mind, another occurred to her with near certainty. If Thomas Colville had found himself a wealthy heiress, Fife must have arranged that as well. Moreover, the connection would somehow benefit Fife.

Deciding that she must help Alice but would have to be subtle about it, Sibylla soon went to change from her riding dress to garb more suitable for supper with their guests. Then she sought out Sir Malcolm and found him having just entered his bedchamber with his manservant.

"What is it, lass?" he asked when she peeped through the doorway.

"Prithee, sir, I would beg a word with you."

Her father nodded to his man, who bowed and left the room. "What, then, lassie?" Sir Malcolm said, adding, "I like that yellow dress on ye."

"Thank you, sir," she said with a smile. "'Tis one of the old ones I left here, but I like it, too, although such a pale yellow is usually better on Alice. I own, I am quite jealous of her. She has grown to be a beauty, has she not?"

"Aye, she's well enough. But I doubt ye came here to praise the lass, so I'll tell ye to your head, Sibylla, I'll have none of your argie-bargle."

"You will do as you think best, sir. I've just realized how little I know of her. She was a bairn when I left and is now old enough to marry. The only pity I see is that she must do so before she has had any opportunity to see and be seen."

"Here now, what are ye saying?" he demanded, scowling.

"I hope I've not said anything to vex you," she said. "Mayhap 'tis only that I'd like to know her better myself before she marries."

"Ye'll have plenty of time for that, for she'll not marry till August. The pair of ye can talk yourselves mute afore then if ye like."

"Nay, sir, for Isabel will be in Edinburgh by now or as soon as makes no difference. I must return to her service."

When he bristled, she added hastily, "It will not do for me to anger her after she has been so kind to me, sir. Also, Murray has offered to escort me. As Lady Murray will likewise be with me, my journey need not trouble you in any way."

"Aye, ye'd be safe in Annabel's charge," he agreed, still frowning.

Satisfied with that response, Sibylla said, "I do wish Alice could go with us. Seeing the court would be such a treat for her, and under an eye as watchful as her ladyship's, she would be safe, too. But doubtless the Colvilles would disapprove."

His frown had grown darker before she paused, and she suspected that by shifting so abruptly from her plan to his, she had unsettled him.

He did not speak for a long moment, and she kept silent.

At last, he said, "Why d'ye think the Colvilles would disapprove?"

With a little smile, she said, "Why, sir, surely you can

see that men will need only to look on our Alice to fling themselves at her feet."

"Aye, well, I'll have none of that!"

"You certainly won't if you keep her clapped up here," Sibylla agreed. "Edward Colville must be pleased that you have, because he surely knows that better and wealthier men than he would leap at a chance to marry our Alice. He won her so easily, I suspect, only because no others had seen her."

"Sakes, she has not been buried here. I took her to Ferniehurst at Yuletide."

Sibylla nodded. "To be sure you did, sir. But one must suppose that nearly everyone at Ferniehurst was a kinsman of ours on one side or the other. And most of the younger men who were there are married, are they not?"

"Aye, they are that," he said, looking thoughtful.

Deciding she had made her point, Sibylla said, "You will take good care of Alice, I know. I just wanted to tell you that I shall accept Murray's kind offer to escort me to Edinburgh. But if you *should* choose to visit me whilst Isabel is in residence there, I can easily provide chambers for you and Alice at the castle."

Her sister could share her room, but she sent a prayer aloft that he would not demand to know if she thought the princess had taken to including gentlemen as her guests. She also prayed that Archie the Grim had not forgotten his promise to house any guest of hers in his gatehouse apartments. As generous as he could be, he might have made the same promise to others and might find himself short of space.

It was not in her nature to worry about things she could not control or influence, and she knew Archie well enough to be sure that if he were there he would find space for

Sir Malcolm. So she went in search of Rosalie and Lady Murray.

"I trust you find everything to your liking," she said when they bade her enter their chamber.

"Indeed, Lady Sibylla, Akermoor seems most comfortable," Lady Murray said.

"Thank you, but pray do call me Sibylla. Praise from one who knows a well-run household when she sees one will mean much to my father."

"I have seen too little to judge how well it is run," Lady Murray said more austerely. "And I should think your charming sister or Sir Malcolm's housekeeper would deserve the credit for its management. In my experience, gentlemen know little of how to run a household smoothly."

"I am sure you are right," Sibylla said. Smiling at Rosalie, she said, "I would ask a kindness of you, my lady."

"Anything you like," Rosalie agreed.

"My sister is sadly envious of your journey to court, so I would beg you to be as tactful as you can if the subject arises. My father's notions on such things are stern, I'm afraid. He believes she should marry before she attends the royal court."

Noting Lady Murray's knitted brow, Sibylla said they must let her know if they needed anything more for their comfort, then suggested they go down to supper.

⁓

Simon enjoyed his tour of Akermoor.

Although he had once believed that Sir Malcolm had misled him about his daughter's willingness to marry, Simon's anger had soon shifted to Sibylla. He now found that he liked her father. Moreover, Akermoor was thriving, so he seized the opportunity to ask questions about matters that had perplexed him at Elishaw.

Sir Malcolm answered them all with hearty good sense, and the two men had spent the entire afternoon together in perfect amity.

Entering the great hall at suppertime with his host, Simon saw Sibylla on the dais, talking with Lady Murray. A short distance away, near the large fireplace, Rosalie chatted animatedly with the lady Alice Cavers.

As they all took their places, servants scurried about with dishes of food and pitchers of what was likely ale for the lower hall and wine for the high table.

They paused where they were while Sir Malcolm said the grace before meat.

Evidently believing he had already talked with Simon as much as courtesy dictated, Sir Malcolm turned to Lady Murray as they sat down, and engaged her in conversation. Simon was amused to see her respond with smiles and arch comments.

Beyond her, Sibylla chatted with Alice and Rosalie.

Simon's ears were sharp enough to hear most of what the others were saying without troubling himself to take part in the conversation. Soon his thoughts drifted to Edinburgh and Fife's summons. Those thoughts proving less than cheerful, he pushed them away only to have them drift back whenever he let down his guard.

Fixing his attention firmly on Sibylla's low-pitched voice and the younger girls' higher ones, punctuated now and again by her throaty chuckle and their giggles, he found the sounds oddly peaceful, even comforting.

From time to time, his host would address a comment to him, and he would reply. Each time Sir Malcolm quickly returned his attention to Lady Murray. Thus, he surprised Simon as they were finishing the meal when he said abruptly, "Sibylla, lass, Murray has asked several times today about our loch. I've been thinking ye could put your riding dress back on and take him to see it afore darkness falls."

"I do not need to change my dress, sir," Sibylla said. "At least an hour of daylight remains, and it is no more than a twenty-minute walk through the woods to the loch. His lordship is fit enough, I think, to manage that without undue exertion."

Simon's spirits lifted. "I'd like that," he said, smiling.

~

The naturalness of Simon's smile startled Sibylla. The only other time she could recall seeing his smile had been the small, rueful one he had offered her the previous night in Elishaw's great hall when she had reminded him of his threat to have Sir Malcolm ask her how she had got out of the castle.

Even that smile had altered his features considerably. This one did much more. When he looked at her, still smiling, every nerve in her body reacted.

Sir Malcolm's suggestion that they go to the loch had surprised her, but she knew his reason for the apparent impulse. He still hoped for a union between them.

Still, she was grateful to escape an otherwise tedious evening, doubtless a prime sample of how it would often be if she had to remain under her father's roof.

Outside, the sun touched a nearby hill to the west, and she knew they would see the sunset when they reached the hilltop. The track up through the pines and beeches was wide enough to walk side by side. As they followed it, Simon glanced back twice.

"What is it?" she asked.

"I expected your father to have someone follow us," he said. "He should not have sent you alone with me like this."

"Should he—or I, for that matter—not trust you?"

"That is not what I mean," he said. "I'm thinking only of protecting your reputation, lass. People talk whenever they hear or see aught to stir talk."

"His men can see us easily enough from the watchtowers," she said. "I suspect, though, that he hopes we might still make a match of it."

Smiling wryly, he said, "You are very blunt tonight."

She nearly told him that if she was blunt, he was unusually cheerful. Resisting the impulse, she said, "He *was* pleased to find me at Elishaw under your protection, for he said as much and hinted— Nay, that is too tame. He would have expressed his hope outright had I not interrupted him to tell him not to be thinking such a thing."

Simon was looking at her feet, just as he had the night they had met at the pond. "Those shoes look too thin for this rough track," he said. "I warrant their soles are slick, too, so take care how you step. How much farther before we see the loch?"

"Just over that low ridge ahead," she said. "I told my father I mean to accept your offer to escort me to Edinburgh," she added, watching for his reaction.

"My *offer*?"

"You did say you'd take me if he gave me leave."

"*Did* he?"

"He did not forbid it. Moreover, you may find your party further enlarged."

She thought his lips twitched, but he said only, "How so?"

"I may have put the notion into his head to take Alice to court."

He did not roll his eyes, but he did look heavenward. "You *may* have?"

"Aye, so I pray you will not discourage him if he mentions such intent. He wants my sister to marry Thomas Colville's younger brother, Edward, but she does not like him. Thomas is now to marry a great heiress, but as Edward inherited their mother's estates, Father believes he will make Alice a good husband."

"I should think he would," Simon said.

"Perhaps, but she can do better, and so I told him. Alice has scarcely met any eligible men. You have seen how beautiful she is, and I think the sweetness of her temperament would appeal to most gentlemen."

"I'll not argue that. But surely your father knows what is best for her."

"I fear he still thinks only of what such a marriage may do for him," Sibylla said. "The Colvilles are as firmly in Fife's encampment as you are, sir."

"Thomas Colville is doubtless much more so than I am by now," he said. "But I am not aware that Edward serves Fife in any capacity."

"Nor did *your* brother apparently serve him."

When he flinched, remorse banished her irritation and she said ruefully, "I should not have spoken so bluntly, sir. But your brother did seek to please you with many of his actions, and it may well be the same betwixt the Colville brothers."

"Don't apologize," he said quietly. "If reminders of Tom give me pain, I deserve it. I'd got him involved in

Fife's attempts to keep an eye on Isabel, and it was I who sent him to Scott's Hall that fateful day."

"We both know you had naught to do with the attack that killed him, even so. He was but carrying word of your father's death to your mother at the Hall."

"Aye, well, the guilt lingers nonetheless. But you need not apologize for aught you say to me, lass. You just speak your thoughts. I like listening to you."

The last statement warmed her. No one had said such a thing to her before.

He had diverted her, however, from her point about the Colvilles.

She said, "You don't like me talking about Fife, sir. Yet he is the reason you offered for me, is he not, *and* the reason my father accepted your suit?"

"I cannot deny that I obeyed Fife's wishes and hoped thereby to gratify him. But I can speak only for myself. I do not know what your father's reason was."

She made a rude sound.

He shook his head at her but said, "Sir Malcolm did talk to Fife. But at the time, you'll recall, I had just come of age. I paid heed to nowt but pleasing my liege lord and my own keen interest in increasing our Murray holdings. But I have gained experience enough to know now that any truth has two sides to it."

"What is the other side of pleasing Fife?"

"That if you please one person, you invariably displease someone else."

"That someone being me, I expect."

"As matters transpired, aye. But you may recall, too, that I did not tell anyone in my family," he said.

"You feared it would displease them?"

"There was dispute between my parents and yours," he

said. "I do not know why, but I'd heard my father speak the name Cavers disparagingly before Fife mentioned a possible marriage. But Fife did not approach my father either. Instead, he waited until shortly before I came of age and put the matter directly to me."

"Do you think he knew what lay between them?" she asked.

"I don't know," he said. "He may have, but looking back, I can see that I thought I was taking control of my life. I felt like a man, and I had a long habit of following Fife's orders. As nothing came of it, it did not occur to me until much later that I *ought* to have talked to my parents before taking such a step."

She understood that. Young men who wanted to make something of themselves made it a habit to obey those in authority over them. Hugh had, but he had admired James Douglas and was proud to follow where James led.

After her years with Isabel, she found it hard to imagine any man of integrity staying loyal to Fife, let alone admiring him. But she knew that many honorable men *were* loyal to him and admired his strength as a ruler. Archie the Grim supported Fife, although Archie had said he did not always trust him.

They continued in silence to the hilltop overlooking Akermoor Loch, an oval body of water a third of a mile long and a quarter mile wide. As they watched, the sun dipped below hills to the west, its last rays gilding the one on which they stood.

As they started down the steep, pine-needle-strewn path toward the loch, Simon said, "Where would your father and Alice stay if they do go to Edinburgh?"

"I reminded him that I have access to Isabel's chambers in the castle."

He chuckled. "You're treading on thin ice, lass. Even if he is unaware that the princess houses no men in her chambers, he will find out soon enough."

"My godfather also keeps rooms there, in the gate-house tower."

"Aye, sure, I should have remembered you can call on Douglas to aid you."

As she took her next step, she looked up at him, wondering if he mocked her. Her right foot, coming down on dried pine needles, slid right out from under her.

Somehow he caught her by one arm and managed to swing her toward him and catch the other. Pulling her close, he steadied her against his warm body. He was not wearing his cloak, but she could smell its spicy scent on his doublet. Indeed, she could detect an underlying scent of lavender.

Heart pounding, and with unexpected heat surging through her, Sibylla pushed against his chest with both hands and looked up at him.

A glint in his eyes was her only warning before he pulled her close again, lowered his head, and captured her mouth with his.

⁓

Simon felt her soft lips yielding against his, and primal instinct surged through him, urging him to overpower her and claim her for his own.

A tiny, nearly unheard voice from the civilized part of his brain gently advised resistance to that urge. Every other fiber of him sided with the urge.

His arms encircled her, holding her close, and his mouth moved against hers as if it would devour her. His mind and body both anticipated her resistance, but none stirred. She pressed her body to his, breasts to chest, hips to hips. Her lips parted beneath his, inviting his tongue into her mouth to explore.

Accepting that invitation, he shut his eyes, savoring sensations that burned through his body, yearning to tear her clothes from her and see her again as he had in the moonlight at the pond. His hands slid up over her back to her shoulders.

With his right palm between her shoulder blades, his left hand stroked the back of her head and pulled off the soft cap she wore and the netting beneath it. Dropping both, he laced his fingers through her thick hair as his right hand moved to cup the nearest breast.

His lips and tongue continued to investigate her mouth as the hand at her breast began to explore, easing over its softness to the tip, prominent now beneath the soft cloth of her bodice. When he rubbed the nipple, she moaned.

He opened his eyes. Hers had shut. Her tongue moved against his.

Her hips moved, too, and he felt himself swell against her.

Aching for her, watching expressions play on her beautiful face, he shifted his hand from her breast to her lacing.

Her eyes opened. As his fingers began to tug, she touched them.

Aching more than ever, he shut his eyes again, this time in a wince.

Groaning his reluctance, he released her and opened his eyes.

Hers were dancing.

"We should go back," he said, his voice sounding hoarse in his own ears. "It is too dangerous here."

"It is, aye," she agreed. "I understand gey well now why you thought my father should not trust you."

"I did *not* say that," he retorted indignantly.

She did not reply, but her eyes twinkled more.

Chapter 10 _____

Despite her amusement, Sibylla knew that to stay where they were would be unsafe. Simon was much more dangerous to her sensibilities than she had realized.

Had anyone told her she would meet a man who could make her react to one unexpected kiss as she had to his, she would have laughed that person to scorn.

She had felt comfortable walking with him through the shady woodland. They had talked easily of matters important to each of them, rather than exchanging socially polite phrases as people who scarcely knew one another usually did.

He had subjected her to none of the flirtatious comments she so often heard from gentlemen in company. Nor had she expected such flummery from him. But neither had she expected him to speak so openly about himself.

Recalling that she, too, had spoken freely stirred another twinge of remorse.

She had spoken only the truth, but it was unlike her to confide her thoughts so easily to anyone else. Particularly to one so quick to judge her, as Simon was.

She gathered information. She did not share it without due consideration.

But to Simon she had spoken as naturally as, in the old days, she might have spoken to Hugh. Thinking of Hugh in the same context as Simon drew a soft smile.

"Why do you smile so?" Simon asked.

He had not said a word since they had started back, and he was looking straight ahead, watching the track. She had not realized he could see her expression.

She answered readily nonetheless, "I was thinking of my brother, Hugh."

"Being back at Akermoor must stir many memories of him," he said quietly. "Sir Hugh was a fierce warrior. You must be proud of him, and miss him sorely."

"I do," she admitted. "At times, as a bairn, I spent more time with him than with my father. I was just thinking that you and he share traits in common."

He frowned. "I doubt we share many. I am skillful with a sword and dirk, and in a tiltyard. But I've fought no great battles and never sought to win my spurs."

Fearing he might think it strange that she compared her openness with him to what she had shared with Hugh, she said only, "The other night at the pond when I saw you with your hands on your hips, scolding me, Hugh came instantly to mind."

His lips twitched, but he said, "I warrant he'd have felt much as I did to see you in such a place. Especially at such an hour."

"He felt exactly the same," she said, smiling reminiscently. "You were kinder to me, though, and not nearly as loud as he was."

"When was this that he scolded you?"

"When I was seven," she said. "He caught me swimming in the loch by myself in broad daylight. Afterward, I couldn't sit comfortably for days."

"You're lucky you could sit at all," he said sternly. "You must have known you were doing wrong."

"I did, aye, but Father would not go with me and Hugh was not home to ask. I asked Father if one of the other men could watch me, but he said no to that, too."

Simon made an odd choking noise.

"I beg your pardon," she said innocently. "I did not hear what you said."

"I was stifling a most uncharacteristic hoot of laughter," he admitted. "Sakes, lass, unless you swam in your shift or some other garment—"

"I swam and still swim as most people do, sir."

"Most Border women do not swim at all," he pointed out.

"I feel sorry for them," she said. " 'Tis most enjoyable, swimming."

"It is gey fortunate for Kit that you were the one who heard her cries."

She glanced at him and saw that he was looking solemn. No sign remained of his amusement, and she could read little in his expression.

He said no more, and she was content to walk beside him in silence.

The castle soon loomed ahead, and when they entered the hall they learned that Lady Murray and Sir Malcolm had sent Rosalie and Alice to bed. The two sat at the dais table with a chessboard between them, chatting amiably over a game of dames.

Isabel and her ladies often played the game, which French soldiers who had fought for the Douglas some years before had introduced to the Scottish Borders.

The French called the game dames after the two female pieces in chess, because each piece could move only one square diagonally as present rules of chess decreed.

Watching Lady Murray jump one of her dames over one of his and remove his, Sir Malcolm said cheerfully to Simon, "Here ye behold me enjoying defeat, lad. Mayhap ye'll give me a game after her ladyship finishes me off."

"She is too good for me, too, sir," Simon said.

"You are welcome to take my place, for I am ready to retire," her ladyship said. "I just hope you do not mean to leave at the first burst of dawn but will let us arise at a civilized hour and break our fast in a civilized manner before we must go."

"As to your leaving," Sir Malcolm said to Lady Murray. "A notion has occurred to me that I'd like to discuss with ye."

"Indeed, sir," she replied with a regal nod.

"The thing is, our Alice feels ill used because I've said she may not visit the royal court until she is married," he said. "Had her mam lived, or were Sibylla married and thus able to look after her there, it would be different. But surely, for an unmarried lass to squire her sister about whilst also attending the princess . . ."

"'Twould not be suitable," Lady Murray agreed when he paused. "Maidens should enjoy such events in the company of mature women who can tell them how to go on, and if possible, with friends their own age. Rosalie, of course, has me to guide her but has no companions her own age."

"So ye said earlier, aye," he said. "It gave me cause to think. What say ye, my lady, if Alice and I were to go with ye to town so she might also benefit from your guidance?

That is," he said to Simon, "if ye'll allow us to join your party."

"You are welcome, sir," Simon said.

Sibylla was careful not to let him catch her eye.

～

Simon noted Sibylla's satisfaction and deduced that she had, indeed, twisted her father around her thumb. After years of seeing his mother do likewise with his father, he recognized the signs. And he swore—as he often had in the past—that when he did find someone to marry, he would not permit her to overset his decisions.

As Sir Malcolm was the victim of their manipulation, Simon felt only mild amusement and willingly joined him in a game of dames after the ladies retired. He found his host both interesting and genial, and less inquisitive than other men who knew of his relationship to Fife and hoped to pry information from him.

He was tempted again to ask Sir Malcolm what had happened between the Caverses and the Murrays that had annoyed his parents so. Recalling the amity he had noted all day between his host and Lady Murray, he wondered if she had been party to the disagreement or had simply supported his father's dislike of Sir Malcolm.

As persuasive as she had been with Sir Iagan, Simon could not imagine that she would have permitted him to hold an opinion with which she strongly disagreed. And, although Sir Malcolm had said they might talk of it later, good manners forbade interrogating one's host. So Simon held his peace.

Despite his concern about Fife's summons, he had been looking forward to the journey to Edinburgh from the moment Sibylla had said she was going. Now that her father was also going, the last thing he wanted was to stir coals with him.

There was one matter, though, in which the older man might aid him.

"As you heard, sir, my lady mother prefers not to travel more than fifteen miles in a day," Simon said as they were putting the game away. "I had hoped to persuade her to ride twice as far tomorrow, because I believe we can make Edinburgh by nightfall if she agrees. However, if I cannot persuade her . . ."

"Bless us, lad, why should ye? Nae female enjoys six or eight hours on a horse, certainly not when she rides in the torturous device they call a lady's saddle as your lady mother does. I'm thankful to say both of my lasses ride astride as young Rosalie does. Still, I doubt Alice will want to ride so far in a day either, and there can be nae reason, for I've an invitation to stop at Penkaet Castle whenever I like. 'Tis nobbut fifteen miles from here, and Winton can put your people up as well as mine. Our lads will sleep rough, but the rest of us will be comfortable."

Simon agreed to the plan with relief as he did not expect them to get away from Akermoor before midmorning. Nor did they. But Lady Murray was in good spirits and the two youngest ladies had become fast friends.

When Alice bemoaned her certainty that she would have nothing stylish enough for court wear, Rosalie assured her that she had enough clothing for them both if necessary. So they were getting on famously.

The Roman camp proved interesting, but they did not delay and forded Ettrick Water a short time later. Before crossing the river Tweed, they enjoyed the midday meal Sir Malcolm's people had provided. Then, for a while after the crossing, they followed an old drove road through low, forested hills.

The pace had grown tedious, and Simon's thoughts drifted as they had before to what awaited him in Edinburgh. Recalling his mother's warning, he wondered just how angry with him Fife might still be, and hoped Elishaw was safe from him.

The Governor had formed a habit of collecting estates to increase Crown holdings—or so he said. In effect, Simon knew that Fife was increasing Fife's holdings, because he controlled nearly everything related to the Crown.

Simon had committed no crime that Fife could condemn. Nor had he ever opposed Fife except when Fife had wanted Rosalie to marry Harald Boyd.

In the end, Boyd had suffered a fatal accident after seriously displeasing Fife. Surely, Simon told himself, Boyd had angered Fife more by his actions than Simon had by refusing to make Rosalie marry the scoundrel.

Moreover, the taking of an estate by the Crown was illegal unless no other recourse existed, and it required the consent of the lords in the Scottish Parliament.

They'd have no reason to consent even if he suffered the fatal accident Lady Murray feared, because his sisters would inherit Elishaw. Two were married to powerful men—Meg to Sir Walter Scott, Laird of Buccleuch and Rankilburn, and Amalie to Sir Garth Napier, Laird of Westruther. Both men were loyal Douglas supporters and could rely on Archie the Grim to back their claims against Fife's. So, the likelihood that Fife would order Simon killed so he could seize Elishaw was remote. However, he could make life wretched for him if he decided to do so.

As they approached Gala Water, rapid hoofbeats behind him made him look back to see Sibylla galloping her horse toward him. She had been riding with the younger lasses since fording the Tweed, and the way she smiled as she urged her mount to such speed for the short distance amused him.

Did she mean to gallop on ahead of them all?

He half hoped she would because it would give him an excuse to put his own horse to a gallop, if only to recall her to order.

But she deftly reined in beside him, still smiling infectiously as she said, "That was wonderful but much too short! I must remember Isabel in my prayers tonight."

He raised his eyebrows. "Why?"

"Because she rarely travels at such a tediously poking pace," she declared roundly. "Do you think we shall reach Penkaet before suppertime?"

"We ford Gala Water just ahead, so I expect we will," he said. "We sent men on, at all events, to warn Lord Winton that we would arrive in time to sup there."

"Do you mind if I ride with you for a time?"

"For as long as you like," he replied.

"I own, I grow weary of giggles," she admitted. "But Rosalie is charming and gey generous, too, to offer to share her clothing with Alice. I left things of mine in Isabel's chambers when we were last in Edinburgh, and told Alice that I had. But she sniffed at wearing my year-old fashions."

"Rosalie is a good lass," he agreed. Digesting the full meaning of her words, he said, "I hope you have enough suitable garments to wear when you attend the princess. It never occurred to me that you might not, but . . ."

Her eyes danced. "Having not lived at Akermoor for three years, I can assure you, sir, it did occur to me. I sent a messenger to Sweethope as soon as I knew Father would let me come with you, and asked them to send me what I shall need."

"What will you do till it arrives?" he asked as they approached the Gala ford.

"I'll be a bit ragged—by my sister's standard, anyway. In troth, I cannot recall what I left, so I may be missing some necessities. But I can hire a sempstress. And I can borrow from Isabel's other ladies. If all else fails, I'm handy with a needle and can cut simple patterns. One learns such things, serving the princess."

In his experience, ladies worried constantly about their attire, so he found her attitude unusual and refreshing. He rarely heeded his own appearance, because his manservant knew what he liked and replenished his clothing as needed. All Simon had to do was approve fabrics and stand for an occasional fitting.

Fife's men, like Fife himself, wore primarily all-black clothing. Otherwise, Simon preferred colors of the forest or hills and enjoyed new fashions, although even in his callow youth, he had spurned particolored hose, absurdly long-pointed shoes, and similar outlandish styles that other young noblemen fancied.

He and Sibylla had ridden for a while in the same comfortable silence they had enjoyed the night before when she said, "Do you know Edward Colville, sir?"

"I've seen him with Thomas," he said. "I cannot say I know him. In troth, I do not know Thomas well. Fife encourages competition rather than amity amongst those who serve him. I warrant he fears conspiracy, but I confess I have sometimes envied the strong friendships of men who fight together."

She nodded. "Hugh's friends were like brothers to him.

And one has only to see Amalie's husband and Meg's together to see the bond they share. Amalie says she thinks Garth would sometimes rather talk to Wat Scott than to her."

Amalie was probably right, Simon thought, especially if pregnancy had turned her irritable, as it did some women. But she loved her husband and he loved her. Simon liked Westruther, too, and thought him a good match for her.

"Why do you ask about Edward Colville?" he asked Sibylla.

"Because Alice confided to Rosalie and me that he *and* his brother are now in Edinburgh," she said with a grimace.

"As he is to marry Alice, would it not be good for her to get to know him better in company?" The thought crossed his mind that he would have liked to know Sibylla better before their aborted wedding.

She said, "Mayhap it would be good had Alice not also confided to us that the man she rather tediously calls her true love will be there as well. She had begun talking solely to Rosalie by then and had forgotten I was there."

"Were you not riding three abreast, with Alice between you and Rosalie?"

"Aye, sure, but Alice looked at Rosalie as they talked. I saw Rosalie's eyebrows shoot up, whereupon Alice turned sharply to me and begged me not to let Father forbid her to speak to this love of hers, whom Father calls a plaguey lackwit, or force her to be more than civil to Edward Colville. I made no such promises, because I know of no way to keep them. But I fear uproar may lie ahead."

Wondering what Rosalie had made of these confidences, he said dryly, "Who is the true love?"

"She also calls him her dearling Geordie. I thought it

better not to stir debate in Rosalie's presence, or encourage Alice by asking for more details."

"I just hope she does not offer young Colville to Rosalie."

A gurgle of laughter escaped her. "Faith, sir, would Rosalie want him?"

"She has declared that she wants to marry as soon as possible," he said.

"Does she know how close she came to marrying last year?"

"Nay, and she has not said what sort of man she seeks. I think it has not yet occurred to her that the man might make a difference to her happiness in the union."

She chuckled again, making him smile. "Wait until she meets Edward," she said. "If he is half as cocksure of himself as Alice says he is, or as Thomas is, Rosalie will quickly see her error. Alice suggested, too, that something has gone amiss with the Colvilles, but she admitted that she has no idea what it may be."

He shook his head. "How can she even know of such a thing?"

"Apparently Edward has visited Akermoor, paying court to her. She said he had not formed any intent to go to Edinburgh, that he left only because Thomas sent for him urgently a few days ago. Do *you* know of any crisis?"

"I know little save that Fife has likewise ordered me to Edinburgh," he said. "But if my sister may take interest in a Colville, I promise I'll learn all I can."

"You care deeply for her," Sibylla said.

"I just think she is still too young for marriage," he said. "My father thought so last fall, and my mother is in no hurry to send her off to her own establishment. Nor would any sensible man want Rosalie for his wife."

"Mercy, sir, why not?"

"Because she kens nowt of housekeeping. Both Meg and Amalie knew much more, Meg especially. But I fear that Rosalie has become everyone's dearling."

"I am sure that anyone as kind and generous as she is deserves all the affection she receives, sir."

⟞

Sibylla saw no reason to mention that Amalie had said that Simon doted on Rosalie. He did not seem the sort of man who doted on anyone.

Her first impression of him, on that long-ago rainy day, had been of a chilly, self-absorbed young man interested only in getting on with the business at hand. At Elishaw, it had taken just a short time to see that he was more complex than that.

He still often seemed chilly, but she was not sure now that the description was apt. To call him a private man, perhaps a lonely one, might be more accurate.

He certainly took his duties seriously, but aside from his displeasure, he did not share his feelings easily if at all.

An image awakened from years before of a pot she had seen blow its lid off when a kitchen maid had failed to shift it to the hob in time. Soup bubbling to the rim had stuck the lid tight, but the contents had boiled until increasing pressure broke the seal, abruptly and violently. The lid flew off, and erupting soup had scalded a maid.

Realizing that she was comparing Simon to a soup pot, she concealed her amusement. He had proven to be more observant of her expressions than most men were, and she doubted he would appreciate the image if she described it to him.

As she continued to ponder his apparent ability to talk comfortably with her, she recalled Amalie saying that she could never tell what Simon was thinking. But Amalie had also described Simon as harsh and had clearly been wary of his temper.

Yet Sibylla had stirred his temper more than once, just to see what would happen or to divert him from a point on which she preferred he not dwell. And she had done so—thus far, at least—with impunity.

He had spoken sharply to her, had even scolded her. But his temper had seemed mild by comparison with her father's or Hugh's—or even her own.

"You seem deep in thought," he said, startling her.

She smiled. "I was thinking about temperamental men."

"Do you number me amongst them? I'd not blame you if you did."

"You did not know my brother well, then," she said. "Nor have you seen aught but my father's milder side. The Cavers temper is renowned, sir."

"Yours, too? I have stirred your displeasure more than once, but I would not describe you as temperamental."

"In a household of explosive men, a sensible woman learns to control her ire. But I confess that I grew more adept at such control in Isabel's service than at home. She does not like discord, but some of her ladies tend to seek faults in others and try to exploit them to their own benefit, so one must ever take care."

"You can tell me little about service in a royal household that I do not know," he said with a wry smile.

"I expect that is especially true in Fife's service," she said.

Their conversation continued in this friendly way as they followed the Gala Water road to Penkaet Castle, where they arrived in good time to dress for supper with their host. Lord Winton and his lady, genial hosts, had done them the honor of hiring minstrels for their entertainment, so the evening was a pleasant one. They all sat up later than they should have, and even Simon smiled more than usual.

Simon watched his mother and the Wintons, surprised that she seemed so at ease with them. Members of Scottish nobility did know *of* one another, but the level of her ease after such a long day suggested she had known them a long time.

Yet when he asked her, she replied, "Oh, no, dearest. They are mere acquaintances. So kind though, and it has been a pleasant day, has it not?"

Sir Malcolm, too, was enjoying himself and revealed no sign of the volatile temperament Sibylla had described. Simon suppressed a smile at his mental image of Sibylla with a spitting temper. She had shown claws once or twice but nothing he would call rage.

Remembering Sir Iagan's rages and the icy fury with which Fife could terrify anyone within earshot, he decided Sibylla knew naught of what she spoke.

Well aware of the effect his own temper had on his sisters, and how quickly it could erupt if he did not keep it firmly checked, he wondered what Sibylla would think if he ever unleashed it on her. Not that he would. He was coming to like the saucy lass now that he knew her better. And with her father at hand, he could enjoy her company and give thanks that she was no longer his responsibility.

The next morning he did come within a hair's breadth of losing his temper when his mother and the other females in his charge all seemed bent on moving slower than snails as they prepared to depart.

While he dealt with any minor task he could find to occupy his hands and thus keep his temper, it occurred to him with force that trouble lurked ahead.

Knowing the road and knowing, too, that Edinburgh Castle lay nearer twenty miles from Penkaet than fifteen, he feared that Sir Malcolm would suggest stopping at Dalkeith Castle for the night, rather than pushing on.

Dalkeith, the Douglas seat nearest the capital, lay some seven miles southeast of it. They would pass within a mile, and he was sure that Lady Murray would accept such an invitation if she had not already done so.

In the hope that she had not, and to ward off the likelihood of its happening later, he seized the first opportunity to speak privately with Sir Malcolm.

"Our journey today is again longer than my mother likes," Simon said. "Nevertheless, sir, I do not want to spend another night on the road."

"Nay, for ye'll want to learn what Fife has in mind for ye," Sir Malcolm said. "I ken that fine, lad. I'd offer to assume the escort of your lady mother and young Rosalie myself if I thought ye'd allow it—or that she would."

"She would not, sir," Simon said. "You and I both know how it would look if you and your tail were to escort her. And she looks askance at gossip, let alone scandal. Mayhap if I knew what stirred that dispute betwixt our families . . ."

To his surprise the older man blushed like a schoolboy but said hastily, "Nay, I told ye, lad, 'twas nobbut bit o' ribble-rabble. In troth, I scarce recall it, but 'twas nowt for making a bard's tale about, so I've nae intention of speaking more on the subject. If Annabel wants to tell ye, she will, but I'll tell ye nowt."

"Very well, sir. It must be as you say. I'll be much obliged to you, though, if you can manage to distract her from talking of time and distance today."

"I'll do that and happily," Sir Malcolm said. "I'm gey pleased that I decided we should come. I'd forgotten what a fine sense of humor your mam has."

Simon stared at him. He had heard many things said about his mother in his lifetime, and he fancied he knew her well. But no one had ever accused Lady Murray of having a sense of humor, and he had never expected anyone to do so.

Whether Sir Malcolm knew what he was talking about when it came to her ladyship or not, Simon was relieved when he did manage to keep her diverted.

By the time they approached Holyrood Abbey at the southeast end of Edinburgh, the sun was low and Sibylla was again riding beside him. Her eyes were bright as her gaze swept westward from the abbey bell tower and upward to Castle Hill. Her expression revealed simple pleasure in the view.

"Do you enjoy life in court circles?" he asked her.

She looked startled at the question but gave it thought before saying, "I like being with Isabel, but I dislike all the intrigue at court. Someone is always plotting something, so one has to watch for pitfalls if only to avoid falling victim to a prank meant to make someone else look bad."

He nodded. Having been party to many such intrigues over the years, if only as an adjunct to a primary player, he knew she was right.

"One must be devious by nature, I suspect, to enjoy such things," he said.

"Are you devious, sir? I would not have thought that of you."

He said, "I don't think I am, but I was raised to be loyal to my liege, and obedient. I was both of those things, and I am still loyal to the Crown."

"And the Crown is Fife," she said with a sigh.

"Aye, the Crown is Fife."

She glanced back. "I should fall back to ride with the other women, should I not? I am surprised that neither her ladyship nor my father has commanded it."

He was reluctant to agree with her but knew he must. "Aye, you should," he said. "You do not want to stir talk, not if you would please Isabel."

She sighed. "She does not dare keep anyone who stirs gossip, lest she give Fife cause to make her leave Sweethope Hill and live with the husband she detests. Even the Douglas would refuse to tolerate scandal in her household."

He missed her company after she fell back with the others, but the castle looming ahead soon turned his thoughts back to Fife.

~

As they rode along the Canongate, past St. Giles, and into the High Street, Sibylla described the royal burgh's points of interest for her sister and Rosalie. The most impressive view of it came as they wended their way up the steep road to the castle with the burgh sprawling below and southeastward to Holyrood Abbey.

Passing under the tall gate tower into the castle precinct, they rode to the easternmost end, to massive David's Tower, containing the royal apartments.

Greeting them just inside, the steward for those apartments solemnly informed Sibylla that the princess Isabel was not yet in residence.

Chapter 11 ——————

Sibylla received the news of Isabel's absence with more equanimity than did other members of their party. Sir Malcolm, showing signs of incipient wrath and ignoring the steward's presence, demanded to know if she had purposely misled him.

Giving him a straight look, she said, "You know me too well to believe that, sir. Isabel said she would come when the court removed from Stirling. That she has not yet done so suggests only that something has delayed her."

"Where will you stay until she does come?" Lady Murray asked.

Smiling at the expressionless steward, Sibylla said, "As one of Isabel's ladies, I have access to her chambers, madam. I shall occupy my usual room."

"Begging your pardon, Lady Sibylla," the steward said. "As ye ken, the princess always sends word a few days ahead, and we've not heard from her yet."

"She did tell you to expect her when the court removed here, did she not?"

"Aye, she did that," he agreed. "And ye're welcome as always, m'lady."

Much as she would have liked to have Isabel's chambers to herself for at least a short time, she said to her father, "Alice can stay with me, sir. Rosalie is also welcome, madam, and you, as well, if you like. I can provide beds for you all until Isabel arrives, but I recall that you do have access to other accommodations."

"We do, aye," Lady Murray said. "In the past, my son has given up his room to his father and me, and I did assume . . ." Pausing, she looked at Simon.

"You are welcome, of course, madam," he said. "I can always find a bed."

"And you, sir?" Lady Murray said to Sir Malcolm. "Where will you put up?"

His annoyance with Sibylla plainly forgotten, he said, "The Douglas keeps chambers in the gate tower, and I use one of his rooms. But I own, it would be better if Sibylla provided a cot here for Alice. And, as I'm thinking the two lassies might like to sleep together"—Rosalie and Alice nodded fervently—"I'd be gey pleased if ye'd agree to look after them all yourself, my lady."

"'Twould be a pleasure for me, sir," she said, nodding.

That exchange leaving Sibylla with no more to say, the other ladies followed her to Isabel's chambers. The rooms were always kept ready for the princess and her ladies, and comprised five bedchambers opening into a larger central solar—two on one side and three smaller ones on the other—on the third floor of David's Tower.

Rosalie and Alice shared one room, leading Sibylla and Lady Murray to opt for separate chambers until the princess's return. Lady Murray had her woman, Alice had brought a maidservant from home to assist her, and the princess always left a chambermaid to look after her rooms, so their baggage was soon stowed.

By then the rooms were redolent of lavender and cloves from scent bags in the Murray ladies' sumpter baskets. Commenting on the pleasant aroma, Sibylla learned that while Lady Murray and Rosalie liked a mix of lavender and cloves in their scent bags, Simon preferred a hefty dose of cinnamon added, as his father had.

When Sibylla told the others they could order food brought to them, Lady Murray announced that they were too weary from their travels to think of attending court that evening. The girls protested, but her ladyship summarily overruled them.

"We shall retire early, my dears, and make our plans tomorrow after we have broken our fast. I know you will agree that that is the best plan, Sibylla."

"Indeed, madam. But, prithee, you two, do not look so downcast," she added. "We are too late to take supper in the hall. Moreover, for a first appearance at court, certain customs apply that you must follow. Your brother will present you to the Governor or to his chamberlain, Rosalie, and our father will present you, Alice."

"What do we say if we meet the Governor?" Rosalie asked.

"Not a word, dearling," Lady Murray said. "You will make your best and deepest curtsy and remain silent unless he addresses you."

"Fife won't," Sibylla said. "He never does." Recalling his aborted attempt to arrange Rosalie's marriage eight months before, she hoped she spoke the truth.

The evening passed without incident, and the next morning, with little else to occupy their time, Sibylla agreed to escort Alice and Rosalie around the castle.

Lady Murray excused herself. "I have been here many times and do not need to wear myself out walking up and down Castle Hill," she said. "But do be sure to show them St. Margaret's Chapel, Sibylla."

Sibylla agreed and, seeing the castle precinct anew through the eyes of her young companions, soon recalled how exciting it had been for her the first time.

A sea mist had blanketed the dawn but lifted before they set forth, to reveal a sky full of drifting white clouds. The air still felt damp but was warm enough for Sibylla to wear only a pale-pink silk tunic and skirt. She wore gloves and a caul, too, because one did so in Edinburgh whenever one was outside. Rosalie had also rejected a heavy wrap, but Alice, less hardy, had donned a gray wool mantle over her dress.

Both Rosalie and Alice showed more interest in the bursts of scenery and the men they saw than in the fine buildings Sibylla pointed out.

Other parties strolled about, gazing at one part or another of the castle just as the three young women were, and usually with someone to act as guide. With her charges showing as much interest as they were in any young man who crossed their path, Sibylla was relieved when the number of other wanderers thinned as they went uphill, until they found themselves alone at the top.

St. Margaret's Chapel sat by itself atop the highest point of Castle Hill. Just fifteen by thirty feet, its exterior was undistinguished for the oldest building in Edinburgh. Explaining that its use was reserved for members of the royal family, Sibylla encouraged her charges to look inside at the columns and lovely carvings on the semicircular apse's arch and the chancel.

Outside again, standing by the chapel, they could see the North Loch just below and the blue-gray waters of the

Firth of Forth in the distance. A breeze blew toward them from the Firth, fresh and tangy with scents of the sea.

Sibylla breathed deeply, listening with only half an ear to her gaily chattering companions until Alice exclaimed, "What is *he* doing here?"

Turning, Sibylla beheld a handsome young man striding toward them with a confident grin on his face. His dark coloring, lanky build, and aquiline features put her so strongly in mind of Thomas Colville that she easily deduced his identity.

"Someone told me you had come here, Alice," he said, walking right up to her, catching her by the shoulders, and kissing her soundly on the cheek. "So you missed me enough to persuade your father to bring you! I'm gey glad to see you, lass, but you should present me to your bonny companions."

Seeing Alice shrink away from him stirred Sibylla's temper. "If we are to talk of manners," she said, "I should think you'd know better than to accost the *lady* Alice in such a rude way."

He threw back his shoulders, put his hands on his hips, and looked down his nose at her. "And who might you be to speak so boldly to a nobleman, my beauty?"

"You would do better to put that question to someone who might present you to me," she said tartly. "Until you find someone of that sort, pray step away from us."

"I do not dance to a wench's command, especially one who would make such a pleasant armful . . . if I were still seeking one," he added with a cheeky grin. "You must not know that I'm betrothed to Alice, which must surely excuse my behavior."

"It reveals only that she is getting a bad bargain," Sibylla retorted. "Come, Alice, we will go back now."

"Nay, come and pray with me," he said to Alice, gesturing toward the chapel.

Keeping her back to him as she stepped between them, Sibylla touched Alice's arm to urge her away, only to feel her own arm grasped rudely from behind.

"By heaven, you'll not dismiss me like a common lackey," he snapped, swinging her to face him.

As he did, she drew her right elbow back sharply, formed a fist, and using the momentum he provided her, drove her gloved fist as hard as she could straight up at his nose. Faintly hearing squeals of dismay from the girls, she watched him lurch backward, catch his heel on a rock, and sit down awkwardly and hard.

When he clapped a hand to his nose, blood spilled into his palm.

Looking at it, he said, "By God, when I get my hands on—"

"Come, ladies," Sibylla said as she stepped nimbly beyond his reach.

Turning from him, back the way they had come, she beheld a familiar, broad-shouldered figure standing on the walkway, looking straight at her.

"Thank heaven," Rosalie murmured.

Sibylla was not sure that Simon's appearance was any blessing. Her cheeks were burning, and her temper was still far from under control. If he thought he was going to wax coldly eloquent over how a lady should behave toward boorish young men, he had better, she told herself, think again.

Walking toward him, aware of the furious man behind her, she did not intend to stop long enough to explain her actions.

"How could you?" Alice asked quietly but with an unexpected tremor in her voice. Thinking she must be on the verge of tears, Sibylla looked at her only to see evidence of suppressed laughter instead.

Rosalie murmured, "Good sakes, I want you to teach *me* how to do that. I never saw *any* female hit a man before."

"My brother taught me," Sibylla admitted. "But I expect I should not—"

"I hope the look on Simon's face is for that ruffian you struck and not for us," Rosalie interjected more soberly than before.

Sibylla was watching Simon and understood her concern. Despite his tawny coloring and stony face, the words "black as thunder" swam into her mind. She remembered Amalie using them to describe what Simon looked like in a fury.

He was not looking at Colville, either.

He was still looking straight at her.

Simon had come upon the scene in time to watch astounded as Sibylla whirled on the apparently unsuspecting man behind her and knocked him flat with one blow of her gloved fist.

As she and the other two lasses came toward him, he strode to meet them and said sternly as soon as he knew she could hear him, "What the devil were you—?"

"Not now," she cut in sharply. "If you must have an explanation, you may have one when we are well away from here. At present, however, you will oblige me by letting us pass and taking care that that ill-bred knave does not follow us."

"I'll see that he does not," Simon said, his ire shifting instantly to the new target. So astonished had he been to see her knock the man down that he had failed to observe the extent of her anger as she approached him.

Or perhaps, he mused, her anger was with him for daring to block her way.

Her victim was on his feet and coming unsteadily toward him, clearly furious. Despite the hand clapped to his face, blood dripped from his nose. Evidently realizing he was only collecting gore, he flicked the hand to one side as if to get rid of the blood. As his angry gaze met Simon's, Simon recognized Edward Colville.

"I suppose you saw that foolhardy wench clout me," Edward snarled.

"I did, aye," Simon said. "She has good aim."

"Well, I'll teach her not to play such tricks with me," Edward said.

"That might not be wise," Simon said.

"Wise or not, my sister has a lesson coming to her, sir."

"Your *sister*?"

"Aye, sure. I warrant you can have no objection to a man punishing his sister. I told her she had no business up here without proper protection, and—"

"She clearly has little need for protection," Simon interjected. In a harder tone, he added, "Before we continue this absurd conversation, Edward Colville, I should tell you those three *ladies* are here under my protection. I trust you will not require me to explain why I used the word 'absurd.' You'd do better to consider what Sir Malcolm Cavers will think of your behavior toward his daughter."

"Look here, I don't know who you are, but if you speak

the truth about your responsibility for Alice Cavers, you know I am betrothed to her. That other—"

"Again I'd caution you to guard your tongue, Colville. Take your tale of woe to Sir Malcolm if you dare, but having lied to me, you will not persuade me now."

"Damn it, what right—"

"As the youngest lass is *my* sister, sirrah, I'd advise you to hold your tongue if you do not want blood pouring from your mouth as well as your nose. I have held my temper so far only with difficulty. Press me further, and I'll happily set it free. Begone now, and do not let me see you annoying those ladies again, or any others."

"By God—"

Simon braced himself hopefully, his hands forming fists.

"Oh, very well," Edward Colville muttered. "I suppose you will tell everyone who will listen to you what she did."

"I do not gossip, certainly not about innocent young maidens," Simon snapped. "But neither do I speak just to hear myself speak."

Brushing past him, Edward strode off angrily down the hill.

Simon followed but felt sure the younger man would not try to catch up with Sibylla—not until he could do so safely, at all events.

Simon had come looking for her . . . for all three of them . . . after learning from Fife's chamberlain that Fife would be unavailable to receive him until later in the day. Deciding then that it would be wiser to talk to Fife before taking his mother and sister to dine with the court, he had gone to relay that decision to Lady Murray.

Learning from her that the three younger ladies had gone exploring, he had strolled in search of them.

His first reaction at seeing Sibylla strike the man had been a mixture of amazement, alarm, and anger. He deplored the impulsiveness of any woman daring to strike someone so much better equipped than she was to win such a match. But underscoring those feelings had been an odd sense of pride and another of gratitude that he had been at hand to see it for himself and stop her victim from retaliating.

Now, as he walked back to David's Tower, reason stepped in and he pondered what he would say to her. Recalling her words as she had passed him, he decided the younger Colville had insulted her or one of the others and that Sibylla had thought the insult severe enough to merit immediate punishment.

Either that or the man had said or done something to snap her temper.

Despite the mastery he now wielded over his own youthful volatility, Simon understood the sudden leap of rage she must have felt to have done such a thing.

Even so, she could not go about Edinburgh doing such things without risking dire consequences. He had to make her understand that straightaway.

Sibylla took her sister and Rosalie back to David's Tower, aware that she would do well to avoid both Colvilles until Edward had time to come to his senses.

As they approached the tower entrance, Rosalie said, "Need we tell my lady mother what happened?"

Hearing Alice gasp, Sibylla said, "You may tell her or

not, as you choose, my dear. I'll not ask you to harbor secrets to protect me from your mother or your brother. He may tell her what he saw, however."

Rosalie shook her head. "He will not. He may scold you—scold all of us, come to that—but he will not do so if she is present. Nor will he tattle to her."

With a squeak of protest, Alice said, "You ought never to have done it, Sibylla. Edward must be *very* angry."

"I expect he is, although he *should* be ashamed of himself. If I am sorry for hitting him, it is only because I should not have done so where others might see me."

"No one was there until Simon came," Rosalie pointed out as they passed through the entryway. "It was just luck, though, that he arrived before Edward recovered his senses enough to vent his anger on you."

"Bad luck, too, though," Alice said, looking sympathetically at Sibylla. "Murray is angry now, too, I think."

"He is, aye," Sibylla agreed. "But Rosalie is right. I own, I did not like to see him scowling at me, but we walked away unscathed only because he *was* there."

Rosalie chuckled. "I warrant you wish he'd been a stranger instead."

Sibylla met her twinkling gaze with a rueful smile. "I may have wished it at the time. But that stranger might as easily have been a friend of Edward Colville's."

That silenced them, leaving Sibylla with her thoughts until they reached Isabel's chambers. Learning then that they would not dine with the court, after all, but that Lady Murray had ordered a small midday repast for them there, Sibylla hoped she had gained a respite from the inevitable confrontation with Simon.

Less than an hour had passed, though, when the chambermaid approached her to say that the Laird of Elishaw had sent her to ask if the lady Sibylla would join him for a stroll round the tower forecourt.

Lady Murray frowned at hearing of this request. "What *is* he thinking?" she asked. "Tell him to come here. To stroll alone with you will surely stir talk."

"Not if I just walk about the courtyard with him, madam," Sibylla said. "We both attend members of the royal family, after all. When the court is in residence, the courtyard is as public as the great hall. Therefore, most observers who recognize us will think only that we meet to relay a request from one royal personage to another."

Sibylla did not include her father in "most observers" and hoped that if he did see them together, the sight would not spur him to tell Lady Murray that they had nearly married. He did sometimes forget his promises, especially if he overindulged in whisky or claret.

Quickly tidying her hair and shaking out her skirts, she went to meet Simon. Not for a minute did she contemplate refusing to walk with him, because she knew he would have his say one way or another. She would gain nothing by delay.

He was waiting quietly if not patiently on the stair landing. "We'll be back soon," he said. "What I have to say will not take long."

Light in the stairwell was too dim to reveal much in his expression, but his demeanor revealed no sign of displeasure. Deciding that he believed he was merely attending to a tiresome duty, she put a hand on the forearm he extended to her when they reached the foot of the stairs, nodded pleasantly to the steward as they passed him, and let Simon take her out into the courtyard.

The sun directly overhead was shining warmly on the

pebbled yard. Two other small parties strolled across the way. Otherwise, the area was deserted.

Doubtless, Sibylla thought, most people were preparing for the midday meal. "You do not dine with the Governor either?" she said.

"He is unavailable until later this afternoon," Simon said. "That is to say he is unavailable to me until then. I do not know if he is here in the castle or elsewhere, but I thought it best that we not subject Rosalie to a possible snub."

"Then doubtless my father will wait to present Alice, too."

In an edgier tone, he said, "You do know that you have made an enemy here today, do you not?"

Grimacing, she said, "If you mean to scold, sir, I cannot stop you. But you will say little that I have not said to myself. I did warn you that I have a temper."

"You must learn to control it."

"I thought I did have it under control," she said.

"What happened?"

"Did you not see?"

"Nay, I crested the hill just as you turned and struck the man."

"Faith, do you doubt that he deserved it?"

He looked at her, frowning. It was not the thunderous one she had seen earlier. Although he rarely showed his feelings, he was an expert frowner, and she suspected he could produce untold varieties. She had, however, begun to identify some of them.

This was his thoughtful frown.

"I saw nowt at first to tell me he deserved it," he said. "But later, when I recalled your words as you stormed past me—"

"I am sure I walked past you with dignity, sir. I do not storm."

"Don't cavil, lass. You cannot warn me of temperament one minute and declare that you have none the next. In troth, I shifted my gaze from you when you asked me— nay, commanded me—to keep young Colville from pursuing you. Only later did I recall your exact words. I do not think you commonly call someone an ill-bred knave without cause. So I will ask you again. What happened?"

"He strode up to us when we came out of the chapel, caught Alice by the shoulders, and kissed her. He'd have kissed her on the lips had she not turned her cheek to him. He then suggested that she had pursued him here."

"Rude behavior," he said grimly. "But hardly actionable. He is betrothed to the lass, after all."

"She shrank from him, sir, and then he rebuked her for not presenting him to her bonny companions."

"I can understand that that angered you, but—"

"Sakes, that was not all," Sibylla said impatiently. "I do not rise to baiting so quickly, I promise you. I reminded him that he owed Alice more civility."

"Calmly."

"Calmly, aye," she said. "He asked who I might be that I dared speak so boldly to a nobleman."

"So . . . calmly *and* boldly," he said. But she had felt his forearm tense.

Careful not to look at him, she said lightly, "Did I mention that he dared to address me as his beauty?"

The forearm tensed more. "You know you did *not* mention that."

"Aye, but he did, so I told him that if he wanted an introduction, he should apply to someone in a position to present him to me. Until then, I said, he should step away from us. I was still perfectly calm, I assure you."

"What did he say next?"

She remembered Colville's words exactly. "That he does not dance to a wench's command, especially one who would make such a pleasant armful."

This time the hand at the end of his forearm clenched, and she detected a near growl. Hoping these signs indicated that she would not have to endure one of his chilly rebukes after all, she kept silent and let Colville's words echo in his mind.

"We must hope no one ever sends the man on a diplomatic mission," Simon said at last. "But I doubt you hit him for that."

"Nay, I said we were leaving, but he told Alice he wanted her to go into the chapel and pray with him."

"He has no business in that chapel," Simon said.

"I did not want to debate that with him," Sibylla admitted. "When I urged Alice to come away, he grabbed me and spun me toward him. He was angry and I . . ." She paused, eyed him speculatively, and gave a dismissive shrug.

"I see." He held her gaze as he added, "Don't tell me that Sir Hugh Cavers taught you that little trick."

Obligingly, she said, "I won't if you don't want to hear it."

"*What* was he thinking?"

"Hugh said that if I were ever threatened, the best plan was to act before the villain suspected I might. He also showed me how to use an attacker's strength against him," she added. "Having no notion what Edward meant by grabbing me so roughly, I . . . It seemed the best course."

When Simon put his free hand atop hers on his forearm, she tensed until he said, "Unless you want to walk all the way to the gate, we should turn back."

Realizing that she had paid no heed to where they were going brought fiery heat to her cheeks. He might have taken her anywhere, for she had kept her attention on him, trying to read his thoughts. She had not expected him to listen so intently or to let her explain without frequent interruptions to scold.

Her father tended to fix on point after point to which he could take exception, making it difficult to explain anything to him. If Sir Malcolm was angry, explanations rarely aided one anyway. What Amalie had said about Simon and her own experience with him had led her to expect similar treatment from him.

"You surprise me," she said when he remained quiet. "I thought you would scold more, but you keep silent, even about Hugh's teaching me."

He glanced at her and looked away but not quickly enough to conceal from her the surprising twinkle in his eyes.

Relaxing, she said, "Now you *laugh* at me?"

"I rarely laugh, lass, but I have done so or nearly done so more times since we met again than I can recall in any such brief period for years. I kept silent because I was trying to think how to impress upon you how great my displeasure would be if you should pass this disturbing knowledge of yours on to Rosalie without, at the same time, putting the notion in your head that you *should* do so."

She chuckled. "Too late, sir. Rosalie has already demanded instruction."

Chapter 12 _____

A group of four was strolling toward Simon and Sibylla, so they walked on quietly until the others had passed them. Enjoying the comfortable silence, Simon remembered some news he had heard in the course of presenting himself to Fife's chamberlain, news he thought would interest Sibylla.

When the group had moved beyond earshot, he said, "I wonder if Edward Colville may have had reason to seek out your sister. Having learned she was here, mayhap he wanted to make a point to her, and to others, by openly declaring his rights. But I heard some news earlier that may interest you—and your father, too."

"I do not mean to tell my father about this morning's incident unless I must," she said. "He would see naught in Edward Colville's behavior to justify my reply."

He was more in agreement with Sir Malcolm than she knew but said only, "Thomas Colville's heiress has evidently changed her mind about marrying him."

She smiled mischievously. "Do not look to me to commiserate with Thomas, sir. I think the lady shows wisdom. Who is she?"

"The lady Catherine Gordon of Huntly," he said. "I do not know the family personally, but her father was a man of wealth enough to interest Fife. 'Tis said Catherine's inheritance includes properties that provide a significant income."

"So, one would assume that the Governor has become her guardian."

"He has, aye, and will act as trustee of her income until she marries."

"Only till she marries?" She looked at him. "That is not his usual habit, is it, sir? The estates his brother David of Strathearn's little daughter inherited did not go to her or to her husband, and Fife married her off straightaway, at the age of six."

"That was different," Simon said. "Margaret of Strathearn is Fife's niece, and David's estates were Stewart estates. Fife considered it his duty to retain them for the Crown just as any family will fight to keep family estates under its control. Recall Isabel's battle to keep Fife from taking the estates James left her."

"Aye, sure, so how did you learn that Catherine Gordon changed her mind?"

"Deduction," he said. "Another chap waiting to learn if Fife would see him told me that her ladyship has vanished. The Colvilles are searching high and low for her."

"But how does someone like that disappear?" Sibylla asked. "She must have an army of servants. Sakes, Fife must know exactly where she is."

"Godamercy, lass, do you blame Fife for everything that goes amiss?"

"Do you believe he does *not* want to add Catherine Gordon's property to the Crown's holdings?" she retorted.

"I don't know what he wants. I've not seen the man for eight months, and he was none too happy with me at the time."

The look she gave him then was troubled. "Fife tends to eliminate people with whom he is unhappy, sir."

"You sound like my mother," he said. "Do you fear he will want my head just because I refused to let Rosalie marry at thirteen?"

"Men have died for irritating him less," she said.

"Fife is too shrewd to order my death without strong cause. And why should he? He could not claim Elishaw, because my sisters would inherit. I'd like to see him try to wrest the estate from Buccleuch and Westruther."

"I hope you are right, sir."

He hoped so, too. Over the years he had seen Fife do many things that more powerful men than Simon had insisted he could not do.

Sibylla saw Simon's expression turn thoughtful and hoped he was reconsidering his position with Fife. As companion to Isabel, she had learned much about the Governor's devious ways and knew better than to assume anything about him.

Fife had long resented the order of King Robert the Bruce that the King of Scots' eldest son must succeed him. Before Bruce, Scots had chosen their High Kings from powerful leaders of powerful Scottish families, and many believed the Bruce's decision was a bad one that had weakened the Crown.

Fife certainly believed he was a better man to rule than

his disinterested, crippled older brother. And many Scottish leaders, including the Douglas, agreed.

But most men of sense also knew better than to trust Fife. They knew he was not a man who exerted himself to avoid or overcome obstacles. He eliminated them.

A question occurred to her. "How *could* Catherine Gordon escape Fife?"

"Sakes, the man does not keep her with him."

"But he must have taken precautions, put her under some sort of guard."

"As far as I know, she was living at Huntly amidst her own people," he said.

"Where is Huntly?"

"Near Aberdeen, a hundred miles or so north of here."

"Thomas Colville is unlikely to have any allies nearby then."

"You take unnatural interest in a man you spurned, lass. Has Colville become more intriguing to you?"

"I pity anyone he seeks to marry, that's all. And I am trying to understand why he sent for Edward Colville to come so quickly to Edinburgh. That detail concerns me because of Alice. I don't trust either of the Colvilles, sir, particularly when I cannot guess what they may be up to. Nor do I trust your master."

"He is not . . . That is, I mean to do what I can to distance myself—"

When he broke off and glanced around, she realized that more people had come outside to walk in the courtyard. Several were nearly within earshot.

"I expect we should return now," she said.

"Aye, we should." His voice hardened as he added, "Do not think that I commend what you did earlier, Sibylla, for I do not. I'll admit you had provocation, but Edward

Colville will remember that you struck him long after he forgets that he provoked you to it—if he ever admits that even to himself."

Understanding despite his stern look and tone that he was concerned for her, she said, "I will take care, my lord, as I hope you will. Prithee, do tell me if you learn more about the lady Catherine Gordon's whereabouts."

"Why does she concern you so?"

"Because if Thomas sent for Edward to help him hunt for her, they may both ride to Huntly. If they do, Alice can enjoy herself here without having to be always looking over her shoulder for Edward, and I may have a chance to persuade my father to undo this dreadful betrothal he has foisted on her."

"Mayhap I should not report what I learn of her then," he said lightly. "My master, as you call him, clearly wants her to marry Edward. He may even expect me to aid the Colvilles in their search for her."

That Simon might have to go to Huntly with the Colvilles had not occurred to her, and the possibility disturbed her. She did not trust them. If they were acting for Fife, his motive in putting them together with Simon might have less to do with finding Catherine Gordon than with arranging for Simon to suffer an accident.

The thought made her shiver before she called herself firmly to order, deciding she was seeing demons where none were yet visible.

Simon was not a fool. He could look after himself.

At least, she hoped he could.

It was as well, she thought, that he had asked only if she had come to find Thomas Colville more intriguing. Had he asked about her spurned suitors in general, she could not so easily have replied.

Simon saw Sibylla to her chambers and then went to his room to change to a black doublet and trunk hose for his meeting with Fife. He had spoken lightly to Sibylla, but as he attached his ceremonial dirk in its sheath to his belt, he wondered if the Governor might send him with the Colvilles to search for their heiress.

He would strongly resist such an order. With raiders wreaking havoc in the Borders, Elishaw and its inhabitants to protect, and his little sister eagerly seeking a husband, it was no time for him to be riding a hundred miles farther from home.

He'd have to be away for a fortnight, perhaps longer.

It occurred to him that he did not want to leave just as he was getting to know Sibylla, either. But he shook his head at himself for letting any lass distract him from his duties, let alone from the ticklish business ahead.

The Governor's high chamberlain escorted Simon upstairs to the room on the second floor that Fife used privately, rather than to his first-floor audience chamber.

The Governor sat by a crackling fire at a large table, facing the doorway. Dark red velvet curtains flanked the tall south-facing window from which sunlight spilled across the documents before him. Rounds of red wax for seals rested in a basket on the table, with the royal seal and other items needed for his duties nearby.

Fife was writing when Simon entered, so the chamberlain remained silent until he set aside his quill and looked up. Then, in a quieter voice than he employed in the audience chamber, the chamberlain said, "The Laird of Elishaw, my lord."

Simon made his bow.

"That will be all," Fife said to the chamberlain.

As Simon straightened, he saw to his astonishment that Fife was awarding him a friendly smile. He had seen that smile before, to be sure, but rarely directed at himself or at any other man in Fife's service.

The Governor could be affable, even charming when he thought it would serve his purpose. He could also be harsh, forbidding, and thoroughly ruthless. His usual manner was chilly, his eye critical, and his fury terrifying when aroused.

Dark enough of hair and complexion to have stirred lifelong rumors that he was less Stewart than his numerous blond, Viking-like siblings, Fife was also of slighter build. He wore his black clothing elegantly, and having reached his fifty-first year, had acquired a dignity of age more plausible than the icy arrogance that had been habitual with him when Simon had first made his acquaintance.

Simon searched Fife's expression for familiar signs of the anger he had expected to see but saw none. Instead of relaxing, he grew more alert.

"We greet you well, I trust," Fife said.

"Thank you, my lord, aye," he said.

"I am pleased that you were able to come to Edinburgh so swiftly and in such interesting company."

Simon was beginning to understand but said only, "Interesting, my lord?"

"Aye, sure, for I am as well informed as ever. In troth, though, most of the castle knows by now that you arrived here in company with Sir Malcolm Cavers and his daughters. This renewal of interest does please me, Simon."

Denial leapt to Simon's tongue, but he bit it back, saying, "I was able to assist the lady Sibylla some days ago, sir. Her horse had run off, so I took her to my mother at Elishaw. Cavers had just come to fetch her when your message—"

"Do you mean to say," Fife interjected, "that you do *not* mean to court the lady Sibylla? She must be grateful if you rendered her a service, and I do still favor such a match. She was perhaps too young before and most foolishly indulged."

"That may be, sir," Simon said, wishing he could think. For Fife to press him to agree that a match with Sibylla was still possible was an unusual tactic. But one did not offer the man a flat denial without knowing the ground on which one stood.

In the Governor's presence, pitfalls could open right beneath one's feet.

"I expect you to do your duty, Simon," Fife said with a direct look. "I'm told that your mother has brought the lady Rosalie to seek a husband. We will see what prospects are at hand. Meantime, may we hope you have at last stopped playing Jack-of-Both-Sides at Elishaw and will devote your loyalty wholly to Scotland?"

"At present, my lord, we are lucky enough to enjoy a truce," Simon said.

"During which, I expect you to learn what you can from your kinsmen to the south. If you keep a close watch on them, those connections may serve us when Northumberland next makes mischief, as certainly he will. I have heard complaints of such already. Pull up a stool," he added with a gesture.

"Thank you, my lord," Simon said, complying with silent thanks that Fife had not asked him directly if he would end Elishaw's neutrality or spy on his English kinsmen. To forestall such questions and the orders that must follow, he said, "The news you have heard of reiving is true."

"Aye, sure," Fife said. "What can you tell me about it?"

"The raids began west of us, near Kershopefoot, whilst snow still lay on the ground," Simon said. "They spread west toward Galloway first, but we've suffered increasing trouble in our area. I must tell you, though, I have found no evidence of an English leader—or one that anyone can name, come to that. My lads have caught no one. Nor have they identified any particular reiver."

Fife frowned. "Mayhap you should investigate more across the line."

"As to that, one of my Percy cousins may soon visit Elishaw," Simon said. "Cecil Percy, Northumberland's nephew, sent a messenger a sennight ago to apply for an invitation. I said he might come whenever he likes."

"This Percy nephew is close to Northumberland?"

"He is, aye, my lord, very close."

"Excellent," Fife said. "You must keep me informed of all he says."

Recognizing signs of approaching dismissal, Simon stood. "I will do all I can, my lord, to learn who is initiating the raids."

"Good lad," Fife said at his most affable. "You must first see to your business here, of course, and we'll see if we can find your sister a husband. So for the present let Douglas and his lot seek your raiders. I am pleased to see you, lad," he added. "And *most* pleased that you have come to your senses."

"Thank you, my lord," Simon said, bowing.

"We will expect to see you at supper."

"I have not yet formally presented my sister Rosalie to the court, sir."

"I see no great need," Fife said. "You must bring the lady Sibylla, too, I expect—and her younger sister, of course."

"As to that, their father escorts them, but I believe we may sup with them."

"Tell my high chamberlain to seat you together," Fife said.

Simon bowed again, murmuring, "my lord," as Fife returned to his papers.

Backing away, Simon left without another word.

In the antechamber, he drew a breath of relief before relaying Fife's order—for such it had certainly been—to the high chamberlain.

Then, after sending a messenger to Isabel's chambers, warning its occupants that they would sup in the hall that evening, he retired there himself for a time to seek friends more in touch than he was with the rumors and gossip of the castle. He knew he would find several who were willing to share all they knew.

Sibylla, Lady Murray, and their charges spent much of the afternoon preparing for the evening ahead. Alice and Rosalie were irrepressibly excited.

At one point, hearing a shriek of laughter from their

room, Lady Murray said, "It must be crowded when all of you who serve Isabel are together here."

"The rooms are small, aye, and often untidy," Sibylla said. "Although the maids try to keep our clothing sorted out, they do not always succeed. However, the chamber-maid did find the things I left behind last time, so I can go to supper with you properly if not stylishly attired."

"If you need anything that I have with me, you need only ask for it."

"Thank you," Sibylla said, hoping her surprise did not show.

Lady Murray had grown less stiff with her during their journey and seemed friendlier to everyone than she had hitherto seemed capable of being with anyone.

As Sibylla ordered water and a tub for their baths and watched Lady Murray with Rosalie and Alice, she noted that her ladyship treated the two much the same, as if Alice were another of her daughters.

Summoning the maid a short time later to help her wash her hair, she let her thoughts wander to Simon. Recalling that he had said his mother had also warned him against Fife, she hoped he did not think she was *like* his mother.

In view of her ladyship's friendlier manner, the thought seemed unfeeling, even silly. Why should she care if Simon treated her like his mother? He was perfectly civil to his mother, and heaven knew he was often not at all civil to *her*.

On the first floor of David's Tower, the fires in the two great-hall fireplaces were roaring and the company already merry when Simon and his party entered.

Because only members of the royal family, their noblest guests, and ecclesiastical dignitaries sat at the long table on the dais that extended along much of one long wall of the hall, the high chamberlain directed them to one of three long, linen-draped trestle tables set perpendicular to the dais.

Between the second and third tables, the arrangement left space for acrobats, jugglers, and musicians who would entertain throughout the evening. If dancing was to take place, servants would dismantle the trestles after everyone had eaten.

Fine steel knives, small dishes for salt, silver cups, and shallow pewter bowls rimmed in silver marked each place, and each place faced the central space so everyone could watch the entertainment.

Simon and the others were none too soon. As they stepped into their places, the chamberlain's hornsman blew for silence, and servants approached with ewers, basins, and towels so they could wash their hands. The royal chaplain soon began solemnly to speak the grace before meat.

Simon had taken the place at one end of their group, with Sir Malcolm at the other end, keeping the four ladies between them. Sir Malcolm declared that Lady Murray should sit beside him and Sibylla beside Simon.

"That way," he added, "our lassies will be well protected in our midst."

Simon had no objection. Having eaten precious little at midday, he was ravenous and appreciated the chaplain's brevity. With the court in residence, despite supper being smaller and more casual than the midday dinner, the ritual of serving was much the same for both and could be tedious.

As they took their seats, the royal pantler and his minions came in with bread and butter, followed by the royal butler and his lads, carrying jugs of wine and ale.

Then, to the accompaniment of pipes and drums, four linen-draped carts rolled in bearing huge barons of beef. These proceeded around the assembly with impressive ceremony and much applause, followed by a parade of servants with platters and bowls of other foods in profusion.

The royal carvers twirled their knives as the beef cart reached the dais, then proceeded with the ritual carving of the roasts onto silver platters for every table.

"Dare I ask if all went well with Fife?" Sibylla murmured to Simon as she took a roll from a basket presented to her.

Glancing at the high table, and aware of Alice next to Sibylla, Simon turned back and said, "We should exchange only civilities here, my lady. You know as well as I do that interested ears surround us here."

"Very well, then. I think your sister is enjoying herself hugely. Do not you?"

"I do, aye," he said, noting a twinkle in her eyes. "I am, myself, come to that."

His answer surprised Sibylla, but she did not comment on it, keeping to such harmless topics as the weather and the castle itself until he stirred a gurgle of laughter from her when, in the same tone in which moments earlier he had remarked on the elegance of the vaulted ceiling, he said, "I like that gown. It suits you well."

"'Tis good that I am not vain, sir, or in a temperamental mood," she replied. "You, with all your experience of court life, must easily see that this dress is two years out of style and lacks every ornamental detail considered necessary today."

"I do know about style," he said. "Style and fashion are what drive women to such absurdities as painting their faces and shaving their foreheads and temples, not to mention plucking their eyebrows until . . . There! Just look at that lass across the way by the wobbly juggler on stilts. She doubtless considers herself a stylish woman, for she has plucked her eyebrows until she looks as if she hasn't got any."

He sounded so indignant that Sibylla had to suppress another laugh, but she said, "Men follow absurd fashions, too, sir. Just note that one with the nipped-in waist and padded chest, trying to look as if he has muscles under that tunic. If he dances, he will be lucky not to trip over those long-piked shoes of his."

"Sakes, lass, I hope you don't accuse me of wearing such stuff."

Her laughter bubbled over then until she could scarcely control it. The mental image of stern-faced Murray of Elishaw striding about in red-silk shoes with points nearly six inches long, a padded orange-and-green-striped doublet, and varicolored hose—one leg lavender, the other bright pink—was too much.

"I'd suggest rejecting the orange stripes," she said when she could talk.

He chuckled, and the sound warmed her.

Still smiling, she said, "That meeting must have gone well."

"Well enough, although I should describe it more accurately as perplexing," he said. "We won't talk of it here, though. Will you try more of this beef?"

They ate until they had assuaged their hunger, and soon afterward minstrels began playing as servants cleared the trestles for dancing and other activities.

When Alice and Rosalie asked if they could join a round dance, Simon said he would permit it if Sir Malcolm would.

"We should offer to join them," Sibylla suggested. "My father will not dance, but neither will he want Alice to do so unless someone keeps an eye on her. I warrant your lady mother will feel the same about Rosalie."

Accordingly, they moved to follow their sisters, only to watch in amazement as Sir Malcolm and Lady Murray went off with them, saying they would dance, too.

"I don't think I have ever known my mother to dance," Simon said.

"I must say, no one would suggest a dispute between our families now," Sibylla said. "Has her ladyship told you yet what caused their disagreement?"

"Nay, and your father told me flatly that he won't if she does not."

"Well, I know he won't tell me," she said. "Still, 'tis strange to see them so friendly, is it not? My father seems years younger of late."

"My mother is different, too," Simon said. Proffering his arm to her, he cast a wary look around the chamber and added, "Prithee, lass, promise me we will not end up playing hot cockles or hoodman blind with our sisters and their friends."

She was about to assure him that neither Alice nor Rosalie would want to play bairns' games even if adults were, when she caught sight of a familiar figure.

"The Douglas is here, sir. I wonder if Isabel came with him."

"He has seen us," Simon said.

Archie the Grim strode toward them. A tall, lanky man in his sixth decade whom many called the Black Douglas, he had retained the darkly tanned complexion of his youth. Although his once raven-black hair had grizzled, his deep-set dark eyes were as bright as ever, and the brilliant Douglas smile lit his craggy features long before he was near enough to greet Sibylla.

As she made her curtsy, he grasped a hand to draw her upright, pressing it to his lips as he did. "God greet you, lass," he said, kissing her next on the cheek. "I hope you are fully recovered from the sickness that kept you at Sweethope."

"I am, sir. But you must have seen Isabel. Did she come here with you?"

"Nay, for I came by way of Hermitage to talk to Fife and will return the same way on Sunday. If Isabel has not arrived, I warrant she must be somewhere betwixt Galloway and here. She expected to arrive this week. Art staying in her chambers?"

"Aye, sir, with Lady Murray, her daughter Rosalie, and my sister, Alice."

"That's good then. I must spirit this young man away for a time. Can you contrive without his escort whilst the two of us talk?"

She agreed, realizing only when the Douglas and Simon had walked away that the others in her party had done so, too. She spied her father and Lady Murray first, watching a troupe of acrobats, and then caught sight of Alice and Rosalie some distance away, where a ring was forming for a round dance.

As she wended her way through the crowd, she saw Alice join hands with a good-looking young man on one side and Rosalie on the other. Rosalie might not have been there, however, for Alice gazed at the young gentleman as if moonstruck.

Sibylla quickened her pace just as the lad pulled Alice from the ring and urged her hastily toward a nearby doorway. Rosalie watched them for a moment, frowning, then abruptly freed herself and hurried after them.

Sibylla followed apace, noting as she did that someone else was watching.

Edward Colville's brow knitted heavily, and he was closer than Sibylla was when Alice and her companion, and Rosalie, vanished through the doorway.

Chapter 13 _____

The Douglas led Simon into a nearby alcove with benches against two walls.

Glancing about, Douglas said, "Heard you were here, lad, and wanted a word. As I've no doubt you ken fine, we've a plague of reiving in the Borders."

"Aye, sir," Simon agreed. "They raided one of my people near Hobkirk just days ago. Those same men, or others like them, threw two bairns into the Tweed. We've caught none of them, but folks who saw them think they were English."

"I'm thinking the Percys may be setting events in motion to shatter this fragile truce we've wrought," Douglas said. "I'll not have that."

Simon frowned. "Do you suspect any Percy in particular as the leader?"

"Nay, we hear only rumors. Would you tell me if you'd heard more?"

"I would," Simon said. "I'd be doing little to maintain

Elishaw's neutrality if I were to conceal knowledge of intent on either side to break the truce."

"You're gey glib on the subject," Douglas said testily. "I'd liefer you'd decide once and for all to side with Scotland, lad. As I told you eight months ago, you cannot straddle yon line for long without vexing *both* sides."

"Aye, perhaps," Simon said. "But if I side with the Scots, Northumberland and his lot may try to seize Elishaw again. They've done it before, more than once."

"I'll see that that doesn't happen. I've beaten Percys afore, and I'll do it again. You've two Scottish goodbrothers now, lad—stout, loyal men. You ken fine that they want you to stand for Scotland as I do, so you think hard on it."

"I have thought, my lord, and I will continue to think. Pray, do you also urge me to pursue the lady Sibylla?"

"I do not. But why do you say 'also'?"

"The Governor learned that my family and I arrived here with Sir Malcolm and his daughters. Fife has made it plain that he expects our marriage."

Archie's grim face softened. "Bless us, lad, but you of all men should know Sibylla will marry where she pleases." His face hardened again as he added, "When you choose sides, Simon, choose wisely. With Sibylla as your wife or none, if I find you're supporting the Percy, I'll hang you as a traitor. And I'll do it without a blink."

With those cheering words and a parting clap on the shoulder that Simon almost did not see coming soon enough to brace himself, the Douglas was gone.

Stepping back into the hall, Simon looked for the others and saw his mother and Sir Malcolm in a ring of dancers. He scanned the room only a few seconds longer before he realized that Sibylla, Rosalie, and Alice had vanished.

Sibylla hurried after Rosalie and Alice, suspecting the lad with Alice must be the lackwit. She lost sight of Rosalie before reaching the doorway, so she kept her eye on Edward Colville and followed in his wake.

He did not look back, for which she was grateful. Having no doubt he would seize any chance to create trouble for her, she hoped to deal with him after they found the girls and not let him delay her now.

Passing through an anteroom and a larger chamber without seeing anyone from whom she might beg assistance, she drew a breath, warning herself to keep her temper. She had given Edward cause to be angry with her, but with Alice and Rosalie at hand, and Alice's young man, she thought she would be safe enough.

On entering the large chamber, she had caught a glimpse of Rosalie's skirt vanishing through the far doorway. But although that chamber opened onto a long corridor, she saw only Edward Colville ahead of her.

He turned abruptly to his left and disappeared.

Sibylla had stayed in Edinburgh Castle many times and knew that a small anteroom opened off the corridor there. The first floor of the tower was a maze of such chambers, often opening from one to another. Trysting couples seeking privacy or to avoid the noisy din in the hall often made use of them.

Reaching the open doorway, Sibylla saw Rosalie facing Edward. Alice and her young gentleman were nowhere to be seen.

Pausing to look up and down the corridor again and wonder where Alice had gone, she dismissed the thought when Rosalie said angrily, "Release me!"

"Och, and why should I?" Edward asked with a sneering laugh. "A pretty wench that wanders unescorted offers invitation to any man she meets, does she not? Where did Alice go?" he added harshly.

Sibylla said with determined calm, "Evidently, Edward Colville, you failed to learn anything from the lesson you received this morning."

He whirled, releasing Rosalie, who stepped quickly away from him. "You!" he exclaimed, scowling at Sibylla. "What business is this of yours?"

"As you saw this morning, I take responsibility for her ladyship," Sibylla said. "You would be wise to let her be."

"Who the devil are you?"

"I am Alice Cavers's sister."

"Sakes, you're the capernoited skit that left Thomas standing like a fool with nobbut the parson and your da when he'd expected to wed you!"

"Mercy, Sibylla," Rosalie exclaimed. "Was he one—?"

Ignoring Edward, Sibylla said hastily, "Come, dearling. We'll find Alice together and go back to the hall. Your mother has doubtless missed you by now."

"We shall *all* go to find your dearling Alice," Edward said.

"No, we will not," Sibylla said. "Come, Rosalie."

"Nay, lassie, you'll bide with me a while longer," he said, catching Rosalie's arm again. "I've a mind to know—"

Rosalie had stiffened angrily when he grabbed her but relaxed as her gaze shifted to a point beyond Sibylla. Seeing her expression change to one of mixed relief and wariness told Sibylla who stood there.

Simon said with measured calm so chilling that it sent

prickles of ice up her spine, "Take your hands off my sister, Colville."

Disturbingly aware that she stood between them, Sibylla moved aside. As she faced Simon, the chill pricked her again, stirring a cowardly wish that she had kept her back to him.

His fury was obvious and directed at all three of them. Doubtless he would save a healthy portion for the missing Alice, as well.

"See here, Murray," Edward said. "I just saw the lass to whom I'm plighted wandering off with some cat-wit. I suspect this lassie kens fine where they went."

Simon said coldly, "If you disapprove of the lady Alice's behavior, speak to her father. But you'd be wise to look to your own behavior before complaining of hers. I've not yet told Sir Malcolm what I witnessed this morning. However, if you do not release my sister's arm at once, I *will* speak to him. I'll deal with you, too, in a way that you won't like," he added. "Do you take my meaning?"

"I'd be none so quick to bear tales to Sir Malcolm," Colville said, releasing Rosalie. "I'll own I'd liefer he not hear about that, but I'm thinking his lass here will dislike it more. I doubt her actions would please him any better than mine."

"Mayhap you are right," Simon said. "But the lady Sibylla *is* his daughter. Displeased with her or not, he will ask why she hit you, and he will believe her, too."

"Mayhap he will; mayhap not."

"I'll see that he does," Simon promised. "So, if you seek to retain your good standing with him, stay away from his daughters unless he is with them. You'd be wise to keep out of *my* path, in any event, for some time to come."

"What I'm thinking is that you're mighty thick with a woman who treated you as badly as she treated my brother."

"Your thoughts are a matter of indifference to me," Simon said. "Your actions, however, are another matter. Come, Rosalie . . . and you, too, my lady." Quietly, he added to Sibylla, "I am indebted to you for interceding here."

Rosalie stared at him as he stepped aside to let them pass into the corridor. Then she looked in wonder at Sibylla.

Aware of what she had just deduced and praying she would hold her tongue, Sibylla murmured, "We must find Alice, sir."

"To your left," he replied. "I saw her peep out of the next chamber. I believe that room adjoins no other, so she cannot have left it whilst I stood here."

Sibylla hurried to the indicated door and pushed it open without ceremony to find her sister and the unknown lad alone in the room.

Stepping hastily away from him, Alice looked guiltily at her.

"What are you doing here, Alice?" Sibylla demanded. "Surely, you know—"

"Not now, my lady," Simon said, touching her arm. "Come away with us at once, Lady Alice. You, too, lad. You have some hard words coming your way, but I'll not leave you here alone to face Edward Colville."

"Thank you, my lord," the young man said fervently, bobbing a hasty bow.

"Do you know me, then?"

"Aye, sir, I do. We've not met, but I have seen you before. I'm George Denholm of Teviotdale. The lady Alice and I . . . well, we're by way of being good friends, sir. So, when she said she had to speak to me—"

"You have both behaved badly, but we'll talk of it anon," Simon said curtly. "At present, we must return to the hall, where you, Denholm, will return her ladyship to her father and beg his pardon."

George Denholm turned pale enough to make Sibylla pity him, but by the look of Simon, all of them would hear what he thought before the night was over.

She saw no sign of the younger Colville when they passed the room where they had found him with Rosalie. But Simon allowed no one to dawdle.

When they entered the hall again, Sibylla's gaze collided with her father's. Distance lay between them still, but when he saw her, his gaze shifted to Alice. He turned briefly away, whereupon Lady Murray came into view, looking sorely vexed.

"May God have mercy on us," Rosalie murmured.

"You don't deserve mercy, lassie," Simon said to her. "What demon possessed you to leave the great hall by yourself?"

"I didn't leave by myself," Rosalie protested. "I followed—"

Sibylla cleared her throat.

Glancing at her, Rosalie said, "I was alone but not completely, I vow. I was holding Alice's hand one minute and the next she was walking away with Geordie."

Simon said, "Geordie?"

"George Denholm, of course. Alice calls him Geordie, so I— I expect I should not do so," she amended hastily, eyeing Simon.

"No, you should not. Nor should you have left here without telling someone where you were going. In troth, you should not leave this hall by yourself for any reason or wander alone anywhere in this castle. All manner of people come here, and some are gey untrustworthy. You have your good name and reputation to protect, Rosalie. I do not want to have to explain this to you again."

"I'll remember, sir," Rosalie said.

"See that you do. We will talk more of this anon."

She bit her lower lip, but Sir Malcolm and Lady Murray were upon them, and Sir Malcolm was already scolding.

"Sibylla, where the devil did ye go, and why did ye take your sister and the lady Rosalie with ye? Sakes, but I turn my back for a moment . . ."

He continued in this vein, and Sibylla waited for him to pause before she said quietly, "I beg your pardon, sir."

Before she could continue, Alice said, "It was not her fault, sir. It was mine."

"Faugh!" he snapped. "Sibylla is the elder. It is her duty— What the devil are *you* doing here, sirrah?" he demanded, taking note at last of the still-pale George Denholm. "You have nae business to be anywhere *near* my daughter."

"I am sorry to have vexed you, my lord," Denholm said. "By my troth, I never meant to do so, but when the lady Alice—"

"Father, truly, it was *my* fault," Alice said fiercely enough to draw notice.

Sir Malcolm gaped at her.

Smoothly, Simon said, "Mayhap it would be better, sir, if we were to adjourn to a more private chamber to continue this discussion." He turned to Sibylla. "The princess's solar would be the wisest place if you will agree to that."

She nodded and led the way with him. Hearing her father curtly dismiss George Denholm, she prayed that the young man would not meet either of the Colville brothers until Edward's temper had cooled.

She had seen no sign of the lackwit about Denholm, however, nor any lack of courage. He seemed pleasant and well-mannered. Looking over her shoulder, she saw tears in her sister's eyes. One spilled over and left a damp trail down her cheek.

Sibylla looked up at Simon. The dimple near his mouth showed, and a muscle twitched in his cheek, warning signs that he had his temper under tight rein.

"In troth, sir," she murmured as they turned a corner, briefly leaving the others behind, "little of it was Rosalie's fault."

"And none of it was yours," he replied curtly, surprising her.

"I should have watched them more closely," she admitted. "I thought our parents were with them when we saw the Douglas, and then—"

"Wait until we are more privy, lass. These stairwells echo all we say."

She bit her lip, then recalled Rosalie doing the same thing and hid a smile.

Simon had that effect on one, especially if one was in the wrong.

~

Simon struggled to control his anger. Of late, he had begun to feel as if his emotions were as wobbly as the juggler's stilts had been. Rage had nearly overcome him when he'd seen the Colville pup's filthy paws on Rosalie. But that was normal.

That he might have spitted the pup had he had his sword was less so. How Sir Malcolm could be thinking of sacrificing a tender morsel like Alice to such a scruff he could not imagine. But if either Colville touched Rosalie again, or Sibylla . . .

Taking a deep breath, aware of Sibylla's darting glances, he forced his thoughts back to Sir Malcolm . . . and to Lady Murray.

Had he not assured Sibylla that he could trust his lady mother to keep a close eye on Rosalie? Had Sibylla and Sir Malcolm not expected her to guard Alice, too? Instead, behaving as senselessly as bairns themselves, his mother *and* Sir Malcolm had joined the dancers. They had shown no concern at all for their daughters.

By making himself breathe deeply and evenly until they reached Isabel's chambers, he was able to open the door for Sibylla and stand calmly aside to let her and the other three ladies enter the solar.

When Sir Malcolm moved to follow, Simon stopped him. "A moment, sir," he said. "There is something you should know before the discussion continues."

"Eh? What's that, lad? I don't mind telling ye I'm sore vexed already."

Pulling the door to again, Simon said, "I am indebted to Sibylla for following Rosalie and Alice, sir. She might as easily have looked for you or me to go instead. Had she done that, Rosalie would have found herself in sad straits."

"Foolish lassie. What had she done? And where the devil was Alice?"

"You will have to ask Alice where she was, sir, but

Edward Colville waylaid Rosalie. When she went after
Alice, he cornered her in a private chamber. Had Sibylla
not followed and diverted him long enough for me to find
them . . ."

"Edward *Colville*? Bless me, what was he doing with
Rosalie?"

"Ask him. I've said enough," Simon said, not trusting
himself to say more. "I'll not tell any man how to manage his daughter or aught else, but I *don't* want Colville
near Rosalie. I have warned him off. If that vexes you,
so be it."

Sir Malcolm grimaced. "He should not have concerned
himself in any way with that lassie. I'll talk to him, never
fear."

Simon nodded and reached for the door latch again,
pausing with his hand on it. "With your permission, sir, I
mean to talk with the lady Sibylla about this, too," he said.
"I must also assume some fault, because I let the Douglas draw me away without making sure Rosalie was safe.
In fact," he added, remembering, "he and I walked off
and left Sibylla without noting whether you or my mother
were nearby."

"Aye, well, our Sibylla can look after herself. She's accustomed to it, what with serving Isabel as she has these
past years. Ye're welcome to speak with her, though, lad.
I ken fine that ye'll do her nae harm. But what was that
feckless Denholm doing with our Alice? That's what I
want to know."

"Ask them." Simon opened the door and gestured for
him to enter first.

Sibylla told the chambermaid to stir up the fire and then to take herself off to bed. "We will sit up and talk, but we shan't need you any more tonight," she said.

Having seen Simon stop her father at the threshold and shut the door, she was sure he was explaining what had happened and hoped he could dampen Sir Malcolm's ire. Then perhaps he would not erupt over everyone as he so often did.

Alice and Rosalie had retreated to a settle near the fire and sat silently there.

Lady Murray watched the chambermaid busy herself at the fire but was clearly gathering her own resources for an unpleasant discussion.

Sibylla held her peace and went to sit on the cushioned bench in the window embrasure. It was chilly there, but she could sit undisturbed until the men came in.

When the door opened at last and her father entered, she noted his heavy frown with a resigned sigh. Then his gaze shifted to Lady Murray, and Sibylla saw him grimace. To her surprise, her ladyship, meeting his gaze, looked rueful.

"Lady Sibylla, I would speak with you now if you please."

Looking sharply at the expressionless Simon, Sibylla felt sudden tension.

Lady Murray bristled. "What is this, Simon? Where would you take her?"

"I have Sir Malcolm's permission, madam," Simon said, the chill back in his voice. "If you have a cloak, my lady, you should fetch it."

She did not question him but went to get the cloak Lady Murray had given her.

Rosalie caught her eye when she returned and gave her

a sympathetic smile. But Sibylla barely acknowledged it, glancing instead at her father to judge whether he might change his mind.

He was gazing gravely at Alice.

Simon held the door for Sibylla, and when she heard him shut it behind her, she breathed a sigh of relief, not realizing until then how much she had dreaded the confrontation with her father. Being long unaccustomed to dealing with his rants, she had *not* wanted to deal with this one.

"This way," Simon said, lightly touching the small of her back.

"Where are we going?" she asked, wondering if she had escaped one scolding only to fall headlong into a worse one.

"Have you seen the view from the ramparts here?"

"Not for a long time and never at night," she said as they reached the stairs.

"If the moon is up and no mist obscures it, we'll be able to see it reflected on the sea. In any event, we'll see the lights of the town and the abbey."

"Will the guards let us up there at night?"

She heard a smile in his voice as he said, "I know you don't like Fife, lass, but there are some advantages to being in his service. Most of the guards know me, so we're bound to find at least one man up there that does."

"They will probably know me, too," she reminded him.

"You can put up your hood if you don't want them to recognize you. But I warrant they will say little if they do."

"The truth is, sir, that I'd liefer they not hear what you mean to say to me."

"I don't shout at people, Sibylla. Anything I may say to you, I will say quietly. But I did not pluck you from that cauldron downstairs to berate you."

"Then why did you?"

"Because I think it is our parents' business to deal with what happened tonight. Neither of us was chiefly at fault. When we walked away, your father and my mother had taken charge of Rosalie and Alice. Therefore, I thought it best that we absent ourselves now and leave them to deal with the consequences."

"My father disagrees with your assessment of where the fault lies, sir."

"I fancy I have adjusted his assessment," Simon said as they reached the upper landing and he leaned past her to open the heavy door onto the ramparts.

His breath tickled her neck, sending unfamiliar tremors through her.

"He did look at your mother as if he was sorry, but I thought he was only sorry that I had failed them both," she said. "Whatever did you say to him?"

Touching her back gently again as he nodded to the nearby guard, he guided her across to the north side of the crenellated battlements. "I told him what Colville did tonight," he said. "I also told him how indebted I am to you for intervening on Rosalie's behalf. I told you the same, and by my troth, lass, it is true. I do blame myself somewhat for what happened, as I know you blame yourself. That's *just* why I decided to keep us out of the scene taking place now downstairs."

"Alice and Rosalie may be wishing we had not left them," Sibylla said.

"Whatever Alice may wish, Rosalie is *not* wishing I had stayed," he said. "Sithee, I want our sisters to understand that *they* are at fault. I don't want them being confused by anyone else's attempt to take blame or cast it elsewhere."

She understood what he had done for her and was not sure how she felt about it. It had been long since anyone had taken her part in a dispute. In the meantime, she had learned to fight her own battles and had forgotten how satisfying it could be when someone else entered the fray to ease that burden.

They stood silently on the parapet between two of the seven-foot embrasures for archers—called crenels—looking out over the four-foot wall between them.

The moon, nearing its half, shone brightly on the North Loch below and the waters of the Firth in the distance. The loch was still and glassy. But the Firth's frothy waves capered like so many tiny white horses across a dark field.

Resolutely, but without looking at him, she said, "I should tell you that Rosalie now knows or at least suspects that we nearly married."

"Edward Colville?"

"Aye, he said I'd ill-treated you just as I had Thomas. I'd told your mother and Rosalie that Father arranged three marriages for me, but did not say with whom."

"It doesn't matter," he said. "I shall have to tell my mother before your father decides he can no longer keep it from her."

Relieved, Sibylla said with a sigh, "'Tis a beautiful night, is it not?"

"Aye, but we cannot stay up here too long," he said.

A rough note in his voice made her turn and look up at him.

Simon wondered what was getting into him. If he had not learned by now that being alone with the lady Sibylla was a mistake, he damned well ought to have learned. At least, here on the ramparts, he should have been able to count on the guards' presence to quell any unseemly impulses that stirred.

Instead, the blasted fellows had vanished to the opposite battlements, doubtless believing they were tactfully giving him privacy for his dalliance.

When Sibylla looked up at him with a tremulous half smile on her lips, his hands itched to touch her and his mouth burned to capture hers. Other parts of him came to life, too, until it was all he could do to ignore the ancient urges wrestling again with his good sense.

He'd been living like a monk since his return to Elishaw, and until Sibylla, no temptation had arisen to alter that state. If it had, he'd had his mother's presence to consider and the swiftness with which news spread throughout the Borders. Lady Murray's determination that he marry one of her English cousins had made it nearly certain that she would hear if he cast a look in any other fair lady's direction.

But then had come the night at the pond and the walk at Akermoor.

"You *were* angry with me, though," Sibylla said abruptly.

His thoughts still at Akermoor, it took him a beat to realize she meant earlier that evening. He grimaced then but felt no need to equivocate. Despite their brief time together, he found her easier to talk with than anyone else he could call to mind.

"I was furious," he said. "I'm no good at describing my feelings, or justifying them, come to that. I have learned to control my temper, usually. But when it does flare, it can do so with such heat that it burns anyone within range . . ." He watched to see if she understood, and when she nodded, he felt a glow of satisfaction.

"An apt description, sir. Shall I tell you how *I* have imagined your temper?"

"Do I want to hear it?"

The moon overhead revealed a twinkle in her eyes as she said, "The way you keep things inside until you spew them out reminded me of a kettle left to boil over the fire until its lid sticks to the rim. Do you know what happens then?"

"The same thing that can happen if I simmer too long without release, aye. What led you to evoke this so-flattering image of me?"

She looked out toward the sea again. "On our journey here, I thought about my first impression of you on the day that was to have been our wedding day."

Bewildered, remembering feeling nothing at first but irritation at her childish prattle, he said, "As a result of *that* memory, you likened me to a spewing pot?"

"Not at first," she said, regarding him more warily. "At first, I saw only a cold, self-absorbed man with no interest in me, wanting to get on with his wedding. I found the prospect of living the rest of my life with him so daunting that I fled."

"Even so, a cold man and a boiling pot do not . . ."

She shook her head. "My thinking was not so particular. I was considering your temperament—how I'd first judged it and what I'd seen since. Especially when—" She caught her lower lip between her teeth.

"Never mind." She was irresistible, looking at him so, and he could easily suppose he had given her good cause at Elishaw to liken him so.

Noting that the guards seemed content where they were and that he and she stood in the shadow of a crenel, he pulled her nearer and lowered his mouth to hers.

With a low moan, she leaned toward him, opening her mouth to him.

Shutting his eyes, he called himself a fool for plunging into something that could lead only to turmoil of one sort or another but savored her taste nonetheless.

Without warning, Sibylla pushed against his chest and tilted her head back with a frown. "You have behaved differently since . . . since this afternoon," she said.

"I don't want to talk more now, and certainly not about me," he said. But when he moved to kiss her again, she slipped from his grasp.

"Moreover," she said, "you *were* angry with me. I saw it in the way you looked at me, as if it were *my* fault that Edward had cornered Rosalie. And, earlier, you refused even to talk to me about your meeting with Fife."

"Sibylla, I explained those things. It would have been unwise—"

"Just tell me this, sir," she said. "When you met with the Governor this afternoon, did he press you to renew your suit with me?"

Stunned by the question, he hesitated. But he could not lie to her.

"Faith, I can see that he did!" Tugging him out under the moonlight, she said fiercely, "Look at me! Now, sir, I challenge you to deny Fife's urging if you can."

He was not accustomed to any woman commanding him, let alone challenging him in such a tone, and would accept it from few men. But he steeled himself to hold his temper as he said, "By my troth, lass, it is *not* as you think."

"Do not equivocate, Simon Murray. I asked a simple question that requires a simple answer. Did Fife urge you to seek marriage with me again or not?"

"He did, aye, but—"

"I *knew* it! Will you tell me you refused him?" Her words dripped with scorn, and when he did not answer immediately, she said, "Well, did you?"

"Don't take that tone with me," he warned her. "I know you are angry, but whatever Fife may have said, I swear it has nowt to do with this. You must—"

"Do not tell me what I must," she said in a voice as cold as any he could produce. "You said yourself that you are still obedient to his will, but I will *not* become another pawn on Fife's board, sir, or yours. I bid you good*night*!"

Chapter 14 ————————

Simon caught Sibylla's arm and held her firmly when she tried to jerk free.

Determined not to let her make a greater sight of herself, he said with what he hoped was his usual calm, "You may go when I know you won't storm off in full view of those men yonder. Here in the open, the moon is as bright as day and you do not want to stir talk of unseemly behavior. I'd prefer to escort you. But if you cannot agree to that, pray have the good sense to walk with your usual dignity."

She scowled at him, then looked at his hand on her arm.

Hoping she understood that he would brook no defiance, he released her.

As she turned away, he saw the effort it took to cloak her anger. He matched his stride to hers, relieved when she made no effort to elude him. At the doorway, she paused to let him pull it open but then moved to go ahead of him.

"I'll go first, my lady, as I should," he said quietly.

He saw her grimace but knew it for a sign of annoy-

ance with herself rather than with him. After living so
long in a female household, doubtless she had got out of
the habit of always waiting for a male companion to go
ahead to clear a path for her across a crowded room or
shield her from a fall down a spiral stairway.

He hoped she was pondering what little she'd let him
say about Fife's remarks and would realize she had misunderstood. She was a sensible woman. If he let her think
now, perhaps he could smooth things between them before she retired.

That hope vanished when they reached the princess's
chambers to find the door open and merry feminine chatter sounding from within.

"Sibylla! There you are!" Rosalie exclaimed, appearing in the doorway with a grin and reaching for Sibylla's
hand. "Only see who has come!"

Simon's first thought was that the princess Isabel had
arrived. However, he quickly recognized voices and realized his error.

Glancing at Sibylla, he knew she had heard them,
too, because she smiled and hurried inside, exclaiming,
"Amalie! Meg! How wonderful to see you! When did you
arrive, and why did you not send to inform us you were
coming?"

Stepping to the doorway, he saw the two elder of his
three sisters greeting Sibylla with hugs. Amalie, rosy and
round with child, seemed especially delighted.

"We just learned you were here," she said. To Simon,
she added, "Did you not know that Westruther and Buccleuch were coming to meet with the Douglas?"

"Nay, although I did see Douglas tonight, and talked
with him. I came to Edinburgh because of a summons
from the Governor."

"Aye, well, they are downstairs in the hall, and they said we should send you to them if we found you. We've already sent Sibylla's father away, and we mean to talk until our husbands send for us to return to the Canongate."

"Where are you staying?" he asked.

Meg said with her wide smile, "Buccleuch has a house there. His brother usually lives in it, but he is away, so we're all staying there. You must visit us."

"I will," he promised.

He bowed, responded when Sibylla thanked him civilly for seeing her safely back, and then left them to their reunion.

Sibylla was pleased to see Amalie and Meg and wanted to hear all their news. Despite her pleasure, though, a nagging voice in her mind kept diverting her thoughts to the scene on the ramparts with Simon.

Until he'd spoiled things by admitting that Fife did expect him to renew his suit, she had let her emotions rule her behavior.

Now she could see how foolish she had been.

She forced her attention back to her guests, but the nagging voice continued sporadically until Amalie said, "But Rosalie, the lady Catherine Gordon is not a woman grown. She is not even as old as you are."

Sibylla stared at her. "What are you saying, Amalie? Catherine Gordon is to marry Thomas Colville. Surely, she must be at least Rosalie's age."

"But she is not," Meg said. "Wat said only today that

the lady Catherine is just seven, a year older than Strathearn's daughter was when Fife arranged *her* marriage."

Stunned but recalling her discussion with Simon on the same subject, Sibylla said, "But Margaret of Strathearn is Fife's niece and her estates Stewart lands! Surely with an unrelated, Gordon heiress, he has to behave differently."

Amalie said dryly, "Apparently not, as he's giving her to Thomas Colville, who is one of his most loyal followers. Just as Simon is," she added with a sigh.

When Meg nodded in agreement, Sibylla felt impelled to defend Simon.

"He supports Fife less eagerly now, I think," she said. "He has been . . ." She paused, unable to say he'd been kind to her, for he had not, but seeking some way to explain that he had changed from the man Amalie had known.

Amalie chuckled. "Rosalie and our lady mother did tell us he rescued you and some child from the Tweed, Sibylla. Doubtless, he felt obliged to treat you civilly for a time. But I could tell at once that you were seething before you smiled and hurried in to greet us. Clearly, Simon had infuriated you."

Annoyed with herself for giving her emotions away when she thought she had controlled them, Sibylla said, "You read too much into a look of weariness, my dear. I own, he was displeased with me, and rightly, but I'm not angry and neither is he. Now, tell me more about Catherine Gordon. Are you sure she is only seven, Meg?"

Amalie said, "Wat did say so, Sibylla. I heard him, too."

"He said Fife used Catherine's age as cause to declare himself her guardian, just as he did with Margaret of Strathearn," Meg said. "He believes—Wat does—that

Fife means to add her estates to the Crown lands and control them, just as he controls Strathearn. But Wat thinks he will find it hard to do. Sithee, Sir John Gordon had other female heirs. And one is married to a man of consequence."

"Even so, if Fife can make Catherine marry one of his own men, he can keep control of her estates if not her entire income—or so Garth said," Amalie told them. "That *is* Fife's usual practice, is it not?"

No one disagreed, but Meg changed the subject, asking Sibylla to tell them more about her daring rescue. "Rosalie said you jumped in after that child."

Sibylla explained briefly but refused to let them draw her into detail, and soon changed the subject again by asking Amalie if she and Westruther were not looking forward eagerly to the birth of their first child, still some months away.

Although Amalie replied with loving exasperation that she would look forward to it more if Garth would cease trying to wrap her in cotton wool, this interesting topic entertained them until Sibylla tactfully suggested that Lady Murray might like some time alone with her daughters.

"Oh, aye," Alice agreed. "I must retire, too, because although I delight in hearing all your tales and reminiscences, I can scarcely keep my eyes open. But may I speak to you in your chamber, Sibylla, before I go to my own?"

"Aye, sure," Sibylla said before bidding everyone else goodnight.

When they were alone inside her room with the door shut, she said, "What is it, Alice? I hope you do not mean to complain to me about whatever Father may have said to you after you ran off as you did with young Denholm."

"Nay," Alice said doubtfully. "That is to say, it is all

horrid, because Father said that if the Colvilles do not discard the notion of allying their family with ours after what I did, he means to move the date of our wedding forward."

"Sakes," Sibylla said. "I had hoped he would understand now why you dislike the match and how unsuitable Edward Colville is to be your husband. The Denholms are perfectly respectable, are they not?"

"They are, aye," Alice said. "But Father is so angry with me, Sibylla, and one cannot blame him. Also, he blames himself for not watching me closer, and that makes him angrier. I know I ought never to have walked away with Geordie as I did, but when he asked me to go, I just went. I did not think at all."

"I am glad you understand that you were in the wrong, love. Not just for going with Denholm but for abandoning Rosalie as you did."

"I know," Alice said. Looking guiltier than ever, she added, "Rosalie knows now that you and her brother nearly married, Sibylla. But I vow, I did *not* tell her."

"Nay, Edward Colville did that," Sibylla said.

"So she said, aye. But she is sure that her lady mother knows naught of it. We know we mustn't tell her, but we do think that you or Simon should."

"Simon has said he will," Sibylla said. "But you *are* growing wiser, love, surely wise enough now to know that you need not marry Edward Colville."

"But I *told* you, I cannot defy Father as you did," Alice said. "You don't understand, because it is always so easy for you to do as you please. But not everyone is like you, Sibylla. *I* am not."

An idea stirred, and Sibylla paused to consider it before she said, "Look here, Alice, are you sure you love

George Denholm? You are not just encouraging him as a way to escape Edward, are you?"

"Nay, I swear! I have loved Geordie for more than a year now, and I loathe Edward Colville. But I don't know what to do," she said. Then, with a sigh, she added, "Mayhap Geordie should just go to Father and demand that he let us marry."

"He can hardly do that whilst you are betrothed to another man. You must break the betrothal first."

"Oh, I couldn't!"

Sibylla sighed. "It is rarely easy to follow one's own course, Alice," she said. "No one can do it for you, you know. You must do some things for yourself."

"Then tell me what to do," Alice begged. "Just do *not* say that I must stand up to Father and *explain* to him."

"It did occur to me that if you love Denholm, you might run away together and get married," Sibylla said. Before Alice could protest, she added, "Sithee, you are past the age of consent, so you do not need our father's permission to wed."

Alice stared at her in dismay. "You must be joking, Sibylla! I could *never*—"

"You sought my advice, and I have given it," Sibylla said, losing patience. "I do not think less of you, dearling, but I cannot help you if you refuse to help yourself. Now, prithee, go to bed and let us both get some sleep."

Scowling mutinously, Alice left the room without another word.

Knowing she had handled the situation badly but with no idea of how to help her sister, Sibylla summoned the chambermaid. As she prepared for bed, her thoughts shifted back to Simon and the abruptness of their parting.

He had kept silent all the way back from the ramparts, but she had sensed more easily than usual with him that he had had more he wanted to say.

She'd cut him off when he'd tried to explain, not wanting to hear him defend his loyalty to Fife. A more civil person, one with a stronger guard on her tongue, would have let him speak. Not, she decided, that anything he *could* say would alter the facts that Fife wanted to see them married and Simon habitually obeyed Fife.

She lay in bed, lulled by the murmur of voices in the solar and thinking of things she had omitted in telling Meg and Amalie about her stay at Elishaw. Recalling Amalie's remark that Simon, having rescued her, felt obliged to treat her civilly, she realized she'd had similar feelings of obligation to Kit. Might Simon's thoughtful gestures have been similar to the small indulgences she allowed the child?

When she'd felt bad at leaving Kit to sleep in the shadowy kitchen, and had let her sleep in her bedchamber instead, had it not been much the same as Simon's unwillingness to send *her* to bed with wet hair after her moonlight swim?

The fact was that, annoyed with him or not, she wanted to share her thoughts with him and tell him all she had learned about the lady Catherine Gordon. When she told herself that she just wanted to hear what he'd say about it all, the voice in her head laughed. He'd say that it was none of her affair, and he would be right.

She wondered if Simon was already aware that Catherine was only seven. He had said he did not know the family, but he might still have known her age. Perhaps Fife's habit of assuming guardianship of little heirs and heiresses was so common that it had not occurred to him to mention it to her. Then she remembered his anger with Fife for trying to marry off the thirteen-year-old Rosalie.

Surely, then, had Simon known Catherine's age, he would have mentioned it.

Even so, she could almost hear him say that while it was one thing to concern herself with Alice's betrothal to Edward Colville, having spurned Thomas herself, she had no right or reason to take interest in whomever Thomas might marry.

He would be right, but she still wanted to talk to him.

On that thought, she slept, only to wake to a drizzly morning that reminded her of their near-wedding day and thus brought Simon to mind again.

As she accepted the chambermaid's aid to dress, she wondered if he would come in search of her as he had before, and demand private speech.

By midmorning she persuaded herself that she had declared her distrust so blatantly that he never wanted to speak to her again.

Deciding to prove to herself, if not to him, that his silence meant nothing to her, she passed time before the midday meal casting dice against Rosalie and Alice while Lady Murray worked at her tambour frame. But when they entered the hall, Simon was not there to impress with her lack of concern.

Nor did she see Westruther, Buccleuch, or their wives.

"Did not Meg say they would all dine with us today?" she asked Lady Murray.

"I thought so," her ladyship said.

Sir Malcolm, escorting them, said, "Doubtless the weather kept them in."

Fife was in his place at the center of the dais table with the Bishop of St. Andrews at his right. Sibylla recognized several lords of Parliament sitting in a string to the right of the bishop.

At Fife's left was a line of noblewomen, wives of the men on his right who had wives. Thomas Colville was with the men, but she saw no sign of Edward.

She still had not seen Simon, either, when Lady Murray announced she had had enough of the din and suggested they return to their chambers.

With nothing more interesting in mind to do, and the girls wanting to learn the game of dames, Sibylla agreed. Simon would find her if he wanted her.

That he was not coming became clear long before suppertime, and it was then that she recalled his mentioning that Fife might send him to Huntly with the Colvilles to search for the lady Catherine. Perhaps he had gone with Edward.

Because of that fear, she had small hope of seeing him when she went down to supper with her three companions. The din greeted them yards from the hall entrance, and when the chamberlain's lad blew his horn and the chamberlain announced them, Sibylla doubted that anyone in the chamber heard him. Clearly, everyone kept inside the precinct by the rain all day had come to supper in the hall.

Her gaze swept the lower hall trestles without finding Simon, but she did see her father beckoning from one, where he had apparently saved places for them.

Lady Murray's smile said that she had seen him, too, so Sibylla followed her and saw Simon at last when she looked toward the dais.

He sat at Fife's right hand. As Thomas Colville sat farther down the table, Sibylla hoped that Edward, still apparently absent, had gone to Huntly alone.

They took their places, and Alice and Rosalie chattered as if they had not a care in the world. If either suffered any lingering ill effects from their confrontation with Lady Murray and Sir Malcolm the previous night, Sibylla saw no sign of it.

They had missed the grace before meat, and minstrels played merrily as a troupe of dancers capered in the open space provided for them.

Sibylla gazed vaguely at them and toyed with her food until someone passing behind her said, "I must ask Kitty Lennox. She is kin to nearly everyone, so she may know that handsome wretch."

Sibylla stopped breathing long enough to become aware of her heartbeat. She did not know Kitty Lennox, but she knew many things about her. Lady Susan Lennox, one of Isabel's other attendants, was Kitty's cousin. And Susan, who was full of just *being* a Lennox, talked of Kitty often. More important to Sibylla, however, was that Kitty Lennox's Sunday name was Catherine.

A chill crept through her as she considered that simple fact and strenuously resisted the next, patently absurd, thought striving to form itself in her mind.

She looked again at the high table. If she had wanted to talk to Simon before, it was as nothing to her desire to do so now.

But Fife was speaking to him, and Simon was listening intently.

She had to think. But the din in the chamber rendered anything but the simplest thought processes impossible.

On one side of her, Alice and Rosalie continued to chatter away. On the other, Sir Malcolm and Lady Murray had their heads together, talking quietly.

Listening with only half an ear as Fife described the Douglas's report to him about the increasing Border raids and insisted Northumberland must be instigating them, Simon had watched as his mother, Rosalie, Sibylla, and Alice joined Sir Malcolm at one of the trestles reserved for the nobility.

He continued to keep an eye on them as he listened and occasionally replied to Fife's questions. As a trio of young women walked past Sibylla toward the main entrance, he saw her stiffen. Her mouth opened, and she turned her head toward him.

Although she looked right at him, he knew she could not tell that he was watching her. He was careful to look as if he kept his attention firmly on Fife.

"I agree with Archie that before we act we must be certain that these raids come from beyond the line," Fife said.

"I assure you, my lord, the Percys want peace as much as we do and support the truce. I'll talk with Cecil Percy when he visits and hear what he thinks of it all."

"I shall be interested to learn what he says," Fife said.

Glancing again at the trestles as Fife went on to another matter, Simon saw that Sibylla's place was empty. Scanning the huge chamber, he saw her alone near the doorway through which his sister and Alice had vanished the night before.

Tempted to swear, he exerted patience until Fife said that for civility's sake he supposed he ought to converse with the woman at his left.

"By your leave then, my lord, I would beg to be excused," Simon said. "Others here and in town may have ideas on subjects we have discussed, and—"

"Take yourself off then, but heed what I've said to you, Simon. I expect you to attend to business here as I suggested, and likewise to learn from those others all that you can of this raiding. I shall depend on you for that, sir. Don't disappoint me. I want know more about it than the Douglas does."

"Aye, sir, I'll do all I can," Simon said despite his certainty that Fife was unlikely ever to know more than Douglas about what happened in the Borders.

Fife turned away, and Simon left the dais, his deceptively long strides covering the distance to the doorway without any appearance of undue haste.

Having taken leave of the others by suggesting a need to use the garderobe, and eschewing Lady Murray's suggestion that she take a maid along, Sibylla headed for the maze of chambers and corridors accessed from the east doorway of the hall.

The area was reassuringly empty, doubtless because the rain had kept folks in town who might otherwise have come to sup at the castle and then sought privacy.

Westruther's and Buccleuch's continued absence reinforced that notion.

Nevertheless, Sibylla resisted the temptation to enter one of the nearer chambers, opting instead to go to the end of the first corridor before peeping into one. Finding it empty, she went into the chilly room, shut the door, and—recalling that she had walked in on Rosalie and Edward Colville in just such a chamber—looked for a bolt or some way to fix the latch in place. Examination revealed only a fragile-looking brass hook that she slipped into an equally fragile-looking ring.

Aware that most people seeking such a room would not want to find anyone in it and would accept any resistance as proof that someone was there, she could be relatively sure to remain undisturbed. She knew she ought to have gone upstairs to think, but she wanted to stay near Simon. He was plainly avoiding her, and she wanted to give herself a chance to speak to him—after she had decided what to say.

Taking a seat on a cushioned bench, she reminded herself that he would reject even the slightest suggestion that Kit might be the Lady Catherine. Trying to imagine why the intriguing possibility had struck her with such force made her want more than ever to talk to Simon.

The plain fact was that she liked talking with him. His mind was coldly logical, whereas she tended to think more emotionally when something engaged her feelings, as she was coming to realize Kit had. He did have an irritating tendency to dispute nearly anything she might say. However, irritating or not, when he did disagree with her, it nearly always sharpened her focus and clarified her thoughts.

She also admired his good sense except perhaps when she disagreed with him. Even then, if only after the fact, she envied his ability to keep his head and think beyond his emotions—if any emotions other than anger ever plagued him.

Focusing her thoughts, determined to think as logically as he would, she recalled that from the first, Kit had taken small notice of the fine quality of the garments provided for her at Elishaw. She had seemed oblivious, as if she had always worn such things. She had also revealed surprising grace and good manners.

As absurd as the idea of her being Lady Catherine seemed, and however illogical, such qualities and attitudes suggested that the little one was better born than they had thought. And if she *was* the lady Catherine, she stood in danger if not of life and limb, then certainly of making a dreadful misalliance.

However, Kit's obvious fear and the fact that both children had ended up in the river Tweed as victims of so-called raiders indicated worse danger.

That, Sibylla decided, was why she had to discuss it with Simon.

But would he talk to her? Well before she had ripped up at him on the ramparts, he had clearly abandoned his vow never to forgive her and had listened to her in a way that few men ever had. Had she destroyed the comfortable way they had of talking with each other by accusing him of still being in Fife's pocket?

He *had* kept his temper after she lost hers and had seen to it that she did not make a fool of herself by stomping off in full view of the castle guards. And he had left primarily because Meg and Amalie had arrived and had told him to go.

Hope stirred.

Reminding herself that he also cared about Kit, she wondered how she might suggest the idea of Kit's being Catherine to him without putting up his back.

Simply seeking his advice did not appeal to her. She had got out of the habit of asking anyone but the Douglas or Isabel to advise her, and Simon was too quick to take control and issue commands if one gave him the least encouragement.

The latch on the door rattled.

Catching her breath, ears aprick, Sibylla fixed her gaze on the door.

Silence.

Her heart pounded at the guilty reminder that the little chamber was no place for any young woman alone.

"Lass, if you're in there, open the door."

Exhaling with more relief than she might have expected to feel at the sound of Simon's voice, she got up and went to open it. But she stepped back at once.

His stern gaze swept the room. "Sakes, are you alone in here?"

Stiffening despite her expectation of the question, she said more sharply than she had intended, "Did you think you would interrupt an assignation, my lord?"

His stern, penetrating gaze shifted back to her. When it met hers, she felt again that strange, intense sense of vulnerability he could stir so easily, as if her innermost secrets clamored to shout themselves to him.

He shut the door and took a step toward her.

She stepped back, saying, "I'm glad you came. I want to talk to you."

"I came because I saw you leave the hall and I thought . . . that is, you looked as if you were . . ." More abruptly, he said, "What compelled you to leave, Sibylla?"

"I told your mother I sought the garderobe," she said, feeling her cheeks grow hot at revealing the lie.

"I don't want to know what you told her. I want to know why you left."

"I'll tell you, but may we sit first?"

"Just tell me. We must not linger here."

She licked her lips, certain it would be useless to tell him what she had overheard and uncertain what else to say. Impulsively, she said, "When we did not see you all day, I thought Fife must have sent you to Huntly with Edward Colville."

"He did not even send Colville," Simon said.

"Are they not going to search near Huntly for the lady Catherine then?"

"Sibylla, such interest in a matter that is someone else's concern can have nowt to do with why you left the hall so abruptly."

"But it does," she said. "That is to say the lady Catherine does. Do you know how old she is, sir?"

"I heard she is too young for Colville. But that is no unusual situation."

"She is just seven," Sibylla said, watching his expression. She thought his jaw tightened but saw nothing else to indicate his feelings.

"That is very young," he said. "But that, too, has happened before."

"Do you know what most people call the lady Catherine Lennox?"

He frowned, clearly holding his temper in check. "I cannot think what that has to do with any of this. Most people call her Kitty, I think."

"Or Kit," Sibylla said, still eyeing him closely.

To her astonishment, instead of bewilderment or an exclamation of flat denial, he remained silent with an arrested look in his eyes.

"What is it?" she demanded. "What are you thinking?"

"Nowt," he retorted. "It just came to me what foolishness *you've* been thinking. Use your sense, lass. Come now, we're going back to the hall."

Chapter 15 _____

Sibylla caught Simon's arm as he turned toward the door. "We must not go yet," she said. "Prithee, sir, you must hear me first."

He turned back, but his eyes had narrowed. "Look here, Sibylla, you are not thinking clearly. I'd wager that Kit and Kitty are common nicknames for Catherine."

"Then why did you look as you did when I told you? And do not say it was because the very idea is absurd. I could see that it was more than that."

He met her gaze. "The last time I replied honestly to a question of yours, you chose to mistake my meaning," he said in the chilly tone she so disliked. "If I reveal the thought that entered my head, I fear you may do it again."

Licking dry lips, she said, "I behaved badly last night, sir. Learning that Fife is again trying to order my life infuriated me. His very interest is intrusive, but I should not have spoken as I did, and I cannot insist that you see this matter as I do. After all, I may easily be wrong. And, too, if Fife does demand that you help look for the lady Catherine, I should not even tell you all I—"

She broke off with a cry of protest when he grabbed her by both shoulders, believing he meant to shake her. He certainly looked as if he did.

Instead, he closed his eyes for a moment, drew a breath, and let it out.

His hands felt hot through the thin sleeves of her silk tunic. Their heat radiated through her until she could scarcely breathe. His grip tightened as he opened his eyes again, but then he eased it, although he still held her.

His voice was calm, almost gentle, as he said, "You may tell me anything. I would never betray your confidence."

"Nor I yours, sir," she said, fighting to keep her voice steady when what she really wanted was to forget Kit and have him take her in his arms and kiss her again.

The thought of how foolish she was to feel so at such an inauspicious time steadied her. Without giving him time to reply, she said, "Tell me first why you looked as you did when I suggested Kit might be Catherine."

His lips tightened, but he nodded. "I'll tell you, but I hope you will consider my words in a context other than as grist for your mill."

Curiosity burning now, she said, "I'll try, I promise."

This time an eyebrow twitched, giving her to realize that, as seldom as his feelings revealed themselves in his expression, she was coming to note even the slightest sign. Reading the twitch as doubt that she could remain objective, she dampened her lips again. She could not promise more than to hear him out.

"Don't *do* that," he said, his voice suddenly hoarse.

"What?"

"Lick your lips. Every time you do it, I want to—" He shook his head. "Never mind. I think I'm just trying to divert you as you have diverted me when I've asked a question *you* don't want to answer. The fact is that Lady Catherine is not at Huntly as I had supposed and has not been for some time. She and a servant disappeared from Oxnam Tower, a Gordon holding not ten miles from Elishaw."

"There! You see?" When his eyebrows shot upward, she said, "Be fair, sir. You must see that had you told me instead that someone had *seen* her at Huntly, it would have proved that she cannot be at Elishaw. But a servant with her . . . That could be her nurse. Surely, we should at least discuss the possibilities!"

Simon gave her a shake then but only to emphasize his point as he said, "See here, lass, the idea of our Kit being a young noblewoman or an heiress of any sort is daft. She may be the right age, but her speech and appearance befit a common lass, not a noble one. There is also Dand to consider. The lady Catherine has no brother."

"Are you sure?" Sibylla demanded. "You said you don't know her family."

He fought a smile. "We both know that a brother would inherit before Catherine would," he said gently.

She grimaced. "Very well, I spoke too hastily for my thoughts to catch up. But mayhap *he* is the servant. Has Kit ever said that Dand is her brother?"

"Certainly—" Doubt assailed him. Had Kit said that, or had they just assumed Dand was her brother? "Sakes, I don't know if she said it or not. But I have certainly referred to him as her brother, and she has never denied it."

"She is afraid to admit or deny anything," Sibylla said.

"But she does not know if his Sunday name is Andrew. If he were her brother, she *would* know. Mayhap he is the nurse's son or some altogether different kinsman. If Lady Catherine was at Oxnam, she clearly has Gordon kinsmen in the Borders."

"Aye, many, but now you are adding facts you've no right or reason to add," he said. "I know nowt about the servant. But the notion that Kit is wealthy remains absurd. Think how common she looks, lass. Think of the clothes she was wearing!"

"She wore boy's clothing," she reminded him. "Oh, don't you see, sir, she has evaded every question about herself. As to her looks, she told me she hacked off her own hair. She is wearing your sisters' cast-off clothes and pays their quality no heed. In fine clothing with her hair grown long again, her appearance will change."

"But her manner and speech will not."

"They already have," Sibylla declared. "You may not have noticed that she speaks perfectly well when she chooses, but—"

"I have noted that," he said. "I have also noted that when she is with you, she walks, talks, and moves as you do. The child is an excellent mimic, Sibylla, striving to be like you. That is all she is."

Her beautiful eyes flashed. "Is *this* how you listen, Simon Murray? Must you dismiss whatever does not match your own opinion of things? What about those awful men throwing Kit and Dand both into the Tweed?"

"Dand said—"

"By heaven, there is no talking to you!" she exclaimed, trying ineffectively to pull away. "I do not know *why* I thought it would help. Unhand me, sir!"

His hands tightened, but although he had to fight harder

than he could ever remember having fought to keep his
temper, he resisted the urge to shake her. "You cannot
leave here if you will do so in a temper," he said. "I'll let
you go when—"

"You will let go at once," she snapped, trying again to
pull free.

He held her easily. He wanted to wrap his arms around
her and hold her close until she calmed. He wished fervently that Fife had never entered his life.

The absurdity of that thought nearly made him laugh.

His gaze shifted past her in what was becoming a familiar need in her presence to conceal amusement lest she
demand an explanation he was reluctant to give her.

Her sudden stillness warned him that he had failed.

In measured tones, she said, "Your behavior is shame-
ful. To invite me to talk to you about anything, then dismiss what I say as if it were of no consequence *and* dare
to laugh at me is unconscionable."

Meeting her angry gaze, he said in all sincerity, "I
admit my amusement, lass, but I deny that it arose from
any such cause. In troth, I was wishing that Fife had never
entered my life when it occurred to me that such a wish
was as daft as any thought I have accused you of having.
He has filled a large part of my life for years. Until these
past eight months, he played a greater role in it than my
family did, so he has done much for which I owe him
gratitude as well as loyalty."

When she remained silent, he added softly, "You do
make me laugh, Sibylla, often. But I am grateful for that
laughter. You have made me like myself again."

Her lips parted softly, and his body came alive. He
drew her nearer.

When she continued to gaze limpidly at him and made

no further objection to his holding her, he slowly lowered his mouth to hers.

She responded as quickly and thoroughly as she had the night before, melting toward him. As his arms went around her, she slipped hers around him.

He savored the taste of her, plunging his tongue into her mouth and caressing her back, easing a hand down to cup a bottom cheek through her skirt.

She pressed harder against him, bringing his cock to full alert.

Sibylla felt him move against her and knew she ought to step away, but she could not have done so if the building had caught fire. She felt as if *she* had.

She did not want to stop. Inhaling the spicy scent of him, she relished the feeling of her palms against his soft velvet doublet and the contrast of the taut, hard muscles underneath.

Her breasts felt swollen and tingly as if pressing against him excited them. As his right hand eased to her left breast, she tensed with unfamiliar sensual anticipation. When his caresses grew more daring, she did not object.

Other men had tried to kiss and touch her, but she had received their attention with speculative interest if she had felt any at all. In general, she had resisted letting them touch her, most strenuously if they had tried to kiss her without invitation.

She had never felt the slightest wish to lure a man to touch her and would not have expected to endure a man who dared hold her against her will. If she did not count Hugh or her father—and one certainly would not count either in such a context—no one but Simon had ever dared to do such a thing.

Now that he had, she could not think sensibly, but she did not want to think. She wanted to take pleasure in what he was doing to her. The rest of the world, as far as she was concerned could just—

"What manner of mischief is this, then?"

Startled, and with Simon hastily stepping back, she looked past him to see Thomas Colville in the open doorway. So engrossed had she become in Simon and what they were doing that she had not heard the latch lift or the door open.

Simon said in his chilly way, "What the devil does it look like, Colville? Get out, and shut that door. You are very much in the way."

"I want to know what you're up to, Murray," Thomas said. "More than once since your arrival you have busied yourself in *my* affairs, so when you left the hall so abruptly, I thought I'd see where you went. I had seen the lady Sibylla leave and had a notion you might follow her."

"Whatever I am doing is no concern of yours. Must I put you out myself?"

Thomas smirked at Sibylla, then turned and walked away.

"That man should think black shame to himself," she muttered as Simon moved to shut the door. "He'd tell a woman she should cover herself after he'd spent half an hour peering down her dress. And his odious brother is just like him!"

Despite his anger, Simon nearly laughed at her choice of words, but he knew that what had happened was no laughing matter. He latched the door, fixing the hook this time before turning back to her.

"I'm sorry I failed to do that before, lass, and for what followed," he said. "But the damage is done. I know a way upstairs from here that will preclude our having to walk through the hall."

"I know that way, too," she said. "But I will not hide away, sir. He saw naught but a kiss, and he should never have—"

"He did what he did, lass, just as we did. And if you think he'll keep silent—"

"Sakes, sir, Fife must dislike his people gossiping as much as Isabel does!"

"He dislikes gossip only when the gossip is about him," Simon said. "Otherwise he thrives on it and exploits it to his own ends. Colville will certainly see that he hears of this, and is likely to tell others as well. In troth, he could make things ugly enough for your father to insist that we marry."

She frowned. "You told Thomas he was in the way, and now you mention marriage after admitting that Fife practically commanded—"

"Don't talk yourself into a fury again," he said. "It may look like that, but you ken fine how it felt for both of us. I did try to make Colville think it nowt but dalliance, but if an ugly tale reaches your father's ears, he will react just as I said."

"Come what may, sir, I won't be forced into marriage. And I refuse to make things worse by creeping about as if I have aught to conceal. I mean to return to the hall, and when it is time to retire to my chamber I shall do so. You may escort me back to the others or leave me to go alone, as you choose."

He searched her expression for any sign that she would listen to reason and saw none. Tempted as he was to toss her over a shoulder and carry her to Isabel's chambers, he knew that submitting to such an impulse would more likely stir just the sort of tale he wanted to avoid. The chance was small that he could get up the service stairs and through the corridors at that hour without meeting other people.

Accordingly, he said, "You must do as you please, lass. I think he is unlikely to tell anyone at once. If he does, he will not shout it from the dais to the entire hall. But I would advise you not to linger long before retiring."

"I suppose you cannot command him to keep silent, or force him to."

"He would not heed me," Simon said. "In troth, Colville has no love for either of us and will do us a mischief if he can. He has long competed with me for Fife's favor and for the past eight months has had Fife to himself. He had done well, too, until his heiress ran away. I warrant he sees my coming here as yet another setback. He'll want to put me in the wrong."

⁓

Sibylla could easily believe both Colvilles capable of spreading false rumors about them. But she thought Simon was wrong about what drove Thomas.

"None of this is your doing," she said. "You have not wronged him. Before he left, he smirked at me as if he had already triumphed. I could feel his enmity."

"He may not like you, lass, but his motives are more self-serving than that."

"Recall that you are not the only man I have humiliated," she said. "When I spurned Thomas, he must have felt as angry as you did, although I was not present to see it. Mercy, but that made it worse! At least you had the chance to shout your feelings at me and threaten to get even."

He smiled wryly. "I doubt that helped me much."

"You may think it did not, but shouting at the person who angers you often does relieve one's anger. You must recall at least that much from days in the past when you let your temper fly free."

Shaking his head, he said, "I remember nowt but the feeling that I had lost control of myself. I disliked that feeling intensely. I still do."

His expression was enigmatic as he added the last three words, but she understood that he regretted what he viewed as his loss of control with her.

"I also humiliated his brother," she said. "And I did it before the girl Edward expects to marry. Can you guess how Thomas feels about that if Edward told him?"

"I doubt Edward would admit a woman had knocked him flat."

"Perhaps not, but can you so easily doubt that he described the incident to Thomas in a way meant to make me look as demented as possible? I suspect he has done that if only to counter any other version Thomas might hear."

"You may be right," Simon said. "But all that matters is what happens next. If you do insist on returning to the hall, we should do so at once."

She nodded, grateful that he would go with her. The

more she thought about facing the Colvilles' smirks, the less she wanted to return alone.

As they walked, she indulged in a wishful vision of Simon having knocked Thomas flat before he could walk away and inviting her with a polite bow to stomp all over the nosy snake's prostrate body.

She glanced up at him again.

"What?" he said.

"I was just thinking," she said. "I'm glad I hit Edward Colville. I have told myself more than once since then that I should not have done it. But now I'm glad."

He chuckled. Then, he put an arm around her and gave her a hug. "I'm glad you hit him, too, lass. I wanted to kill Thomas Colville tonight. The feeling was so strong I was afraid to step toward him, lest I do it."

A happy little bubble rose within her, and she nearly put her arm around his waist. But he released her before she could, and she thought better of it.

When they entered the great hall, she felt visible to everyone in the vast chamber. A glance at the dais revealed Fife still sitting at the high table.

He looked at her, and Thomas sat beside him where Simon had sat earlier.

When they found the others, Lady Murray said, "I was about to send someone to look for you, Sibylla. How is it you find yourself with Simon?"

"He found me, madam," Sibylla said. "I was wondering, though, how much longer you want to stay. The noise . . ."

"Indeed, it is as if we had tried to sup inside a drum whilst its owner beat on it," her ladyship said. "I don't mind telling you my head has begun to ache. But if you want to stay longer, my dear, I shall endure it."

Rosalie and Alice looked pleadingly at Sibylla, but she did not hesitate.

"We need not stay on my account, my lady," she said. "I shall be glad to retire. Perhaps if it is sunny tomorrow we will order our horses out and explore the town," she added for Alice and Rosalie's benefit.

Neither seemed much appeased by the offer, but Lady Murray rose, saying, "We four can look after ourselves, my lords. You may stay here if you like."

"Nay, then, madam," Sir Malcolm said, rising and extending his arm to her. "Ye'll no be denying us the pleasure of escorting ye."

Sibylla glanced at Simon to see if he meant to come, too.

Receiving a reassuring nod, she placed a hand on his arm. With Rosalie and Alice ahead following Sir Malcolm and Lady Murray, they left the hall.

⟶

"If you please, Sir Malcolm," Simon said, as the two of them paused to let the ladies precede them up the stairs. "We should talk privately."

"Sakes, lad, what can you want to say that you cannot say to me now?"

"It is no subject to discuss in this din, or anywhere in the open."

"Aye, but sithee, I'd hoped for a pleasanter time tonight than yestereve."

"I don't blame you, sir. I do see that you take pleasure in my lady mother's company. But we should speak."

Sir Malcolm's eyes twinkled. "I hope ye don't want to put a stop to it, lad."

"By no means," Simon said. "I do suspect, though, that your friendship is of longer standing than I had thought. Might it have been the cause of the long dispute between our families?"

"Now, now," Sir Malcolm said. "If there were ever a subject unsuited to a stairwell, that is one. Another time, lad, another time. Sakes, I should think that whatever ye may want to say to me can wait."

Having intended to tell him what had happened so he could help deflect the results of any rumors the Colvilles might stir, Simon gave the matter more thought.

With Alice's betrothal at stake, he reminded himself, Sir Malcolm might have a greater interest in appeasing the Colvilles than opposing them.

The decision was taken from him as they reached the ladies' solar, when Lady Murray said to Sir Malcolm, "It chances, sir, that we unearthed the dames-board and its pieces today. Unless you have made other plans—"

"Nay, nay, madam, I am at your service, as always," he said. "Will ye stay to see fair play, lad?" he asked Simon with a grin.

Smiling, Simon said, "No, sir. I trust you will not take advantage of her."

The twinkle in Sir Malcolm's eyes became more pronounced than ever as he said confidingly, "'Twould take a braver man than I am."

Lady Murray looked at them in astonishment, and Simon was only surprised that she did not call him to order.

It was not his habit to make such remarks, but he liked Sir Malcolm and something about the man had stirred a response that, for him, bordered on levity.

Bidding them all goodnight with a lingering look at

Sibylla, he went back downstairs, wracking his brain for a way to protect her from the storm he foresaw erupting around them. For, whatever Sibylla might think, he held no illusions.

Although he had prided himself on his control over himself and his emotions, he had lost control of both. But he would not suffer the consequences. People rarely blamed the man even in cases of rape. Certainly, no one would blame him for stealing a kiss. They would blame Sibylla for allowing the theft.

He knew the Colville brothers were likely to concoct tales to account for Edward's blackened eyes and to make what Thomas had seen seem much worse. If such stories spread, it would be Sibylla's word against theirs.

In such instances, custom favored the male version every time. But if he supported her, people would think he did so only out of chivalry.

Returning to the hall, he saw to his relief that Fife had gone. He likewise saw no sign of Thomas or Edward Colville.

Sibylla was safe for the moment, and although he wished on one hand that the princess Isabel were there, he was relieved on the other that she was not.

Had she been there, they might seek her advice. She liked and admired Sibylla, and was kind and generous to her ladies. But as a princess heading a household of women, and with a brother like Fife generally at odds with her, Isabel had to protect herself. If the Colvilles succeeded in sullying Sibylla's reputation, Isabel would be unable to help her without risking her own.

At last, deciding he would need a clear head for whatever was to come, Simon retired to his room, slept fitfully, and awakened early the next morning feeling as gloomy as the overcast day outside.

Dressing, he went to the hall to break his fast. Before he had been there ten minutes, knowing smiles and glances told him things were as bad as he had feared.

Despite its being Sunday, Fife had assigned him duties the previous night that would not await his convenience, so he spent the hours before the midday meal dealing with as many as he could in his usual efficient way. But the hours were rife with reminders of what lay ahead.

People eyed him as they talked behind their hands. One woman pointed him out to another. More than one jesting remark as he passed stirred his temper, but he took care to maintain his usual controlled demeanor until, on his way back to the hall, he rounded a bend in a corridor and nearly collided with Sir Malcolm Cavers.

"Here, I've been searching this whole place for ye, lad. D'ye ken what they're saying about ye and my lass?"

"I do, sir. May we find a more private place to discuss it?"

"Tell me first, is this what ye were going to divulge to me last night?"

"I had hoped that I might," Simon admitted.

"Then I wish I'd not put ye off."

"Sakes, sir, had I not decided it could serve no useful purpose, I'd have insisted, so do not blame yourself. Has Sibylla come downstairs yet?"

"She has, aye, but she and the other lassies ordered horses out, and I've sent some o' my lads with them so they can explore the town and ride in the abbey park. They also mean to call on your sisters, so we'll no see them afore supper."

Simon nodded, and they said no more until they

reached his room. It was small by comparison with the princess's chambers, but the door was a good, solid one that fit its frame well.

"If we keep our voices down, sir, no one will hear us talking here," he said.

"Aye, well, I'll contrive to keep from roaring at ye then. But what were ye about, lad, to compromise my lass so?"

"The details are unimportant, sir," Simon said, having no wish to steer the man's uncertain temper toward Sibylla by telling him she had left the hall alone, prompting him to follow her. He was not even sure, in good conscience, that his reasoning had been so noble. Firmly, he said, "The fault lies with Thomas Colville, who is certainly the source of any rumors you have heard."

"By the Rood!" Sir Malcolm exclaimed. "How does he come into this?"

"He followed me," Simon said. "We have both served Fife for years, and Colville is ambitious. I believe he seized the opportunity to do me a mischief."

"Aye, well, as ye've now assumed your duties at Elishaw, I doubt the man can hurt ye much with Fife. These devilish rumors will do mighty harm to Sibylla, though. What are ye meaning to do about that?"

"What have you heard, sir?" Simon countered. "In troth, no one has dared speak plainly to me. I thought it better to ignore the looks and snickers."

"What I hear does *not* redound to your credit."

"I kissed Sibylla. That is all, I swear."

"Faugh," Sir Malcolm snorted. "The tattlers claim much more. In troth, lad, I'm thinking ye'll have to marry my lass after all, to protect her good name."

"I'm willing enough," Simon said, realizing the statement was perfectly true. "But I doubt that anyone can persuade Sibylla to marry me."

Sir Malcolm sighed. "She's damnably stubborn, is that lass."

"She is, aye, and I fear that her stubborn nature may lead her to insist on living with the consequences of this. With any other woman, those consequences would drive her to accept marriage, especially as one will certainly be dismissal from Isabel's household."

"Sakes, I'd not thought of that till now, but I've nae doubt ye're right," Sir Malcolm said, rubbing his forehead.

"Fife watches Isabel's every move," Simon said. "He watches particularly for aught suggesting immorality in her household, because it would give him cause to insist that she live with the husband the Douglases provided for her."

"Fife does not approve of women living on their own," Sir Malcolm said. "Bless us, though, who can blame him for that? I don't approve of it either."

"Fife will learn of this soon if he has not done so, and he already urged me to renew my suit with Sibylla," Simon said. A knot of anger formed in his stomach as he realized that Fife might be in league with the Colvilles, but he said only, "I'd like to discuss this with Thomas Colville, but he seems to have disappeared."

"I heard that Edward left Edinburgh yesterday, so mayhap Thomas followed him," Sir Malcolm said. "I'm thinking I should find another man for my Alice."

"I agree," Simon said. "I'm not one to bear tales, sir, but . . ." He described the incident at St. Margaret's Chapel, and as he did, an idea stirred in his mind.

His experience of Sibylla had shown him that any logical discussion they might have about the situation was unlikely to end as he might hope or predict.

Marriage was, in fact, the only honorable way they had now to resolve the problem quickly and with minimal fuss. Although there were obstacles to his idea and the idea itself went against his sense of propriety, it was the only possibility that had occurred to him. He did not doubt her feelings for him or his ability in the long run to persuade her of his own. However, by the time he could ease her doubts and overcome her stubbornness, the damage to her reputation would be irreparable.

Even if he could work out the logistics, Sibylla would remain the greatest obstacle. Perhaps, though, if he could arrange to give her little choice and still let her make the final decision, the thing could be done.

It would take luck and considerable preparation. But nearly everything he'd ever done for Fife had required those things, and he had nearly always succeeded.

This time he would be doing it for himself and, whether she liked it or not, for the woman on whom he had so long thought only of wreaking his vengeance.

Chapter 16 _____

Sibylla enjoyed her day away from the castle. The early morning gloom had given way to a bright azure sky filled with nimble white clouds, and the previous day's rain had left the air smelling fresh and clean. The two men-at-arms Sir Malcolm had provided for the ladies' protection trailed tactfully behind them, and Alice and Rosalie found much in the thriving burgh to fascinate them.

One fascination proved to be young George Denholm, but Sibylla took the "chance" meeting in stride and agreed to his polite suggestion that he join them to ride in the abbey park. Alice looked adoringly at him, but to the lad's credit, he chatted as much with Rosalie and Sibylla as he did with Alice.

Drainage in the abbey park being poor as always, the horses' hooves splashed along its paths, but no one minded.

Denholm took reluctant leave of them at Buccleuch's house in the Canongate, where, despite being bereft of his company, all three ladies looked forward to dining with Meg, Amalie, and their husbands, both of whom Sibylla liked very much.

She also enjoyed Meg's devoted servant Sym Elliot, a lad of twelve or thirteen summers with a shock of red hair, who rarely left his mistress's side except to aid with the serving or to harry the other servants to do this or that for her or her guests.

Talk at the table was desultory until Buccleuch dismissed the servants. As he did, Sibylla caught Westruther's stern gaze on her. He smiled then, looking friendlier.

Sir Garth Napier, Lord Westruther, had served as one of Isabel's knights, so Sibylla knew him better than she did Buccleuch, well enough to know that Garth had something on his mind. The friendly smile was much more customary with him than the stern, measuring look it had replaced.

She glanced at Buccleuch, but he was talking to Rosalie. Wondering if the two men, or Garth alone, had already heard rumors, Sibylla would have liked to ask them but did not want to endure the discussion that would follow if she did.

Meg and Amalie engaged her in conversation, and although she caught Garth's sober gaze on her twice more, his comments were unexceptional.

When she and the two girls took their leave, he and Buccleuch saw them off with affectionate farewells and assurances of welcome whenever they should choose to visit, leaving Sibylla to wonder if she had imagined Garth's concern.

She adopted a lighthearted mood with her companions until they reached their chambers, where Lady Murray informed Alice and Rosalie firmly that they would want to rest if they were to enjoy the evening ahead.

"I should rest, too," Sibylla said as the others turned obediently away.

"Sit down, my dear; I want a word with you first," Lady Murray said.

Both Alice and Rosalie glanced back, doubtless made curious by her tone, but Sibylla nodded and took the seat Lady Murray indicated. When the door to the girls' chamber closed, she steeled herself for the rebuke she expected.

However, Lady Murray sat, too, and said in her usual way, "As you may have guessed, I have heard some rumors about what occurred last night. You need not fret, my dear. Simon has explained what happened, and I believe him. We raised him to know his duty, and he has accepted responsibility as he should."

"But I don't want him to," Sibylla said without thinking.

"Don't be tiresome, my dear. It is the only answer."

Understanding better than ever where Simon had come by his certainty that he always knew what was best for anyone in his orbit, Sibylla gathered her wits.

"We were both at fault, madam," she said. "Indeed, if anyone was more so, it was I, for I did the very thing—"

"Sibylla, I do not require to know more. The only facts that matter are that you were with Simon and someone saw you. I know you did almost none of the things of which you stand accused. Even if you were a young woman who would do such things, Simon would not be party to them. I know my son, and I have come to know you this past sennight. I've no right to tell you what to do, but I would counsel you to be sensible. I want you to know, too, that I'll not stand in your way."

"Thank you, madam," Sibylla said. Overwhelmed and wondering what Lady Murray had heard, she realized she lacked the nerve to declare to her ladyship's face that, gratified though she was, she could not marry Simon.

Her ladyship stood. "You will doubtless take your supper here tonight."

"Nay, madam," Sibylla said, relieved that she had not lost all her nerve. "'Twould give credence to the worst rumors, so I'll act as I always do. If people choose to titter behind their hands or fans, they will do so. I cannot hide forever."

Again surprising her, Lady Murray nodded majestically and said, "Then you should rest for an hour or so. You do not want to be tired."

What Sibylla wanted was to see Simon, because if Garth knew, Buccleuch did, too, and either might confront him. But Simon did not appear for supper.

Many people did gape or point, making it clear that the rumors had spread. A more cowardly woman would have turned tail and run. As it was, Sibylla was sure the increasing scandal meant she would end up back at Akermoor under her father's thumb. This time even Archie Douglas would refuse to help spare her that fate.

A message arrived from Isabel on Monday, declaring her intent to arrive in two or three days, but they still saw nothing of Simon. His mother said she thought he had gone out of town on an errand for Fife. Continuing to behave as if nothing had happened, Sibylla nevertheless retired earlier than usual Monday night.

Alice and Rosalie invited her to ride again Tuesday morning, but she had no taste for exercise and did not want to miss seeing Simon if he came to see her.

When midday came without him, she went down to dinner with the others but took no appetite with her. Her father talked to her then, but he accepted her refusal to marry Simon with no more than a grimace and did not bring up the subject again.

She had no doubt, however, that he would say more in days to come.

At supper, after a long, lonely afternoon, she toyed with her food and strove to make polite conversation. Simon did not appear or send any message.

The noise in the hall was deafening as usual, and long before the others were ready to depart, Sibylla ached for her bed. As soon as Fife took his leave, she arose and bent to bid her father and Lady Murray goodnight.

"If you'll wait a half hour longer, lass, we'll go up with you," he said.

"Nay, sir, I'm for bed. No one will trouble me tonight, for I'll ask the steward to have someone escort me upstairs. I'll be perfectly safe."

It felt comfortably familiar to have a man-at-arms follow her upstairs again, albeit for perhaps the last time. The sense of being alone yet safe was almost heady. At the door to Isabel's chambers, she thanked her escort and bade him goodnight.

Entering the solar, she found to her surprise that the chambermaid had failed to light the lamps and candles, or stir up the fire.

Ambient moonlight through the uncurtained window and glowing embers on the hearth provided light enough to seek a candle to light from the coals. She had taken only two steps when a heavy cloth enveloped her from head to toe.

An arm of steel snapped around her arms and upper body, holding her while what felt suspiciously like rope looped around her below it and tightened.

In seconds, she was off her feet, slung over a broad masculine shoulder like an unwieldy sack of meal. His shoulder bruised her ribs, but her struggles were useless.

Then, abruptly, the scent of cinnamon and cloves penetrated her outrage. She inhaled carefully and detected the slight scent of lavender, as well. Simon!

When he turned toward the door and she heard the latch click, she opened her mouth to scream, then shut it again, hoping she was not making a fatal error. That the sternly controlled Simon could do such an outrageous thing awoke a host of emotions, including fury that sent blood racing through her veins and set every nerve atingle.

Then doubt stirred. Most people of means used scent bags in clothes kists and sumpter baskets. Who knew how many mixed cinnamon and cloves with lavender? If her abductor was *not* Simon, she was in much greater danger than she had believed.

It had to be Simon, doing as he deemed best again without consulting her. He would learn his error, because she'd tell him exactly what she thought of such tactics. In the meantime, she did not want to draw anyone else's attention if she could help it.

Until Sibylla wriggled again as he carried her down the deserted service stairs, Simon feared she had fainted from the shock of what she must surely believe was an assault. When she did move, he wondered why she had not screamed. He had been prepared to deal with that but was grateful that her silence made it unnecessary.

Slipping out of David's Tower through a postern door shadowed by the huge bakehouse that served the castle at large, he made his way swiftly, depending on his black clothing and coldly stern demeanor to protect him and his burden.

One guardsman dared to approach him, but the yard's torchlight was sufficient to reveal Simon's all-black clothing. A warning scowl sent the man scurrying, unwilling to confront one of Fife's so easily recognizable, generally ruthless men. At times, Simon mused, the reputation did prove useful.

Inside the nave of St. Margaret's Chapel, he carefully set his burden on her feet and unwrapped her, noting in the glow of the cressets, as he whisked the blanket off her, the angry flash of sparks he had expected to see in her eyes.

"I knew it was you!"

"Then why didn't you scream?"

"Sakes, because we'd already stirred enough gossip without stirring more. How dared you snatch me up like that!" She glanced warily toward the archway and the altar beyond before adding, "By heaven, you deserve flogging if you brought me here thinking I'd marry you. Had you done me the courtesy to ask, I'd have said I won't have you! I told my father as much. Must I shout my refusal to the world?"

"You need only tell me," he said calmly.

"This should not be happening," she said with a frustrated sigh. "We did none of the things of which those horrid rumormongers accuse us, and so—"

"Did we not?"

"Nay, sir! Do *not* flatter yourself."

He remained silent, holding her gaze until blushes suffused her lovely face.

Sibylla ignored the fire that swept through her body, ignited by the memory of his touch and his stirring kisses. Fighting to hold on to her anger, she said, "Other men have kissed me, and no one demanded that I marry any of them. There can be no need for us to marry, and I will not have it."

"If you are certain of that, you need only say so."

She eyed him suspiciously. "What do you mean?"

"I mean just what I said. I did bring you here tonight because I've obtained special license for the bishop to marry us here. I thought—"

"You did *not* think, for you had no right to do that. I *gave* you no right."

"Sibylla—"

"You gave me your word on the ramparts the other night that Fife had naught to do with . . . with your kissing me," she said. "But how can I know that he has not ordered all this, as usual? That would explain why you told Thomas he was just in the way and why Fife stared so at me afterward. The two of you both showing up in that disastrous room, both serving Fife, could quite easily mean you were all—"

Her words ended in a shriek when he gave her a rough shake.

"Stop it," he said harshly. "I know you are angry, but *you* know that I blame myself for what happened and would *not* conspire with anyone against you, let alone with Fife or Colville. Use your sense, Sibylla, if you still have any."

"But how else can you have acquired a special license

for so hasty a marriage if Fife did not provide it? He organized everything last time."

He was silent, and a twinge of wary guilt stirred in her, but she suppressed it. She knew too much about the wily Fife not to suspect his involvement.

At last Simon said quietly, "I paid a large fee, Sibylla. One may pay a fee to any bishop and be married in the Kirk without banns."

Stunned by that news but determined to speak her mind, she said, "Still you arranged this without discussing it with me. You said you respected my opinions, but you acted without a word to me, snatching me up as if I were a bundle you had forgotten to pack. Sakes, you carried me here in no more than my tunic and skirt."

"So, tell me, lass, art angry with me because I should have given you time to dress more appropriately before abducting you or because I carried you here?"

"Both," she snapped. "Am I never to make my own choices? If I *were* fool enough to marry you, Simon Murray, would I not be far less in your household than I am in Isabel's? Do you still seek penance from me?"

"I do not, nor would you *ever* be less to me than to Isabel," he said. "But if you think I will always tolerate this sort of volcanic eruption from you, I'd advise you to think again, lass. I'm having all I can do not to answer in kind."

"Aye, sure," she retorted. "Gentlemen may erupt whenever they like."

"Even if that were true, I doubt it would daunt you, but I think we can find more entertaining ways of erupting together. God knows, we have only to look at one another . . ." He paused, capturing her gaze as he could do so easily. "The bishop is waiting, my wise and charming vixen," he said softly. "So what say you? Art truly opposed to the whole notion or just furious with me?"

It wasn't fair that when he looked at her as he did now, he seemed to see right to the part of her she had so carefully and for so long kept hidden from others.

As that thought formed, another struck. She could see him as clearly.

Those fathomless green eyes pulled her down into him until she felt as if she knew him in so many ways that the small bits she did not yet understand became insignificant. In the ways that counted, they two could almost be one person.

And that person would be Simon.

"I . . . I can't," she said, and for once, she found it easy to look away first. "You would swallow me up, my lord."

He moved both hands back to her shoulders. "Listen to me," he said, stern again. "You reject my promises, saying you cannot know I will keep them."

"I know you mean to keep—"

"But you *do* know what you face if we don't marry," he went on inexorably. "Your reputation will be destroyed, Sibylla. Isabel will dismiss you, because she has to protect *her* reputation. Next and worse, your father will order you home to Akermoor, and he will keep you there this time. The alternative is marriage to a man who cares for you and believes you will make him an excellent wife."

"A man who swore to wreak vengeance on me. Can you deny that?"

"Of course not. We both know what I said, but you know I no longer feel that way. What I shouted then was as childish and ignoble as you said it was."

"And now, you think you are behaving *nobly* by rescuing me?"

Simon did not pause to think but for once in his life said the first words that came into his head. "You are wrong about what I think and how I feel."

"I do not—"

"There is nowt about this that a person of sense would call noble," he interjected. Noting the resultant flash in her eyes, he added hastily, "I'm sorry to interrupt you again, but I must say this whilst the thoughts remain clear in my mind. The fact is that before I pulled you and young Kit from that river I'd have believed myself incapable of ever doing what I've done tonight. But since that day, I've done many things I never expected to do."

She did not reply, but sparks still glowed in her beautiful eyes, diverting him because they were as lovely when she was angry as when she smiled. "I will never tire of looking into your eyes," he murmured before he realized he was not thinking the words but was saying them aloud.

She shut her eyes. When she opened them again, her expression had not softened. "You seem to mean that," she said. "But Fife will doubtless reward you well if you succeed in this."

Anger flashed in him, but the words hurt, too, and he knew he deserved them, because she had begun to trust him. That she no longer did was his fault.

Had he been wise enough not to admit Fife had pressed him again to marry her . . . But she had guessed as much, and he could not have denied it without lying.

How could he expect her to trust a liar?

Her hand on his arm stopped this painful train of

thought, and he realized he had looked away from her to stare blindly into space.

As he fought to suppress his warring emotions, she said quietly, "I should not have said that. I do see that you had no thought of Fife just now, whatever influence he may have had on your actions tonight."

"I don't suppose you will believe that he had none."

"Nay, for you told me yourself that he'd encouraged you to try again. At the least, I'd suspect his words had put the idea into your head. You will not tell me, I think, that you entertained any thought of marriage whilst we were at Elishaw."

He remembered watching her wade into the forest pond with the moonlight blazing down on her, turning her beautiful skin to alabaster. He had thought briefly then that, had they married, he might have enjoyed her magnificent body for several pleasurable years. But regretting a loss of pleasure for himself hardly meant he had thought then of marrying her, for he had not.

"Tell me what you are thinking," she urged gently.

"It was nowt," he said in the same tone, meeting her gaze with more ease than he usually felt when she looked at him so. "I can tell you that, although I had no clear thought today but to protect you, my reasons were selfish and had nowt to do with Fife. They had to do only with my own desires . . . and my deep regret that actions of mine have caused trouble for you."

To his surprise, he got a wry smile. "There were two of us in that room, sir."

"Aye, sure, but a more sensible man, especially one who has prided himself on controlling his emotions, as I have, would not have lost his wits—as I did."

"Did you truly lose them?"

"I did, aye. There can be no other explanation for such foolhardiness. We both know that men roam here as they please. Since I had taken note of your departure from the great hall, it was nowt but loss of good sense to think that no other man had seen you go. Still, when I get my hands on Thomas Colville—"

"Nay," she said. "Do not blame him. Recall that I humiliated him, too. Mayhap you should have fellow feeling for him."

"I don't, nor will I develop any," he said tersely. "I was as much a lackwit the day we nearly married as your sister's chap, Denholm, is now. So much did I think of myself then that I thought you should feel honored by my suit. That you might cast me to the wind never entered my head until you did."

"I was younger than you and terrified of what lay ahead," she said. "My father took no heed of my tender years when he negotiated those marriages for me. Had I not seen for myself that you take greater care with Rosalie . . . Indeed, sir, it was only when I saw how kindly you treat her that I began to like you a little."

He smiled. "Rosalie does not thank me. I just hope she won't elope with the first callow youth who flirts with her."

"A number of practiced flirts have already done so," Sibylla said.

"I know, but despite my mother's lapse, I do trust her to deal with them." He looked into her eyes again. "I want you to marry me, Sibylla. I don't think I have ever wanted anything in quite this way before. If you say no and then suffer for your refusal as we both know you will, I'll never forgive myself for my part in it."

Sibylla nearly agreed on the spot. She knew she was angrier with the situation than she was with Simon, and she had known it for some time. But with all that had happened, her temper had snapped the moment she faced him.

She did not know of any man other than Hugh who would have dared treat her so fiercely or so decisively with no apparent fear of consequence. And Hugh had been her brother, duty bound to protect her. Simon was *not* her brother.

"What say you, lass?" he asked again. "You know better than most that I cannot force you—in troth, that no one can. But I can say honestly that I do want more than anything to have you for my wife."

"But why?" she asked. "You have said you want me, but what do you mean by that? Why do you want to marry me, Simon?"

"Because you make me laugh," he said without thinking.

Indignation rendered her speechless for a moment before she said, "What a thing to say to me! Do you expect me to believe that you find me so amusing that you cannot bear to live without me, sir?"

"You know better," he said, using two fingers of his right hand to tilt her chin up. "Look at me."

Sibylla had never been shy in her life, but the gentle amusement in his voice made her feel shy now. His touch disturbed her in other ways, too, as it always did.

The hand on her shoulder was warm, as were his fingertips on her chin. He had taken off his gloves, if he had worn any. But simple warmth was no cause for the tingling sensations that shot through her body, warming her all through.

She licked her lips as her eyes met his and then, remembering how lustily he had reacted to that before, caught her lower lip between her teeth. His pupils were so large that his eyes looked black. The tingling within her increased.

"What *did* you mean then?" she said, sounding breathless even to herself.

"I meant that I like to be with you, that I like knowing when I wake up in the morning that I'll see you during the day and that we'll talk together. I've missed all that these past two days whilst I was making all my arrangements."

"And avoiding me," she said.

"Aye, but moments ago, you expressed doubt that I respect your opinions. You need not."

"No?"

"No, for I don't just respect them; I value them. I think we've become good friends, lass, more quickly than one might expect, given how we met. A marriage that follows friendship must be more likely to survive than one that does not."

"I expect so," she admitted, wondering why the thought of friendship with Simon did not delight her, then calling herself a fool. Men married women every day without a semblance of friendship between them, simply because the marriage would increase the man's wealth and property. Marriage was much more often a matter of property or power than of gentler feelings.

"So I'll ask you one more time," he said, both hands on her shoulders again. "What say you, Sibylla? Will you marry me?"

She swallowed hard, knowing she was going to say

yes. First, though, she could not resist a small test of how much he valued her opinions.

"What of Kit, sir? I do still believe she may be the lost Catherine."

"I know you do," he said. "I doubt there is anything to such a notion, but one thing you said that we did not discuss much has stuck tight in my mind."

"What?"

"Those men did try to drown her or, if Dand's account is true, she was so afraid of them that she chose to fling herself into the Tweed rather than let them catch her. We must make it a point to get more answers out of the bairn this time."

"Then, if I do marry you, may we leave at once afterward?"

His eyes crinkled at the corners, and his lips twitched in the way that she had come to recognize as his expression of considerable amusement.

He said, "I promise you, we'll leave first thing in the morning for Elishaw. We cannot go tonight without looking as if we are fleeing. As it is, our hasty marriage will stir more questions. But I can deflect most of them by saying I acted as I did because, after we'd stirred such a flap, you feared everyone would think I was marrying you just to save your reputation."

"I don't think much of that reason. You're making me sound noble now."

"Nay, I am using a bit of the truth and their own evil thoughts to persuade them," he said. When she continued to frown, he added, "*Or*, we could say that I abducted you because just the thought of the grand wedding my mother would have planned made me quake in my shoes—which it would, lass, I promise."

"I believe you, but that also would give us better reason to leave at once for Elishaw, would it not?"

"Nay, for my mother would have my head on a charger if I left without attending the supper she has organized for us. By the way, I hope you don't object to a few guests at our wedding."

Reaching automatically to smooth tendrils of loosened hair back under her beaded net and straighten the net, Sibylla exclaimed, "Guests! Who?"

He smiled, and she marveled again at how a smile lightened his features.

"Wait here," he said. "I'll fetch them."

He went only as far as the door, opening it and gesturing. Hearing a giggle that sounded distinctly like her sister's and being sure that Lady Murray, Rosalie, and Sir Malcolm would be with her, Sibylla quickly shook out her skirts, kicked the dark blanket aside, and gave thanks for dim lighting that would conceal the worst of the wrinkles in the dress she had worn since midday.

She was glad she had done so when the four she had expected to see came in followed by Amalie, Meg, Westruther, Buccleuch, and two of Buccleuch's lads whom she recognized as Meg's devoted servant Sym Elliot and the large captain of Buccleuch's fighting tail, oddly known as Jock's Wee Tammy.

Amalie came to her at once. "I've brought you a present," she said.

Sibylla smiled warily. "Did Simon tell everyone about this but me?"

"Aye, sure," Amalie said, grinning. "He wanted proper witnesses, and he needed Garth and Wat to watch the stairway. And he knew he dared not marry you without us. Besides, you're staying at Wat's house tonight. We've plenty of room, and you'll be much more comfortable than you would be in Simon's room—or your own if you dared, and with my lady mother so near. But here," she added, handing Sibylla a small vial. "You did this for me, remember?"

Sibylla took the vial, pulled out the stopper and sniffed. It was her own favorite fragrance. Giving Amalie a hug, she said, "Thank you. I'm sure I need to daub some on straightaway."

"Aye, well, don't use it all. Meg ordered a bath for you when we return."

"I'm glad you're here." Sibylla looked around at the smiling faces, realizing how much she would have abandoned had she tried to endure the scandal.

The Bishop of St. Andrews entered then with a lad garbed as an acolyte following in his wake and carrying a prayer stool.

The prelate said serenely, "The hour grows late. Shall we begin?"

Sibylla looked at Simon, who smiled at her but said not one word.

She looked next at Sir Malcolm.

"Don't look to me to decide, lassie," that gentleman said bluntly. "Ye may be putting a hitch in my own rope with this match, but I cannot deny that I still think it an excellent one for ye."

Glancing next at Lady Murray to see her looking uncharacteristically self-conscious and avoiding her gaze, Sibylla thought she could guess her father's meaning. Suppressing a smile, she said calmly, "Aye, my lord bishop, let us begin."

Chapter 17 ——————

The wedding ceremony was over so quickly that Simon could barely accept that he was marrying. Because of the late hour and the few witnesses, the bishop offered only two brief prayers in lieu of a nuptial mass. Then, blessing the bride and groom, he had them face their guests and presented them as husband and wife.

As he did, Simon saw Fife standing just inside at the rear of the nave.

"I must present you, my lady," Simon murmured.

The bishop, overhearing, said, "Indeed, you must, my son. I should have told you the Governor would be here. He said he desired no ceremony and would come in quietly. But in troth, with such haste and informality, I forgot to mention it."

Simon thanked him for marrying them. Then he escorted Sibylla to Fife and said with a slight bow, "You do us honor, my lord. May I present my lady wife?"

"Indeed, you may, although I have known the lady Sibylla for years," Fife said softly. "Isabel will miss your companionship, my lady. She arrives in a day or two, though, so you will have good opportunity to take your leave of her."

Rising from her curtsy, Sibylla said only, "Thank you, my lord."

"She will be pleased to know that you can remain here with her for a time," Fife went on. "That may appease your disappointment at learning that I have a task for your husband that will take him away from you for a sennight or two."

To Simon, he went on, "I had not realized you meant to wed so quickly, sir. But I want you to go to Huntly, for we learned today that the lady Catherine may have gone home. I think it unlikely myself, but the Colvilles have returned to Oxnam to stir their searchers there to greater activity, so I need someone I can trust to search Huntly and its environs thoroughly, in the event that the rumor is true."

"With respect, my lord, I *have* just this moment married," Simon said. "If the lady Catherine is at home, she is safe and will stay for a time. If you permit, I would take a few days to get to know my lady wife better before I must leave her."

"'Tis a reasonable request, especially as Isabel has not yet arrived," Fife said, smiling again at Sibylla. "We may even receive word tomorrow that the Colvilles have found Catherine in Jedburgh or Kelso. I shall grant you four days as a wedding gift, Simon. I must also offer my felicitations, sir. This marriage pleases me well."

Nodding to them both, he gestured to the bishop and left the chapel with him, the little acolyte hurrying after them.

Simon's lips felt dry and his skin prickled. Knowing what Sibylla must be thinking, he did not want to face her. But he knew he must.

Turning to her, he said quietly, "Lass, we will talk of this later."

She nodded, saying nothing. But two small lines had appeared between her eyebrows. He was sure Fife's comments must have raised her doubts again. But he did not want to fratch with her in front of the others and was grateful for her silence.

To his further relief, she turned with a smile to receive their hugs and blessings, and they all trouped out together to collect their horses.

Half an hour later, they arrived at Buccleuch's house in the Canongate.

Sibylla had chatted with Amalie, Meg, and the two younger girls on the way, but she had not said a word to Simon.

It was not, he thought, an auspicious beginning for a man's wedding night.

~

Sibylla looked fondly around the table in Buccleuch's house at the people gathered there for a light wedding repast. She smiled at the ubiquitous Sym Elliot as he hurried hither and yon and then saw Garth grinning at her.

"You knew something Sunday afternoon," she said to him.

He nodded. "Wat and I went up to the castle Sunday morning to meet with Douglas before he left for Hermitage," he said. "The rumors flying about the place dismayed us. When you came here to dine, I saw that you were tense and unlike yourself. We knew something must have happened, although we did not believe most of what we heard. Not about you, at all events," he added with a twinkle in his eye.

Beside her, she sensed Simon stiffening, but he said, "I'd not blame either you or Buccleuch if you'd believed me capable of rape or worse, given what little you knew of me. But it is good that I won't be at the castle for some time now. I'd likely lose patience and throttle someone."

"Aye, sure, and it's as well that you came to us before we looked for you," Garth said. To Sibylla, he added, "He told us what happened and what he hoped to do. We'd meant to follow Douglas but agreed to delay when he said he would marry you tonight. However, he did not explain how he meant to get you to the altar until the last minute, when he needed us to watch the stairs for him."

"I heard Fife say that he's sending you to Huntly, Simon," Buccleuch said.

"Aye, he did say that, but he's given me a few days here first," Simon said.

Words of protest leapt to Sibylla's tongue, but she stifled them. Men always put duty first. But something had been troubling her about Fife's behavior in the chapel. For a shrewd, clever man, and a ruthless one, his behavior had been odd.

The last, fleeting look she had seen on his face had been one of triumph.

She had thought he was gloating about having contrived at last to bring about her marriage to Simon. But he had directed that look at Simon. She wanted to talk it over with him, but it was hardly a suitable time or place for such a discussion.

Everyone at the table was a friend, and now a kinsman as well. But she dared not speak the words that had leapt to her tongue, not with Alice and Rosalie there.

Simon had said nothing about anyone else going with them to Elishaw. So, it was likely that Lady Murray and

Sir Malcolm would be staying in Edinburgh with Rosalie and Alice. Either of the latter two might repeat what she heard here. Indeed, Alice would likely share all she knew with George Denholm.

The general conversation had turned to Catherine Gordon, eliciting heated opinions of the uneven match with Thomas until Meg said, "Sibylla, I've ordered a hot bath for you, so you may come with me and we'll leave the men to talk. And you, sir," she said sternly to her husband, "will send her husband up soon as well."

"I will, aye," Buccleuch said. He smacked her backside as she passed, adding with a grin, "Recall that I am your lord and master, lass, and behave accordingly."

She put her chin in the air. "Aye, my lord, when I choose."

Sym Elliot, appearing at her side, said, "All's prepared above, mistress. I'll tell them now in the kitchen to be sending the hot water up straightaway."

He hurried away, intent on his mission.

"We're coming, too, Meg," Amalie said, getting up. "You don't mind if all your sisters help you prepare for your wedding night, do you, Sibylla?"

"Nay, just promise me that Sym does not mean to oversee it all," Sibylla said, smiling. As the others burst into appreciative laughter, she turned to Lady Murray and said, "I hope you mean to come, too, madam."

Color tinged Lady Murray's cheeks as she said, "I will certainly come if you'd like me to, my dear. It is kind of you to include me."

Sibylla saw Amalie exchange an astonished look with Meg, but neither said a word. With the younger two chattering as they went up, the others held their peace.

In the tidy bedchamber to which Meg led them, a fire

burned on the hearth with a large, empty tub sitting before it. A tall wooden screen stood at one side.

"This is our chamber," Meg said. "But it will afford you warmth for your bath and some privacy. The chamber you are to share with Simon lacks a fire, but we'll put you to bed after your bath. So he can bathe in here, too, if he likes."

The hot water soon came, and to Sibylla's relief, Sym bowed and left.

Arranging the screen around the tub, Amalie said, "We were all going to ride with you tomorrow, because Garth and Wat are going to Hermitage to join Archie if he is still there, or ride on after him to Threave if he has gone. We'll ride as far as Hawick with them, and then I mean to ride to Scott's Hall with Meg for a visit with her bairns. But I expect you won't be going with us if Simon has to go to Huntly."

"You are welcome to stay here, Sibylla," Meg said as she undid the back lacing of Sibylla's tunic while Sibylla deftly twisted her hair into a topknot. "Wat's brother is away and no one else will be using it for a month or so."

Sibylla thanked her but said, "I have no clothes with me. I've been wearing old ones and borrowing things the other ladies left in Isabel's chambers."

"Aye, well, you have your own clothing now, my dear," Meg said with a chuckle as she swept a familiar yellow woolen robe up off the bed and waved it at Sibylla. Your husband arranged to intercept a big bundle of your things from Sweethope Hill yesterday afternoon and had it delivered here to us."

"Sakes, I've been watching for that carter every day," Sibylla said. "But I never spared a thought for him today—not until I found myself in the chapel."

Lady Murray said, "It was clever of Simon to remember you had sent for clothing. Gentlemen frequently forget to concern themselves with such trifles."

Amalie chuckled. "Sakes, but Simon surprised us all. Who would ever have expected him to do such a mad thing as to abduct you, Sibylla? I did not believe it until I saw him carry you up the hill and into the chapel."

"Mercy, were you all standing there watching?"

Laughing, they nodded. When Sibylla was nearly ready to get into the tub, Lady Murray suggested that someone make sure all was ready in the other chamber.

Meg smiled at her and said, "To be sure, you have not seen yet where they are to sleep. Come, and I'll show you. Amalie will stay to help Sibylla, and mayhap if we take these two chatterers with us, she can relax in her bath."

When they had gone, Sibylla seized the opportunity to say to Amalie, "I don't mean to stay here if I can avoid it, and I suspect Simon won't either, because we've something rather urgent to attend to at Elishaw."

"Sakes, but he'll have to stay," Amalie said, handing her the soap. "Fife said so. Besides, he'll have to ride to Huntly soon. What can be so urgent at Elishaw?"

"I should not say more without leave from him," Sibylla said. "And, prithee, do not ask him. It is important, though. If he cannot go, then I must."

"Well, he won't go, so I hope whatever it is can wait, because I doubt that Garth or Wat will let you ride by yourself from Hawick to Elishaw." She grinned. "Any other time, I'd go with you, but I dare not whilst I'm with child. As it is, Garth tries to make me use a horse litter now when we travel, but I won't do it."

"Tell me something, Amalie. Have you ever known

your brother not to keep his word once he's given it—if it is in his power to do so?"

"No, but even if he gave it, he did not do so *after* Fife gave his order, so . . ." She ended with a shrug, and Sibylla, afraid she might be right, said no more.

The others soon returned, and she let them wrap her in her yellow robe and brush her hair while she dabbed on some scent. When they escorted her to the other chamber, she let them tuck her into bed. Then she begged them to leave.

"I love you all, and I hope you will forgive me," she said warmly, looking from one smiling, sisterly face to another and then to the more sober one of Lady Murray. "I shudder at the thought of so public a bedding."

Her three good-sisters and Alice agreed, laughing as they went and threatening to demand every detail on the morrow. When Lady Murray had shepherded them out, she shut the door and turned back to Sibylla.

"Do not fear that I mean to stay, my dear, for I shan't. I did want to tell you, though, that I believe you will suit our Simon very well as his wife."

Startled but grateful, Sibylla said, "Then you cannot be the reason my father told me my marriage was putting a hitch in his rope. As you had said you would not stand in the way, I doubted that was it, but I knew not what else it could be. I trust you will not think me impertinent if I say I hope he can make all smooth again."

"Dear me," Lady Murray said, turning pink again. "'Twould be dishonest to deny that we have formed a tenderness for each other, my dear Sibylla. But with you and Simon marrying, Sir Malcolm becomes, by law, Simon's father, and I your mother. So he fears that we have fallen into a prohibited degree of kinship. I am not so certain, but he will look into it. I believe he meant to ask the bishop tonight had Fife not taken the man away so quickly."

"What if my father is right?" Sibylla asked, easily able to picture them married. They would complement each other well, because he was a good landsman and she would revel in managing the household at Elishaw and looking after him.

"He will seek papal dispensation, I warrant," Lady Murray said. "It is so often necessary these days in any event."

"What caused that dispute, my lady?" Sibylla asked. "Will you tell me?"

Color suffused the older woman's cheeks, but she squared her shoulders and said, "It was little more than what happened between you and Simon, my dear, with one trifling difference. We were both married, you see, and my husband walked in."

"Mercy!"

"Just so. Iagan was livid, and . . . and when Malcolm tried to take the blame and said he was just stealing a kiss, Iagan knocked him down. He would not hear Malcolm's name mentioned, and I'm afraid that over time, I accepted Iagan's belief that it *was* Malcolm's fault. Then he walked into the hall at Elishaw and I was . . . But I am talking too much now and should bid you goodnight, my dear. I just wanted to tell you that I approve of this match. You make Simon so much happier."

Without awaiting a response, she left the room.

Sibylla lay back against the pillows and tried to imagine her father kissing another man's wife, or Lady Murray another woman's husband, only to startle awake at the click of the latch and a chuckle that sounded like Garth Napier's.

A moment later the latch clicked again, and then there was silence.

She opened her eyes and saw Simon, wearing only a pair of breeks, his tawny hair curling damply, the muscles of his powerful torso clearly etched in the glowing candle-light. Her heart pounded, and nerves and other parts of her body that usually did not disturb her came eagerly to life.

⁓

When Simon entered, he thought she was asleep and stood still for a long moment, gazing at her. One naked arm lay atop the coverlet, which had slipped low enough to reveal her smooth shoulders and the soft swell of her fine breasts.

Her skin looked golden. The candles on the stand by the bed had turned it so and had set highlights dancing in her hair. She had left its long tresses unplaited, which he thought a more encouraging sign than her silence earlier.

The room was plain but tidy. The bed looked large enough for comfort and sturdy enough to accommodate a lustful couple. His lips curved at the thought, just as she opened her eyes and looked at him.

He could not read her expression, but he thought she colored a little as she said, "I think I must have fallen asleep."

"I hope you don't want to go back to sleep," he said.

"Nay," she said, sitting higher on the pillows and tugging the coverlet up over her breasts. "I want to talk."

"I know you do, lass. About what Fife said—"

"Simon, has it occurred to you that his behavior was most unusual? Recall that soon after Thomas walked in on us he was sitting next to Fife in the hall."

"Aye, he was, and I've no doubt he told Fife what he had seen, and little doubt that he exaggerated it all to put me in the wrong."

"Or mayhap to twist the truth because Fife told him that a stolen kiss would not be reason enough for us to feel obliged to marry," she said.

"Look here, lass, I ken fine what you think about Fife, but I swear to you, I offered to—nay, I *arranged* for us to marry because I wanted to marry you."

"Duty, sir?"

"*No*," he said savagely. "Not duty!"

"Your lady mother said you knew your duty."

"*Did* she?" He dashed a hand through his still-damp hair and pressed his lips together, struggling to reclaim his calm. But he wanted to throw something or shake someone—his mother. He glanced away but forced himself to look back at Sibylla.

She was eyeing him expectantly, her soft lips parted.

"Lass . . . Sibylla, I don't know what I can say to persuade you that Fife had nowt to do with my decision, or with my wanting you."

"I know," she said softly.

"But how *can* you know? His very words to me earlier tonight had to sound as if we had conspired together to bring about that wedding."

"It did sound exactly so," she said. "But does it not occur to you that such clumsy behavior is not at all like Fife?"

Simon relaxed. He had expected to have to persuade her of that himself and had feared she would be in no mood to listen. "We're going to Elishaw," he said.

Still in that soft voice, she said, "I told Amalie we would go with them."

"Sakes, you *are* a witch."

"Nay, but I have lived for years in the shadow of Fife, sir. Men have called him coward, but none has suggested he is inept. Our unloved Governor is shrewd and subtle in his acts. He would not behave as he did tonight without purpose, so we must ask ourselves what that purpose is."

"We can talk about it later," he suggested.

But she went on. "He ordered you here to Edinburgh, away from Elishaw. What reason did he offer for that, and what reason to send you farther away now?"

"I agree that we should discuss all that, lass, but I do not understand how, from such thoughts, you deduced that we would ride to Elishaw with the others."

"'Tis simple, sir. You promised me we would go to Elishaw, and I believe you are a man of your word. It will have to be a quick trip—for you, at least—because you will still have to ride to Huntly. Fife is too dangerous to defy outright."

"We'll see," he said, smiling. "But for the moment—"

"Wait," she said.

"I don't want to wait."

~

Sibylla wanted to know more but wondered if it was worth it to press him more on their wedding night. In truth, with him standing there looking as he did, she was finding it harder than usual to think. She did not want to anger him.

They could fight later if necessary. For now, she wanted him to come closer.

He said gently, "Even Fife will not cavil if I explain later that I wanted to get you away from those lying rumors. I'm hoping we can reach Elishaw in just over a day as we need not concern ourselves with my lady mother's notions of travel."

"Mercy, 'tis more than thirty miles, is it not? And what of Amalie?"

"Garth will see to her. She takes too many risks, he says, but he can handle her easily when he must. And we've decided to take the main roads, because we can cover the distance faster and change horses more easily. So it will be longer but quicker."

She had not thought of changing horses. Isabel traveled fast, but her men-at-arms led a string of extra mounts in case someone's horse injured itself. The ladies rarely needed an extra one. But they rarely traveled even twenty miles in a day.

"I do see that you might ride to Elishaw and back in four days' time, sir, but do you mean you may *not* go to Huntly at all?"

"If you are right and Kit is Catherine, that question will be moot, will it not?"

"Aye, but you do not believe she is."

"I think she may have information that can help us find Catherine. Even ruling out that possibility will help. In any event, I can send word to Oxnam, so the Colvilles can go to Huntly if need be, and I'll tell Fife the activities of the raiders keep me at Elishaw. In troth, lass, he cannot expect me to continue much longer in his service now that I am responsible for a border stronghold."

She had no idea what Fife expected of him, but she knew enough to be sure the Governor had some plot in mind. Simon had twice rubbed his bare arms, though, and with a damp head and no shirt, she knew he must be getting cold.

"You should come to bed, sir. We can talk more tomorrow as we ride."

"Aye, sure we can, lass, but I cannot trust myself to touch you until I can be sure we have talked enough to ease your mind. This marriage has been gey sudden, and you were sorely vexed with me."

"I was furious," she said. "But I agreed to this marriage, and if I must ride all day tomorrow, I need to sleep." Trying to sound casual and not shy about the duty that lay before her, she said, "I warrant you have another activity in mind, though."

"I do, aye," he agreed. He took a step nearer before pausing to say, "Art sure of this, Sibylla?"

Relaxing, she drew back the covers and scooted over to make room, saying, "Am I to understand you will now submit to *my* wishes, sir?"

"You may hope," he said, unfastening his breeks and letting them fall.

She stared. He was certainly ready for her.

<hr />

Simon heard her gasp and saw her eyes widen. In the candles' glow, her huge pupils made them look black. But black or their usual silver, they were like glass, and he could see the nearest candle flame reflected in them.

Her beauty stunned him as it always did, and the anticipation of touching her stirred his cock again as strongly as it had when she had told him to come to bed.

Without hesitation, he got in and shifted himself to look down at her as he shoved the covers away, baring her splendid body so he could gaze on it as he once had by moonlight. Again the primeval urge that had nearly overcome him the first time he had touched her sprang to life, and before she could draw her next breath, he had her in his arms and his mouth had claimed hers.

When she moved against him, his tongue swiftly penetrated the soft inner recesses of her mouth. He stroked her body, savoring its smoothness as he continued kissing her. His left palm cupped a breast, finding it firm and just the right size. Fingering its erect nipple, he heard her moan, and her hips moved toward him.

His urges increased, shouting at him to take her. But he restrained himself, recalling her maidenhood, and shifted his lips to the nipple, suckling gently. She squirmed, and he relished her soft gasps and mews.

He had expected maidenly resistance, but she displayed none. And although she had yet to learn how to please him, he could wait for that. Pausing sometime later, he raised his head and saw that although her lips had parted, her eyes had shut.

"A good wife does not fall asleep too soon on her wedding night," he murmured provocatively.

Her mouth quirked into a smile. "Don't stop," she murmured. "I had no notion that a man could make a woman feel like this."

"Dearling lassie, I can make you feel much more. For example . . ."

Sibylla sighed as his lips moved from one breast to the other and back again, gently nibbling and sucking. Then his hot breath warmed a nipple, his wet tongue laved it, and she stopped breathing to savor the sensations sweeping through her.

She paid vague heed to his hands as his tongue stroked her eager flesh.

Her hands caressed and explored him everywhere she could reach. She had known his body was hard and muscular, but she had not known his skin could feel soft and smooth, that his stomach would feel rock hard, that he would have so much hair, or that the hair on his chest would feel so soft and springy.

His lips and tongue brushed across her belly, making her gasp again and wonder how it would taste to do such a thing to him.

Her fingers laced themselves in his hair as if they thought they could stop him doing aught she did not like. A bubble of laughter rose in her at the thought. She doubted he would do anything to which she or her body would object.

A large hand moved to where her legs joined, cupping her there.

Surprised, she stiffened, her fingers tightening in his hair.

His kisses continued, moving upward to her breasts again, while his hand stayed where it was, quiet but confident of its right to be there. He suckled again as a bairn might, then eased back up to capture her mouth.

Realizing she was pulling his hair, she untangled her fingers and shifted that hand to his shoulder.

As she did, his hand below moved and a finger penetrated her there, making her gasp again and grip him with both hands, her fingernails digging into his flesh.

He moaned softly against her lips but uttered no other protest. His tongue continued to explore her mouth and his fingers below stayed busy as he eased over her more, his body hard above hers.

Her fingers gripped him again when he moved his left knee between her legs, easing them farther apart. Soon he was on all fours with both knees there, and when she reached a hand to touch his belly and began to stroke there as he had stroked her, he caught the hand and put it up by her head, pressing it into the pillow as he eased himself down to her with his weight on that elbow.

All the while, his fingers below kept busy, rubbing her there so she could think of nothing but how he was making her feel. Her body arched. His fingers stopped, and something larger touched her.

Gasping, she went perfectly still.

It was like slipping a living sword into a hot velvet sheath, he thought as he began to ease his way in. She was hardly the first woman he'd had, but never before had he been with one whose every breath, sound, and movement excited him.

The little gasp he had heard and the way she had stilled made him want to plunge right in. But experience had taught him that resisting that impulse led to greater pleasure for both partners. He could not imagine that the sensations firing through him could intensify, but if such a chance existed, he did not want to lose it.

He paced himself carefully, keeping his eyes open, watching her as he eased himself farther and farther into her softness.

Her eyes were nearly shut, her eyelids fluttered, and he could feel her begin to relax beneath him. Then his cock met resistance.

Her eyes opened wide.

"Am I hurting you?" he murmured.

"A little, but it will pass, will it not?"

"Aye." He stroked a breast with his free hand. Realizing he still held her hand against the pillow, he let go of it.

Easing gently out and back in again, he repeated the movements slowly for a time as the pressure built within him. But when her hips began lifting to meet his, he could stand it no longer. Moving faster, then faster, he forgot all save energy and sensation, feeling the inner tension increase until the moment of climax, when his breath exploded from him, leaving him raggedly gasping, leaning on his elbows, gazing into the face of his beautiful wife.

Tears glistened in her eyes.

"Faith, lass, I *did* hurt you!" He brushed a tear away with his thumb.

"Nay, 'tis only . . . we are truly married now, are we not?"

"Is that so bad?"

"In some ways, not at all," she said, smiling softly. "But 'tis easier to remember you shouting at me in the kirk that day than to think of you as my husband."

His sense of humor stirred, and he said dryly, "Well, if it is any comfort, I don't feel that way anymore. I think you will suit me well as a wife, lass."

To his surprise, she sighed and said, "Your mother said the same thing."

"*Did* she? I own, I did not think of pleasing *her* when I arranged all this. If I thought of her at all, it was with relief that our marriage would put an end to her persistent notion of wedding me to one of her English cousins."

"Sakes, I should be grateful that she approves of me," Sibylla said.

"It will go easier for us if she likes you, lass. We both know that."

~~~

Sibylla was glad Lady Murray had blessed their marriage, but the jolt of disappointment she'd felt when Simon had so casually said she would suit him as a wife had surprised her and stolen much of the delightful languor she had felt.

He did not linger but got up, cleaned himself at the washstand, and then brought back a damp cloth for her. There was a little blood, but she had known to expect it, and Meg would not cavil over a few drops on the sheet.

When he climbed back into bed, he put an arm around her and drew her close, saying, "We've a long day tomorrow, lass, so we'd best sleep now."

With an ear against his chest, she could hear his heart beat. In minutes he was sound asleep, breathing deeply. She soon slept, too.

When she awoke the next morning, the curtain was open, letting gray dawn light into the room, and Simon was gone.

Sitting up in bed, remembering that he thought of her as little more than a friend who would suit him as a wife, she wondered if she would regret marrying him.

Chapter 18

Simon soon returned, and his warm smile eased Sibylla's doubts. She felt self-conscious going downstairs to break her fast with the others, but everyone greeted them cheerfully and seemed intent only on departing as soon as possible.

After a hasty meal, they were soon ready and mounted.

With Buccleuch's, Westruther's, and Simon's men—and all their servants—following, they made a large party. Buccleuch's inaptly named captain, Jock's Wee Tammy, took charge of the long tail of men, while Meg's devoted Sym Elliot took charge of everyone else, giving orders to the other servants as if he were their steward.

Pausing by Sibylla, he said, "I had them put everything for Elishaw together, me lady, and told the laird's man. So when ye leave us, all will be in order for ye."

Smiling, Sibylla thanked him, having to remind herself that Sym was not yet as old as Rosalie. His confidence and demeanor were those of an old family servant.

At Simon's suggestion, and to draw as little attention as possible, their party followed the track through the abbey woods until it met the main road south.

Sibylla rode with Simon until she saw that he paid more heed to Buccleuch and Westruther than to her, and urged him to ride with them. "Truly, sir, you are much in the way here," she said cheerfully. "I want to talk with my new sisters."

He gave her a rueful smile but accepted her suggestion, and she did not mind. Amalie was full of energy and laughter, her mood contagious, and without Lady Murray and the girls, they traveled fast, passing Penkaet Castle before midday.

Sym rode to and fro on his apparently tireless pony, checking on his mistress and the other ladies, and on the servants behind them.

The road was wide enough most of the way for them to ride three abreast and still leave room to pass travelers they met without difficulty. However, their pace slowed considerably when they reached the winding, narrow track through the hills.

They stopped after a time to rest the horses and take their midday meal. Afterward, Sibylla dropped back to ride alone, hoping the slower pace would give her time to think. But after only a few minutes, another horse eased up beside hers as Sym Elliot said, "Ye'll no mind an I ride wi' ye for a bit, will ye, me lady?"

"You don't fool me, Sym. You just want to ride nearer your mistress."

"Aye, well, I'm sworn to look after me lady Meg. The others, especially them great louts behind us, can look out for themselves. But I've no seen ye since last fall, and now me lady says ye've gone and married her wick— That is ye've wed the laird, her brother, wha' she says I must now call the laird or Murray o' Elishaw."

"What did you call him before?" Sibylla asked him.

"I'm no to say it again, so I canna tell ye," he replied with a virtuous air.

Reining back to let Amalie and Meg draw farther ahead, Sibylla murmured, "I shan't give you away, Sym. But I think you ought to tell me, don't you?"

"Why?"

"Well, if you think he may behave badly, should I not protect myself?"

He eyed her thoughtfully for a moment, then said, "Aye, that's true. I dinna ken that he's bad, but the man's a Fifer, ye ken. As ye've served wi' Princess Isabel as our lady Amalie did, ye'll ken fine what a buttery-lippit scoundrel *that* one be."

"But you should not say so when anyone else can hear you," she said gently.

"Hoots, I ken *that* fine. I like me skin, sithee. But the sort o' huggery-muggery he and his gallous lot get up to be enough to make a good man weep!"

"Did you call the Laird of Elishaw a hugger-mugger, Sym?"

His blue eyes twinkled. "As I'm recalling, it were '*gallous* hugger-mugger' that chawed Himself into a fizz."

"Buccleuch?"

"Aye, sure, who else? Said I'd nae business saying that Fife be a sneakster headed for the gallows and he'd skelp me good did he hear me say it again. I'm gey bigger nor what I were, but he's one as can still do it," he muttered.

She wondered what Simon would think about a twelve-year-old imp of Satan calling *him* a sneakster bound for the gallows. But although she felt an urge to defend her husband, she said only, "Men do change, Sym."

"Aye, sure, and I ha' seen him look after ye fiercely, but even so—"

"I doubt the Laird of Elishaw is bound for the gallows," she said.

"Aye, well, there's time enough yet for him. And if he *don't* hang through serving the Governor, his luck'll change gey quick does he kittle the man again."

Aware that Simon *had* angered Fife and was now treading on more dangerous ground with him, Sibylla decided to change the subject. She had already said more than she ought to a lad as skilled as she was at prying information from others.

At a brief loss for a safer topic, she asked how he liked his lady's eight-month-old daughter and the young heir to Buccleuch, now two and a half.

That subject proved fruitful enough to keep Sym chatting amiably until Jock's Wee Tammy rode up and sternly addressed him.

"Cease your nash-gab now, lad," Tammy said. "Take yourself back wi' the other men, and stay there till the mistress wants ye."

Sym looked as if he might object. But when Tam's lips tightened, he said to Sibylla, "I'd best go, me lady, but if ye ever need someone to ride like Auld Clootie for ye, dinna forget that, unless me lady Meg needs me, Sym Elliot's your man."

"I won't forget," Sibylla said. Then, as he turned back to ride with the men-at-arms, she said, "Don't scold him, Tammy. In troth, I do enjoy his company."

Tam said, "He's an amusin' scruff, to be sure, m'lady. But do we no squash him now and again, he gets above himself. Aye, and here's the laird comin' to see why ye're entertainin' so many menfolk, so I'd best be goin' along, too."

As he turned back to join his men, Simon reined his

black in beside Sibylla's bay and said, "I know that lad. But I cannot recall where I saw him."

"He is Sym Elliot, your sister Meg's devoted slave," Sibylla said.

"Aye, sure, Wee Sym. He has grown since last I saw him."

"Bairns do that, sir, but I doubt Sym grows fast enough to suit himself. He told me Buccleuch can still skelp him, as if that is how he measures his size."

"I do recall that he's a cheeky one," Simon said.

"He is," she agreed, suppressing a grin.

"What?" he demanded.

"He has small opinion of Fife, or of men he calls Fifers."

"In which group he certainly counts me."

"And other gallous hugger-muggers," she said.

"Sakes, if those were his words, he *deserves* skelping," Simon said. "Aye, and so do you if you encourage such impertinence."

"One does not have to encourage Sym," she said with a chuckle.

He smiled and said, "I came to see if you might be growing tired. But I must say you don't look it. Even Meg is drooping, and Garth is threatening Amalie with a horse litter. But you look as if we'd been riding for just an hour or so."

"I don't flag easily, sir. Traveling too slowly wearies me quicker. If we ride all the way to Elishaw, though, I'll fall asleep the minute I lay my head down there."

"We've some distance yet to Selkirk, and Hawick lies eleven miles beyond. The others plan to stay the night at the Black Tower there, if you'd like to do that."

"Do you want to stay in Hawick?"

"If we go on to Elishaw, darkness will fall before we arrive, and yonder moon is already dropping to the horizon. So we'd have to carry torches through the forest, and I'd liefer not. But I ken fine that you're gey fretful about Kit."

"'Tis only a few hours betwixt tonight and tomorrow morning," she said. "I expect that by the time we reach Hawick, I'll be ready for supper and a good bed."

"I don't know about a *good* bed or even one for the two of us," he said with another smile. "Buccleuch says we're more likely to have the men all in one chamber and lasses in another. But I don't doubt we'll all be glad to rest."

When their party rode into Hawick at last, they were all looking forward to supper and bed, and lost no time in finding both.

Early the next morning, Simon and Sibylla dressed quickly, broke their fast, and bade the others fond farewells. They reached Elishaw two hours later.

Jed Hay, Simon's captain of the guard, greeted them in the bailey with visibly rueful surprise as he motioned gillies to tend the horses. "Sakes, laird," he said, "I told your cousin ye were in Edinburgh. He rode on earlier to find ye."

"Cecil Percy?" Simon said as he dismounted and moved to aid Sibylla.

"So he said," Jed said, frowning. "But ye should ha' met him on the way."

Sibylla noted Jed's frown, saw him glance warily at Simon, and thought Jed seemed more worried than such a minor mischance warranted.

"How many in Percy's party, and when did they leave?" Simon asked.

"He had six men. They were up afore dawn, sir, and away soon after."

"We must have just missed them," Simon said. "We stayed the night in Hawick but we, too, were up and away betimes."

"I expect they rode past the town without entering," Sibylla said.

"'Twould be sensible," Simon said. "Hawick has but one entrance and is rife with Douglases at any hour. I was not expecting Cecil so soon," he added.

"They came yestereve," Jed said. "Percy said ye *were* expecting them, that he had news for ye and would ride on to Edinburgh to find ye. I did tell him that, truce or nae truce, he'd be wise to ride under a banner other than his own. But he did say he had your safe-conduct and would trust that to protect them."

Sibylla, watching Jed closely, said, "Have you aught else to tell us?"

He gave her a wary look, then licked his lips and said to Simon, "There is summat, aye, laird. That lad, Dand, wha' our lads plucked out o' the Tweed . . ."

"What about him?" Simon asked impatiently when Jed hesitated.

"He had an accident, sir."

Sibylla felt a chill sweep through her.

"What sort of accident?"

"They said he were still gey weak from the river and from bein' sick. He got up in the night, they said, and . . . and he did fall down the stairs, laird."

"Mercy," Sibylla breathed as tension gripped her.

"How badly was he hurt?" Simon demanded.

Jed grimaced.

"He's dead, isn't he, Jed?" Sibylla said.

Jed nodded, gave her another look, and then turned warily back to Simon.

Before either man could speak, Sibylla said urgently, "Where is his sister?"

Jed grimaced again. "We dinna ken, m'lady. Nae one has seen her today."

"We'll find her," Simon said, reaching to touch her hand.

She said flatly, "We're too late, sir. They've taken her."

Simon stifled a curse and forced himself to say calmly, "What would Percy want with her, lass? Doubtless, she's just upset by what happened. We'll find her."

"I hope you are right," Sibylla said, her tone suggesting strong doubt.

Seeing Jed look from Sibylla to him and back in puzzlement, Simon said, "I should tell you, Jed, that the lady Sibylla has become my wife."

"Then I wish ye both happy, laird. Welcome to Elishaw, m'lady."

"Thank you." Turning back to Simon, she said, "We must not dally, sir. I fear she is not here, but if she is, we must find her."

"Jed," Simon said, "did you see any bairn with the Percys when they left?"

"Nay, laird."

"Were you on the gate yourself?" Sibylla asked him.

"Aye, m'lady."

Sibylla said, "Do you *know* Cecil Percy, Jed?"

With a wary glance at Simon, he said, "I canna say I

do, my lady. But they did carry the Percy banner and had the laird's message with his signature. I saw that myself. I recall, too, when that messenger came to beg the laird's leave to visit."

Simon's first impulse had been to cut the questions short and find Kit, so he could sort things out about the boy's death. However, Sibylla's last question raised a new one in his mind. "Describe the man who called himself Cecil Percy, Jed."

"Aye, sure, laird. He were as tall as ye, I'm thinking, and built much the same, too. Sithee, though, he wore a helmet coming and going, and I never did see him inside, because I ate my supper late in the kitchen."

"Did you note what color his hair is?"

Jed thought before he shook his head. "Nay, sir. I'd guess it were brown, because his eyebrows were, but I canna say for sure."

"Send men up to the lads on Carlin Tooth and the Pike to ask what they've seen," Simon said, putting a hand to Sibylla's back. "We'll go inside now, lass."

"Wait, sir," she said. "Jed, did the men wear jacks-o'-plate or light armor?"

Jed's eyebrows shot upward. "Jacks, m'lady."

"And cloaks?"

"Aye, good, thick, long ones," he said. "It were cold last night."

"Come along, lass," Simon said. "No one carried Kit out under his cloak."

She did not reply, but another thought stirred him to turn back and say to Jed, "Tell those lads to come down from the peaks only if they've aught to report. If not, they must bide with the watchers. I want at least one man on each peak till I say otherwise. If one comes to report, send another up straightaway to replace him."

"Aye, sir. D'ye expect trouble?"

"We'll prepare for it just in case," Simon said. "We've eased our watch on the peaks since the truce, so remind those lads to keep a keen eye at night, too."

Urging Sibylla to the entrance, he saw the worried look on her face but said no more. He was certain that once word spread of their arrival, Kit would show herself.

Three hours later, at midday, they still had found no sign of her.

Tetsy and another maid had prepared Dand's body for burial, and tears sprang to Sibylla's eyes when she saw him. He looked pale and thin, and she strongly believed that his death had been no accident.

But when she said so to Simon as they dined, he patted her shoulder and said, "You're letting your imagination run amok again. No one else has said such a thing."

"Prithee, sir, stop dismissing everything I say without giving it a thought," she said testily, her temper barely in check. "The way Jed Hay kept saying 'they said,' as he told us what happened, he clearly suspects villainy just as I do."

"I don't dismiss everything you say," he said.

"You do it often enough, and something is amiss in all of this," she insisted. "The least you can do is discuss it with me as if I had a brain in my head."

"Sibylla, I have never questioned your intelligence."

Ignoring that tempting subject, she said bluntly, "Did

Jed Hay's description of your Percy cousin fit the man you know? You asked for no other details."

His temper had visibly bristled at her tone, but after a momentary silence he said calmly, "I don't know Percy well, lass. But as I recall, he had hair just a bit darker red than Sym Elliot's. That is why I asked the question. However, I don't remember if his eyebrows were red or brown, so Jed's reply was not much help."

"What about their apparel?" she asked, eyeing him intently.

He shrugged. "They wore what Borderers wear—jacks-o'-plate, helmets, and heavy cloaks against the chill. There is nowt to question there."

"Is there not?" she asked. "I'm told the Percys wear light armor like that which the French provided for many of our own Border nobles years ago. Wat Scott and others who were at Otterburn said Hotspur and many of the Percys wore it."

He frowned. "You may be right," he said at last. "But we've no proof that our visitors were other than Cecil and his lads, and we did expect them, albeit not so soon. I do recall enough about Cecil Percy to suspect he is not one who marches to my mother's piping, so his early arrival need not mean much."

"But whilst they were here, Dand died in a fall that apparently none of your own servants witnessed. And Kit vanished."

"Sibylla, listen to me—"

"You say they cannot have spirited her out under a cloak. I say they may have if they dosed her with something to keep her still. Moreover, the very fact of this odd visit, added to her disappearance, tells me she *must* be Thomas's missing heiress. Dand was just a lad trying to protect her. Sakes, but Fife must have called you to Edinburgh to get you out of the way for it. He arranged for those men to do as they did last night."

"Godamercy," Simon exclaimed. "What will you think of next?"

"If I am wrong, where is Kit? We have looked everywhere."

"One must suppose she managed to slip out of the castle and went home."

"But if Dand was not her brother—"

"You don't know that," he interjected testily. "In any event, I have never believed those two did not know where their home is, yet they said nowt of it to us."

In truth, Sibylla had suspected the children knew where their people were, and she saw that Simon's temper had frayed to near breaking. She did not want to fight with him. She wanted to find Kit and learn the truth about what the villains had done.

"If your visitor was honest, he had news for you," she reminded Simon. "Should he not learn soon that our parties missed each other, and turn back?"

"If he inquires on the road, he will, although most folks would speak only of Buccleuch," he said. His expression softened. "I'm sorry if I sounded angry, lass."

"You did, aye, but I ken fine that you are unaccustomed to disagreement. In troth, you discourage it in much the same way that Fife does," she added frankly.

"So now I am like Fife?" he said, raising his eyebrows.

"Aye, sometimes," she said. "You display the same icy demeanor that he does when you are angry, and sometimes when you are not. You said Kit imitates me, after all, and youngsters do often acquire attitudes from adults they respect."

"I don't know about that, but I will agree that Fife behaved oddly," he said. "Also, the Colvilles have been in this area searching for Kit. If they learned that we had a child here who *might* be their missing heiress, and if Fife saw some way he *might* somehow be able to use that as legal cause to seize Elishaw . . ." He paused.

"We need to learn more," she said.

"We do, aye," he agreed. "At the least, I must go to meet Percy if he does return, or send someone on to find him and bring him back."

"Will you leave straightaway then?"

"Aye, and return for supper if I meet him before Hobkirk as I suspect I will."

Sibylla doubted that, but she encouraged him to make haste. "And prithee, take a score of good men with you, sir, lest you meet danger. I may fratch with you more than either of us likes, but I am *not* ready to be a widow."

Simon left within the hour, taking his best tracker and a dozen men-at-arms.

Other thoughts had come to him as he got ready, thoughts he had not shared with Sibylla. He was sure she was wrong about Kit, but he suspected she was right about Fife, who had a network of agents to attend to his more secretive affairs.

The closest Simon had come to being part of the network was some years before when he'd agreed to ask his brother Tom, a talented lute player, to serve as minstrel in Isabel's household, so Tom could keep an eye on her for Fife.

Thinking of those agents, and the supposed raiders throwing the children in the river, he recalled the rider Dand had described, whose meeting with the raiders had hurried them all away shortly before Simon and his men arrived on the scene.

Simon realized the raiders might easily have taken cover then and followed his party back to Elishaw. If they recognized the Murray banner, they might just have watched and reported to the Colvilles or Fife that he had saved the children.

If Fife *was* involved in the affair, one thing was certain. His motive was more complicated than just to make sure of Simon's continued loyalty to him.

⸻

Sibylla did not believe Kit had left the castle voluntarily. But much as she believed the strangers were responsible for the child's disappearance, she could not be sure they had taken her with them. Accordingly, she summoned the housekeeper and Tetsy to organize a more thorough search.

"I want every kist and cupboard turned out," Sibylla said.

"Mercy, madam," Tetsy said. "I didna say nowt wi' the master here, but if them men last night didna find her, how can we?"

"Do you mean to say they were looking for Kit?"

"One came where we sleep. But she wasna there, and he didna believe I knew nowt. I were so afeard, I fainted dead away. When I awoke, he'd gone."

"Look again, anyway," Sibylla said. "We must be sure she is not here before the laird will do more to find her."

As she left them, she felt a niggling sense of something she or someone else had said that was not right. She had sensed the same thing, talking with Simon, but she could not recall what had caused it then either.

Annoyance with herself reminded her she had been irked with him because he'd interrupted her in the midst of telling him that they'd looked everywhere for Kit, offering the information as proof that the visitors must have taken her.

But they had *not* searched everywhere. And she had not tumbled to that fact even when Simon had suggested Kit might have slipped out of the castle unseen.

Descending to the kitchen, Sibylla noted that two scullions were still working at the far end of the kitchen. The bakehouse chamber, however, was empty.

Without hesitation, she stepped into the alcove, shifted the latch hook, and began to open the door to the tunnel. It met immediate resistance, heavier than the small sack of walnuts she had set against it before.

"Kit, it's Lady Sibylla," she murmured. "You're safe now, love. Come out."

The sound of a gusty sob from within brought a huge sigh of relief.

"No one else is with me, lassie," Sibylla said. "Come quickly."

If Kit did not come quickly, she emerged before anyone walked into the bakehouse or past the archway.

"Be the laird vexed wi' me?" she asked in hushed accents.

"Never mind that," Sibylla said, drawing her toward the stairway. "And don't say another word until we reach my chamber." She had little hope that they would get that far without meeting anyone, but the Fates, for once, were kind. Reaching the door to her room, she pushed it open and almost walked into Tetsy.

"Och, m'lady, ye found her! Where was she?"

"That is not important now," Sibylla said. "I do need to talk with her, though. Prithee, go and tell the others we've found her."

"Aye, mistress, but I've turned out all them kists. I'll just put everything—"

"Go along. Kit will put those things away."

"Aye, sure, mistress. She ought no to ha' hidden herself that way, and so I hope ye'll tell her." Giving Kit a stern look, Tetsy hurried out and shut the door.

"She's vexed," Kit said dolefully. "I like Tetsy. I'd no want her to be angry."

"She will come around," Sibylla said. "How did you find that place?"

"I saw ye . . . you, the night you went through the wall," Kit said. "You thought I was asleep, but I did no like the kitchen wi' ghosts dancing on the walls as they do." She shivered. "And when ye went through the wall, ye didna come back, so I came here and slept. When I woke, ye were here! Be ye a witch, m'lady?"

"Nay, but why did you hide there, Kit? Did you not hear us calling for you?"

"Did ye? I didna hear," Kit said. "I kept yon door off the latch for a time, but then I heard men calling me, and I feared they'd see it were . . . was open. So I shut it. Then I was gey afeard to open it again, nae matter how fearsome it got inside."

"But why did you hide?" Sibylla asked again.

Tears sprang to Kit's eyes. "'Cause the b-bad men

hurt Dand," she sobbed. "He ran from them, but a big 'un caught him at the stairs and swung him over them, saying he'd better tell them. When Dand wriggled to get free, the man just let go."

"You saw that?"

"Aye, for I'd come up them stairs we just used. I heard a man say he were dead. Then another man said, 'Odds sakes, then we'll ha' to find the lassie ourselves.' I kent fine they meant me, so I hied me back downstairs to hide in the black room."

"Did you stay by the door the whole time?"

Kit sniffed and wiped her nose on her sleeve as she muttered, "Aye, sure. Sithee, I couldna feel the back wall, and did I keep seeking it, I feared I'd no find my way back to the door. I feared nae one would find me, and I were gey hungry."

"Did you know the men who hurt Dand?"

"They were the ones from that day at the river. The one wha' threw him downstairs said it served Dand right for no telling them where to find the lassie—me! They said summat more, too, m'lady, afore I shut the door."

"What was that?"

"They said they had enough wi' just the bairns—Dand and me—being here to make the laird see sense. Did he no see it, they said, they'd fix him for good."

A chill swept over Sibylla. Grasping the little girl gently by the shoulders, she peered into her eyes as she said, "Kit, your Sunday name *is* Catherine, is it not?"

Kit shrugged. "Everyone just calls me Kit."

"But you are the lady Catherine Gordon of Huntly, are you not?"

"Nay, mistress."

"Don't lie to me, Kit. This is very important."

Kit burst into tears.

Certain that she was Catherine, frightened witless and grieving for Dand—whatever their relationship might have been—Sibylla exerted herself to console her.

When only sobs remained, Sibylla said, "I shall ask you no more questions now, but heed me well, Kit. The laird is my husband now, and I must find him, because if those bad men mean him harm, I must do what I can to stop them."

"Ye'll leave me here again?"

"Aye, but I know you'll keep safe this time. You're to stay with Cook or with Tetsy until I get back. If those bad men should return without the laird or me, you do as you did before and hide in the black room. Can you do that?"

"Aye, if Cook and Tetsy will let me."

"Don't ask them. Just take care that nobody sees you go in and then no one will seek you there. But I'll know just where to find you when we return."

"Prithee, dinna be all night about it," Kit said gloomily.

"I'll try, but if aught frightens you, you go there and stay till I come for you."

Chapter 19 _____

Having seen Kit safely into the care of the cook and Tetsy, Sibylla found Jed Hay in the bailey, drew him aside, and said, "I want messengers sent to the Douglas at Hermitage, Jed, and to Buccleuch's people at Scott's Hall, too."

"Aye, sure, m'lady. Will ye tell me what sort o' messages we'd be sending?"

"I've evidence that the laird is riding into a well-laid trap," she explained. "All these incidents occurring at a time when Douglas and the Percys are trying to maintain the truce between our two countries seems suspicious to me."

"Sakes, m'lady, if that be the case, we should prepare for siege here and no be sending more o' my men from the castle. The laird would say—"

"Jed, *after* you send the messages to Douglas and to Scott's Hall, you may do as you see fit to protect Elishaw. But, prithee, answer me this. If a troop of men should arrive here flying the royal banner, would you refuse them entry?"

He frowned. "Me orders are to do nowt to endanger

the castle's neutral position, m'lady, so I canna deny entry to men flying the royal banner. Why, it would ha' to be a troop led by the King or the Governor, would it no?"

"Aye, sure," Sibylla said, stifling a sigh. "But that is what I fear may happen. If it does, it means the Governor may try to seize Elishaw. And *that* we must not allow, certainly not without the laird's knowledge and agreement."

"Nay, but how—?"

"I am the laird's lady now," she interjected before he could protest further. "I must take responsibility for what happens in his absence, just as his lady mother would if she were here in my stead. So you *must* send those messengers, so Douglas and Buccleuch's people will send men to aid us."

"But the Douglas may already have left Hermitage for Galloway," Jed said.

"I know he did not mean to stay long and that Buccleuch is with him," she said. "'Tis why I'm sending to the Hall, too. But are you sure they've already gone?"

"The Douglas meant to stay but a night or two," he said. "If Buccleuch is with him, he'll have some of his own men, too. As for sending to Scott's Hall, 'twould be two days afore they could get to us even if I was to send a man straightaway, and they'll likely have gey few to send. To raise more will take even—"

"We need more men here, Jed, and Elishaw's own ladies Meg and Amalie are at the Hall. If our man does not find them at home, tell him he must relay my message to Dod Elliot, Buccleuch's captain of the guard."

"I dinna ken that I should—"

"You will send men to both places," she said firmly. "The Douglas is my godfather, Jed, and Buccleuch is good-brother to the laird and sworn to aid him in such a case. His people know that and will come if they can. Meantime, the laird is riding into deadly peril. I mean to go after him, but first I must know that you will do all you can to keep anyone from entering Elishaw without his leave."

When he hesitated, she looked him in the eyes and said with all the authority she could muster, "I *am* mistress here, Jed. I cannot take time to explain everything I have learned to you, or how I've learned it, but I am as certain as I can be that this castle is in danger and that your master's life is threatened, too."

Jed licked his lips. "I've seen, aye, that ye ken things others do not, m'lady."

"Good," Sibylla said, grateful for once that her long habit of acquiring facts wherever she could often stirred rumors that she was a witch. "I want two men to ride with me—good men. Indeed, if Hodge Law did not go with the laird, I want him with me. He is a good man for tracking the others, is he not?"

"The best I have wi' Jock the Nose gone wi' the laird. And Hodge do be here."

"I shall leave the choice of the second man to you and Hodge. But I want them ready to depart as soon as possible," Sibylla added. "Don't fail me, Jed."

"I'll send Willy the Horn," Jed said. "If ye find the laird, 'twould be best an ye can let him know straightaway that ye be friendly." He hesitated.

"What is it?" Sibylla asked. "If it is aught I should know . . ."

"Aye, well, I were just thinking on the laird, mistress, and what he'll likely say about this decision o' yours to ride after him."

"I know what he'll say," she said. "But to send someone

who does not think this matter is urgent will just persuade him that it is not. I can make him see it as I do."

"Aye, perhaps, mistress. *If* he will listen to ye."

Sibylla smiled grimly. "I'll make him listen, Jed. I must. But I must also know I can rely on you to keep all visitors at bay. Will you promise me?"

"I'll do what I can, mistress. But ye should ken that if the Governor demands entrance or his grace the King does, I canna deny either man."

"Then for mercy's sake, say the gate is stuck!" Sibylla exclaimed, knowing that the King of Scots was nowhere near Elishaw, but fearing that Fife might already be near and awaiting his chance. "I do not care how you do it, Jed, but you must not let the Earl of Fife inside our wall with a force of his own men."

He looked doubtful, but she could spare no more time for him or conceive of any argument that could make him hold firm against Fife.

She could only hope that Fife's practice of keeping his own hands clean of any mischief he stirred would keep him in Edinburgh, and that anyone else he might send to seize Elishaw for the Crown would fail to make Jed open the gate.

Twenty minutes later she found her two escorts waiting in the bailey with their own horses and a fresh one for her. When she greeted them, big shaggy-haired Hodge Law firmed his lips into a stern, disapproving line and nodded.

But the lanky, towheaded man known as Willy the Horn grinned at her, revealing a mouthful of crooked teeth and a light of eagerness in his brown eyes as he said, "Jed said we'll ride after the others, me lady. I been fair fidgeting for that!"

"Good lad, Willy," she said as she mounted. "Hodge, I want to go as fast as we can, so I'll rely on you to see that we don't lose their trail."

"Aye, mistress," the big man replied.

As they rode out through the gateway, she signed to Willy to fall in behind and drew her mount close to Hodge's.

"I suspect you think this poor payment for dragging wee Kit and me out of the river, Hodge," she said quietly. "But I am glad to have you with me."

"Sakes, mistress, ye could ask aught o' me and I'd do it. But if ye're thinking the laird will thank us for this, ye're nobbut seeking your sorrows *and* mine own."

"I know, but his life is at risk, Hodge, and he does not know it," Sibylla said. "I cannot just sit at Elishaw and pray for him. That is not my nature."

"Nay, mistress, I ken that fine, and so does he. Sakes, he said as much to me. Still, he'll be gey fierce when he sees us, and I'm thinking ye've never seen him in full fury, or ye'd take the greatest care no to light that fire."

Sibylla assured him she would do all she could to prevent setting the laird's temper alight, but she knew as well as Hodge did that her likelihood of success was small. Simon was already irritated that she had refused to agree with him about Kit. He was also sure he could protect himself *and* manage the unpredictable Fife.

He would not thank her for following him. Most men, in her experience, were loath to accept even much-needed help from the women in their lives. And despite her confidence that Fife meant to seize Elishaw, she might easily be wrong.

That Fife had arranged all that had happened since the day she'd met Simon was impossible. That he had arranged for a man to pose as Cecil Percy at Elishaw after Percy had applied to visit was possible, though, however unlikely.

The Murrays had made no secret of the expected Percy visit. She had heard Rosalie speak of it at court and knew Lady Murray might have done so as well. And Fife was wholly capable of using such knowledge to gain entry to Elishaw.

But could he have acted quickly enough to be threatening Simon now?

Whether he had or not, the fact remained that Hodge Law was right about Simon's likely reaction to their riding after him. Remembering comments Amalie had made about Simon at Sweethope Hill, she was wondering if he might do more than scold her when Hodge's voice interrupted her thoughts.

"Sakes, Willy," he exclaimed. "A bairn could follow these tracks!"

Looking from one to the other, Sibylla said, "Why should the laird and his men be hard to follow when they'd have no cause to cover their tracks?"

"'Tis no *their* marks that set me to wonderin', mistress," Hodge said. "Sithee, I were with Jock the Nose when the laird said to see if them Englishmen would be hard to track. We saw straightaway that one o' their ponies had an odd front hoof, so Jock were right gleeful, and me, too."

"Aye, sure, for it would make tracking them much easier."

"It does, aye, but now I'm thinkin' ye may be right in suspectin' mischief. These tracks ha' turned eastward, sithee, and south toward the line. If them Percys was ridin' toward Edinburgh, why be they a-headin' back toward England now?"

"Because they are not going to Edinburgh," she said.

"Aye, they're devious, is what," Hodge said. "But dinna tell me the man ridin' that pony doesna ken the beast be easy to track. Nor his master neither."

"They intended to let someone follow them," Sibylla said.

"Aye, that's what I'm fearing," Hodge said with a grimace.

"Then I'm right, lads, and we must ride faster."

～

Simon, too, had wondered about the shift in his quarry's direction. For a time, the visitors' tracks had led them northwest toward Hobkirk, just as he'd expected.

The shifts eastward and then south had come after they were beyond sight from Elishaw's ramparts and before they'd left the forest for more populated areas where they'd have drawn notice. They were heading toward Carter Bar crossing and Redesdale, and had been for some time. The borderline lay less than a mile ahead.

He sent two lads on ahead to see what they might see on the other side.

From the outset, he and his men had asked the few folks they'd met if they had seen other riders, and if so, whether they had a child with them.

Most had seen the riders, but none had seen Kit, making Simon sure that he had been right and Sibylla wrong to think the visitors had abducted Kit.

He smiled at the thought. He was fond of her and hoped

she was safe, but no matter what Sibylla had said, the wee lassock was *not* the heiress Catherine Gordon.

Whoever the lass was, the men he was following had behaved oddly.

He cast his mind back to the message from Cecil Percy, trying to remember if the messenger had said anything about his master being in a hurry or having in mind a more distant destination than Elishaw.

"He did not," Simon muttered to himself, recalling that his mother had written later, telling Percy to bring his daughters and perhaps his sons with him.

Lady Murray would not have told Percy to bring his daughters if she'd had any hint that he was doing more than paying a family visit. Amusement stirred as he imagined how Cecil would react to meeting Sibylla after receiving what amounted to an invitation to present his two daughters as potential wives for Simon.

In any event, whoever Elishaw's visitors had been, he doubted now that Cecil was their leader. Unless, his inner voice instantly suggested, Cecil and other Percy chieftains *had* been responsible all along for the raids into Scotland.

He rejected the thought at once. Northumberland, the Percys' leader, was getting on in years and supported the truce. Moreover, his son Hotspur, the Percys' finest warrior, had left England for adventure elsewhere. Without Hotspur to lead them, Simon doubted the Percys *could* have organized so many successful raids.

He would have liked to discuss his thoughts with Sibylla, because he had formed a deep respect for the wide range of knowledge her years with Isabel had gained her. He had a feeling, though, that she would say he was just coming around to what she had understood from the minute they reached Elishaw.

Faith, but she had made him angry! Having prided himself on learning to control his temper—indeed, to control all his emotions and thus avoid giving any man the satisfaction of disconcerting him—he found it especially irritating that she could stir his temper with just a look, a word, or a tone of voice.

That she could stir other emotions and sensations as easily was a different matter and one he was willing to explore further. True amusement stirred then, and he realized he already missed her.

She could make him laugh, and it had been too long since anyone else had, but she did it easily. She was an excellent listener, and knowing that she was at Elishaw, he looked forward more than he had in years to going home again.

He felt guilty about letting his temper keep him from easing her concern about Kit, and for failing to explain clearly that Fife's delight in their marriage had not meant he'd had anything to do with it. He hoped she did know that but wanted to be sure. Moreover, he had not spent nearly enough time in bed with her.

"Laird!"

Torn from his musing by the shout, he saw the two lads he had sent ahead riding toward him hard. Motioning his men to rein in, he continued toward the two.

"Laird, there be a large force o' men just over yon hill," one of the riders shouted as soon as they were within earshot.

"How many?"

"Three score or more, laird," the man said as they reined in.

"Longbows?"

Both men shook their heads, as the spokesman said, "We saw nae longbows, sir, but they be armed, o' course. And they be flying the Percys' blue lion."

Simon frowned. If Cecil Percy had wanted to draw him into ambush, surely he'd have found a simpler way. And why would he do it at all? Other Percys might be up to mischief, but the whole situation irritated Simon.

With a truce in force and his innocence and Percy kinsmanship to protect him, there was one sure way to find out if they were friendly. As he waved the rest of his men forward, he told the two with him to stay put.

"Conceal yourselves well and see what occurs," he said. "Don't show yourselves unless you hear battle raging or fail to hear from me within the hour. In either event, make haste for home and tell them the Percys attacked us. Then tell my lady wife to send for the Douglas and tell him what happened here."

Watching the two men vanish into a nearby thicket, he said to his standard bearer, "You and I will ride ahead of the others, Rab. Recall that we are at truce and stay calm. You others will follow at a distance—not too near, nor yet too far. I don't want to look like an army. Sithee, we merely follow cousins who paid us a too-short visit and then apparently missed their way to the Edinburgh road."

One of the men stifled a snort, and Simon ignored it, turning his horse and urging it toward the hilltop.

From there, he could see the men-at-arms and horses below. It was a large contingent, but no one was mounted, and they gave no appearance of lying in wait.

"Wait here until we've ridden about halfway down to

them and then follow slowly," he said just loudly enough for the lads behind him to hear.

"Laird, that banner be a different color blue than the one our visitors had," Rab said quietly. "The other was gey lighter, sir. And from here, it looks as if the lion on that one yonder be lying down. The other stood wi' his forepaws high."

"Hand me the pennant, Rab," Simon said. "You fall back with the others."

"But, laird—"

"Do as I bid you, lad," Simon said.

As he rode slowly downhill, he heard a voice below shout, "There be those damned raiders now! Have at them, men!"

Ignoring the shout, Simon kept to his steady pace, eyeing the Percy banner. It looked just like one his mother had stitched on a cushion in her solar. She had also stitched cushions with the Murray crest, as well as Buccleuch's and Westruther's.

When a helmeted man whose bearing and light armor declared his nobility snatched up the Percy flag, flung himself on a horse, and rode alone toward Simon, Simon shifted his reins to the hand holding his own banner and took off his helmet.

Seeing the rest of the Percy men snatch up arms and run to their horses, he felt his stomach tighten and wondered if he was being a damned fool.

"The line lies just yonder, m'lady, 'twixt them two boulders," Hodge said gruffly. "I'm thinking we should no cross it."

"Sakes—" Willy began, only to stop when the larger man scowled at him.

"Don't be foolish, Hodge," Sibylla said with an understanding smile. "We've come this far, so the laird will be furious no matter what we do. But 'tis gey strange, I'll admit. Why *would* someone stay overnight at Elishaw, saying he'd come from England, only to return to England?"

"I dinna ken, m'lady, but it canna be for any good purpose."

"Just so," she said. "And we may be the only help at hand. If the laird has ridden into a trap, we must learn how far he got and how many attacked him."

Hodge did not argue, leaving her with her thoughts, which were of no comfort. Not only was Simon at risk, but she was sure now that Kit and the castle were in danger, too. And she still felt that, somehow, Fife lay behind it all.

She knew she might be putting her own life at risk by crossing into England. But, with the truce in place, she did not think any Englishman would harm a woman riding with two armed escorts, or consider her a threat to English peace.

Indeed, she thought with a wry smile, she might be safer meeting an Englishman than meeting her husband.

Simon was going to take a much dimmer view of her actions.

One thing was certain, and that was that the Douglas could not possibly arrive in time to be of use. The messengers Jed Hay had sent could not even have reached Hawick yet. Bitterly, she recalled the many times people had named her witch just for knowing something they thought she ought not to know.

She only wished she were one.

Her fear for Simon had increased with each mile and was much the same as his would doubtless be for her. But men who charged into danger without thought or care for consequence scolded their womenfolk just for putting a foot wrong.

The thought that someone might kill him before she could see him again—no matter how angry he was—terrified her. Telling herself she'd feel the same about anyone who might die in such a case did not help. Simon's safety was an altogether more important matter than anyone else's.

Examining these unfamiliar feelings, she muttered, "Faith, but I've fallen in love with the arrogant creature!"

"What's that, m'lady?" Hodge said. "Beg pardon, but I were keeping a keen eye on them tracks ahead and I didna hear ye properly."

"Is there something amiss with those tracks?" she asked, having no wish at all to repeat to him what she had muttered.

"I'm thinking those riders stopped here and bided a wee time," he said. "Ye can see how the ground be churned up."

"But they rode on."

"Aye, yonder up that hillside," he agreed, pointing.

"Then we must go, too, and quickly," she said, spurring her mount and trying to ignore the wave of anxiety sweeping through her.

The sun was setting, and from the crest of the hill, all she could make out milling round its base were men and horses, a large contingent of mounted, armed men flying a Percy banner. Then, riding toward them, she saw a lone rider carrying the Murray banner, with fewer than a dozen horsemen following him.

A half mile to the west, in a thickly wooded area beyond sight of the men below, she saw more mounted men-at-arms—many more than she could count.

"Hodge, they're going to attack him, just as we'd feared!" she cried. "Willy, blow your horn. If you care for the laird, make us sound like the King's whole army!"

Willy put the horn to his lips.

~

Simon watched the man riding toward him and searched in the increasingly uncertain light for some hint of his identity other than the banner he carried. Not until the other reached up and swept the helmet from his head to reveal a weathered face, tousled coppery hair, and graying sideburns did Simon relax.

He waited for the older man to draw rein, letting him set the distance between them. Then he reined in his own horse.

"Identify yourself, sir," the other snapped.

"Simon Murray of Elishaw, sir. Are you Cecil Percy of Dour Hill?"

"I am, though I own, I'm astonished you'd guess it. If you are indeed Simon Murray, you've not clapped eyes on me for nearly a decade."

"No, sir, I have not," Simon said. He eased his mount forward. Noting the other man's increased tension, he added coolly, "The last time I saw you, I believe, we were both at Alnwick during a brief truce. Your hair was redder then. That is the only time my lady mother has visited Alnwick—or I, come to that. You bear a strong resemblance to her."

Cecil Percy rode closer then, but his stern look did not

alter. "What the devil have you been up to, cousin, leading raids against honest English landowners?"

"That boot's on the other foot, sir," Simon said. "My people have suffered many losses since the snows began to melt. We suspect English raiders, Percys."

"Then we must talk. But if you do not come a-raiding, why *do* you come?"

"To learn why you paid Elishaw such a hasty visit last night."

Above them on the hill, a horn sounded the royal Stewart call to arms.

Snatching the horn from Willy's hand, Hodge snapped, "Nay, ye daft fool!"

"But he must frighten off those villains, Hodge," Sibylla protested.

"Ye told him to make us sound like his grace's own army, m'lady. He did blow the *Stewart's* call to arms, and— *Ay de mi*, look yonder!"

Sibylla followed his gaze and saw that instead of turning tail, riders in greater numbers were emerging from the woods to the west. Having thought them ambushers, she recognized the large red heart on the Douglas banner with a huge sense of relief. Then she turned to Hodge and saw that he felt no relief at all.

Reality struck hard when she looked back at all the men below with Simon, and realized how close together the Murray and Percy banners appeared.

"Mercy, but the Douglas cannot have received my message yet," she exclaimed. "He must think that Simon is conspiring with the Percys."

"Aye, and wi' the Governor, too, thanks to Will here," Hodge snapped.

Willy said indignantly, "But I thought—"

"Give Willy back his horn, Hodge," Sibylla commanded. To Willy she said urgently, "Blow the Murray notes now, Willy, and keep blowing them."

Leaning forward, she gave spur to her horse, and without a thought for safety or consequences, urged it headlong down the hill toward the oncoming army.

When she realized it would be a close-run race and that her long cloak might conceal her sex, she flung it back and snatched the netting from her hair, letting the long tresses fly free.

The Douglas banner meant that Archie was leading them. She could only trust that he would not allow his men to ride a woman down.

~

Simon, hearing the Stewart call to arms, immediately suspected that Fife had followed him or had sent an army of his men to do so. When the notes changed abruptly to the Murray call, he knew not what to think.

"Look yonder, my lord," one of the Percy men shouted, pointing west.

Simon and Cecil Percy turned as one, to see an army approaching fast.

Percy exclaimed, "The Douglas! In faith, Murray, ye've set a trap for me!"

"Not I, cousin, but I begin to think someone has set one for us both."

Just then, movement above on the hillside diverted his

gaze. Seeing one rider with a larger one in pursuit, he exclaimed, "What the devil is this!"

Percy said, "Whoever they are, they're riding straight at the Douglas."

"Hold your men here, and tell them to keep their arms sheathed," Simon ordered savagely, wheeling his horse and spurring hard.

As he did, he was not surprised to hear Percy shout his lads to arms instead. But he could not stay to explain. He had seen the rider, fairly flying down the hill now, snatch off her net and let her hair fly free. The last tiny doubt of her identity, a doubt to which he had clung fiercely, vanished at the sight.

Terror that her horse would stumble and send her crashing to the ground, or that the oncoming army would ride her down, clashed hotly with his own furious determination to get his hands on her himself.

He spurred harder, but he knew already that only God could save her.

The Douglas horns blew, urging the Douglas army forward at speed.

Chapter 20 ⸻

Sibylla heard the Douglas horns as she neared the bottom of the hill but kept on toward the enormous army. To her left, she caught a glimpse of the eastern force with a single rider leading it before focusing on the leaders to the west, trying to judge their speed. Her intent was to ride between the two forces if she could do so in time, and try to stop the carnage before it began.

At the bottom of the hill, still some fifty yards from the Douglas's army, she saw the leader of the Percy lot closing fast on her and spurred harder toward the Douglases. Her swiftly seeking gaze spied Archie the Grim just as he raised a hand.

The notes of the Douglas horns changed abruptly and the horses slowed, but they were near enough that several dashed by on each side of her.

She reined her horse in hard, shut her eyes, and held her breath as the noisy sea of horseflesh and riders flowed around her.

Aside from still-jingling harness and blowing horses, an eerie silence fell.

She opened her eyes to find Archie the Grim, the Black

Douglas, in front of her, his expression revealing just how he had come by both names.

"My lord," she said hastily, "it is not—"

"Be silent," Douglas snapped. Then, "Let him through, lads."

A prickling sensation shot up her spine, telling her who the "him" was.

Straightening, Sibylla raised her chin. She would have liked to explain the whole thing to the Douglas first, but his forbidding expression kept her quiet.

He was not quiet. "Have you lost your senses?" he demanded, his face too close to hers and choleric with fury. "Do you know how near you came to death?"

"I—"

"Silence!" he roared. "I do not ask questions to hear your prattle but to keep me from snatching you off that horse and putting you over my knee!"

"That is my right now, my lord," Simon said with icy calm from much too close behind Sibylla for her comfort. "She is my wife."

She dared not look at him, so she fixed her gaze on Douglas, reassuring herself that Archie at least would not make good his threat. His expression still suggested otherwise, but at last he shifted his gaze to Simon.

"By heaven," he growled. "I've a mind to hang you both if only to ease my temper! I *told* you what I'd do if I caught you conspiring with the Percys."

"By my troth, sir, I have not done that," Simon said. "I cannot tell you why Cecil Percy is here. We were getting to that when the horns interrupted us."

"Aye, *Stewart* horns," Douglas said. "You've no right, unless Fife be with you, to be blowing such."

"I did not order it," Simon said. "To my ken, Fife is nowhere near here."

"That was my fault, my lord," Sibylla said, her eyes still on the Douglas but only too aware that Simon was within arm's reach of her. "I told my hornsman to blow as if the King's whole army were behind us. He . . . he misunderstood."

Stunned silence greeted her explanation.

"As . . ." She swallowed. "As soon as I realized what had happened, I told him to blow the Murray notes instead. I'd seen the Percy men below and a host of riders to the west, so I thought the Percys had lured Simon into ambush. That's why I—"

"Enough," the Douglas said curtly. He turned to Simon. "I expect I'd better hear what you have to say."

Movement of riders wending through the mass behind Douglas soon revealed to Sibylla that she had more to face than Archie's temper and Simon's.

Meeting first Buccleuch's harsh gaze and then Garth's reminded her that they both regarded her as a sister now, subject to their authority as well as Simon's.

With an inward sigh, she looked back at the Douglas.

He had turned to Buccleuch and Westruther. "You two should also hear what Murray has to say," he said.

"With respect, my lord," Simon said. "I'd ask that Cecil Percy join us. Unless I much mistake the matter, he has concerns about this incident, too."

"Aye, sure, why not?" the Douglas said with more than a touch of sarcasm. "At least his men, though armed to the teeth, are holding their peace."

Sibylla, shocked to think the leader of the visitors to Elishaw had been Cecil Percy after all, and wondering where else her thinking had gone amiss, turned to catch a glimpse of Percy only to find her gaze locked with Simon's instead.

⁓

Simon had had all he could do not to snatch her off her horse right there in front of God and two armies and use her exactly as Archie had suggested. His fingers fairly itched to grab hold of her. But when she turned, and her silvery gaze met his, all he could think was how blessed he was that he hadn't lost her.

Such thinking, however, being clearly unacceptable under the circumstances, he forced icy calm into his voice to say, "Do not expect thanks for this, madam."

"I am not so foolish, my lord," she said. "I know that when you decide on a course, you remain certain you are right even when events prove you wrong."

"We will talk later," he promised, turning to watch Cecil Percy approach.

Behind Percy, four men-at-arms flanked two others, whom Simon recognized with astonishment and a sense of irony as the Colville brothers. Casting a glance at Sibylla, he saw that she had recognized them, too.

As her gaze met his, her lips curved wryly, making him sure that, believing Kit was Lady Catherine, she had leapt again to conclusions—this time about the Colvilles. The two might well be involved, but he had yet to see evidence of it.

Nevertheless, as he heard Douglas order his men to fall back and give them space to talk, he looked forward grimly to hearing what the Colvilles would say.

Sibylla watched the Douglas's men move a short distance away and saw, too, that Cecil Percy's men likewise moved back—except for the four right behind him who stood with Thomas and Edward Colville.

She studied Thomas, trying to read his expression. With so many other horses moving, she did not hear one approaching her until Westruther's voice sounded practically in her ear.

"So you've been riding like Auld Clootie again, as young Sym would say."

Managing not to jerk her reins, she turned to him and said, "I did as I thought necessary, sir. Not that I expect you or Buccleuch, let alone Simon, to accept that."

Garth's bright blue eyes twinkled. "Simon is the only one that need concern you, lass. But I'll wager you do have some unpleasantness coming your way. I'm a gey tolerant fellow, myself, but if Amalie were to—"

"Amalie is with child, sir. I am not." It occurred to her as she said it that she might be, but she took care not to let that thought show on her face.

Garth was shaking his head. "Try telling that to Simon and see where it gets you," he said. "I'm sure you had cause, Sibylla, and I've reason of my own to be glad you are quicker to act than to think. I wish you luck, lass."

"As long as neither you nor any of the others mean to make me miss hearing what is said here, sir, I shall remain content for now."

"Nay, we'll keep you near, lass, especially Archie. Wat and I did tell him of your marriage. But as you and I both heard when he spoke to you, he still looks on you more as a daughter than as Simon's wife. He may have more to say to you anon. But for now, he will keep you close to him for your own protection."

Sibylla nodded but knew the Douglas would not protect her from Simon. The journey back to Elishaw would be discomfiting no matter what happened here.

Simon could wreak his vengeance on her at last, with every right to do so.

⁓

Cecil, encouraged by Douglas to speak his piece, said, "I was in the area for private reasons when I came on this chap, Colville, and his men. He warned me that Scottish reivers were on their way to harass my people again and steal their beasts. We waited with him until Murray and his men appeared. Colville said they were the reivers. I met Murray, and we'd begun to speak when events transpired as you saw."

Simon watched the Douglas shift his fierce gaze to Thomas Colville. "You say you know of raiders attacking here in England," Archie said. "Where are they?"

"I fear they are here, my lord," Thomas said, gesturing to Simon.

Simon saw Sibylla bristle, but she wisely held her tongue.

He said evenly, "You know that is not true, Colville. But you and my cousin have now said enough to make me certain that your trail, not his, is the one we followed here from Elishaw. You stayed there last night under false pretenses."

"I am not surprised that *you* would make such an accusation," Thomas said with disdain. To the Douglas, he added haughtily, "It is wholly untrue, of course."

Keeping tight rein on his temper, Simon said gently, "You will hardly be foolish enough to insist on that. You must know that one of your men rides a pony with a mis-shapen hoof that we can easily identify."

Thomas glanced at Edward, their expressions showing that they did know.

Simon added, "My own experience proves to me that a man may do things in obedience to his liege lord, or a brother, that he would not do on his own. If you two set things in motion at someone else's command to draw me into a trap you expected my cousin Percy to spring for you, you'd be wise to admit it."

When both Colvilles remained silent, Douglas said curtly, "If you've aught else to say, lads, say it now or I'll be drawing my own conclusions."

"It was not like that," Thomas said. "We had nowt to do with bringing the Percys here, though I'll admit we used the Percy name to gain entrance to Elishaw."

"Why?" Douglas asked.

"I knew that Lady Murray"—Thomas glanced at Sibylla—"the dowager lady Murray, that is, was a Percy, so I thought . . . that is, my lord suggested that the name would gain us entrance. When these Percys appeared un-expectedly today, I told them what we have suspected for some months now—that Murray of Elishaw is behind the raiding both here and throughout the Scottish Borders."

"Is that notion Fife's or yours?" Archie asked bluntly.

"Both, I'm afraid, sir. We have come to see that Murray pretends to remain neutral merely to cover more dis-reputable activities that increase Elishaw's wealth."

Sibylla snapped, "That, Thomas Colville, is a fiendish lie, and you know it!"

"Hush, lass," Simon said. "Nobbut what she speaks the

truth, Colville. Are you prepared to swear that you lied to my people at Elishaw and gained entrance there with no idea but that you'd find stolen sheep and cattle in my bailey?"

"You know that was not my purpose," Thomas said. "I don't deny that my lord Fife would be content had we found such, but you know very well that I sought something far more valuable."

Impatiently, Douglas said, "Well, Murray, is there aught to what the man says?"

"Nay," Simon said without taking his eyes off Thomas. "I thought nowt but that Cecil Percy had come a bit earlier than expected to Elishaw."

"That is true, my lord," Sibylla said. "However, I did suspect mischief."

"That's enough, madam," Simon said. "Leave this matter to us."

"Nay then, I'll hear her," the Douglas said. "Go on, lass."

Sibylla said, "You have heard of the missing heiress, Lady Catherine Gordon, my lord. The Colvilles have been searching for weeks for her."

"I am betrothed to the lady Catherine, my lord," Thomas protested.

"I did hear that, aye," Archie said. "And a travesty I thought it, too. Do you mean to say you gained entrance to Elishaw to search for your wee heiress there?"

"Aye, for you see, my brother had seen her with Murray," Thomas said.

Simon kept silent, wondering how Edward Colville would explain that.

But Sibylla said angrily, "Remember the lad Dand, Thomas Colville, and tell the whole tale! If Edward saw us with Kit and Dand, my lord, then he and his men are the villains who pitched the poor lad into the Tweed. So terrified was Kit of them that she hurled herself into the river after him rather than let them catch her."

Simon turned to hush her again, but Douglas flicked a hand, silencing him.

Edward Colville, Simon noted, was silent but deeply flushed.

When Sibylla began to go on, Thomas cut her off, saying, "Murray, do you allow *all* your womenfolk to run their mouths so? That's a fine tale, my lady, but my brother will tell you 'twas simply by accident those children fell into the river."

"Is that so?" Sibylla asked Edward scornfully.

"Aye, it is," he muttered without looking at her.

Thomas said, "For Murray to pluck them out and carry them back to Elishaw like more of his ill-got beasts was nobbut theft. Edward rode at once to tell me he had them. I informed my lord Fife, and we decided that rather than set siege to Elishaw to regain what was mine, we'd try a less martial way first."

Douglas said, "Why did you not simply ask Murray to give her back?"

The Colvilles looked at each other again.

Furiously, Sibylla said, "Because they never thought of that! They and their master had other plans in mind. So they got in by lying, then took the opportunity to cross-question poor Dand about Catherine's whereab— No, Simon, I will *not* be silent. You do not know this part. *Then*, Thomas Colville, when Dand would not tell you where Catherine was, one of you pitched him down those stairs to his death."

Shock stopped Simon's breath in his throat.

Sibylla saw Simon's ashen face and wished she might have broken the news more gently to him. "Aye, sir, it is true," she said to him quietly. "They did it in the dead of night, after our lads were asleep, but there was a witness."

"Kit?"

"Aye, she is safe. You were right about that."

"There, Douglas, I told you they had her," Colville said.

Simon said, "We do have a wee lass at Elishaw, my lord. But I'd swear on my life that she is *not* Catherine Gordon. The lad the Colvilles evidently killed—"

"That is a *damnable* lie!" Thomas exclaimed. "I'll admit we did threaten the boy when he refused to tell us where the lass had hidden herself. But it was only by the most regrettable accident that he fell down the stairs."

"You swung him over the stairs, threatening to throw him," Sibylla said.

"Be silent, damn you! You cannot know such a thing to be true."

"I've heard enough," Douglas said. "Take them, lads, and if they have other men yonder amidst Percy's lot, seize them all."

"With respect, my lord," Percy said. "We *are* in England, and many of us could have died here today. I'd like the privilege of hanging them myself."

"Nay, we'll keep them," Douglas said. "You've little evidence to show, whilst it seems we can prove murder and attempted murder against them. Also, when we chat with the Colvilles' men, I believe one or two of them, to save their own skins, will tell us more about the other raids. I'm guessing they had much to do with them, too."

Buccleuch said casually, "I own, Percy, I remain curious about your presence here. You've a large tail for a man just out for a day's ride."

Cecil Percy glanced at Simon. "I was on my way to Elishaw," he said. "In response to a *very* odd summons."

Visibly puzzled, Simon said, "Summons?"

"Aye, sir, for I received a message from your lady mother, suggesting—nay, commanding—that I set the exact date for my requested visit to a few weeks hence and bring my daughters with me, mayhap my sons, too. The tone of her message indicated that you were ready to seek a wife"—he flicked a glance at Sibylla—"and might soon be seeking a husband for the lady Rosalie as well. I was in no way averse to discussing such possibilities, even an alliance, with her. However, as I had not . . ."

He paused, glancing uncomfortably from face to face and back to Simon.

"Sakes, sir," Simon said. "I'd assumed that Fife used your name because he'd somehow intercepted your message to me! Are you trying to tell us that you did *not* request my permission to visit Elishaw?"

"I did not. I cannot deny that I'd readily accept an invitation, but I'd sent no messenger, so . . . Sithee, I did wonder if Annabel had perhaps imagined I had."

Sibylla put a hand to her mouth, but seeing Simon stiffen, she reached it out to touch his arm as she said, "Pray, sir, is that all you wondered about her?"

Percy had a charmingly rueful smile, and he flashed it as he replied, "In troth, my lady, one does not like to suggest . . . I have long admired the way Elishaw has maintained its neutrality in hard times. Indeed, I had the greatest respect for Cousin Annabel, because knowing Sir Iagan, too, one saw clearly that . . . well, that she . . ."

". . . that she ruled the roost," Douglas said bluntly.

"Just so," Percy agreed. "So you see, to receive *such* an odd message, one suggesting possible *marriages* betwixt our families, I desired to . . . uh . . . be sure that Annabel had not gone . . . that is to say, that she was still in full possession of . . ."

A shout of laughter erupted from Buccleuch. "Save us!" he exclaimed. "You wanted to be sure before engaging in talks of marrying your offspring to a Murray, that she had not gone mad and might thus pass her madness to the Percy line!"

"Just so, my lord," Percy said with a distinct note of relief in his voice.

As Buccleuch, Westruther, and Douglas roared with laughter, Percy added hastily to Simon, "As you might understand, cousin, I knew that such an inquiry would require a personal visit and . . . and much tact. I dared not entrust it to another."

Simon was struggling visibly with his own emotion, but Sibylla was not sure if it was anger or amusement until he caught his lower lip between his teeth.

He gave up the struggle then and joined the others in their whoops.

~

Shaking his head, Simon said when he found his voice again, "I promise you, sir, my lady mother is in full possession of her senses. She can be a little trying at times, due to her habit of seeking to manage everything in her orbit. But that habit has served us well today, I think."

"Aye, it has that," Douglas agreed, still chortling. "For,

sithee, in a more roundabout way, her meddling likewise brought me here."

"I did wonder about your presence, my lord," Cecil admitted.

"Aye, well, the Governor of our Realm taught me the value of efficient watchers. Thanks to mine, I got word yestereve of a large English band of Percys moving toward the border. Your men, in fact, sir," he said. "My lads kept track of you, and I set out early this morning to intercept you. When I saw Simon with you, and the Murray and Percy banners cheek by jowl, I feared he had decided against neutrality at last and had thrown his lot in with the wrong side."

"I am a Scotsman first, my lord," Simon said. "But I believe in peace and want us to do all we can to keep the present truce as long as it will hold."

"I agree," Cecil said firmly.

"Then we're of one mind, the five of us," Douglas said, including Buccleuch and Westruther with a gesture. "I'm thinking we need to do summat, though, to make it easier to stop mischief makers like this lot we've taken today."

"I'm agreeable, sir," Cecil said. "And I'd surmise that Northumberland would likewise agree. Have you aught in mind to accomplish that?"

"I do," the Douglas said. "I've thought on it for a time now. But I'm thinking we should discuss it more together. All of us," he added with a look at Cecil.

"We're together now," Simon said. "And Elishaw is nobbut an hour or so away. I suggest that we go there and talk more."

This being agreed to by everyone, the leaders collected their men and their prisoners and set out together without delay.

Although Sibylla doubted that Simon would fly into her amid such a host of men-at-arms, she remained wary as the long train of riders followed the river Rede through the hills toward Scotland. She and Simon led the cavalcade with Archie, Buccleuch, Percy, and Westruther. The others all followed them.

She wanted to talk with Simon, even to argue with him, but he rode silently, looking straight ahead. Douglas rode at his right, the other three lairds behind them, leaving the captains of their fighting tails to keep order among their men.

They were nearing the Carter Bar crossing when Garth eased his big bay next to hers, smiled, and said quietly, "Tired, my lady?"

"Not yet," she said, almost as wary of him as she was of Simon. "If you have aught to say to me, sir, just say it," she said, wishing she could say the same thing to Simon, albeit not in present company.

"Nay, I've no cause to take you through the boughs," Garth said in his normal tone. "Had you not meddled today, the Colvilles would doubtless have stirred more strife. To my mind, you did well . . . for a lass."

Shooting him a sour look, she said, "Do you say such things to Amalie, sir?"

Grinning, he said, "I wanted to see how tired you really are. Tell me more about this bairn at Elishaw. *Might* she be the lady Catherine?"

She glanced at Simon, sure he must be listening. But he continued to look straight ahead, his jaw set hard enough to reveal the dimple near his mouth.

Turning back to Garth, she said, "I think she may be

Catherine Gordon, but she will not admit it." Glancing at Simon again, she saw his jaw relax.

"I see," Garth said. "She might be keeping silent to protect herself. I'd wager that, with all the fuss and to-do, she must be terrified. But at least she won't have to worry any longer about marrying Thomas Colville."

"Don't depend on that," Sibylla warned, wishing she could be as sure that Alice need not marry Edward. "Fife will still have much to say about all this, and I have seen him at work, sir. So, too, have you."

"Aye, but if you think Archie will forgive the murder and attempted murder of two bairns, whoever they may be, you are mistaken. And now that the Percys are involved, Fife may find it impossible to protect the Colvilles."

At that, Simon said curtly, "If the Douglas does not hang them, I'll do it myself, Fife or no Fife."

"They are mine," Archie said flatly, showing that he, too, had been listening. "But you're in the right of it, Garth, lad," he added. "If Sibylla's young witness can say the Colvilles put them in that river and caused that lad's death, I'll hang them."

"She did say that," Sibylla assured him.

Simon remained silent, and when Westruther dropped back to ride again with Percy and Buccleuch, Sibylla had all she could do not to look at her husband again, to try to judge what he was thinking.

$\sim$

Simon could not decide what to say to her. One minute he wanted to shout at her for risking her life, the next he marveled at how self-possessed she was.

Even now, she rode with her head up, looking as regal

as the princess Isabel ever had and as if she had not a care in the world, although she certainly knew he was furious with her. Considering how angry she had made him, she ought to be trembling, but he was strangely pleased that she was not.

He wished he had not invited all the others to Elishaw. They would be damnably in the way there.

As he imagined sundry unlikely methods for disposing of them, a rider appeared in the distance, approaching fast.

Simon recognized him as one of his lads from Elishaw and told the Douglas, who signaled a halt.

"Laird, the Governor has come," the rider said as they met. "We did see him coming, and Jed Hay said I should hie m'self off and tell ye, 'cause her ladyship did say we ought no to let him inside. But Jed said he dared not keep him out."

"How many are with the Governor?" Simon asked.

"Dunamany, laird. I dinna ken how many, but it did look as if they would fill the bailey and more."

"How did you find us?" Douglas asked.

"I were on the Pike earlier, m'lord. We saw ye crossing into Redesdale, and we saw the laird head that way, too. So when I come down just as the Governor had come and Jed said I should find ye and tell ye, I rid here to find ye."

"Can you tell us aught else?" Simon asked.

"Nay, that be all Jed said to tell ye, save it looks as if he means to stay—the Governor. He told Jed to shut the gate and stand down as soon as his own lot was inside. Jed signed to me to take off then, so I did."

"Good lad," Simon said. He turned to see Douglas frowning heavily.

"How many men did you leave behind?" Archie asked.

"Not enough to prevent Fife from doing as he pleases, whatever it may be."

"Aye, well, I warrant we've enough here together to change his mind if he plans mischief," Douglas said, still frowning. "It may lead to trouble, though."

Glancing at Sibylla, Simon drew a breath and let it out. "With respect, my lord," he said. "I'm thinking we'd be wiser not to corner Fife inside Elishaw. He looks on you as a friend and ally, which is gey useful to us here in the Borders."

"You speaking as a Borderer, lad, or as a Murray?"

"Both, my lord. I'll admit that I'd liefer Elishaw not find itself under siege. For one thing, that bairn is in there with Fife and his men, and my people are, too."

He saw Sibylla open her mouth and shut it. "What is it, lass?" he asked.

She looked at the others, still hesitating, until the Douglas said, "Don't be shy now, Sibylla. I'll listen to anyone with something to say."

"In troth, my lord, I believe the Governor's intent in all of this has been to seize Elishaw," she said. "Simon angered him months ago, when he refused to let Fife arrange Rosalie's marriage to his own man, and Fife has not forgotten. Nor does he ever forgive an injury." Her gaze met Simon's and held it. He knew she was reminding him that he and Fife had once shared that trait.

"So you believe he means to declare Elishaw forfeit to the Crown," Douglas said thoughtfully. "What grounds can he offer to accomplish that legally? Thanks to Colville, we ken fine what grounds he *meant* to offer—that Simon was threatening the truce by leading the raids—but that is now provably false."

"Fife does not know that yet," Simon said. "I would

suggest a more subtle method of relaying that information to him if you will agree to it."

"Spit it out, lad. I cannot agree or disagree until I ken your reasoning."

"I think we should sit down with the man and seek his advice," Simon said. "I suggest we walk into the hall as if we'd been inside the wall all along. We'll tell him we've learned who is behind all the raids, that we have the villains by the heels, *and* that we've done it all with the Percys' aid—as a matter of strengthening the truce. I think he'll have to accept that appearance of things."

Archie grimaced. "That might work, aye. But if the gates are shut and the devious bastard has seized the castle, how do you propose we stroll in to see him?"

"There is a way, my lord." Simon turned to Sibylla, looked her in the eyes, and said, "Is there not, sweetheart?"

She gazed steadily back at him and said, "Perhaps so, my lord."

Turning back to Douglas, who looked bewildered—as well he might, Simon thought—he said quietly, "I mean to ride ahead with Sibylla for a time, my lord, and talk. But I swear, before we reach Elishaw, all will be in train to surprise Fife."

Chapter 21 _____

As Sibylla reined her horse around to go with Simon, her gaze met Garth's. Noting the twinkle in his eyes, she deduced that he thought she was in for it, believed she deserved it, and found amusement in those thoughts.

She raised her chin higher, but the truth was, she wondered what exactly Simon had decided to do.

"If you don't lower your chin, madam wife," he said without looking at her, "you are likely to let your beast walk into a bog or trip over a boulder."

Her lips twitched, but she quickly controlled them. She had not minded Garth's silent enjoyment of what he believed would be well-merited rebuke from her husband, but she was not daft enough to let Simon think she laughed at him.

Hoping to divert his attention and even disarm him a little, she said, "Under like circumstances, I'd do it all again, you know. I know that I've vexed you, and that you are unlikely to forget or forgive me quickly. But will you tell me what you mean to do—and perhaps be kind enough to tell me just how angry you are?"

He flicked her one of the cool glances that she had

come to realize he used to conceal his deeper feelings. Then he said, "You should thank the Fates that an army surrounded us when I caught up with you. Come to that, you should thank them for protecting you from Archie's wrath."

"I trust you will not be the sort of husband who rants at his wife or beats her whenever she makes a decision without first consulting him," she said.

"For some time today, I contemplated just such a future for myself," he admitted. "But we have a more important matter now to discuss."

"In your opinion, perhaps. But, in mine—"

"We can parley as much as you like when this is over," Simon said. "You won't persuade me that you mean to issue threats or ultimatums now, however."

"I won't?"

"No."

The flat, uncompromising reply did draw a smile from her. "Thank you," she said, satisfied that his anger was under control, at least for the moment. "I rarely do threaten people or issue ultimatums. But I do want to know more about this plan of yours, because I doubt it can be what it seems to be."

"What does it seem to be?"

"To enter the castle secretly and confront Fife. But surely, the two of us would have no effect on him other than to make him shut us up in your dungeon."

"I had not considered any such thing. In troth, I had no—" Breaking off, he pressed his lips together as if he were annoyed with himself, and she knew why.

"You did not mean for me to go in with you," she said matter-of-factly.

"Of course not. Don't be daft."

"How will you stop me?"

"I'll leave a man to guard you if I must."

"Just one?"

A hint of a smile touched his lips as he said, "Two or three, if necessary."

"Where will you leave me?"

He looked at her then. "I see your point," he said. "As I don't want to reveal the tunnel's existence, let alone its entrance, to any of the men-at-arms, I'd have to trust you to stay by the pond or wait whilst one of the others takes you back to our men."

"So you do know about the tunnel," she said. "Sithee, I had decided that you did not. But if you do, why do you need me?"

"Because I don't know where the entrance at this end is, only that it must be near the pond," he said. "You wore soft shoes that night, so I doubt you'd walked far, and from just one brief visit you could not have known about the pond to stroll to it from anywhere else in the woods. As soon as I learned about the tunnel—"

"You knew naught of it that night then."

"Nay, it was only afterward that I discovered there'd been rumors of one. But I could scarcely quiz everyone at Elishaw. So I asked my mother if she knew a way out besides the gate. She told me where it starts, but we all left for Edinburgh the next day. As I've had no opportunity to explore it, I must rely on you."

"But you cannot want to take the others with you, and you cannot go alone."

"I'll take Douglas, Percy, Buccleuch, and Westruther with me."

"Mercy, how secret will it be then?"

"Sibylla, I want peace, so our people can plant crops

and expect to harvest them without watching them trampled to dust by raiders first. Douglas wants to improve the way we redress grievances across the line, and Northumberland will listen to Cecil Percy, who supports that notion. What better way to show them *we* mean to cooperate than to let them know of our siege tunnel?"

"Aye, sure, until the plan fails and the English besiege us."

"Sakes, I mean to destroy that tunnel. It seems a daft idea anyway, providing a way in as well as out. But enough of this. We're already within view of the Pike, and they'll soon see us from the ramparts. I mean to leave the men with their captains just up ahead and take those I named in with me. You'll wait for us well away from—"

"No," she said.

"By heaven—!"

"Elishaw is your home, sir, and your plan may succeed, but there is every chance that Kit is in that tunnel now. I *won't* let you terrify her, which you would certainly do if you all crept up on her in the dark. I'm going with you."

His jaw tightened until she heard his teeth grating, but he reined in and motioned the other lairds to rejoin them. It was growing darker.

"You've answered only one of my questions," she said as she watched the four urge their mounts toward them. "But I suspect you're even angrier now."

"We'll find out when this is over," he said curtly.

A tingling thrill shot through her, making her wonder what manner of fool she was that such a statement could make her look forward to that discussion.

Simon stopped the cavalcade in dusky shadows before anyone on Elishaw's ramparts could catch sight of them. Leaving their men and the prisoners to wait with their captains, the five leaders and Sibylla walked with him toward the forest pond.

He led the way with Sibylla a pace behind him. As they went, he discussed his plan quietly with the other men, aware that she listened and wondering at his complaisance to her presence. When he realized he was accepting her silence as approval, he wondered even more at himself.

He knew her well enough to be sure that although she might exercise tact in such company, she would speak up at once if anything they said struck her amiss. The thought was more reassuring than annoying, which told him he had come to believe in her good sense—more often than not—and truly to respect her opinions.

The other men seemed to approve his plan.

Douglas said only, "We're putting a lot of faith in just letting the man know that his plot to provide legal grounds for seizing Elishaw failed."

"He'll bow to a subtle approach, sir," Simon said. "But if we had to force our way in or lay siege to the castle, he'd dig in his heels, because news would quickly spread that he'd no cause to seize it. Fife's public face is that of a law-abiding ruler. Had he been able to argue that I'd broken the law, endangered the truce . . ."

"Aye, sure," Buccleuch agreed. "Fife's most dangerous when he's cornered. 'Tis better to provide him a way to leave quietly with his dignity intact."

That they accepted Simon's reasoning and respected his knowledge of Fife stirred an unfamiliar sense of simple pride.

Into a silence, Westruther muttered, "Our light is fast fading, my friends. We must hope Fife has not got his devil's imps lurking in shadows to waylay enemies."

Buccleuch chuckled, but Douglas said testily, "We're not enemies of the man. He's done all he can to undermine *my* authority, but I don't want all-out war with him, for although he may not be the best choice to lead Scotland, he's the strongest one available. Even so, we can be sure he's the one behind these raids because he's tried similar tactics in the past, and they must stop."

"One would think he'd learn from his errors," Buccleuch said.

"He's no tactician, though," Westruther said. "We also know that."

"Aye, *and* that he's a coward," Douglas said. "We'll rely on such traits now to discourage his mischief for a time."

Percy said, "I don't understand what he'd hoped to gain from such raids."

"First," Buccleuch said, "he wanted to make it seem that Douglas authority in the Borders had weakened, because Fife has always resented the fact that the Douglas is more powerful than any Stewart. Next, to provide himself with legal cause to seize Elishaw, he wanted to make Simon appear to be behind all the raids."

"But such raids could lead to armies gathering," the Englishman protested.

"Aye, sure, but Fife never sees clearly past his own goals," Westruther said. "Some go so far as to say he *hopes* the two countries will become one—with himself appointed to govern the Scottish part for the English king."

"Sakes, does he suppose Richard of England would

name any Scot to such a post?" Percy demanded. "I vow, he would not."

"We ken that fine, but Fife tends to reckon as if his opponents will do just as he imagines they will," Buccleuch said. "He is a shrewd politician and a ruthless one, but it never seems to occur to the man that his opponent in battle might think for himself and have another outcome in mind."

With a chuckle, Westruther said, "Perhaps we ought not to speak so freely of Fife's failings with Murray and Percy. Percy may be an enemy again one day, and Simon may feel obliged to submit to Fife out of nobbut habit."

Sibylla's hand slid warmly into Simon's.

Giving it a squeeze, he said mildly, "I'd expected someone to suggest that long since, Garth. In troth, for years I thought Fife was leading Scotland effectively and followed him all in all. But when I came to see how freely he expected to use our Scottish noblewomen and Scottish lands for his own purposes, and how easily he can dismiss assault and murder if such crimes benefit him . . ." He paused, then said, "I am loyal to the Crown, but my first loyalty is to Elishaw, to my family, and to the cause of peace if we can strengthen this truce."

"What if we cannot?" the Douglas said.

"In that event, my lord, I am yours to command, as is Elishaw," Simon said. "I understand that, in most ways, my parents and grandparents wanted what I want. So I accepted their neutrality, but now . . ."

Turning, he said directly to Cecil, "I hope that you, especially, will understand what I say now, cousin. Sithee, with things as they stand, and men no longer sure of who serves which side, we who lead them—on both sides of the line—must make clear where *we* stand and do all in our power to bring peace to the Borders."

"We'll never stop the reiving," Buccleuch said.

"We won't as long as many of us are involved in it ourselves," Simon retorted. When Buccleuch just smiled, he shook his head at him.

Archie said, "Wat's right, though. We *won't* stop the reiving any time soon on either side, even amongst the nobles. 'Tis why I want an arrangement to address grievances across the line. We do it in some cases now with our wardens' meetings, but we need a better system that will serve both sides fairly and efficiently."

They fell silent then, each with his or her thoughts, until they came to the clearing. Keeping to the trees, they skirted the pond.

When Simon saw Sibylla pause opposite the memorable granite slab from which she had waded naked into the pond, he said, "Well, lass, which way?"

Sibylla saw Garth look curiously at Buccleuch and then at Simon.

Simon ignored him.

"Beyond that boulder yonder, sir," she said, pointing. "I'm not sure I'd have recognized it if it were not as dark as it is, but another large boulder lies beyond it, and the opening beyond that." She still was not sure she'd find the entrance, but by lining up the boulders with the tall tree at the end of the pond, she did so easily.

"We'll need light," Douglas said as he peered inside.

"I have a torch and a tinder box," Simon said.

"The torch may be an encumbrance," Sibylla said.

"The passage is narrow, and Garth will have to duck. I left candles a bit farther inside," she added.

"Did you, indeed?" Simon said. "How many?"

"I don't recall; three perhaps."

"I hope someone means to tell me how her ladyship kens more of this place than its lord does," Garth muttered.

Simon explained as he found the candles and reached for his tinder box. When he admitted that Sibylla had found the tunnel after being in the castle little more than twenty-four hours, the other men had to struggle to muffle their amusement.

"You'll have to destroy the tunnel now, lad," Douglas said. "It won't do to leave it, because even Fife is bound to figure out how we must have got in."

"I ken that fine, my lord," Simon said.

After he lighted the candles, he handed one to Sibylla and motioned for her to lead them. "Stop well before the door at the other end, lass," he said quietly. "We'll open it, and you will stay in the tunnel until one of us comes to fetch you."

That, she decided, would depend on whether they found Kit in the tunnel, but she knew better than to say so to him then. His tone had said he would brook no argument, and although he seemed willing to forgive some things now, he would find it hard to forgive a wife who defied him in front of Douglas and the other lairds.

The only sounds were their feet padding softly on the hard-packed floor until her quick ears caught scuffling sounds of a presence ahead.

Raising a hand to warn Simon behind her, she paused.

Softly then, she said, "Kit, it is the lady Sibylla. I'm here, love."

A shape unfolded from the deep shadows a few yards

ahead, and with a cry, the child ran into her arms. "Och, but when I heard ye coming, I thought the deevil were after me," she exclaimed as she buried her face against Sibylla. "There be bad men inside, me lady! I'm gey glad ye came!"

"*This* is Colville's lady Catherine?" Buccleuch said over Simon's shoulder.

"Nay, then, I'm not!" Kit protested, clinging harder than ever to Sibylla.

"I promise you're safe now, Kit," she said. "No one here will harm you, so you can tell us the truth."

"But I did! I'm nobbut plain Kit!"

"She *is* telling the truth, lass, as I've said all along," Simon murmured. "Quiet her and stay with her, whilst we go in and deal with Fife."

Sibylla nodded. Spilling wax to hold her candle, she drew Kit close.

~

"Does she truly think that bairn is the lady Catherine Gordon?" Douglas whispered as they emerged from the tunnel into the empty bakehouse chamber.

"Aye," Simon replied. "And the Colvilles apparently thought so, too."

Gesturing for the others to wait, he moved to the archway and looked into the kitchen, where servants were preparing to serve supper in the hall.

As he took in the bustle, a gillie saw him and stopped in his tracks.

Simon motioned him over. "Tell Cook and the others to keep busy but to stay out of the hall until I send someone down with other instructions," he said.

The lad nodded fervently. "I'll tell 'em, laird. But, sithee, sir, there be dunamany men-at-arms above."

"All will soon be well again," he said, hoping he spoke the truth. He hoped, too, that if anything did go amiss, Sibylla would have the sense to get Kit and herself safely out of the tunnel before battle erupted.

He told himself she would simply return to the men with Kit and explain what had happened. Then, shaking his head at what he suspected was wishful thinking, he shoved all thought of her to the back of his mind and led the way up the service stairs to the hall.

The sight of Fife in his black-velvet elegance sitting in what Simon still thought of as Sir Iagan's two-elbow chair stirred his temper. He suppressed it, warning himself that if ever he had learned to stay cool in a crisis, this was the time to prove it.

"Ready?" he asked the others.

The Douglas nodded, his dark scowl fiercer than ever.

Westruther and Buccleuch smiled grimly and nodded.

As a gillie approached Fife with a jug, Simon stepped through the servants' archway and onto the dais, saying, "Welcome, my lord. Forgive me for not being at hand to greet your arrival, but I trust my people have seen to your needs."

Fife turned sharply, nearly knocking the jug from the pop-eyed gillie's hand.

"Murray! Where did you spring from?"

"As you see, sir, we will not be supping alone tonight," Simon said. "I have brought distinguished guests to sup with us. Is that my best claret in that jug, lad?"

The gillie recovered himself enough to nod and say, "Aye, laird."

"Then fetch more mugs and pour some for each of us.

Then you may set the privy screens and leave us till I shout for you. We've much to discuss."

Although Simon had rarely known Fife to lose his poise, he came close now.

"Douglas! Buccleuch! What the . . . ?"

They ignored him. Buccleuch and Westruther took seats on either side of him, while Douglas and Simon drew stools to the lower-hall side of the high table and sat to face him. Percy, following Simon, drew one up next to his.

When one of Fife's captains stepped onto the dais, Archie said in what was more akin to a beastly growl than anything human, "Send him away, my lord."

Fife did so with a gesture, but he had collected himself enough to say coldly, "What is the meaning of this? How dare you—!"

Simon interjected gently, "How dare I enter *my* hall to sup with *my* guest? Although I did not invite you, my lord, you are ever welcome at Elishaw. However, I fail to understand why you did not send to let me know so I might have prepared more properly for you. My lady wife will be distressed to have missed you."

"Do not forget who I am," Fife said to him. "Or that I control—"

"That's enough of that," Douglas said, unimpressed with Fife's bluster. "Here are the plain facts, sir. You will be pleased to know that we have caught the men responsible for raids on both sides of the line and will hang them as the traitors they are for stirring strife that might have led to war with England. There is nowt in that business that need concern you. However, as two of them are the Colvilles who have pretended to seek the lady Catherine Gordon in these parts—"

"Pretended?"

"I say what I mean and dislike interruption," the Douglas said. "But aye, pretended. To that end, they threw a local lad into the river Tweed a fortnight ago. When that did not kill him, they came here and threw him down the stairs."

"What the devil was such a lad doing here?" Fife demanded.

"My men rescued him from the river and brought him here, sir," Simon said. "He was exhausted, and remained sickly and weak. The Colvilles gained entrance here last night through a ruse. Believing the lad knew the lady Catherine's whereabouts, they threatened him. When he could not help them, they killed him."

"Surely, you cannot think I had aught to do with such a travesty."

"Such a thought never occurred to us," Simon said, looking into his eyes, daring him to challenge the lie. "We know how strong your principles are. We know, too, just how much value you place on human life . . . and on a person's legal property rights."

Douglas waited a beat before saying gruffly, "The important thing is we've put an end to this raiding and can now set up a way to deal with such mischief in future. I've made a list of my own notions, and the five of us mean to discuss them, sir. Percy here has agreed to present the result to Northumberland for his support."

"What sort of notions?" Fife demanded.

"Bless us, sir, there be nae need to trouble you with the details," Douglas said. "We ken fine how busy you are, but I'll meet with you anon to discuss it when we have put more form to our thoughts. In troth, if you'd like to adjourn with me to Hermitage tonight, we can talk there."

Fife's eyes narrowed as he shot a glance at Cecil Percy. "I expect the five of you did not ride over this evening from Hermitage, however," he said.

"Faith, my lord, I am a poor host," Simon said, shaking his head. "I have neglected to present my cousin Cecil Percy of Dour Hill, England, to you. He is cousin to Northumberland and to my lady mother. We have spent much of the day with him, as he did aid us in capturing the ill-willed Colvilles. His men and the Douglas's are camped in my woods now, awaiting instructions. When we learned that you were here, we came at once to tell you that we had caught the raiders."

A sardonic gleam appeared in the Governor's eyes. "It does not please me to find you in company with a Percy, Simon—let alone to have brought one, as you say, to sup with me. You must strive to do better by the ruler of your realm."

"I will, aye, sir," Simon said, choosing his next words with care. "Given due warning in future, I promise you Elishaw's hospitality will be all that you expect."

Fife's glance flicked to Percy again and back to Simon. "Tell me, will the Percys find as warm a welcome here as I shall?"

"That must depend, sir, on the state of the truce between us. That truce is of paramount import, as you will agree. We must do all we can, together, to preserve it."

"Answer me plainly, sir," Fife said. "If hostilities arise again, will those at Elishaw continue to play Jack-of-Both-Sides, or nay?"

"We have likewise discussed that, my lord, all of us here. Elishaw is at heart a Scottish holding, and in such a case will stand with Douglas for Scotland."

"With Douglas," Fife repeated.

"Aye, and with the realm."

"I see."

"The truce is all-important, sir," Simon repeated.

Fife looked at Buccleuch. "You are quiet for once."

"I've nowt to add," Buccleuch said.

"So you agree with Murray?"

"He is my good-brother, my lord. I'm sworn to support him."

"He is my good-brother as well, sir," Westruther reminded Fife.

Having given little thought to his own friends or foes while serving Fife, Simon felt an unexpected rush of gratitude for the men who stood with him now.

Fife nodded. "Very well. I shall rely on you all to see that the Borders remain at peace. I do have one other question to ask you, Murray."

"Aye, sir?"

"I ordered you to Huntly to seek news of my royal ward, Catherine Gordon, then most generously granted you four days' leave to enjoy your bride. Shortly thereafter, though, I learned that you had left Edinburgh and that the lady Catherine was here at Elishaw. To be exact, that you keep her here as your hostage."

"I suspect one of the Colvilles told you that, my lord," Simon said. "The lady Catherine is not here, nor has she been here."

"I'm told you rescued *two* children from the river. Will you swear to me, on your word of honor, that you did not bring a female child here a fortnight ago?"

Simon said, "The second bairn is a lass, sir. But she is of common birth and speech, and cannot be the one you seek."

"I would know that for myself," Fife said. "Fetch her to me."

A flash of russet cloth in the service archway caught Simon's eye, but as the arch was behind Fife, he knew the Governor had not seen it. He also knew who was there and hoped Sibylla had put Kit somewhere safe. The last thing he wanted to subject the already terrified child to was an inquisition by Fife.

Douglas said to Fife, "Do you know the lady Catherine personally, sir?"

"I am her guardian. Of course, I do."

"I have heard that her hair and eyes are an unusual color, and I have seen the lass Murray rescued. Ask him what color they are, for hers are unusual, too."

Fife looked grimly at Simon.

"Her eyes are pale blue, sir," Simon said, reluctantly trusting Douglas to know what he was doing. "They are so light as to appear almost colorless at times."

"So you see," Douglas said. "She cannot be Lady Catherine. *Her* eyes and hair were described to me as symbolic of her fortune, both being golden."

"This bairn has flaxen hair," Simon said. "She must be asleep by now, too. She has been terrified, sir, has lost her brother, and so far has been unable to help us find her family. I warrant she has suffered enough without haling her from her bed."

"As to sending Murray off to Huntly for any reason," Douglas said without giving Fife time to reply, "it is a poor time to be sending the master of any Border stronghold so far to the north, sir. I need him here to discuss our plan for redressing grievances across the line and to deter further raids in the meantime."

Simon said, "I would also submit, my lord, that as

you've suspected me in Lady Catherine's disappearance, you will prefer to send someone else to Huntly. In any event, with respect, my duty now lies here at Elishaw with my wife and family."

Fife nodded and got to his feet. "The question of anyone going to Huntly becomes moot if Colville is not to marry Catherine. She will turn up somewhere, and I'll deal with her and those concealing her when she does. Douglas, I have supped and you have not, so I suggest you stay to see to your hunger. But I would ask you to return to Edinburgh in a month's time to discuss this plan of yours."

"Thank you," Douglas said. "As you ken fine, Murray here is but two days married and doubtless finds us all in his way. I do mean to take my supper with him, which will give you time to get on your way. Then I'll be leaving, too."

Chapter 22 _____

On the service stair landing, Sibylla heard sounds of Fife's departure and waited to hear what the other men would say when he had gone. Beside her, Kit waited silently, her small hand clutching Sibylla's.

Having been unable to bear being blind and deaf to what was going on above, and hearing no one in the bakehouse chamber, Sibylla had slipped out of the tunnel, and with the child as her shadow, had crept up to the landing.

She knew it was likely that someone in the kitchen had seen them. But no one had called out to her and she had not looked to see if anyone was watching, suspecting that anyone who did see them would think she had simply used her rumored witch's powers again to appear from the supposedly empty chamber.

Again, the rumors could prove useful.

When Fife ordered Simon to fetch Kit, the child had spun round to dash back down the stairs, and Sibylla nearly missed catching her. Having hoped that in moving so quickly she had not revealed their presence, it was annoying to hear Simon raise his voice to say, "He has gone, my lady. You may come in now."

Kit grabbed Sibylla's skirt with both hands.

Dampening suddenly dry lips, Sibylla bent close to her and said quietly, "We will go in together, love. Nay, do not speak. Just listen to me. The Douglas is here. He is the most powerful man in Scotland, and he will keep you safe. He is kin to me, and I promise he will let no one hurt you. I think I was wrong and you are not the lady Catherine, but I think you do know where she is and the time has come for you to tell us. The Douglas will keep her safe, too."

But when she straightened, Kit clung to her skirt, trying to hold her back.

"Sibylla?" The warning note in Simon's voice said his patience was waning.

She said, "Kit, have I ever lied to you?"

Looking at the floor, the child shook her head.

"Then, come." Sibylla held out her hand.

Kit looked into her eyes then, and she gazed steadily back.

At last, Kit took her hand and they stepped through the archway together. A gillie passed them and hurried down the steps toward the kitchen, doubtless to tell them to begin serving supper to the lairds on the dais. The lower hall was nearly silent. Few lingered there other than those clearing up or coming late to supper.

The men at the high table stood, Garth and Buccleuch on the nearer side and Simon, Percy, and Douglas with their backs to the lower hall.

Simon moved around the table toward Sibylla and Kit.

"This is Kit, my lords," Sibylla said, fixing her gaze on Douglas and thus avoiding Simon's eye and the others' as well. "She will talk with us, but I did promise her, my lord Douglas, that you will keep her safe."

"I will, aye," Archie said, his harsh face softening. "Come to the table, lassie. You are not the lady Catherine, but I'm thinking you must look summat like her."

Holding tight to Sibylla's hand, Kit went nearer, regarding Douglas solemnly as she said, "Why do you think I look like her, my lord?"

"Because you are also gey fair, and the men who interfered with you the day you went into the river thought you *were* Catherine, did they not?"

Squeezing Sibylla's hand harder, she nodded. "They were bad men."

"They were, aye. Why did they accost you?"

"Accost?"

"Why did they stop you?" Sibylla said gently.

"We had stopped already," Kit said. "The river stopped me, and then Dand found me, and he were sore vexed and shouting, so the bad men found us both."

"Dand was not your brother then."

"Nay, there's just me and me mam and . . ." She looked up at Sibylla.

"And Catherine?" Sibylla said.

"Aye, we've always been together till now. But Mam and Cat went across the river. Mam said the people seeking us looked for a woman wi' two wee lassies, so I must stay with Dand and his kin. But I didna like it there, so I cut off my hair, put on some old breeks o' Dand's, and went to find me mam and Cat."

"So that's why you were dressed as a lad," Sibylla said.

"Aye, but Dand found me by the river, and the bad men heard me shrieking and kent I was a lassie. They said they'd been seeking me and called me Catherine. I said my name *wasn't* Catherine, and Dand said I was his sister. But one o' the men knew Dand's people and said he didna *have* a sister, that he'd never seen me before. They said either I was Catherine and me mam was near or I was the other one left behind, 'cause being Catherine's nurse, Mam wouldna leave her for nowt."

Sibylla looked at Douglas, raising an eyebrow. When he nodded, she said, "Did they discover which it was, Kit?"

"The one as threw Dand said she wouldna let Cat roam about as I had either."

"Why did he throw Dand in the water?"

Tears welled in her eyes. "He believed me when I said I didna ken where they'd gone," she said. "But he said Dand must know 'cause he was older, or his people did. So I screamed at them that Dand didna ken nowt, that me mam hadna told *any*one where she went, so no bad people could find her. But they thought he *must* know, so the man wha' did all the talking said he'd throw him in the river if he'd no tell them. But he knew nowt, so he could say nowt, and so they did."

"Dand told me you ran and jumped into the water on your own," Simon said. "Did you think you could help him?"

She looked down. "Nay, I just ran so they'd no catch me . . . and 'cause I wanted gey fierce to get across the river to Mam and Cat. But the water took me, and then the lady caught me and you brought us here, laird. Then the men came and . . ."

The tears spilled silently down her cheeks, but she said no more.

The Douglas said, "We'll find your mam for you, lass, and I'll see you safe, and your mam and Catherine, too. Do you know Dand's family name, or kindred?"

She shook her head hard. "They dinna ken nowt, and I canna go back there. They'll be sore vexed wi' me 'cause it be my fault he's dead—for running away!"

"Nay," Archie said. "You'll come with me, and I'll see all safe. I'm thinking, if you know that your mam and Catherine crossed the river, you ken where they are."

She shook her head again, the tears falling unchecked now, silently.

Sibylla opened her mouth but shut it again when Simon put a hand on her shoulder. He said, "We'll keep Kit here overnight, my lord. I can meet you for our talk tomorrow at Hermitage and bring Kit with me. I warrant, as frightened as she has been, a good night's sleep here in familiar surroundings will do her good."

"Aye, lad, that's a good notion," Archie said. "In troth, Hermitage is nae a good place for a bairn."

Sibylla did speak then, saying gently, "Mayhap, my lord, if Kit *can* remember Dand's family name or where you *might* find her mother, she could stay here until you do. I warrant you'd travel more easily without a bairn to trouble you."

The Douglas gaze held hers until she saw understanding of her tactics dawn. He nodded then and said without looking at Kit, "But she'll bide here only as long as she will talk to you, lass, and *only* if she can tell you what we need to know."

Nodding, Sibylla said, "She can sleep with me tonight, and we'll talk."

"Nay," Simon said, his hand firm on her shoulder. "You may sup with her upstairs and talk whilst you eat, but she'll sleep better if you put her to bed in Amalie's chamber. Tetsy can stay with her there, so she'll not be alone."

He spoke evenly, but Sibylla detected an implacable note. When she tried to read his expression, he leaned close and murmured in her ear, "After I bid farewell to our guests, I'll expect to find you in my bedchamber, madam, where *we* will talk. Do not make me look for you."

"No, my lord," she said in a normal tone. Heat flooded her cheeks then as she realized not only that Simon might misunderstand her, or choose to misunderstand, but that the others must think she disagreed with him about Kit. In an attempt to recover, she said, "Putting Kit in Amalie's bed is an excellent idea, sir."

Noting a grin on Garth's face and wry disbelief on Buccleuch's, she squeezed Kit's hand and said, "We'll leave you to your supper now, my lords. Come, lassie."

"Be the laird vexed with us?" Kit murmured as they started up the stairs.

"Nay," Sibylla said, adding silently, *only with one of us.*

As the thought formed, she heard Douglas say, "We'll sup quickly and save most of our talking for Hermitage, so you can tend to your lady tonight, lad. If you're wise, you'll get on her gey fierce for that chancy bit of mischief today."

Sibylla paused long enough to hear Simon say, "Have no fear, my lord. I can promise she won't try to face down an army again."

Although she allowed herself a wry smile at the unlikelihood of such a necessity arising, she was aware that only a dafty would feel optimistic about what Simon would say to her. After he'd had his say, though, was another matter.

When Kit's small hand slipped into hers again and she realized the child had also heard what the two men had said, Sibylla's focus shifted and she said quietly, "We'll talk a little now, Kit, and it will all come right. You'll see."

Squeezing her hand, Kit nodded, still solemn. "I hope ye're right."

~

The Douglas kept his word and haled the others off with him when they had supped, and Simon went with them to the bailey.

No sign of the Governor's presence remained there. He would travel only to Jedburgh or Kelso, but the moonless night was clear with a blanket of stars, so once out of the forest, he and his men would see their way easily. Not being Border bred, Fife would keep his torches lit and thereby miss much of the brilliant display.

Archie, on the other hand—moon or no moon—was famous for traveling as swiftly by night as by day. He rarely ordered torches unless the night produced an overcast sky. With less than eight miles between Elishaw and Hermitage, and a good track, he and his men would make speed.

Simon's impatience stirred when Westruther paused to adjust his saddle.

Percy and the Douglas talked to each other as they waited for him, but Buccleuch eased his skittish mount nearer Simon and said with a grin, "It has been an interesting day, has it not? Elishaw has apparently acquired another strong-minded mistress, and an intrepid one at that."

"We'll soon see how intrepid she is," Simon said. He

had meant to sound grim but realized belatedly that he was smiling.

Wat Scott chuckled. "I wish you joy of her and offer my felicitations yet again. Your marriage promises to be as lively as mine."

"And mine," Westruther said as he mounted. He was smiling, too.

Simon watched until the gates began to swing shut and then turned and hurried upstairs to his chamber, wondering if his wife would be there or had dared to defy him again. He would not blame her much if she'd managed to get the truth out of Kit at last. They'd all seen that the bairn knew more than she had told them.

When he opened his door to find candlelight blazing within and a cheerful fire on the hearth, he stepped in with a sense of anticipation, expecting to see that Sibylla had kept Tetsy or one of the other maids to protect her from the wrath she expected to face. But he saw no one he need send away, and she seemed not to have heard the latch click.

She wore a light yellow robe and stood in one of the two window embrasures, its curtain half shut, gazing out at the starlit sky.

When he shut the door, harder than usual, she turned and took a step toward him. Her robe fell open, and Simon's breath caught.

She wore not a stitch of clothing under it, and was apparently oblivious of her magnificent body, for she made no move to cover it.

His mouth and lips felt dry, and if his heart was still beating he had no sense of it. Every bodily function had evidently ceased save one.

Sibylla had wanted to surprise him, and his stunned look told her she had.

"Did you expect to unman me, madam?" he said.

"In troth, my lord, you do not appear to be at all unmanned."

His lips twitched.

Evidently, he was no longer angry with her. He was just as clearly not thinking of Kit or the Douglas, or of anything save her lack of clothing.

"Come here," he said hoarsely.

She walked toward him, but he met her halfway, putting both hands on her shoulders. "Do you know what the Douglas expects me to do?" he asked.

Feigning innocence, she said, "Nay, what?"

"This," he murmured, scooping her into his arms and carrying her to the bed.

As he put her down on it, she said demurely, "Art sure Archie meant you to ravish me, my lord."

"If he did not, he thinks me a fool," he said, stripping off his jack and shirt and reaching for the lacing of his breeks.

He did not wait, nor did he take time to pleasure her first but took her swiftly and powerfully. Even so, her body was ready for his and took fire the minute he touched her. She responded with enthusiasm, learning quickly how to stimulate him more, and urge him on. She also learned how she could tease him to make him even wilder for her until she lost control of herself and of him.

When they lay back again, sated, he drew her close so that her head rested in the hollow of his shoulder. He was still breathing heavily, but after a few quiet moments, just as she began to fear he might have fallen asleep as he had before, he said, "Archie told me to get on you gey fierce for what you did today, sweetheart. I warrant I followed his instructions."

She chuckled. "I can vow that you did."

He was silent for a time, making her wonder if he would say more about the incident but not wanting to spoil their contentment by encouraging him. His breathing had quieted but he was definitely not asleep.

"What did you learn from Kit?" he asked.

"Enough to tell me that her mother was indeed Catherine's wet-nurse," Sibylla said. "Catherine's mother died soon after her birth, and Kit's mother, Lucy Aiken, had had Kit just a month before. She raised the girls together."

"Why wouldn't Kit tell us about her before?"

"She said that she and Dand had sworn a solemn oath to tell no one they even knew Catherine. Kit said her mam was terrified of being caught."

"Aye, she must be still. Fife would certainly charge her with abducting Catherine, and even young Kit is wise enough to fear her mother might hang."

Sibylla had not thought of that. "They *won't* hang her, will they?"

"Douglas promised to protect her," Simon said. "He'll see that she comes to no harm. What else did you learn?"

"As best I could make out from the bits Kit could tell me, after Catherine's father died and Fife assumed her guardianship, Lucy Aiken and the girls continued to live at Huntly with everything much as before. But when Fife arranged Catherine's betrothal to Thomas and decided the Colvilles should take charge of her, they told Lucy that Catherine would no longer need her."

"So Lucy ran off with her," he said.

"Aye, Kit said her mam and Catherine were both gey upset. Sakes, but Lucy was the only mother Catherine had ever known and the girls were closer than most sisters. I warrant Kit was gey upset, too."

"How did they get to Oxnam Tower?"

"That happened before they learned the Colvilles would take Catherine. Kit said only that they'd had to leave Huntly, so I warrant Fife ordered the move."

"Aye, it makes sense if she was to go to Colville."

"When they ran away, they went to Dand's family, kinsmen of Lucy's on this side of the Tweed. But when the Colvilles got too close, Lucy took Catherine and fled back across the Tweed to other kinsmen, leaving Kit. Kit remembers her mentioning Melrose but does not know if Dand's family knows where Lucy went."

"Aye, well, the Douglas will find her. We've Aikens on our land, come to that, so the name alone will help. Folks will tell Archie much that they would not have told the Colvilles. We'll find them, sweetheart."

"I'd like to keep Kit here until we do," Sibylla said.

"Aye, sure," he murmured. "I've a strong feeling that the place will seem a bit empty, anyway, until we have bairns of our own. I expect your father and my mother to make a match of it and keep Rosalie and Alice with them at Akermoor."

"Do you mind if that happens?"

"Nay," he said. "Your father finally admitted that the dispute was his fault, because he was already married to your mother when he met mine. It seems hard to imagine my mother stirring such passion in any man, but he swears he had only to see her to lose his wits over her."

"She was married then, too," Sibylla said. "She told me

your father caught them together and knocked my father down."

"Did she?" He chuckled. "Sir Malcolm did not tell me that. He said only that he and my father had had a falling out, that it was all his own fault, and that she had been furious with *him* for making her the focus of such attention. I'd not be surprised if she played that part so convincingly that she persuaded herself it was true."

"Until they met again, at all events," Sibylla said. "If they do marry, I expect she will much enjoy setting the household at Akermoor to rights, for all that Father believes it runs smoothly now."

"Aye, she will," he said. "I have great respect for her, but I do look forward to making decisions about Elishaw without always wondering what she will say."

A small silence ensued.

At last, Sibylla said, "Do you fear that I may be too much like her?"

His arm tightened around her and then he raised himself on his elbow and leaned over her. "Nay, sweetheart, I don't fear you. At first, I did think you might be like her. But I can talk with you, and even when we disagree, we soon seem to find common ground. The fact is that when I am with you, I like myself and I want to know what you think and hear what you will say."

"I often find myself wondering what you will think or say about things, too," she said. "But we can make each other fiercely angry, too."

"Aye, you're gey lucky you had an army to protect you today, but after the way I infuriated you in Edinburgh . . ."

"I'm content now," she said. "I'm not sure why I was so angry then, come to that. It all just seemed to boil over and spill out when you took the blanket off me and I saw where we were. It felt as if I were watching it happen, listening to some other woman snarl at you."

"Aye, well, mayhap we both lost our wits, sweetheart." He bent then and kissed her on the lips, gently.

"That's the fifth time you've called me sweetheart tonight," she said.

"Do you count such things?"

"Nay, but you had never done so before. You said only that I'd make you a suitable wife, just as your mother had said to me."

"I can see that you mean to plague me with that. You should remember instead that I also told you I wanted *you* for my wife more than I'd ever wanted anything else. Do you know why I was so angry today?"

"Aye, sure, because I rode like a harridan into the midst of the Douglas army. I didn't know what else to do. I feared they'd kill you for conspiring with the Percys."

"And I thought you would kill yourself. If you had, sweetheart, I'd have wanted to die, too. Sithee, you have become precious to me. I never knew I could care so much, could love someone so much. But I have only to see you—"

"Kiss me, Simon. You talk too much, and I want you to make me feel as only you can make me feel."

"I vow, my heart, I can make you feel much more."

"Braggart. Prove it."

He did.

Epilogue

I, Annabel, take thee, Malcolm, to my wedded husband . . ."

"That's me grandame!" the three-year-old heir to Buccleuch and Rankilburn, who stood beside Sibylla, said clearly into the pause.

As the bride continued with her vows, Sibylla looked down at her husband's beaming nephew, smiled back at him, and raised a finger to her lips.

Wat Scott, on his other side, bent and whispered in his son's ear.

Robbie Scott nodded once, listened, then nodded again, whereupon Wat lifted him up and held him so he could see better. Sibylla smiled again when she saw the little boy put a hand over his mouth as if to remind himself to keep still.

". . . in sickness and in health, to be bonlich and buxom in bed and at board . . ."

Hearing Lady Murray, soon to be Lady Cavers, promising to be meek and obedient, Sibylla glanced at Simon and found his gaze waiting to catch hers, his eyes as brimful of amusement as she knew hers must be.

He put a hand to the small of her back and rubbed it, plainly not caring a whit if people behind them saw him stroking his wife. As she leaned into his hand, to savor its warmth, she thought how different it all was from four years before.

It was the same wee kirk, and less than a fortnight short of the anniversary. But no rain fell today, and wedding guests packed the kirk, so it was much warmer inside. Also, the bride and groom looked happy to be there.

Geordie Denholm stood on the other side of Simon with Alice beside him and Rosalie next to Alice. Geordie and Alice were not yet betrothed, but the Colvilles were no longer an issue, the Douglas having hanged both for their crimes. Sir Malcolm's lady had said she thought Geordie would do very well for Alice, so Sibylla and Simon considered that matter settled.

The Douglas was present, too, in the front row of guests. The two-year-old truce, amended to include his new rules for resolving grievances across the line, would, they hoped, continue for at least the original ten years. The reiving had not stopped, but families deprived of their beasts were more apt to see justice now.

Cecil Percy had brought his wife and family to visit Elishaw in May, and his eldest son had taken a strong liking to Rosalie. Rosalie, having learned in Edinburgh that there were many fish in the barrel, had kept the lad at arm's length.

Simon thought she was turning into an accomplished flirt, but Sibylla knew that Annabel remained confident of another English alliance.

The priest murmured to the bridal pair, and they turned to face their guests.

"I present to you Sir Malcolm and Lady Cavers," the priest said solemnly.

The piper skirled a tune, and they came down the steps to receive the felicitations of their guests.

"How are you feeling, Sibylla?" Amalie demanded as she approached. "I saw Simon rubbing your back."

A mother for more than two months, Amalie had regained her usual figure. Her son was with his nurse at Akermoor, where the whole family was staying.

Sibylla grinned at her. "I'm fine," she said. "Sakes, I'm barely three months along, but your brother is already proving to be as certain of what is good for me as Garth was when you were with child. I marvel now that you did not murder him," she added, with a teasing look at Simon.

"Take care, my love," he said, smiling and holding her gaze. "If I hear much more of that, I'll put you to bed as soon as we get back."

"Aye, sure, you may, but only if you promise to join me there, my lord."

With that, surrounded by laughing kinsmen and merrily chattering friends, they followed the newly married couple outside into the sunny street.

Dear Reader,

I hope you enjoyed *Border Moonlight*. Its title derives from a mixture of old reivers' cries, particularly those of the Scotts of Buccleuch and Scotts of Harden.

The lady Catherine Gordon of Huntly is a product of the author's imagination, although her "father," Sir John Gordon of Huntly, was the last in the male line of the Gordons of Huntly. The author also took literary license with the date of his death, moving it up a few years from 1408. He was succeeded by his sister Elizabeth, who married a Seton. His descendants have held Huntly Castle since then.

The Earl of Fife ruled Scotland until his death in 1420.

The truce to which Scotland and England agreed in 1389, nearly a year after the Battle of Otterburn, was re-negotiated in 1391 to include Archie the Grim's rules for redressing grievances across the line. Despite those rules, reiving had become such an integral part of Border economy that it continued for two hundred years. After the union of Scotland and England, stiffer Elizabethan laws finally put an end to it.

The river Tweed rarely behaves as it did in *Border Moonlight*. It is generally a calm and beautiful river, the fourth longest in Scotland with the second largest watershed. As a point of trivia, according to the *Encyclopedia of Scotland*, although tweed cloth is produced in some Tweed towns, the name does not derive from the river. It comes from a "misreading in London of the Scots word 'tweel' or 'twill.'"

If you wondered about bridges, the Tweed was bridge-free from Berwick all the way to Peebles through the year 1654. Few bridges existed in the Borders, because Borderers saw them only as rash invitations to invaders.

The Abbot's Ford mentioned in *Border Moonlight* belonged to Melrose Abbey and lay about three miles west of it. Sir Walter Scott, the poet, built his home there and called it Abbotsford. The cluster of shiels or huts the abbey provided for pilgrims near the confluence of Gala Water with the Tweed grew to be the town of Galashiels.

The game of dames, which dates to as early as 1100 in southern France, was an early form of what the British call draughts and Americans call checkers. It derived from chess and was played on a chessboard. For more information, see *Board and Table Games From Many Civilizations* by R. C. Bell (New York, 1979) or *Birth of the Chess Queen* by Marilyn Yalom (New York, 2004).

My primary sources for Douglas history were *A History of the House of Douglas,* Vol. I, by the Right Hon. Sir Herbert Maxwell (London, 1902), and *The Black Douglases* by Michael Brown (Scotland, 1998).

Other sources include *The Scotts of Buccleuch* by William Fraser (Edinburgh, 1878), *Steel Bonnets* by George MacDonald Fraser (New York, 1972), *The Border Reivers* by Godfrey Watson (London, 1975), *Border Raids and Reivers* by Robert Borland (Dumfries, Thomas Fraser, date unknown).

As always, I'd like to thank my wonderful agents, Lucy Childs and Aaron Priest, my terrific editor Frances Jalet-Miller, Art Director Diane Luger, cover artist Claire Brown, Senior Editor and Editorial Director Amy Pierpont, Vice President and Editor in Chief Beth de Guzman, and everyone else at Hachette Book Group's Grand Central Publishing who contributed to making this book what it is.

I'd also like to thank copyeditor Sean Devlin, a master of the craft.

If you enjoyed *Border Moonlight*, please look for *Tamed by a Laird* at your favorite bookstore in July 2009. In the meantime, *Suas Alba!*

Sincerely,

Amanda Scott

http://home.att.net/~amandascott
amandascott@worldnet.att.net

Don't miss the start of
Amanda Scott's thrilling
new series!

Please turn this page
for a preview of

Tamed by a Laird

Available in mass market
July 2009

Chapter 1 ————————

Seventeen-year-old Janet, Baroness Easdale of that Ilk—but Jenny Easdale to her friends and family—was trying to ignore the hamlike hand on her right thigh of the man to whom, just hours earlier, she had pledged her troth. To that end, she intently studied the five jugglers performing in the center of Annan House's lower hall, trying to decide which of them might be her maidservant's older brother.

Since Jenny's betrothed was drunk and she had no information about Peg's brother other than that he was a juggler in the company of minstrels and players entertaining the guests at her betrothal feast, her efforts bore no fruit.

Reid Douglas squeezed her thigh, making it more difficult than ever to ignore him. And, as all five jugglers wore the short cote hardies and varicolored hose favored by minstrels of every sort, she saw little to choose between them.

"Give me a kiss," Reid muttered loudly and too close to

her right ear, slurring his words. "'Tis my right now, lass, and I've had none o' ye."

She glanced at him, exerting herself to conceal her disdain. He was nearly four years older than she was and handsome enough, she supposed, and doubtless all men got drunk from time to time. But Jenny had not chosen Reid and wanted nothing to do with him.

However, Lord Dunwythie—her uncle by marriage—and his lady wife, Phaeline, had made it plain that Jenny's opinion of Reid Douglas was of no importance whatsoever. Had her father still been alive, perhaps . . .

"Come now, Jenny, kiss me," Reid said more forcefully, leaning so near that she feared he might topple over and knock her right off her back-stool. His breath stank of ale and the quantities of food he had eaten, and she shrank from the odor.

"What's this?" he demanded, frowning. "Now ye're too good for me, are ye? Faith, but I'll welcome the schooling of ye after we've wed."

Meeting his gaze, she put her hand atop the one on her thigh, wrapped her fingers around his middle finger, and bent it sharply upward. "Pray, sir," she said politely as he winced and snatched his hand away, "have the goodness to wait until after the wedding to make yourself so free of my person. I like it not."

"By my faith, ye'll pay heavily for such behavior then," he snarled, putting his face too close to hers again. "Just a month, Jenny lass, three Sundays for the banns, then six days more till I become Easdale of Easdale. Think well on that."

"You are mistaken, sir," she said. "Although others may address you then as 'my lord,' I shall remain Easdale of Easdale. My father explained to me long ago that when

I became Baroness Easdale in my own right, my husband would take but a pretender's styling until he and I produce an heir to the barony. Your title will no longer be a mere styling then, but you will *not* become Easdale of Easdale unless I will it so. And I have seen naught in you yet to make that likely."

"Aye, well, we'll see about that, but a betrothed man has rights, too," he snapped. "Ye'll soon be finding out just what they are, too, I promise ye."

"Here now, lad," Lord Dunwythie said from Reid's other side, putting a hand on the younger man's right shoulder and visibly exerting pressure. "Lower your voice. Ye've had too much to drink, which can surprise no one, but—"

"A man's entitled to drink to his own betrothal, is he not?" Reid interjected, shrugging his shoulder free and shifting his heavy frown to his lordship.

"Aye, sure," Dunwythie replied mildly. "But he should not treat his intended lady unkindly. Nor should his actions distract his guests from the entertainment—which, I'd remind ye, I've provided for them this evening at great expense."

Realizing that their discussion had drawn the attention of the powerfully built gentleman at Lord Dunwythie's left, and unexpectedly meeting his enigmatic dark gaze, Jenny raised her chin a little and returned her attention to the jugglers.

Sir Hugh Douglas had sharp ears. Despite a desultory conversation with his host that now and again required his dutiful attention, his younger brother Reid's muttered words to his betrothed had drawn his notice before Lord Dunwythie had even glanced toward the two.

Hugh was observant, too, and he'd noted a spark in Janet Easdale's eyes that he had easily identified as anger. When he saw his brother snatch his hand out from under the table, he guessed that Reid had taken an unwanted liberty. Reid was clearly inebriated, but it looked as if the lass could manage him. He'd noticed little else about her other than a pair of deep dimples that appeared as she hastily turned away, but Reid's behavior was no real concern of Hugh's in any event.

He liked the lad well enough, although he had seen little of him over the years. Reid had been their sister Phaeline's favorite brother from birth, years before she had married. The lad had been ten when their mother died, and Phaeline had insisted then that he'd do better to live with her at Annan House than at Thornhill.

Their father had not objected. Nor had Hugh. At the time of his mother's death, he was serving as squire to his cousin Sir Archibald Douglas. After winning his spurs on the field of battle two years later, he had continued to follow Archie.

He had done so, in fact, until the King of Scots had sent Archie to France as envoy to the French court. Hugh had married shortly thereafter, and he and his beloved Ella had been expecting their first child when his father died.

Ella and their wee daughter had died just a few months after Hugh's father did, and in his grief, he had been content to leave Reid with Phaeline and devote his efforts to his Thornhill estates. Having had an opportunity to observe Reid closely for the past two days, he decided that Phaeline's upbringing left much to be desired, but he found it hard to care much. In truth, he had found it hard since the deaths of his wife and daughter to care much about anyone or anything except Thornhill.

He saw a gillie heading their way with a jug of claret. Dunwythie saw the lad as well and motioned him away. Then he turned to Hugh and said quietly, "Mayhap if you were to invite the lad to stroll with you, sir, his head might—"

"Sakes, don't talk about me as if I were not here," Reid said in a tone more suited to a sulky child than to a man soon to marry. "I'm going for a walk, and I don't need Hugh to mind my steps for me." Turning to his betrothed, he said curtly, "Don't wander off before I return, lass. I will escort you to your chamber myself."

Hugh saw that the command annoyed her, but she said calmly, "I never wander, sir. Prithee, take time to enjoy your walk."

As Reid ambled off, she glanced at Hugh, and this time he noted that her eyes were an unusual shade of soft golden-brown, almost the color of walnut shells. They were also beautifully shaped and thickly lashed. Her caul and veil completely covered her hair, but her rosy cheeks glowed softly in the candlelit hall. And her dimples were showing again.

Dunwythie's voice jarred him as the older man said, "I've been meaning to ask if ye ken the reason for this new tax that Maxwell is demanding, Hugh. He has seen fit to impose it even on those of us here in Annandale, though he surely must know that we have never recognized his jurisdiction over us."

"I ken little other than that I had to pay it," Hugh said. "As Thornhill lies on the river Nith, I am well within his jurisdiction. But for all that he says he is acting at the royal behest, I expect the truth is he needs the gelt to rebuild Caerlaverock."

"Aye, sure, and with Archie Douglas building his own

castle on the river Dee, we'll have them both trying to put their hands in our purses. I'm willing to support the Douglases, see you, because we need their strength here to keep the English at bay. But Maxwell has twice proven that he cannot hold Caerlaverock against them, so I've told him I'll pay nowt of this snickering he demands."

He went on, but Hugh listened just closely enough to respond appropriately. He could scarcely advise him. Maxwell or no Maxwell, his own loyalty remained with Archie Douglas, now known to all as Archibald "the Grim," Lord of Galloway. And as Archie defined Galloway, it included most of southwestern Scotland.

In the entertainers' clearing below the dais, a tall juggler wearing a scarlet robe longer than any of the others wore had just stepped forward. He looked older than the others did, too, certainly too old, Jenny thought, to be Peg's brother.

Apparently plucking a long dirk from thin air, the man flung it high to join the six balls already flying upward from his hands and back again.

As his audience emitted a collective gasp, another dirk joined the first. Two white balls then flew from his agile hands toward the high table on the dais, one to the ladies' end, the other to the men's.

The younger of Jenny's two Dunwythie cousins, fourteen-year-old Lady Fiona, leapt up and captured the ladies' ball with a triumphant cry. At the other end of the table, one of the men put up a hand almost casually to catch the second one.

By the time Jenny looked again at the jugglers, the

older one had six daggers spinning through the air. She had no idea where they had come from or what had become of the four balls he'd still had when she had looked away.

Musicians had played from the minstrels' gallery throughout the afternoon and now into the evening. But as the dirks flew ever higher, each one threatening to slice the juggler's hands when it descended, the music slowly faded. Soon the hall was so quiet that one could hear the great fire crackling on the hooded hearth.

Clearly oblivious to the juggler and the increasing tension his skill had produced in his audience, Phaeline, Lady Dunwythie, said in her usual placid way, "Our Reid is much taken with you, is he not, Janet, dear?"

Concealing her irritation as she turned to her uncle's round-faced, richly attired second wife, Jenny said quietly, "Reid is ape-drunk, madam."

"He is, aye," Phaeline agreed.

"Such behavior does naught to recommend him to me."

"You are young, my dear. So is he. But he will soon teach you how to please him, and I cannot doubt that you two will deal well together."

"I fear the only thing that pleases him, madam, is my inheritance."

"That may well be true, although he is not blind to your attractions," Phaeline said without a blink. "One must be practical, though. My lord might have preferred our Hugh to marry you, because 'tis Hugh who is Laird of Thornhill. But as Hugh swears never to marry again, and as Reid must be provided for until *he* inherits Thornhill, one could say that your betrothal simply arranged itself."

Resisting the impulse to glance again at the dark-eyed

gentleman at Lord Dunwythie's right, Jenny said, "But Sir Hugh cannot be much older than Reid is."

"That is, unfortunately, also true," Phaeline said. "Hugh is just five years older, and that is a difficulty, is it not? Hugh is perfectly aware of it, too. So one might expect him to have provided an adequate allowance for Reid. But he has refused to do so, saying that Reid would do better to win his spurs, and mayhap even an estate of his own. I confess, that did vex me until—"

"Until my lord Dunwythie assumed guardianship of me and my estates," Jenny said, widening her eyes. "Mercy, but you are blunt, madam."

"'Twas providential, though, as even my lord was quick to see."

Jenny did not bother to point out that it had proven other than providential for her. She knew she would be wasting her breath.

Applying to her uncle to support her against Phaeline's wishes would likewise prove useless. His lordship exerted himself in all ways to please his wife, because he still hoped for an heir. Phaeline was thirteen years younger than he was, but although they had been married for fifteen years and she had several times been with child, she had produced only their daughter, Fiona.

Lord Dunwythie's first wife had been Jenny's maternal aunt Elsbeth, who had died in childbed, just as Jenny's mother had. Elsbeth's daughter, the lady Mairi Dunwythie, was now eighteen. She sat at Phaeline's left with Fiona to Mairi's left.

Should Phaeline fail to produce a male heir, Mairi would, at his lordship's death, inherit the ancient Dunwythie estates and become a baroness in her own right just as Jenny had upon her father's death.

However, Phaeline had recently declared that she was pregnant again.

Leaning nearer, Phaeline said, "Reid was wrong, you know."

Jenny looked at her. "Wrong?"

"Aye, for today is Friday, so your first banns will be read Sunday, just two days from now. Thus, your wedding is but three weeks hence . . ."

". . . and two days," Jenny said, stifling a sigh of frustration.

But Phaeline was no longer listening. Looking past Jenny, she said to her husband, "Prithee, my lord, I would take my leave of you now. In my condition, I need much rest, so I mean to retire. You need not escort me, however," she added graciously. "You and our guests must continue to enjoy yourselves as you will."

Dunwythie stood when she did, as did everyone else at the high table. Those in the lower hall were watching a troupe of players rush into the central space and paid no heed to those on the dais.

Summoning a gillie, Dunwythie told him to see his lady safely to her chamber. As soon as she had gone, everyone sat down again and his lordship resumed his conversation with Sir Hugh.

Mairi immediately changed her seat to the one by Jenny, whereupon, Fiona—doubtless fearing as usual that she might miss something—moved to Mairi's.

"Art reconciled yet to this marriage they've arranged for you, Jenny?" Mairi asked as the players took places to start their play.

"Resigned, I expect, but scarcely reconciled," Jenny said. "'Tis of no use to repine, though, now that the betrothal is done. Phaeline is most determined."

"I think Uncle Reid is handsome," Fiona said brightly. "You are lucky, Jenny. I just hope I can find someone like him one day."

"You are welcome to *him* if you like," Jenny said.

"Sakes, I cannot marry my own uncle," Fiona said with a giggle. "But I do think you will come to like him in time, don't you?"

Mairi said, "Don't tease her, Fee. It is not kind when you know that she does not like him."

"But I don't understand *why* she does not," Fiona said.

"We can talk about that later," Mairi said. "For now, if you wish to stay with us, you must keep silent. Otherwise, I shall tell our father it is time you were in bed."

"You would not be so mean," Fiona said.

When Mairi only looked at her, she grimaced and subsided.

Jenny had returned her attention to the players and was wondering what their lives must be like when Mairi said, "That tall juggler was astonishing, was he not?"

"Aye, he was," Jenny agreed. "You know, Peg's brother is a member of this company—one of the jugglers. Don't you wonder what it must be like to travel about as they do and see all the fine places and important people they must see?"

When silence greeted her question, she looked at Mairi and saw that she had cocked her head and her gray eyes had taken on a vague, thoughtful look. She said at last, "Do you know, Jenny, I cannot imagine how they bear it. No bed of one's own, only pallets on a stranger's floor, and traveling, traveling, all the time."

"But the only traveling I have done is to move here from Easdale, whilst you have traveled with your father and Phaeline," Jenny said. "You said you enjoyed it."

"Aye, sure, for we stayed with kinsmen everywhere we stopped. That was fun, because they were all eager to show us how well they could feed and house us, and provide entertainment for us. But these minstrels must *provide* the entertainment wherever they go, and if they displease the one who is to pay them, they go unpaid. They may even face harsh punishment if they offend a powerful lord. It cannot be a comfortable life, Jenny. I much prefer my own."

"Aye, well, *you* don't have to marry your odious cousin," Jenny said.

"I am thankful to say that Reid is *not* my cousin," Mairi reminded her.

"He is as much your cousin by marriage as Fiona is mine," Jenny said. "He clearly cannot wait until I have to marry him, and he just as clearly expects to become master of Easdale. Sithee, *that* is bound to create difficulties, because he knows naught about managing such a large estate, whereas my father trained me to do so. Such a marriage cannot prosper. I am sure of it."

Fiona said, "Still it will be better than if they had decided to wed you to Sir Hugh, Jenny. Only think what that would be like! He *is* accustomed to managing estates and would not care a whit that you can manage your own. Why, he scarcely says a word to us. Indeed, he is so solemn that my mother said one could light a fire between his toes and he would simply wonder if one had built it to burn properly."

Jenny laughed but took care not to look again at Sir Hugh. Fiona's portrayal was an apt one, for Sir Hugh Douglas was unlike any man Jenny had met. He did not flirt with her or tease. Nor did he laugh or make jest with his friends. She had heard Phaeline say, too, that once

Hugh made up his mind, he never changed it. He would just fold his arms across his chest, she said, and pretend to listen. But one's words would have no more effect on him than drops of water on a stone.

"I don't want Sir Hugh, either," she said firmly. "I should infinitely prefer to choose my own husband."

"But you don't know any other suitable men," Mairi said. "Had Father taken you to Glasgow, or to Edinburgh or Stirling, I warrant many men more suitable than Reid is would have paid court to you, for you are beautiful, wealthy, and—"

"Have mercy!" Jenny interjected, striving to keep her voice from carrying to anyone but Mairi and Fiona. "It is too late even to be thinking of such a course. Moreover, whilst I do not count my worth low, Mairi, my looks are not at all what fashion decrees. At least, so Phaeline has told me. And she, you know, takes good care always to know about such things."

"That is true, Mairi," Fiona said. "Mam does know what people like. You recall that she said only yesterday that she fears one reason you have not yet contracted a marriage is that men consider your fairness unfashionably insipid."

Mairi smiled. "My coloring won't matter a whit if your mam fails to produce a son, dearling. As for Jenny's beauty, although she counts it low, others will not. Had your mam not decided to wed her to your uncle Reid before anyone else could clap eyes on her, Jenny would find many eligible young men eager to admire her."

Desiring to change the subject, Jenny said, "Reid will return shortly, and I do not want him near my bedchamber, so I think I must go before he gets back."

"Sakes, Jenny, you cannot leave your own betrothal feast!" Fiona protested.

"I am feeling very decisive tonight," Jenny said. "So I think I will."

"Then we should go, too," Mairi said. Before Fiona could protest, she raised her voice a little and said to Lord Dunwythie, "Forgive me, sir, but Jenny would like to retire now. I think Fiona and I should go, too, if you will excuse us all."

Jenny glanced toward the lower hall, half fearing to see Reid Douglas already lurching drunkenly toward her between the trestles. She did not see him, but when she looked at her uncle, she realized that he had been watching her.

"D'ye want to seek your chamber now, lassie?" he asked.

"Aye, sir, I do."

He nodded and observed the lower hall for a long moment before turning back to meet her gaze again. "I'll see that ye're not disturbed then."

"Thank you, my lord," she said with deep sincerity as she made her curtsy.

Hurrying from the hall with Mairi and Fiona, she cast one more wistful glance at the minstrels and wondered again what it would be like to be one.

⁓

Hugh was bored, so when the play ended, he lost no time in bidding his host goodnight. He did not want to spend the next hour exchanging polite phrases with other guests, most of whom were doubtless as eager to be away as he was if they lived near enough to go home, or to seek their chambers if they did not.

The hour was still early, and he was not yet ready for bed, especially as he was sharing his brother's chamber. So he went outside for fresh air instead, taking care to avoid the forecourt, where other guests would be taking their departure.

The air was crisp, the moon high, and he could hear the surf in the distance, for Annan House sat atop a hill overlooking Solway Firth. By walking a short distance, he obtained a fine moonlit view of the water. The tide was surging in.

He stood there until he grew chilly. Then, reluctantly, he went to his brother's room, found it still empty, and went to bed, expecting Reid to disturb him on his return. Instead, he slept deeply until a clamorous knocking at the door awoke him.

As he opened his eyes, his host entered and said abruptly, "Jenny's gone. Your brother is still in a stupor in the lower hall where he passed out last night. Not that I would send him after her even if he were sober. The lad lacks discretion."

Sitting up, Hugh said, "Where would she go?"

"Heaven knows," Dunwythie said. "No one saw her leave."

"But why do you come to me?"

"I cannot go after her without creating the devil of a stir, and your brother would create a worse one. Nor can I send any of my men. You'll have to go."

"Sakes, sir, but this is no concern of mine," Hugh said firmly.

THE DISH

Where authors give you the inside scoop!

From the desk of Julia Harper

Dear Reader,

So many books to read, so little time! Do you find that you have trouble deciding which book to pick up next? Should you read that cat mystery your mother keeps shoving at you or the new zombie book your sister loved so much? And then there are those ubiquitous lists of "classic" books that you must read before you die. What is a reader to do? Well, never fear, I've just made your reading decisions a little easier with the following comparison of my new book, FOR THE LOVE OF PETE (on sale now), and one of those books you really should've read in freshman lit:

A Handy Dandy Guide, comparing my new book, FOR THE LOVE OF PETE, with William Faulkner's AS I LAY DYING

	AS I LAY DYING	VS.	FOR THE LOVE OF PETE
First line of book:	*Jewel and I come up from the field, following the path in single file.*		*Things finally came to a head between Zoey Addler and Lips of Sin the afternoon he tried to steal her parking space.*

Heroine:	**Addie Bundren,** who is dying	**Zoey Addler,** who is *alive* and on a mission to rescue her kidnapped baby niece.
Hero:	Several choices here, but I'm going with **Anse Bundren,** who needs false teeth.	**Dante Torelli,** hot, if uptight, FBI agent. His teeth are all intact.
The Plot:	Well, Addie dies and her family has to bury her. They're not very good at it.	Dante Torelli is an undercover FBI agent assigned to protect a mob informant and his family. But the informant's hiding place is blown and a baby girl is snatched by a ruthless hit man. Now, Dante must save the toddler, uncover the traitor in his department, evade various bad guys, and deal with Zoey, the toddler's sexy aunt, all before the biggest mob trial in Chicago's history, set to begin in just three days.
Love Scene:	I'm not sure there is one, but Addie did once have an affair with the preacher who's going to bury her.	Woohoo!

| Ends: | SPOILER ALERT! One of Addie's sons gets sent to an insane asylum, but at least her rotting body is saved from a flooding river by another son. Yea! | Happily (and with more hot sex)! |

There! Didn't that make your decision a little easier?

xxoo,

Julia Harper

www.juliaharper.com

♥ ♥ ♥ ♥ ♥ ♥ ♥ ♥ ♥ ♥ ♥ ♥ ♥ ♥

From the desk of Lisa Dale

Dear Fellow Bookworms,

Do you ever get the feeling that life is too complicated? That you just want to get back to the things that matter most?

I do. That's why I wrote my first novel, SIMPLE WISHES (on sale now), about a woman who makes an impulsive mistake that forces her to leave her New York City apartment and escape to her deceased mother's cottage in the country.

It probably won't surprise you that I wrote much of the novel in my grandparents' cabin on a drab dirt road in Pennsylvania. Every morning, I would get up, make tea, do a bit of reading, and write. You can see pictures of the cabin on my blog, www.Book Anatomy101.com.

Some of the stories in SIMPLE WISHES come from real life. For example, once, my grandfather's collie ran away and I was the lucky one to apprehend the fugitive. When I found him he was barking and running in circles around a tree. I bent down to grab his collar and when I looked up, there was a *huuuge* black bear staring down at me from a branch above my head! Gives new meaning to the phrase: *barking up the wrong tree*.

Unlike me, the hero of SIMPLE WISHES, Jay Westvelt, is totally accustomed to living in the middle of nowhere. He's a rough-around-the-edges recluse and a brilliant artist, and he's intrigued when a prickly yet captivating city slicker moves in next door. Adele has to admit her attraction to Jay, but because she plans to return to the city, she can't let herself fall in love. She vows their relationship is nothing more than a fling—but little does she know that Jay has vows of his own.

SIMPLE WISHES is about what's most important to us as women—getting over the past, and sorting the things that matter from the things that don't. I'd love to hear about your *simple wishes*. Visit my Web site at www.lisadalebooks.com and leave a note on my "Wishing Well" to share a kind wish for yourself, your friends, your family, or the whole world.

Happy reading!

Lisa Dale

♥ ♥ ♥ ♥ ♥ ♥ ♥ ♥ ♥ ♥ ♥ ♥ ♥ ♥ ♥

From the desk of Amanda Scott

Dear Reader,

Lady Sibylla Cavers of BORDER MOONLIGHT (on sale now) has to deal with Simon Murray, Laird of Elishaw, a man who never forgets a wrong . . . or forgives one.

However, Sibylla, like most of my heroines, is a capable, intelligent woman who knows her own mind. By the time she's finished with Simon, he's not sure which end is up. That is not to say she wins every battle, but she does hold her own.

I think the reason I enjoy creating strong, independent heroines is that I come from a long line of strong, independent women. Since most of my many Scottish ancestors hailed from the Borders, I often tell people I have horse thieves hanging from nearly every branch of the family tree. I have certainly used many examples from that tree to create my heroines—and a number of my heroes, for that matter.

Thanks to a little nepotism, my triple-great-grandfather, Andrew Scott, whose father came to America from the Borders, became the first—and from 1819 to 1821, the only—superior, or supreme, court judge for the Arkansas Territory. His older brother, John Scott, was one of the first U.S. senators from Missouri and named the state of Arkansas. Their wives were sisters, daughters of lawyer John Rice-Jones, a Welshman who served as commissary general to George Rogers Clark's northwest expedition, among many other accomplishments.

All were strong men, definitely, but their wives and daughters were strong, too. They had to be to cope with those men. One of my favorite stories about Judge Andrew Scott concerns a duel he had in 1824 with another judge shortly after Arkansas outlawed dueling. After an argument over a game of whist, they fought their duel on "Mississippi soil" in order not to break the law. Judge Andrew left a letter for his wife, Eliza—the usual "to be opened in the event of my death" letter.

I have a copy of it. After expressions of much

praise to Eliza as the perfect wife and mother, he added a P.S. telling her to give their youngest son, George (the only son still at home), to the judge's brother to raise.

My grandfather first showed me the letter when I was about ten or twelve. Even then, I did not doubt what Eliza's reaction to that last sentence must have been. It is my firm belief to this day that the letter still exists because of Eliza, not Andrew. He'd certainly have had less reason to keep it, let alone to pass it on to one of his sons to treasure.

Andrew had a legendary temper. During the argument, he is said to have thrown a candlestick at the other judge. But Eliza definitely held her own with him. After she read that letter—and I have no doubt that she did—I'd wager he endured an uncomfortable few minutes at best. My grandfather said she probably "snatched the man baldheaded."

I grew up with many such tales from my grandfather, so perhaps you can understand why, when I need examples of strong women for my heroines, I often look no further than the Scott family history.

Enjoy!

Amanda Scott

http://home.att.net/~amandascott/

Want to know more about romances at Grand Central Publishing and Forever? Get the scoop online!

GRAND CENTRAL PUBLISHING'S ROMANCE HOME PAGE

Visit us at www.hachettebookgroup.com/romance for all the latest news, reviews, and chapter excerpts!

NEW AND UPCOMING TITLES

Each month we feature our new titles and reader favorites.

CONTESTS AND GIVEAWAYS

We give away galleys, autographed copies, and all kinds of fun stuff.

AUTHOR INFO

You'll find bios, articles, and links to personal Web sites for all your favorite authors—and so much more!

THE BUZZ

Sign up for our monthly romance newsletter, and be the first to read all about it!